BOUND BY DARKNESS

THE ALLIANCE SERIES BOOK 3

BRENDA K DAVIES

To all the lost souls out there.

CHAPTER ONE

The streetlights played over the sidewalks and alleys as Killean stalked an outlying area of Boston for his prey. The prey he was hunting had left his rundown building ten minutes ago. The man may be some of the worst the human race had to offer, but still hesitant to take this irrevocable step, Killean hung back from going after him.

Now he was stalking the man through this downtrodden area of the city where he spent more time avoiding rats, feces, and garbage than he did people. Boards covered most of the windows of the dilapidated buildings.

Killean stepped to the side to avoid a yellow food wrapper the wind blew across the broken sidewalk. It caught on a chain-link fence and flapped in the breeze. The crinkling of the paper was the only sound on this forsaken stretch of night-drenched land.

Shoving his hands in his pockets to ward off the unusual chill in the mid-May night, Killean's thoughts drifted to the letter he'd left for Ronan only hours ago. With that letter, he'd most likely severed his bonds to the only family and friends he'd had for centuries, but though he tried not to think about them, his written words replayed in his mind on an endless loop.

My mate is one of the hunters taken by Joseph and his Savages. I've tried to leave her to her fate, but I can't. What we're doing isn't working, and we both know it won't. The only way I'm going to find her is to go into their world. It's the only chance I have of saving her.

I WILL come back from this.

K

And he *would* come back from this, somehow. He didn't care what it took; he would *not* become one of the monsters he'd spent his entire life hunting and destroying.

But the only way to find her is *to become a monster.*

That was true, but he would do whatever was necessary to enter the world of the Savages and find his mate. And he would be strong enough to pull himself back from the killing once he located her. He didn't let any doubt of that creep into his mind; if he did, he wouldn't be able to go through with this, and then his mate would be lost forever.

My mate.

He shuddered as he recalled the beautiful hunter with her clover-colored eyes and shining auburn hair pulled into a bun. He'd never wanted to encounter his mate; he far preferred life alone and not having a woman interfering in it. However, he'd always figured that if he *did* stumble upon her one day, he would merely avoid her and not complete the bond.

After encountering his mate, he'd done well at avoiding Simone as she made things easy on him when she split off from Nathan's faction of hunters and left with another group. As far as he was concerned, it was good riddance until Joseph captured her.

Then no matter how much he didn't want a mate and certainly not a *hunter* one, he knew he couldn't leave her to the fate Joseph intended for her. He was a selfish bastard, but he could never live with himself if he didn't try to save her from Joseph's nefarious clutches, even if she was a hunter.

His life had been far from easy, but being saddled with a *hunter* mate was one of the cruelest blows fate ever dealt him. At least the horrors in his past had ended; this one could last for an eternity as he assumed that Joseph, or one of his Savages, already turned her into a vampire.

If she'd remained mortal for a few more years, or married another hunter, Killean didn't know how he would have reacted to that knowledge, but he'd been determined to let her live out her mortal life, far from his immortal one. Then Joseph went and fucked up his plans.

And now Simone was most likely a vampire.

The reminder she'd probably been turned by someone else caused his hands to clench until the veins in his forearms stood out. Not only had the Savages most likely changed her, but they'd probably done so in the most excruciating way possible and thrived on her agony as well as her powerful, hunter blood.

He wouldn't have turned her; he would *never* have let their bond progress that far, but the idea of someone else doing it made him want to tear the heads from every pathetic human scurrying past him.

Depending on how far Joseph's cruel transition of vampires into Savages had progressed with Simone, it could already be too late to save her. She could already be a Savage. Plus, from what he'd seen of the pristine little hunter, he doubted she'd be able to survive what Joseph and the Savages would do to her with her sanity intact. She'd reminded him of a doll when they first met; he imagined she was a broken one by now, but he still had to try and save her.

Turn around. It's not too late for you. There is no reason you should sacrifice everything you've known for a woman you kissed once and whose kind you despise.

His steps slowed until he stopped. A thin woman pushing a shopping cart that clattered in and out of the cracks nearly crashed into him. She gave him the finger and cursed him with a mixture of English and some other language that he couldn't quite place before shoving her cart around him.

Standing in the middle of the sidewalk, Killean considered what he was doing. He owed Simone nothing. Their relationship hadn't progressed to a point where he would be lost without her. He could live out the rest of his life without her and remain the same, or nearly the same, as he'd felt like crawling out of his skin since their kiss.

At night, his dreams were plagued by the beautiful hunter and the things he wanted to do to her. Their kiss had been the first time in nearly a hundred years a woman aroused him. His dreams had left him hard and on the verge of climbing out of bed to search for her. He spent the rest of those nights lying in bed, cursing himself, fate, and her.

Then she was taken, and the dreams stopped because he barely slept anymore. In the time since they captured her, he'd done nothing more than pass out for fitful bouts of sleep before rising to search for her again. Worry consumed him for a woman he didn't know.

Their relationship hadn't progressed far, and he may be able to go on for centuries without her, but he could never forsake his mate to a fate worse than death.

But sacrificing yourself for her?

He didn't know what else to do or how else to get her back. In the week since Joseph captured the hunters, the Alliance had hunted for them, but they'd smacked into nothing but dead ends. There was still a chance Killean could save her from becoming a

Savage, but if she stayed with Joseph much longer, that chance would vanish.

That knowledge propelled him into motion once more.

Fuck! He owed Simone nothing, yet he continued until he tracked down the human he sought in an alleyway. Killean slid away from the dim glow of the streetlights to stand in the shadows cast by the two buildings while he watched the human he'd marked for death.

This man and nine others were on his list of possible victims. He didn't plan to kill them all before seeking out Joseph, but he wanted options if it did become necessary for him to kill so many.

Once he decided this was the course of action he would take to find Simone, he spent a few hours yesterday researching some of the worst of humanity. This man, Arlo Holt, was arrested for rape five days ago. It was his sixth arrest for the crime, and yesterday, it was the sixth time his victim dropped the charges. Killean didn't know what Arlo did to those women to get them to change their minds, but he suspected it was nothing good.

And those were only the six women who reported him, Killean was sure there were more who hadn't. Not only was rape one of Arlo's favorite pastimes, but he also had a penchant for assault and battery, robbery, drug possession, drug dealing, and DUIs.

If he had to kill, then Killean would at least keep it to the worst forms of human life. It was a small piece of twisted, moral judgment—and he was the last vampire who should be passing judgment on anyone—but he could live with himself if he stuck to men such as Arlo.

Arlo spoke in a low whisper with a young kid who resembled a walking skeleton instead of a human being. They stood between two dumpsters overflowing with trash and rats that didn't care about the presence of the humans. The skeleton handed Arlo some money and received a small bag of white substance in return.

The skeleton slunk away with his head bowed. Arlo started toward Killean and was nearly on top of him before he realized Killean was there. The man, in his mid-twenties, came to an abrupt halt when he spotted Killean.

"I'm closed for the night, buddy," Arlo's racing heart belied the bravado of his tone.

"I'm not here for what you're selling," Killean replied.

Arlo's hand fell to the gun tucked into the waistband of his jeans. Killean followed his movements, but he didn't try to stop him from pulling the gun. He didn't care about the weapon; he was far more interested in Arlo's blood.

His fangs throbbed as his gaze fell to the vein in the side of the man's neck. He regularly fed on humans, but this was the first time he'd be able to let go of all the restraint he'd kept himself under for over four hundred years. The first time he could give in to the impulse to kill that had obsessed him for most of his life.

Before Simone haunted his dreams, graphic images of murder, death, and copious amounts of blood sliding down his throat had filled them. He'd woken from them drenched in a cold sweat, with his fangs fully extended, and his fingers digging into the mattress to keep himself from launching out of bed, fleeing into the night, and slaughtering every human he came across.

On those nights, his dreams were so vivid that he woke with the coppery scent of blood in his nostrils. Over the centuries, they'd nearly hurled him to the brink of madness more times than he could recall, but because of Ronan, and the mission he'd accepted when he joined with Ronan, Killean somehow kept himself from unleashing his murderous impulses.

But tonight, if he went through with this, he wouldn't have to restrain himself anymore. In his life, the only thing that excited him more than this knowledge was the kiss he'd shared with Simone.

It could already be too late for her. You don't have to do this.

But as he thought it, he knew there was no other recourse.

"Hey, asshole, get out of my way," Arlo said and waved his gun at Killean.

Killean seized Arlo by his shirt and propelled him into the brick wall of the nearby building.

"What the fuck, man?" Arlo complained, and lifting his gun, he pressed it against Killean's chest.

Before Arlo could pull the trigger, Killean gripped the barrel and wrenched the gun from his grasp. Arlo's eyes rolled as sweat beaded his forehead and he squirmed in Killean's grasp. The rapist and drug dealer punched Killean in the cheek.

Killean could have dodged or blocked the blow, but he gladly took it, and the next one Arlo delivered. The punch of a human was nowhere near as strong as the many he'd received from Savages over the years, but he welcomed the blows. He planned to end this man's life, the least he could do was take a few punches from him.

"Get off me, man!" Arlo yelled.

"Calm down," Killean commanded as he allowed his ability to manipulate the minds of others to slide free; Arlo's struggles eased when Killean took control of him.

Killean breathed in the scent of Arlo's blood. Unlike his customers, drugs didn't taint Arlo's blood, and the coppery tang of his blood called to Killean. His fangs lengthened and saliva filled his mouth as his heart raced with excitement. Killing Arlo would finally set him free of the constant struggle dominating his life since he became a fully matured vampire at twenty-four.

Don't do this! You can find another way!

The tiny piece of conscience he still had pleaded with him, but his conscience had never been much guidance in his life. His loyalty to Ronan, and his mission to destroy Savages had kept him on the straight and narrow, until now.

Ronan. His friend, his mentor, and the man who had saved his life more times than Killean could recall. The man who would ruthlessly hunt Killean and strike him down for choosing this path.

I will *come back.*

No one has ever come back from being a Savage before.

And no one has ever endured the things I have and survived before; if anyone can do this, I *can.*

"Easy," Killean said when Arlo started to thrash again.

He'd inadvertently pulled back his control over Arlo while wrestling with this decision and asserted it again. He may be about to step over the threshold from vampire to Savage, but he wouldn't inflict unnecessary suffering on another, at least not yet. Who knew what he would do after he killed, but for now, he would retain this piece of his barely there humanity.

Realizing he was going around in circles with himself and he couldn't stand here all night, Killean pushed Arlo's head to the side and sank his fangs into the man's throat. Arlo remained unmoving and unaware of what Killean was doing as he eagerly consumed the blood until Arlo's pulse weakened.

Stop!

Killean's fangs almost retracted as he neared the line between what he was and what he would become. Then Simone's eucalyptus scent, and the sweet taste of her lips, danced across his memory. His mate was trapped and being abused. This man's life was nothing compared to hers.

And who are you to judge that?

I am no one. I stopped being someone when I was a child.

But for those few seconds, while he stood on the beach with Simone in his arms, he'd been *someone* again. For the first time since he was seven years old and his world fell apart, he'd felt as if he finally belonged somewhere, and that was with *her*.

No matter he despised her hunter blood, no matter he would never claim her as his mate, he couldn't abandon her to Joseph.

Instead of stopping, Killean bit deeper and Arlo sagged against him. Arlo's heart thudded, stopped, thudded again, and then gave one more limp beat before ceasing.

A moment of panic descended over Killean as he irrevocably stepped away from his old life and into this far more turbulent and uncertain one. Who and what would he become now?

He would return from this, but he didn't kid himself into believing he could ever be the man he'd been before committing this act. This death of a human would forever change him, but what it would transform him into remained to be seen.

The panic vanished when power unlike anything he ever experienced rushed over Killean and the last of Arlo's life filled him.

Gasping, Killean pulled back to stare into Arlo's sightless blue eyes. Guilt tore at his insides as he released the man and let the body slump to the ground.

But despite the self-hatred and uncertainty battering his brain, he gathered Arlo's body, disposed of it, and went in search of the next name on his list.

One victim would not be enough to make him a Savage.

CHAPTER TWO

Chained to the wall, the cold concrete floor leached the heat from Simone's body. She had no idea where she was, and she'd given up caring. The parts of her that weren't freezing hurt so bad it felt like someone was taking a knife and slicing it across her vertebrae before leisurely flaying the skin from her bones.

In the beginning, she'd welcomed the times when these monsters would come, undo their chains from the wall, and take them to the bathroom. Now she dreaded those breaks as it felt like her legs would shatter whenever she walked. She couldn't recall the last time she showered, and her stench filled her nostrils. She'd always been meticulous about her appearance and upkeep, but if it meant she didn't have to move, Simone didn't care if she ever showered again.

The chains of some of the other hunters imprisoned with her rattled as they shifted position, but she didn't move. Moving only brought more misery. Instead, she remained huddled while her scorched skin felt like it would crack and fall off her body. Except her skin wasn't burnt, it just felt that way. Her flesh was the same as always, or almost the same.

Before these Savages captured her, her skin had been that of a hunter, and now it belonged to a monster. A *ravenous* monster.

Her cramped stomach spasmed at the thought of feeding the beast, but what it required to fill it was no longer the food that sustained her for her entire life. Now only blood would suffice to ease this awful gnawing in her belly.

Without thinking, Simone went to bite her lip and whimpered when the fangs that descended days ago sliced her bottom lip for the hundredth time. She wasn't sure if it really was a hundred times or not, but her mouth was so raw it sure felt that way. The taste of her blood made her stomach cramp tighter and did nothing to ease her endless hunger.

A hunter nearby started crying, and another barked at them to shut up. Those were hunters talking to each other that way. *Hunters!*

She'd never heard her kind speak to each other in such crass ways. Hunter society was one of politeness, respect, and propriety. Hunters did not exhibit such crude language and disrespect. Hunters did *not* tell each other to shut up.

But these hunters were turning on each other like a pack of rabid dogs. Her hunter family was spiraling into this pit of desolation with her, and it was breaking them. She wanted to cry for those who had perished in the raid that landed her here, and for the fellow hunters trapped in this nightmare with her, but she didn't have enough fluid in her body to produce tears.

Simone's thoughts drifted to her mother. She knew her mother wasn't here, but was she somewhere safe, or did she die during the raid the Savages launched against the hunter stronghold?

They were questions she might never know the answers to as there was nothing she could do while chained in this place.

Nothing she could do until she was free, but she had no idea *how* to get free.

In the beginning, some of the hunters tried to escape when they were unchained to use the bathroom, but their struggles never amounted to anything more than being bloodied by the gleeful Savages who beat them. Now no one had the strength to resist anything done to them.

Simone had tried to run once, but the ease with which they subdued her, as well as the hands grasping at her breasts while her captors unnecessarily groped her, humiliated her into submission. She hadn't resisted again.

And besides, Simone had no idea where to go if she did get free, she'd simply needed to try. She would have hated herself if she didn't, because she knew what these Savages planned for her and everyone else here. They were going to starve her and her fellow hunters until they were so mindless they didn't care who they killed to get blood.

In the beginning, she was determined not to become one of them. Then that sick monster, Joseph, had some of his fellow bastards hold her down while he drank from her. The excruciating agony of the experience nearly drove her insane. Not only had he drained her until she teetered on the brink of death, but he'd forced his putrid blood down her throat afterward.

She recalled only anguish when he finished and the transition took over. All her bones had felt like they were breaking before fusing back together. Her muscles twisted and bent into something else. Yet somehow her body retained her Simone shape, but she wasn't the same Simone.

Everything she'd always known was gone, and now there was only cold, anger, terror, and *hunger*. The rare times she slept, she dreamed about the blood they'd given her when she first woke from the brutal change her body endured. It was the only substance given to her since she awoke, but she recalled the sweetness of it on her tongue and the strength of it filling her.

She hated herself for it, but she'd greedily consumed every drop of that blood and been thirsty for more.

Things had been horrific so far, but they were only going to get worse. Once they set her free, Simone didn't doubt that no matter how much she tried to resist, she would jump on the first human she came across and sink her fangs into their throat.

Even as she hated herself for the weakness, her heart raced with excitement at the thought of blood. If she could reach the vampire chained next to her, she would sink her fangs into his throat too, fellow hunter or not, it no longer mattered. The beat of the hearts surrounding her had become another form of endless torment as she listened to the blood pulsing through her neighbor's body.

But they were chained in such a way that she couldn't reach him, and they couldn't get at each other. She had a feeling they'd be tearing one another apart otherwise. She quivered at the horrific image while she licked her upper lip over the blood such carnage would produce.

A small commotion amongst the others barely penetrated the blanket of depression and starvation enshrouding her. Footsteps thudded against the concrete floor, and it wasn't until those closest to her scuttled further into the shadows, that she tried to lift her head. It felt like a fifty-pound weight was tied to her skull, but somehow, she got it upright.

When her vision blurred, she blinked at the approaching group of men coming down the long tunnel until she could finally see again. Her eyes drifted to the tall man in the center of the group. There was something oddly familiar about him...

She frowned as she tried to recall where she'd seen him before, but starvation made it difficult to process her memories.

Then the man slowed as he approached her, and she realized he was *naked.*

She hadn't believed it possible, given everything she'd been through since being taken by these monsters, but Simone blushed and diverted her eyes from him. However, in those few seconds, the image of his lithe, chiseled body was burned into her mind. It was the first time she'd ever seen a nude man.

"Hunters," Killean sneered. Though he showed open disdain to the Savages holding him captive, fury churned in his gut as he gazed at his chained mate.

The word and the familiarity of the voice caused Simone to forget about her embarrassment and lift her head again. Curiosity tugged at her as she was struck by the whim to see more of him, but Simone kept her gaze off the naked man's body and focused instead on his ruby-colored eyes.

Then like Moses parting the Red Sea, the fog clouding her memory pulled back. *Killean!*

The scent of ocean air drifted over her as she found herself standing back on the beach with this man before he kissed her. Simone almost felt alive again as she recalled the delicious heat of his lips on hers and the thrill of her first kiss.

She'd never experienced anything like the intensity of his kiss. It had been amazing until it ended. Then he'd looked at her like she was some disgusting form of slime before ordering her back to the hotel. She'd been so humiliated and angry, and she'd never wanted to see him again.

But seeing him here brought a surge of hope rushing up from the bleakness encompassing her life. This man was one of Ronan's Defenders! Had he come here to free them? She'd given up hope of being discovered so many hours ago, but had someone finally found them? Were they going to be set free?

Her hope vanished when she took a good look at the vampire with the scar. That scar sliced straight down from his deep brown hairline, through his right eyebrow and eyelid, to the center of his cheek where it stopped. How he hadn't lost his eye when he endured the injury, she didn't know, but he hadn't.

The last time she'd seen him, his eyes were the color of gold; now they were the red color she associated with monsters. Then he'd been one of Ronan's men, an ally to the hunters, but now he stood in the center of her enemies, and he didn't wear chains.

She didn't understand what was happening or why he was here, but instinctively she knew he wasn't the same vampire she'd encountered on the beach. She sniffed at the air; however, trying to differentiate his resin scent from the garbage stench of the rest of these monsters was impossible.

Killean held Simone's white-blue eyes before turning away. Unlike a vampire, whose eyes became red with emotion, hunger, or loss of control, a turned hunter possessed that striking, white-blue color.

If he didn't stop looking at her, he would go to her, tear the chains from her thin wrists, and rip her away from the others. He wanted to demolish this place with his bare hands, shred the Savages closest to him, and rain down Hell on all those who'd harmed her, but he was vastly outnumbered, and they would stop him before he could free her.

And if he tried to free her, he would give his real purpose for being here away. He'd sacrificed himself and his relationship with the Defenders to make it here; he wouldn't let it be for nothing. No matter how much it killed him to do so, he had to restrain himself from going after her.

The image of her wrists chained to the concrete wall next to her head, and her white-blue eyes, haunted him as the Savages started walking again. He gritted his teeth and forced himself to continue with them.

The last time he'd seen Simone, she was prim and proper in her ankle-length dress with her hair in a bun. The sun's rays playing across her hair brought out the strands of copper, mahogany, and vivid red in it. Her demure dress and placid demeanor did nothing to hide her beauty, but judging by the ardor of her kiss, they did conceal a passionate woman yearning to break free of the confines placed on her by her hunter heritage.

He'd barely recognized the woman trapped here. Dirt and blood caked the black, floor-length dress she wore. Streaks of brown and red marred her delicate features, and her previously glorious and bound hair tumbled around her shoulders and down her back in lank, greasy locks that appeared to be a dank brown rather than the glorious auburn they were.

She was as far from the ice princess hunter image she'd portrayed on the beach as she could get. Simone was no longer a pretty dolly, and though he'd always believed he would relish the sight of a humbled hunter, he *loathed* the broken air surrounding her.

He had to get her out of this place, but first, he had to stay alive, and to do so, he must keep walking away from her. These Savages were taking him to Joseph, and if anyone could see through the new role he was trying to portray, it would be his fellow fallen defender.

Trying to portray? You've killed seven men in the past two nights.

The reminder of that death didn't bother him as much as it had in the beginning. He'd killed those who deserved it. Four were child molesters set free because of overcrowded jails or technicalities, two were convicted rapists on the streets for the same reasons, and the other was Arlo.

He'd fed on one of the rapists hours ago, and when he finished, he felt ready to try his hand at tracking down these Savages and handing himself over to be brought to Joseph. At first, he'd been afraid they might try to kill him, and he'd have to destroy them and find different Savages, but after a phone call, they agreed to do it.

Killean suspected they'd called Joseph and their leader demanded they bring Killean to him. If it were a setup, Joseph would get the chance to destroy one of Ronan's men, and if it wasn't, Killean could be a significant asset to whatever Joseph planned.

When the call ended, the Savages bound, gagged, blindfolded, stripped, and searched him before shoving him into the trunk of a car. He had no idea where they were, as they'd driven around for hours. These bastards had either taken the most confusing route they could before bringing him here, or they'd left Massachusetts far behind.

Wherever they were, he was alone here, and if he couldn't convince Joseph he was one of them, he would die soon.

CHAPTER THREE

Killean glanced at the concrete walls surrounding him as the Savages slipped out the door behind him. The room they'd led him into was circular, and the gray walls were bare. Like the hallway where Simone was chained, recessed lights set into the concrete ceiling cast a dim glow across the desk in the center of the room and the man sitting behind it.

Everything he'd seen of this place had a bunker feel to it. Judging by the scent of damp earth he detected beyond the walls, they were underground. However, instead of the stale air of the old sewer tunnels where a nest of Savages had been discovered, the air here was fresher and, he suspected, filtered. The temperature in the place was also comfortable and must be as regulated as the air.

They may be below ground, but this was most certainly no sewer tunnel or any other tunnel running beneath the city. But then they could be far from Boston.

"Killean," Joseph purred.

Rising from the black leather chair he'd been perched on, Joseph stood behind the massive, walnut desk in the middle of the room. Joseph planted his hands on the desk and leaned forward as his gaze ran over Killean's naked frame. Killean suspected part of the reason they'd stripped him was to intimidate him.

It hadn't work. He'd endured far worse humiliation and degradation in his lifetime; this was nothing in comparison.

Holding out his arms, Killean turned in a slow circle before facing Joseph again. "Do you like what you see?" he asked.

Joseph's smile revealed the tips of his glistening fangs. With his golden-brown hair brushed back from his face, the narrowness of Joseph's features was more noticeable. At six foot two, Joseph was an inch shorter than Killean but stockier in build and about ten pounds heavier than Killean's two-hundred-ten-pound frame.

"Ah, Killean, I never would have guessed *you* had a sense of humor," Joseph murmured.

That was because he didn't have one.

"So why have you come to us?" Joseph inquired when Killean didn't respond.

"You know why."

"Do I?"

Killean hadn't spent much time with Joseph when they were Defenders. Joseph had spent most of his time in the training facility with the recruits, most of whom were turned vampires rather than purebred ones.

At the time, turned vampires were allowed to train with the Defenders to fight Savages, but only purebred ones made it into their inner circle. That changed when Joseph started creating Savage vampires and the Alliance formed. After he turned Savage, Joseph had recruited some of his old trainees to join his new cause.

"I am moving on from Ronan," Killean stated.

Joseph surveyed Killean again. "You are one of Ronan's most loyal supporters."

"I *was*," Killean corrected. *And I will be again.* "But not anymore."

Joseph's gaze dipped to the scar on Killean's chest. Killean didn't look down at the faint white circle almost directly over his heart; he'd seen the thing too many times over the centuries.

"And why is that?" Joseph inquired.

Killean glanced away in what he hoped appeared to be shame. Acting had never been a skill of his. He'd never seen a reason to pretend about anything; he had no choice now. "I slipped up and killed."

"You killed a human?" Joseph inquired.

Killean met Joseph's eyes again. "Yes."

"Ronan would forgive one slip up."

"It was more than one."

"Ah," Joseph murmured as he lifted his hands from the desk and formed his fingers into a teepee beneath his chin. He studied Killean with an air of amusement. "Did you slip up, Killean, or did you give in to your desires? We may not know each other well, but I've never seen you with a woman, so they are not what you wanted most after maturing. Perhaps you seek pain, but I believe bloodlust and killing are what you battled over the years."

Joseph's attempt at trying to have some insight into him made his blood boil, but he'd thrown himself into this game, and Simone's life depended on him playing it well. "I slipped up, and then I gave in."

"It happens to the best of us. Once we get a taste of the power killing gives us, we only want more." Joseph licked his lips as he lowered his hands. "It is *such* a rush."

Killean's fangs tingled as he recalled the flow of hot, fresh blood sliding down his throat along with the life force of his victims. It disgusted him, but excitement slid over his skin as the memories of those deaths danced through his mind. Though

Killean would never admit it to the prick, Joseph had guessed right about him and his bloodlust.

Upon reaching maturity, all male purebred vampires experienced three things: they stopped aging, their power increased every year they grew older, and they started to want incessantly for something *more*. Some sought out sex as often as possible, others pain, while others craved blood or killing. Some female purebreds also experienced it, but not on the same level as the men.

When he stopped aging, Killean's thirst for blood and killing amped up tenfold. It had taken everything he had not to give in and slaughter everyone he encountered after maturing, but the centuries-old words of his father, also a purebred, stopped him from doing so.

When he was a boy, Killean's brother once asked their father why he didn't kill the humans he fed on? Killean had lifted his head from the book he was reading to hear his father's reply.

"Because killing them would make me a monster, son," his dad replied as he ruffled his brother's hair. "And we don't want to be monsters, do we?"

"No, we don't," his brother solemnly replied, and Killean gave a brisk nod of agreement.

His father had looked back and forth between them while he continued speaking. "No matter what becomes of you when you grow older, you must never give in and kill those weaker than yourself. You must *never* kill a human unless it is necessary for your survival. It would make you less of a vampire. Do you understand?"

"Yes, Papa," they replied in unison.

His father never revealed what happened to vampires who killed humans before he died, probably because they were children when he passed, but his warning guided Killean through the turbulent years of his twenties, thirties, and forties. And then, when he was fifty-two, exactly four hundred years ago, he encountered Ronan.

Ronan had taken him in and taught him more about himself and the nefarious impulses he battled. He trained Killean to focus his bloodlust on killing Savages and given him an outlet for his dark urges. With the Defenders, Killean finally found a place to belong and friends who became family over the years.

If it hadn't been for Ronan, Killean would have eventually caved and started killing, but Ronan saved him, and Killean would always be grateful for that. And now, not only had he let his father and Ronan down after all these years, but he'd become the one thing he'd vowed never to be.

Self-loathing swelled within him, but then he recalled Simone chained to the wall and the desolation in her white-blue eyes. There had been no other choice. He may not be able to get her out of here yet, but he'd located her, and that was much more than he would have accomplished had he remained as he was. And now that he'd found her, he would get her free.

"Hmm," Joseph murmured as strolled out from behind the desk. His eyes reddened with every step he took toward Killean. "You know, when a turned vampire becomes a Savage, they still don't possess the ability to scent a Savage like us purebreds can."

Killean's shoulders went back as Joseph neared and the increasing scent of garbage wafted to him. The rotten aroma wasn't as strong as before Killean turned into a murderer, but it was there. *This* ability of the pureblooded vampire was the reason he'd chosen to kill instead of trying to fake his way through this. He hadn't known if a purebred retained their ability to scent out a Savage or not once they became one.

He still didn't know. Just because he could detect the aroma of refuse on Joseph and the other Savages, didn't mean all purebreds retained the trait. He might not have killed enough yet to drowned out the stench of the monsters among them.

Then Joseph stopped before him and leaned close. Hatred slithered through Killean. He was a killer now too, but this piece of shit was the reason he stood here. If Joseph had been strong enough not to give in to his impulses, if he'd never declared war against Ronan, hunters, the human race, and everything they'd always known, Simone wouldn't be here, and neither would he.

No matter what happened, Killean wouldn't allow this monster to live.

Joseph stopped only a couple of inches away and sniffed him. Killean managed to keep his revulsion from showing on his face as Joseph rocked on his heels, clasped his hands behind his back, and grinned.

"Well, Killean, your aroma certainly has changed."

So, Joseph can *still scent Savages even though he is one.* And Joseph had murdered far more humans than Killean, so that meant the trait never vanished.

Killean killed those humans in case Joseph retained this ability, but he felt no relief that their deaths hadn't been unnecessary. If Joseph scented a Savage on him, that made Killean one of them.

Not one of them. I will come back from this!

He told himself this repeatedly, but he didn't know how accurate it was anymore considering he was already impatient to feed again.

CHAPTER FOUR

Joseph sauntered away from him, around the desk, and opened a door on the other side of the room. "Bring my friend some clothes," Joseph commanded the woman standing outside the door. She hurried away as Joseph turned to another woman. "Bring us some refreshments."

"Right away," she murmured.

Joseph closed the door, lifted a wooden chair from the shadows beside the door, and set it at the desk and across from his chair. "Sit, Killean," Joseph said as he walked over and settled into his chair.

Killean glanced at the closed door behind him. He could feel Simone out there, suffering. But the only chance they had of making it out of this mess was for him to learn more about what was going on here and the weaknesses of this place. After his betrayal, he would return to Ronan with as much information as he could gather.

Killean strode forward, pulled out the wooden chair, and settled onto it. Questions spun through his mind, but he'd never been much of a talker. Smelling like a Savage or not, he would draw Joseph's attention if he started peppering him with questions about his plans and who was the *real* mastermind behind this. No one in the Alliance believed Joseph was working alone in this.

Killean remained mute while he folded his hands and rested them on his bare stomach. Joseph's mouth quirked in an amused smile that vanished when a knock sounded on the door behind him.

"Come in," Joseph called.

The door opened to reveal the second woman Joseph had spoken with. In her pale hands, she clutched a glass decanter full of blood. Placing two glasses on the desk, she poured the liquid into them. Killean's nostrils flared when the scent of it hit him.

"We'll go hunting in a bit," Joseph said as he pushed one of the glasses toward Killean. "Until then, this will have to suffice."

Killean rested his fingers on the glass to push it away; instead, he found his hand gripping it, but he didn't recall giving his fingers the command to do so. *Refusing will only make Joseph suspicious.*

But that wasn't why he was holding the glass. No, he was doing that because the blood called to him like a siren called the ships.

What am I becoming?

What you made yourself into.

It was the truth, but before killing, he'd been sure he could control himself better than this. He felt no control as he lifted the glass and sipped the room-temperature blood. It was not the live, warm vein he craved, but it helped to ease some of his burgeoning hunger.

The first woman returned with a set of clothes. When her gaze raked over him, it lingered on his crotch, and she licked her lips. Killean didn't acknowledge her stare or try to cover himself.

Like almost all the women he'd encountered over the past hundred years, she held no interest for him.

The only woman who had ever mattered was chained to a wall in the next room.

Joseph's serving woman, or whatever she was, placed the clothes on the desk in front of Killean; he ignored them. He wouldn't give Joseph the satisfaction of putting them on now. Killean took another swallow of blood and steadied the trembling in his fingers when he set the glass on the desk.

"Leave us and the blood," Joseph commanded the two women.

The woman set the decanter on the desk and followed the other one out of the room.

When the heavy metal door closed behind them, Joseph clasped his hands before him. "Does your abrupt change of loyalty have anything to do with the fact Ronan and the hunters are working together?"

Killean kept his face blank while his mind reeled from Joseph's question. How did Joseph know they'd formed an Alliance with the hunters? But he supposed any of the hunters chained up out there would willingly spill the information if they believed it might save them.

Idiots.

Killean hadn't planned to reveal this information to Joseph, but if the Savage already knew about the Alliance, then he would use it to his advantage.

"I have never hidden my dislike of the hunters," he said.

"No, you haven't," Joseph agreed. "We rarely worked together, and even I knew you harbored a greater dislike toward them than the rest of us. Perhaps it has something to do with your scars."

Inwardly, Killean seethed at Joseph's attempt to analyze him; outwardly, he remained utterly composed.

"Ronan should have taken your feelings into account when agreeing to work with them," Joseph said. "It cost him one of his most loyal and vicious fighters."

"There is no stopping Ronan when he sets his mind to something."

"Very true. So, tell me, where is Ronan hiding now?"

Killean had expected questions such as this and prepared for them. He hoped he was a better actor than he believed. "And how would I know? As soon as I left, Ronan would have changed locations. Maybe before he became mated he would have stayed, but he'd never risk his mate by keeping her somewhere Savages could find."

"Then where *was* he, Killean?" Joseph inquired with a lethal gleam in his eyes.

Killean smiled as he leaned back in his chair. "I'm sure you can understand that, for now, I will be keeping some things to myself, Joseph. I will not divulge all my info to you as I'm sure you have plenty you will keep from me too. Unless you intend to tell me your exact plans for those hunters and all the others you're turning into Savages as well as where we are?"

Killean practically saw Joseph's desire to destroy him burning behind the Savage's eyes. But instead of trying to attack, Joseph leaned back in his chair and rested the tips of his entwined fingers against his chin.

"While I still have some knowledge you want, I have a better chance you'll keep me alive," Killean continued.

"I plan to keep you alive anyway. Two fallen Defenders working together to bring down Ronan is far better than one, but I understand your reasoning."

"Good. Once we establish a more mutual trust, we can discuss this again."

Joseph smirked. "That shouldn't take long. Do you really think Ronan moved?"

Killean wasn't sure, but he doubted it. They'd just established a shared compound with the hunters; it would be difficult for them to pick up so many lives again and relocate them, but Ronan would do anything to keep Kadence safe.

Maybe he was wrong, and they had left, or perhaps he was only hoping Ronan had enough faith in him to delve into this world of Savages and return from it without betraying the Alliance.

He didn't know if he deserved any faith as he gripped the glass and brought the blood back to his mouth.

Simone lifted her head when the hunter beside her shifted. She looked toward where she'd seen Killean vanishing into the room where the Savage who'd done this to her always went. She hoped they both choked on the next person they ate.

"Simone," someone croaked; their voice was so dry it could have belonged to a mummy recently roused from the dead.

Gradually turning her head, she met the gaze of Dallas as he stared at her from inhuman, white-blue eyes. She'd forgotten he was the one chained beside her. Those eyes should freak her out more than they did, but she couldn't bring herself to care about the strange color on the man she'd briefly considered her leader. When she left Nathan behind, it was to follow Dallas to a stronghold he established in New Hampshire.

She never should have left Nathan and the others, but her battered pride compelled her to go. Pride, a sin she'd believed herself above experiencing, and something she never realized she possessed until Nathan chose a vampire over her. She'd never been in love with Nathan, but she'd spent most of her life with the expectation she would marry the leader of all the hunters. All those in their stronghold had believed the same thing.

But the blow her life took that day was nothing compared to the devastating mess she found herself embroiled in now. Even if she had been prideful when she was raised better than to give in to such a shameful emotion, and when she should have been happy Nathan found love instead of wallowing in the imagined life she lost, she didn't deserve *this*.

No one deserved this.

And now Killean, the only man she'd ever kissed and who made her feel a hint of passion about anything in life, was one of the monsters keeping her here. Tears clogged her throat, and if she wasn't as dehydrated as a raisin, she might have cried for the first time since finding herself here.

Hopelessness and self-pity swamped her. She hated herself for the emotions, but she couldn't shake them. She saw no way out of this debacle, and she dreaded becoming one of the foul-smelling creatures keeping her here.

Even if she could come up with an escape plan, she'd never been a fighter. She'd taken some of the self-defense classes Nathan imposed on the women in the stronghold after Kadence ran away, but she'd hated every second of them.

She was born and bred to become a wife, not a fighter or killer. Cooking and sewing were where she excelled. She'd been the epitome of the perfect student and destined to be the mother of the son who would one day rise to take his father's place as the hunter leader.

Then Nathan fell in love with another, and all her dreams crumbled. She left the stronghold so she wouldn't have to be reminded of that every time she saw Nathan and Vicky together. She left so she wouldn't have to take another class on how to punch, kick, and stab something.

She left because, if she wasn't going to become the wife of the leader, she planned to resume her old life as much as possible.

She'd never liked change, and the changes Nathan was implementing on the hunters were too much for her.

But they were far less than the changes shoved onto her in this hellish place. And soon, if she didn't do something, she would become one of these monsters and what remained of the woman she was would be destroyed forever.

"Simone," Dallas croaked again.

"What?" she asked and was appalled to discover her voice sounded as bad as his.

"That vampire they brought in was one of Ronan's men, wasn't he?"

Simone tried swallowing to wet her arid throat; it was pointless. "Yes."

For a second, hope shone in Dallas's eyes. "Do you think they sent him in search of us?"

Oh, how she wished that were true, but though she was many things, some of which she hadn't realized until recently, she wasn't delusional. She'd seen Killean's eyes, and though he was nude, he wasn't chained. Recalling his cruel dismissal of her after they kissed on the beach, she knew if anyone was going to join these monsters, it was him.

"No," she rasped. "He's here for an entirely different reason."

Noise on her left drew her attention to Killean and Joseph when they emerged from the room. Killean had clothes draped over his arm, but he remained as bare as the day he was born. Again, she felt a hideous blush creeping up her cheeks and ducked her head. What was it about him that always unsettled her so much?

Killean stared at Simone's bent head as her shoulders hunched forward. Her profile revealed the delicate slope of her slender nose, high cheekbones, and the curve of her full, pink lips. In his lifetime, he'd encountered numerous beautiful women, but none had affected him as she did.

He felt no desire for her, not while she was like this, but protective urges he'd never known he possessed rolled through him. He wanted to go to her, draw her into his arms, and shelter her from this atrocity, but he was caught in this hideous pit of helplessness until he could figure out a way to get her free.

"They're future puppets and nothing more," Joseph said. "Come, let's hunt."

Killean forced his attention away from Simone to follow Joseph past the hunters; all fifty of the ones taken from the New Hampshire stronghold were here. Some of Joseph's flunkies trailed them down the long, concrete corridor. No other rooms or tunnels branched off this one, and every ten feet a recessed light cast a dim, yellow circle onto the concrete. A hundred feet from the end of the corridor, the line of hunters stopped, but empty chains continued to dangle from the walls in wait for future victims.

When they reached the end, Joseph stopped outside the large steel door there. "You should probably dress for this," Joseph said. "I don't care if you run around naked for the rest of your life, but you'll only draw the attention of the humans we hunt, and not in a good way."

Killean couldn't argue with that, and since he was ready for more than blood in a glass, he lifted the brandy-colored shirt he'd been handed and tugged it on. It was constricting across his chest and shoulders, and the sleeves ended an inch above his wrist, but the jeans fit well, as did the socks and boots.

"I'm sure you'll understand that you'll be blindfolded and put in a trunk again," Joseph said when he finished dressing. "And that once we get where we're going, you will be watched. You are not to ask anyone any questions about where we are or try to escape. I'm sure you understand that these rules will be enforced, and you will be monitored until a more mutual trust is established."

Everything inside Killean rebelled against the knowledge that he would have no freedom outside of this place, but he gritted his teeth and replied. "Of course."

Joseph gestured to the Savages, and they tied a blindfold around his eyes before slipping a sack over his head and pulling the string tight around his neck. Killean didn't protest that they cut off some of his air supply; he was sure it was done on purpose, and he would not give them the satisfaction of bitching about it.

The door clanged open and fresh air washed over him. Killean scented the air to try to decipher some clue as to where they were, but all he smelled was grass, the sharper aroma of wild animals, and a nearby fresh water supply. He heard no nearby traffic, but crickets chirruped loudly, and the wings of bats or birds fluttered overhead.

"This way," Joseph said.

Someone grabbed his elbow and guided him forward. Instead of asphalt or stone, grass crunched under his feet as he walked. Wherever they were, it was a rural area, and he suspected it was far from the city. He stopped when his knees bumped against the bumper of a car and someone guided him into the trunk.

CHAPTER FIVE

KILLEAN STARED at the weak light in the ceiling as he lay motionless with his arm draped across his forehead. He was slipping further down the rabbit hole of Savagery and tonight hadn't helped him.

They'd driven for at least an hour before finally stopping. Before removing him from the trunk, they pulled the sack off his head but kept the blindfold on until they stood outside the back door of a small nightclub. Killean never glimpsed a license plate or the name of the club before the door opened and he was led inside.

He'd been brought to the club to hunt, and with Joseph and two other Savages monitoring his every move, he had to kill. It was what they expected of him; it was why he was here. And if he didn't kill someone, then they would destroy him, and Simone would be lost.

Seething with resentment, Killean stalked the fifty or so patrons of the club in search of one who would fit some of the criteria he'd used for his other victims. After an hour, he witnessed a man slip something into a woman's drink, but unlike his other victims, he knew nothing else about the man. It had to have been a drug the man used; he *had* to have been planning to rape the woman, but Killean didn't know for sure.

However, it wasn't guilt plaguing him as he swung his legs off the edge of the cot and planted his feet on the floor to sit up; it was his lack of remorse that bothered him. It didn't help that hunger was beginning to churn in his gut again.

Killean's hands gripped the metal edge of the cot as he took a deep breath and shoved himself to his feet. The only furniture in the room was the cot with its pillow and a thin, wool blanket. The room was nothing more than an eight by eight cell with concrete walls that felt like they were closing in on him with every passing minute.

Reclaiming the jeans he'd tossed on the floor beside the shirt, Killean dressed and opened the heavy, steel door. He poked his head into the hall and glanced up and down the nearly two-hundred-foot-long corridor. About fifty closed doors lined both sides of the hall; Joseph's cronies filled many of those rooms.

No one had told him to stay in his room when he was brought there earlier. He saw no reason to remain when he might be able to learn more about this place while everyone else was in their room or elsewhere.

Stepping into the hall, he closed the door on room number twenty-two before striding down the corridor. Beneath his bare feet, the concrete floor was cold, and he made no sound as he walked. He waited for doors to open or for someone to stop him, but no one did.

He still had no idea where they were located, but he believed this to be a bomb shelter or bunker of some sort. Whether it was built years ago, or Joseph and his organization recently constructed it, Killean didn't know.

In the middle of the corridor, Killean stopped at the open doorway leading into the main hall where the prisoners were chained. He should stay away from Simone until he had a better chance of getting her out of here, but he found himself irresistibly drawn across the threshold and into the hall beyond.

He glanced down the row of hunters, and his eyes settled on Simone. She had her knees against her chest and her cheek resting on them as her chained hands remained above her on the wall. The man beside her shifted, and his head rose. When his white-blue eyes locked on Killean, his mouth parted.

Killean wanted to go straight to Simone, but knowing cameras were probably focused on him, he walked over to the first hunter and knelt in front of the man who recoiled as far as he could get. Killean inspected the man before moving onto the next who snapped and lunged at him.

He made his way slowly down the line, inspecting each hunter as he went. His excitement grew the closer he got to Simone. Most of the hunters cowered from him, a few showed no reaction, and the rest tried to attack him. He kept expecting a Savage to come and pull him away, but no one did. Though, he had a feeling they were monitoring his every move.

He paused at one of the hunter women before Simone and cupped her cheek. When she turned her head away from him and whimpered, Killean quickly lowered his hand. The woman had endured enough without having to suffer his unwanted touch, but he hadn't wanted to touch her. He *did* want to touch Simone though, and he had to set a precedent before he reached her and did so. He touched two more women who lunged at him with their fangs snapping.

And then, finally, he was in front of her. Anger filled him as he gazed at her slender frame, dirt-streaked countenance, and dirty hair.

You've seen her. She's fine. Go before someone finds you here.

He should leave and not look back; instead, he found himself remaining before her as she lifted her head to stare at him. At first, she didn't seem to see him as her strangely colored eyes remained unfocused. Then she blinked, and those eyes widened on him.

Pulled irresistibly toward her, Killean rested his fingers against her cheek. Despite the abuse she'd endured and the grime caking her skin, her flesh was softer than a feather against his. Some of his newly reawakened hunger ebbed as the touch of her calmed him in a way he'd never experienced before.

Never had he wished to hold and protect someone as badly as her.

Awe filled Simone as Killean caressed her cheek and the red bled from his eyes to reveal their striking gold color. That color was nearly identical to the color of a tiger's eyes, but she suspected he could destroy someone faster than any tiger; yet, he touched her with unfailing gentleness.

And the weirdest part of all was she *liked* it. She should spit in his face, recoil from him, yell at him to go away, or try to attack him. He was the *enemy*! She should *not* be turning her cheek into his touch or inhaling the resin scent of his skin.

Had she been mistaken about this man? Was he here for some reason other than to be a beast who thrived on killing innocents? She had to be wrong as no monster could be so tender toward another, or at least all the ones she'd seen here couldn't.

Simone's eyes closed as his scent enveloped her, but beneath his natural, woodsy aroma, she detected the rot of a Savage.

No! She inwardly moaned. He *was* one of them; there was no denying or hiding that smell, yet she still found her lips resting against his palm as tears burned her eyes. No matter how hard she tried, she couldn't deny this man made her feel something she'd never felt before him—passion.

It surprised her to discover she felt it more as a vampire than she had as a mortal hunter. His nearness caused her skin to tingle with electricity as his touch warmed her to the tips of her toes. She was so cold before; now his body heated hers.

Killean closed his eyes as he leaned forward. He almost cupped the back of her head to draw her close to him, but he didn't dare. Up until now, he could attribute his actions to curiosity over the turned hunters, but if he kissed her, there would be no denying there was something more between them.

Killean turned his attention to the thick chains binding her to the wall. By the looks of them, they were specially designed to keep a vampire restrained, and not just any vampire, but a hunter turned vampire. Starved, they were weakened, but turned hunters were stronger than a human who became a vampire. Joseph wouldn't take any chances either; these chains would be strong enough to keep *any* vamp secured, even a purebred.

With the essence of life flowing through his veins, Killean was stronger than he'd been before, but he didn't know if he was strong enough to break these bonds. And he didn't dare try without being certain; besides, if he could get her free of this place, what would they discover outside?

For all he knew, they were in the middle of nowhere and could break free only to plunge into an open field with nowhere to run or hide. In which case, with as weak as she was, they would be caught and brought back before they got far. Once recaptured, they would torture and kill him, which would leave Simone forever at their mercy.

No matter how badly he wanted to free her, he couldn't risk it until he knew more.

Simone's fangs throbbed when she detected the pulse in Killean's wrist. Her scorched veins felt like they were breaking apart and turning to ash as each beat of his heart teased her with the possibility of nourishment. She didn't want to hurt him, but his blood smelled *so* good!

Only a little taste to make it stop hurting!

No! No! No! She would not drink his blood! She wouldn't, *couldn't* be one of them!

But no matter how forcefully she told herself this, her lips skimmed back and her whole body hummed with anticipation of tasting him.

Before she could sink her fangs into his flesh, his hand dropped and he rose. Startled out of the trance his pulse lured her into, Simone lunged after her food source, but the chains pulled taut and yanked her back. A wail of anguish rose in her throat and strangled there.

Killean stepped away from Simone when Joseph glided into the hall. He didn't look at all surprised to see Killean standing there as a smirk curved his cruel mouth. "Killean," he greeted.

"Joseph," he replied.

Simone's eyes darted between the two powerful creatures. In here, misery was her ever-constant companion, but the undercurrent of tension between them caused fear to coil in her belly. However, this time, her fear was for Killean and not herself.

"What brings you here?" Joseph inquired.

"I was curious about the hunters; how they react to the change, what they're like, and how far gone these prisoners are in their hunger," Killean replied.

"Why?"

"Because it's a fascinating process, and there is nothing like watching those who believe they are untouchable fall. And the hunters have believed themselves above us for far too many years." He waved a hand at Simone. "I want her."

Joseph glanced at Simone. "Ah, yes, she is a beauty, more so before the chains, of course. She's a bit too dirty now for my liking, but nothing a shower and some blood won't fix. I changed her myself."

Killean had been striving to remain impassive, but this revelation caused his jaw to clench. If Joseph changed her, then he made sure the experience was horrific for her. She never should have known the agony that came from having her blood drained against her will and the change forced on her, but more than that, she was supposed to have been *his* to change.

Or *not* change, he reminded himself.

They would never complete the bond, but *no* other's blood should have entered her, especially not *this* bastard's. Joseph would have made it degrading for her, and Killean knew how it felt to be helpless against the abuse of another. He'd wanted to comfort her before, but now the impulse was almost impossible to withstand, but he did. She deserved better than this, and she would have it once he got her free and returned her to her brethren.

Joseph's abuse of Simone was yet another reason Killean would make his death *excruciating*.

"What do you want with her?" Joseph asked him.

The truth of that could never be revealed, so Killean gave Joseph the only answer he knew the asshole would understand. "I want to fuck her."

Simone recoiled at Killean's coarse words. She didn't know why she was shocked; he was a vampire after all. They were *all* ruled by their desires, and *none* of them cared who they trampled to get what they wanted.

Had she been idiotic enough to believe there might be something more to this beast than bloodlust and carnal pleasure? Yes, she had, and now she had to fend off the disappointment threatening to strangle her. She'd briefly hoped he might be an ally in this place, but he'd just become a bigger threat than anyone else here.

"Why, Killean," Joseph purred, "I don't recall ever seeing you with a woman."

Killean shrugged. "Things have changed."

"Ah, yes." Joseph's gaze raked him from head to toe. "It's

amazing what else awakens in us when the bloodlust is sated. However, these specimens are off limits until they complete their change into something of true beauty."

Beauty? Simone wondered. Did this monster actually see himself and his followers as things of *beauty*?

"Beauty?" Killean inquired, astonished to hear anyone refer to a Savage in such a way.

"Don't you find it a thing of beauty to be yourself finally?" Joseph asked. "Don't you think it's wonderful not to have to fight your instincts and *true* nature anymore? Freedom is beauty, Killean, and we are free."

He must be further gone than he'd realized as some of what Joseph said rang true with him. There was beauty in freedom, and for those minutes when he'd given into his darker nature and killed, he'd been free.

So far, he hadn't truly given into his Savage nature, but he'd experienced those minutes, and they were *wonderful*. If he ever gave in completely, it would be the most freeing experience of his life, and he couldn't deny it sounded amazing. There was also some beauty in death, the eternal slumber, the peaceful oblivion of never suffering again, and he was delivering it to the humans who deserved it.

If he continued only to kill those who hurt others, then wouldn't he be doing something good for this world? And if Simone became a Savage too...

The image of her coated in the blood of those they killed together filled his mind. But instead of tempting him further, the visualization made something within him recoil.

No, *not* Simone. She could never return to what she'd been before, but she was too pure to ever become such a monster. The idea of him being the one who led her down such a warped path was unthinkable.

He could forgive himself for the choices that brought him to this place, but he would never forgive himself if he trapped her here with him. And Killean would never forgive himself if he turned against Ronan and became what Joseph was, but if he kept killing, he probably wouldn't care about that anymore, and he could be *free*.

No! He would not cave; he would not become one of these things. He'd come here for Simone, and he would get her out of this.

"Freedom is beauty," Killean murmured because it was what Joseph wanted to hear and because the words were right.

"Yes," Joseph said and slapped him on the shoulder. "Come, I've plenty of other women I can offer you."

Killean didn't move as the idea of touching anyone other than Simone caused his stomach to turn. "I want this one."

Joseph's eyes narrowed. "Why *her* in particular?"

Killean considered how to respond as he may have just given away too much. "I knew her when she was a hunter, and the little bitch thought she was better than vampires. I think it's time she learns what it's like to have one between her thighs."

Joseph smirked when Simone whimpered. She'd known Killean was revolting, but his words proved he was worse than she believed.

"It would be a good lesson to learn," Joseph agreed, "but not yet. When her transformation is complete, you can have at her, but until then, she remains chained and is only allowed short bathroom breaks. Those are the rules."

"Rules are meant to be broken," Killean said. He wanted to get Simone alone, give her at least a little blood to strengthen her, and assure her he would find a way to free her. He also wanted to learn if Joseph, or any of the other Savages in this place, had violated her. What he would do to them if they had would make what Vlad the Impaler did to his victims look like fun.

"Not this one," Joseph stated.

The glint in Joseph's eyes told Killean not to push it anymore; he was lucky Joseph had bought the shit he was shoveling. Killean suspected this rule was not one of Joseph's making. Joseph would happily take the chance of a hunter getting free if it meant he could abuse them further; they were no fun to play with when chained like this. Someone else was pulling the strings here, but who?

"Come," Joseph said. "Let's find you a woman."

The appearance of two Savages spared Killean from having to think of an excuse to get out of that hideous possibility.

"We have company coming," one of them said.

Joseph's shoulders went back as he gave a brisk nod. "Escort Killean to his chamber."

Joseph's abrupt change in demeanor piqued Killean's curiosity, but he had no choice; in this, he had to obey.

"I can find the chamber myself," Killean assured him.

He didn't look back at Simone as he turned away; he couldn't stand to see what his words had caused her to think of him. If he somehow succeeded in getting her out of this mess, they'd both hate him by the time it was over.

Good. She's a hunter; I don't care if she never speaks to me again.

It was one of the rare times in his life that he'd lied to himself.

CHAPTER SIX

Aside from the hall where the hunters stayed, the corridor where he slept, Joseph's office, and the large communal bathroom with showers that the Savages took him to after returning from the hunt last night, Killean knew little about this place. He decided to spend the next day trying to learn more about their location and the exits from it.

He made sure to look merely curious while he explored as he discovered cameras hidden in some of the lights of every hallway. They would expect him to explore and learn; if they had a problem with it, they would stop him, but so far they'd left him alone.

His exploration also helped him keep his distance from Simone. Still, he couldn't rid himself of the incessant pull he felt to go to her and get her out of here. But he'd discovered no way to do that yet.

Returning to the bathroom, he discovered another circular room near it. The hair on his nape rose as he gazed inside the room. He saw no instruments of torture, but the drains in the concrete floor didn't bode well for those brought here.

Turning away, he padded down the hall and back toward the corridor where he slept before branching off down another hall. This new hallway ran along the backside of Joseph's office and housed more closed doors with numbers beside them.

Though he already suspected more bedrooms lay beyond, he had to confirm his suspicion before moving on. He didn't glance at the camera as he turned the knob and poked his head inside one of the rooms.

The room beyond was identical to his except no clothes littered the concrete floor, and the bed was neatly made. The rooms along his hall were almost all full, but he'd only seen enough Savages in this place to account for the occupancy of those rooms. Most of the ones along this hall were probably empty and waiting for their time to be filled.

Gazing down the long hall, Killean calculated twice as many rooms were lining it as the one where he slept. This place could house a hundred and fifty Savages comfortably; more if they doubled up in the rooms. And this may only be one of many bunkers or shelters or whatever this place was that Joseph had.

What is going on here? What are they preparing for?

The end of the world.

He almost snorted at the melodramatic thought, but the cold certainty Joseph and his followers might be readying themselves for such a thing stopped him. The path Joseph was taking was one that could destroy everything vampires and hunters had spent thousands of years trying to protect. Joseph's course of creating so many Savages and decimating the hunters could alert the humans to their existence, which might result in total anarchy.

Shit. It was such an inadequate word to describe the dread churning in his gut.

Killean closed the door and continued down the hall. Toward the end of the corridor, the space between four of the rooms grew larger. Killean tried the knobs but discovered them locked. Stepping back, he gazed at the identical doors as understanding dawned.

These four doors housed larger bedrooms, one of which was most certainly Joseph's. At least one of the other rooms had to be occupied by the guest Joseph greeted the other night. Killean didn't know if the other two rooms were empty but locked to keep out Savages looking to upgrade, or if other prominent figures in Joseph's army slept behind them.

Killean resisted kicking the doors in to learn more; that would only earn him a detour from his explorations. Turning away, he strode to the end of the hall and turned left; it was the only option given to him.

He stepped into the doorway of another circular, concrete room, but this one was twice the size of the empty room and Joseph's office. About twenty feet separated him from a metal shelf set in front of some see-through plastic sections about waist-high off the ground.

The setup looked familiar to him, and it took him a minute to realize the plastic and shelf were part of a human serving area. He'd seen cafeterias resembling this over the years, but without servers behind the plastic dividers ladling out food, and no people pushing their trays down the metal ramp, he hadn't immediately placed what it was.

Also, when he'd seen places such as this before, there were tables in the room where the humans ate, but aside from the serving area, the room was only empty space and concrete floor. His steps didn't make any noise as he glided across the room to explore beyond the serving area.

When he stepped around the serving area and walked past some cutting tables, he discovered a metal stove and a large, double refrigerator. He opened the fridge and found it empty. Still, if this room was here, then it had a purpose and it wasn't to feed Savages. Whatever this place was, it seemed humans originally built it and not vampires.

Bomb shelter. It had to be. But not one built in the fifties and sixties when fear of nuclear war was at its highest, and even vamps were concerned about what the imbecilic humans would do next. Vampires could survive many things, but they had no idea what nuclear fallout would do to them. If vampires did survive, it wouldn't be pleasant, and it would wipe out most of their food supply.

No, this shelter was newer than those uncertain days, or at least it was more recently updated than the heyday of the Cold War.

And then he realized the Savages *could* have recently had this place constructed to serve as an emergency shelter if it became necessary. They would require a food supply if they locked themselves in here, and they would have to keep that food alive by giving it nourishment. Keeping humans alive in here would be difficult, as some of the Savages would give in and kill some of their supply; he also suspected those Savages would be slaughtered in return.

He couldn't imagine anything more horrible than being locked beneath the earth with a bunch of Savages who weren't allowed to kill their limited food supply.

Walking around the fridge, Killean discovered the room went another twenty feet back. He strolled past the appliances and to the back wall where he opened the door of a pantry to reveal thousands of canned goods stashed inside. He had no idea how much people ate, but there seemed to be enough here to keep them going for months, maybe years.

He closed the pantry door and strolled over to the walk-in freezer taking up most of the back wall. Not only did the freezer contain enough blood to keep a hundred vampires alive for at least a year, but it also held plenty of meat and perishables for humans.

He tried to process everything he was seeing, but his gaze kept returning to the bags of frozen blood. Saliva filled his mouth as he licked his lips; what he wouldn't give to sink his fangs into someone's throat, rip it out, and bathe in their blood. Memories of last night's kill danced across his mind as his body thrummed with excitement.

What he was becoming should repulse him; instead, he found himself pondering when he'd be able to hunt again. He craved the rush of blood filling his mouth, the life slipping into him, and the power it brought. All he wanted—

Stop!

Killean rubbed at his temples as the demon part of him clamored for more death. *Must control it.*

But he felt as if he were spiraling farther away. *Simone! You're here for Simone!*

Drawing on that reminder, Killean gathered the tattered remains of his self-control and finally lifted his head again. He kept his gaze away from the blood as the chilly air flowing over his skin further helped to clear his mind.

If the freezer was fully functional, then they had to be powering it somehow. The same could be said for the lights and the hot water in the showers, but until seeing this freezer, he'd never really thought about a power source for this place. Either they had a self-contained electric grid here, or they were hooked into a natural gas line that wouldn't be affected by a disaster.

But then, if the world went to shit, he doubted anyone would choose to be plugged into combustible gas... so, their own power source fueled this place.

"What are you doing back here?"

Killean almost jumped at the sudden intrusion, but he kept

himself from doing so as he turned toward the Savage standing behind him. How had he not heard the man approach?

Because you're losing it.

And that was true.

"Exploring," he replied as he closed the freezer door. "What are *you* doing back here?"

The man crossed his arms over his chest. "Joseph sent me for you; he says you're to go to him now."

Killean bit back the retort of, *I don't give a fuck what he says,* but such a reply wouldn't go over too well, and he had a role to play. Never had he chafed against the responsibilities placed on him by being one of Ronan's men, but Ronan never treated him like a dog meant to jump when he commanded.

"Now!" the man barked.

Before Killean could think, he lashed out and seized the man's throat. Lifting the Savage off the ground, Killean smashed him into the concrete. The impact shattered the wall and created a perfect, man-sized indent. He bared his fangs as he thrust his face into the man's.

"Don't you *ever* talk to me like that again," Killean snarled.

CHAPTER SEVEN

Killean's fingers dug into the man's flesh, cutting off his air supply and spilling blood. The man's feet kicked against the concrete as Killean's gaze latched onto the red trails streaking his pale flesh. The man choked, and his face turned florid as Killean resisted sinking his fangs into the Savage's throat and draining him dry.

He hadn't been able to stop himself from attacking one of Joseph's men, but he could stop himself from killing one of them. Killean shoved the man's head off the wall and released him. The Savage slid to the ground and nearly collapsed, before locking his legs underneath him.

"Joseph will kill you for this!" the Savage spat at him as he grasped his throat.

Killean grabbed the man by the scruff of his neck and hauled him forward. The Savage was only an inch or two shorter than him, yet he couldn't break free of Killean's grasp as Killean dragged him across the kitchen and out into the hall again. While he was here, he had to play nice and go along with Joseph, but he wouldn't tolerate some little pissant thinking they could order him around.

A couple of startled Savages stepped out of their way when Killean stalked into the hallway where he slept, but no one tried to stop him. Killean kept the man's head down and his body hunched over while he propelled him into the hall with the hunters. His gaze flicked to Simone who didn't look at him, but neither did any of the other hunters as they huddled into themselves.

Killean tore his attention away from Simone's increasingly gaunt face as he dragged the man up to Joseph's door and used the Savage's head to knock on it.

"Come in!" Joseph called.

Killean opened the door and shoved Joseph's lackey inside. The Savage stumbled and nearly crashed into Joseph's desk before righting himself.

"What is the meaning of this?" Joseph demanded as he rose to stand behind his desk.

"We had a disagreement, and he believes you'll kill me over it," Killean replied with a scathing look at the man he'd hauled in here.

"I did what you commanded me to do, sir! He" —the man pointed a finger at Killean, but when Killean growled at him, the guy quickly lowered it— "was taking his sweet-ass time."

"I won't be commanded by some pawn," Killean said, and when he stepped closer to the man, the Savage edged away.

While here, Killean would do as told when it was necessary, but to survive in this world, he had to take a stand. Joseph wouldn't expect him to meekly take orders from someone who didn't possess his kind of power or breeding; it would raise suspicions if he did. In this treacherous, unfamiliar world, *every* move he made could be the wrong one.

Killean stared at Joseph while he waited to see if he'd played this hand right. For all he knew, Joseph had sent this man to ruffle Killean's feathers and bait him into a trap. But had the trap just snapped closed and killed him or set him free?

Joseph smirked as he returned to his seat and rested his hands on his stomach. "Leave us, Andre."

Andre looked like Joseph had told him to fly away as he started to sputter a protest.

"Get out!" Joseph spat, cutting off anything Andre was trying to say.

Andre scurried past Killean and out the door; it banged shut behind him.

"I won't tolerate insolence here," Joseph said.

"Understandable, but I won't tolerate these newbies thinking they can order me around. I am a powerful, centuries-old pure-bred, and they are simply a means to an end for whatever you're planning."

"True," Joseph agreed as he leaned forward. "Our breeding is far superior to theirs, but they are a necessity."

"For what?"

"You are far from ready for that information."

Killean's teeth ground together in response to Joseph's condescending words. If the other Savages wouldn't pounce on him and tear him apart before he could flee with Simone, Killean would go for Joseph in the hopes of putting an end to those plans. But he'd never survive this place, and he'd never learn who was really behind whatever Joseph was doing here.

"Why did you want me?" Killean asked.

"We are going to hunt!" Joseph declared, and settling his hands on the desk, he pushed himself to his feet. "We must both be well fed for tomorrow."

"And why is that?"

"Because the hunters are ready. Tomorrow night we will be taking some of them out and setting them free to slaughter."

Joseph strolled out from behind his desk and clapped Killean on the shoulder before leading him toward the door. Killean's skin crawled at the contact, but something more had the hair on his nape rising. He had to figure a way to save Simone before tomorrow.

~

Hungry. So hungry.

Someone had taken a match to her veins, and as if gasoline instead of blood filled them, they'd set those veins afire. She couldn't think about anything other than the flames devouring her and her burning hunger. Yanking on her chains, she tried to break herself free, but they wouldn't let her go.

The chains rattled; she jerked more angrily as strange noises filled her ears. Was she making that sound? She scented blood. Was she tearing her skin? Did it come from someone else? Whatever the answers, she didn't care as she sniffed at the air like a hound on the scent.

Blood. Blood. Blood.

Her head throbbed; her vision blurred. She was dying, but she couldn't die. She could only feel and suffer and *hunger*.

Nearby steps caused her head to tip back. It took a few seconds, but her gaze finally settled on the scarred man with the deep brown hair. *Name? Can't remember. Don't care. Blood. He has blood! And his blood smells so good!*

Her eyes latched onto his neck and the blood pulsing through there. *NEED!*

Something pierced her bottom lip, but the temporary discomfort was nothing compared to the inferno raging through her body.

Killean went to kneel in front of Simone before catching himself. He wanted nothing more than to offer her some comfort, but at his side, Joseph was speaking with one of his followers. Simone stared at him, but her white-blue eyes burned with hunger and Killean knew she didn't have any idea who he was or what was going on anymore. She was lost in the haze of bloodlust and starvation.

I won't let you be lost forever, he vowed.

Blood trickled from the skin she'd torn away from her wrists in her attempts to get free. Her fangs had shredded her bottom lip, and the fine blue veins in her cheeks and eyelids were visible as her skin had become nearly translucent. The once elegant angles of her high cheekbones looked about to break through her skin.

"Looks like this little bitch is getting the comeuppance you wanted her to receive," Joseph said in his ear.

I am going to kill you, Killean promised as he reined in his temper.

"Yes," Killean murmured.

Simone sniffed at the air as her teeth snapped. The composed, beautiful hunter he first encountered had been replaced by this animalistic, broken version, and though he hadn't liked her doll-like perfection, he *loathed* this.

"After tomorrow, she could be yours for the taking."

After tomorrow, Killean would make sure she wasn't here.

"Come, let's hunt," Joseph said.

It took everything Killean had to put one foot in front of the other away from Simone. Frustration and rage boiled within him as the blindfold and hood were placed on again before they led him outside.

Simone watched the men stride away from her. They'd taken the tantalizing scent of their blood with them, but the aroma lingered.

I want... hunnnngry... Blood. Blood. BLOOD!

CHAPTER EIGHT

Killean paced the small confines of his cell from one end to the other. He'd found and killed a man last night who was bragging to his friends about the number of girls he'd banged.

When one of the friends quipped, "Yeah, but how many of them were awake for it?"

The man had shrugged and replied, "Who cares as long as I am?"

Killean made sure the man was awake and feeling it as he sucked the life from him.

Yet, the blood and death of last night hadn't eased his foul mood or calmed his bloodlust. They'd only increased with every passing hour as night approached. He'd been here for three days and he still had no idea how he was going to save Simone.

Stopping, he drew back his fist and drove it into the concrete wall. Dust rained down, the wall and his knuckles cracked. The broken bones didn't deter him from hammering the wall until his blood streaked it and piles of dust lay at his feet.

Pulling his hand back, he watched as his flattened knuckles popped back up and shifted into place. He flexed his already mending bones as his broken skin knitted itself closed. Consuming the blood of innocents had increased the rate with which he healed. Unable to look at his hands anymore, he lowered them and gazed at the blood coating the wall. He couldn't scent the Savage on himself like he could the others, but that blood was as tainted as he was.

Turning away from the wall, Killean stalked over to the door, flung it open, and strode into the hall. No one else was about, but he knew better than to go to the hunters again. He didn't know if he could stop himself from trying to tear Simone free, and if he kept showing an interest in her, it would only make Joseph suspicious of him.

But he didn't know where else to go. There was no gym where he could unleash some of his pent-up energy. There was no one he could kill, and that was what he longed for most.

Arriving at the end of the hall, Killean turned and headed for the kitchen. He had no idea what he planned to do there, but before he was halfway to his destination, a hooded figure in a black cloak striding toward him caused him to stop. The being stood well over seven feet tall and hunched over to avoid hitting its head on the ceiling. Leaner than him, the cloak swallowed much of the creature and all its face.

However, its imposing height was not what stopped Killean in his tracks. No, what glued his feet to the floor was the vast amount of power wafting from the creature; it electrified his skin and caused the hair on his arms to stand up.

He'd spent most of his life working with Ronan, the oldest vampire in existence and a fifth-generation purebred, but this thing made the power Ronan emitted feel like child's play.

What is this thing?

He had no guesses about that as the being bared down on him. Killean didn't recall thinking about doing it before he was stepping out of the creature's way. The being's head turned toward him, and its stare latched onto him like a tick on a dog.

From beneath its hood two, white-blue eyes burned out of the blackness at him. If this thing had a face, Killean couldn't tell as those glowing orbs became all he could see. They seemed to bore into his soul, stripping him bare to reveal everything about him, including the real reason he was here.

He waited to be struck down by this beast—and that's what this thing was, a beast who could knock his head from his shoulders with one swipe of its hand. But apparently, this powerful being didn't possess the ability to learn all the secrets of another as, instead of killing him, it turned away.

Killean didn't realized he'd stopped breathing until the creature broke eye contact and swept past him. He stood, staring at the wall where the creature had been before turning to gaze after it. The ends of its cloak trailed along the ground as it moved with a grace that made it appear to be floating over the floor. Give this thing a sickle and it would embody the image of the Grim Reaper.

He didn't know what it was, but it had to be the company Joseph received the other night. He also had no doubt it was the brains behind everything Joseph was doing recently. It wasn't a typical vampire, not with those eyes.

Before Ronan was born, a hunter must have been changed into a vampire. Only a hunter heritage would explain those eyes, and only vast age would explain the creature's power and the still electrified feel of his skin. That thing had to be at least a couple of thousand years old and stronger than all of them.

The Alliance had a more grueling battle ahead of them than they'd anticipated, but seeing this creature helped him understand Joseph's ambition to turn more hunters into Savages. This *thing* was most likely seeking to have more of its kind with it, and it would know how powerful a hunter could become once they were turned and groomed for mayhem.

But what was their goal once they had an army of Savages?

He was no closer to learning the answer to that question, and he suspected he'd have to be here for months before Joseph revealed it to him. If he had his way, he wouldn't be here after tonight.

When the creature vanished from sight, Killean forgot about the kitchen and followed it. He watched as it turned into the hall where he slept before entering the corridor with the hunters.

Killean's pace increased as he hurried down the hall. He had no doubt this thing could kill him as he easily as a fly, but he didn't want it anywhere near Simone.

Stepping into the hall with the hunters, he discovered the creature gone. He stood there, gazing back and forth between Joseph's office and the shadows engulfing the steel door at the end of the hall, but he didn't think it had left.

He almost went to knock on Joseph's door, but he had no reason for doing so. He glanced at Simone to make sure she was okay, or as okay as she could be, before slipping back into the hall.

No matter what it took, he had to get them free of here tonight if possible. He didn't have much to report, but Ronan had to know about that thing's existence.

"WHAT IS GOING TO HAPPEN?" Killean asked Joseph as he stood beside him in the hall of hunters.

"We're going to take some of them from here, turn them loose, and let them feast," Joseph replied.

"But won't they feast on *us* once they're unchained?"

Joseph grinned at him and clasped his shoulder. He was far

too touchy-feely for Killean's liking, but it was probably a good thing as it meant Joseph was buying his act.

"That's what I like about you, Killean, you think ahead. None of these other imbeciles"—he waved a hand at the Savages gathered before some of the hunters— "considered that possibility the first time they did this. They didn't even bother to try to take control of their minds before unchaining them. Of course, those prisoners were humans and vampires we'd caught and transitioned, and not hunters, so these will be feistier and more fun."

Joseph licked his lips as he stared at his captives like a proud papa. "I allowed those captives to feast on a few of their jailers to teach them a lesson. Some of the hunters who were captured overseas have already transitioned, and the Savages in charge of that have followed the guidelines I gave them. They've suffered no losses and had success."

Simone's stronghold wasn't the only one the Savages attacked and imprisoned hunters from; three others had fallen around the world. With the amount Joseph had killed, Killean doubted he could make the journey overseas to where two of those strongholds were located. The more innocents a vampire killed, the harder it became for them to cross large bodies of water.

So that meant Joseph had more lackeys running programs such as this and possibly more underground hiding places around the world. There may even be more creatures such as the one Killean encountered earlier running those overseas programs.

"If things keep up and you continue to prove yourself, you will rise to become my second-in-command," Joseph said.

Well yippee, fucking do dah. Killean hoped his smile didn't look as fake as it felt.

"It would be fitting for Ronan to be taken down by two of his former men. Oh, how the mighty will fall," Joseph murmured.

Not going to happen, Killean thought. Ronan was the rightful king of the vampires, and it would take a lot more than Joseph to defeat him.

"We'll keep the hunters restrained," Joseph said. He held up a black hood and a strip of cloth. "Gagged, bagged, and chained, they can't put up much of a fight. It would be much easier if we could control their minds, but even as vampires, the hunters retain their ability to keep us shut out."

"And then what happens?" he asked.

"And then we escort them from here and allow them to play," Joseph purred. "I already have the perfect venue picked out for them. We're only taking half of them tonight; the other half will go tomorrow. It will make them easier to contain, and once they see human prey, they usually go for that, especially if the prey is running and screaming. And if not, we have another way of controlling them."

Killean's gaze locked on Simone and the Savage standing across from her. The female vampire grinned at Simone like she was a treat the Savage couldn't wait to devour. Judging by the hood and gag in the vamp's hand, Simone was one of those who was going tonight.

Excitement and dread rippled through him. Joseph hadn't said whether Killean would be going with them or not. If he wasn't there, then he couldn't stop her from killing, but Joseph could refuse to let him go. He had to proceed cautiously, or everything he'd sacrificed might end up being for nothing.

"The girl," Killean said, forcing his next words out as a question rather than the command he wanted to issue. *Humble yourself.* It went against everything he innately was, but he gritted his teeth and continued. "Can I have her?"

Joseph glanced between him and Simone, and for a second, Killean feared he'd given away too much when it came to her.

"You really have a thing for this girl," Joseph murmured. "Why?"

Killean held Joseph's gaze while he replied. "As I told you before, she believed herself above vampires, and I want to watch her fall. I despise all hunters, but that icy little bitch was more self-righteous than the rest of her asshole brethren."

"Did she spurn your advances?"

"I'd never make a move on one of *them*," he spat the word in the hopes of selling the lie.

He *had* kissed her, and for one blissful second, he forgot all about his past, all the death he'd witnessed and delivered, and experienced lust as well as peace again. When it was the two of them on the beach, he'd held heaven in his arms before recalling she was nothing more than the serpent tantalizing Eve with the apple.

"Hmm," Joseph murmured as he rubbed the scruff lining his jaw.

Killean had to sell his tale more if he were going to get his way. "She was supposed to marry the leader of the hunters."

"Nathan," Joseph stated.

"Yes, but when he chose a vampire over *her*, the knowledge repulsed her, and she didn't hide it. This little bitch mistakenly thinks she's better than us."

Killean's fingers dug into his palms as he made himself put Simone down. *You're doing it to save her life.* But it didn't matter, she was *his* mate, and the words went against his vampire instincts to protect her.

"The hunters did a number on you, didn't they?" Joseph inquired.

Killean couldn't stop his fangs from extending as he held Joseph's curious gaze. No one knew his history, and he would keep it that way.

"They've done a number on far too many vampires," Killean replied.

"Hmm." Joseph looked at Simone again. "You're right; they

have. I think you've earned yourself a little treat. She can be yours to keep leashed until she's ready to be set free, but you are to do everything *I* say with her, Killean, or I'll kill you."

I'd like to see you try. "Fair enough," Killean said.

Joseph led him over to the female Savage and spoke with her as Killean stepped in front of Simone. She looked at him and blinked before baring her fangs like a wild animal caught in a trap. It was as if Simone no longer existed, and if Joseph had his way, she *would* cease to exist in more ways before this night was over, just as Killean already had.

Following Joseph's instructions, he knelt before her and rested his hand on her head to hold it still. Simone snapped and lunged at him while the female Savage bent beside him. Dried blood from her brutalized lip caked Simone's chin and fresh blood trickled from her raw wrists as she jerked against her chains. Her dirty hair whipped around her shoulders as saliva dribbled from her mouth.

Killean had thought he wanted to kill before, but it was nothing compared to the impulse thundering through him as he watched his mate unravel.

Timing the closing of Simone's jaws, the Savage slipped the gag into her mouth. Killean held Simone steady when she tried to recoil and strangled sounds issued from her. He didn't know if he wanted to draw her into his arms and hold her or tear this place down more.

A little while longer. He kept repeating this in his head while she gazed at him with accusation and hatred. *I'm sorry. I wish there were another way.*

The Savage tied the gag behind Simone's head far too tight for his liking, but he couldn't loosen it without drawing attention.

"Move your hand," the woman commanded and waved the black hood at him.

When Killean pulled his hand away, the woman slipped the

hood over Simone's head and pulled the string around her neck. Before Killean could grab her again, Simone threw herself backward, and her head cracked off the wall with a loud *thwack.* Blood pounded in his ears when the Savages around him laughed, and Simone issued a strangled whimper.

Stay in control. It's her only chance.

"Time to go!" Joseph announced and slapped Killean on his shoulder.

Killean almost snapped at the hand, but he restrained himself as Simone's wrists were unchained from the wall and handed to him. Gripping the chain, he realized they were one step closer to freedom.

CHAPTER NINE

Joseph took Simone's chain from him when they stopped in front of the door at the end of the hall. Killean almost closed his hand around the links and refused to let go, but he relented to Joseph's second tug as the Savage's surrounding him stared unrelentingly at him.

Joseph took the chain, and another Savage stepped forward to blindfold and hood him. At least this time when they led him outside, he wasn't shoved into a trunk. Instead, they turned him and pulled his hands behind his back. Cold metal touched his wrists before a set of cuffs clicked shut.

Stronger than the handcuffs used for humans, these weren't built to restrain a purebred. He could break them, but by the time he did that, the Savages would be on top of him. His head was shoved down, and they pushed him into the backseat of a car.

The front doors opened and closed before the other back door opened. A scuffle sounded, and then the car sagged as more weight entered the car. The rank stench of body odor filled his nostrils, but beneath it, he detected a crisp, eucalyptus scent.

Even before her skin touched his, Killean knew Simone sat beside him. When another weight settled into the car, she was pushed more firmly against him, and a door slammed closed.

"Hold still, bitch," a man grumbled.

Killean's wrists flexed against the cuffs as the car started. "Where are we going?" he inquired.

"You'll see," Joseph replied from the passenger seat. "It will be a bloody treat for all of us."

Despite his determination not to give in to the Savage nature he'd awakened, Killean's fangs lengthened, and saliva rushed into his mouth at the prospect of witnessing whatever Joseph had planned. Closing his eyes, he inhaled a tremulous breath as he strove to suppress the demon seeking to control him.

It would be so easy to give in, let Simone go through this tonight, and remain a Savage with her. Maybe, if he gave in completely, he wouldn't care about her hunter heritage anymore, and they could feast on blood and humans and...

And what? Stay with Joseph and work to destroy Ronan?

No!

His eyes flew open, but all he saw was the back of the blindfold. Ronan had given him a purpose for living when there'd been none, and in doing so, he saved Killean's life. Killean betrayed him by becoming this *thing* he was now, but he would not betray him further.

After at least an hour of driving, the car turned. Judging by the ruts and the change from the tires humming across asphalt to the ping of sand and rocks dinging off the undercarriage, they'd driven onto a dirt road. Killean sat up a little straighter and leaned instinctively closer to Simone as they neared their destination.

She'd remained unmoving throughout most of the journey, but now she sniffed at the air and whimpered as her chains rattled. "Quiet," the man on the other side of her commanded, and Killean recognized his voice.

"She knows it's almost playtime, Andre," Joseph replied.

"If she had a shower, I wouldn't mind playing with her," Andre replied, and the others in the car chuckled.

Killean's head turned toward his old friend Andre as he marked the Savage for death. Then the car came to a stop, and the distant thump of dance music floated to him. Doors opened and closed before the one beside him flung open. A hand clasped his arm and pulled him from the seat. They turned him so his chest pressed into the hood of the car while the cuffs were unlocked. When the metal fell free, Killean drew his arms forward and rubbed his wrists together as they tugged the hood free.

"You can take off the blindfold," Joseph said.

Killean removed it, and his eyes went to the building behind Joseph. In the black velvet of the night surrounding the structure, the lights inside and outside the building were a bright homing beacon. The sign over the door marked the place as Trowbridge Hall. Small white lights were twined around the banisters of the wheelchair ramp as it wound toward the door.

Six windows faced the lot, and from within, light shone against the billowy, white curtains covering the glass. The silhouettes of the people inside moved across the curtains, and laughter resonated from within. A cold pit opened in his stomach when he thought of the oblivious humans who had no idea death lurked outside their door, watching them.

Two floodlights were on each corner of the single-story building and lit up the first fifty feet of the parking lot, but the last fifty were cast entirely in shadow, and that was where Joseph had parked. As Killean watched, ten more vehicles, with their headlights off, pulled into the lot and parked behind Joseph's car.

Nestled beneath a cluster of red maples, the hall was situated off a dirt road. He didn't see any homes along the street, only woods. Glancing behind him, Killean saw more forest. He tried to find something familiar in his surroundings, but the pines, oaks, and maples could be in any town along the east coast. However, the woods were thick enough that if he got the chance to break away with Simone, he might be able to lose himself in them.

It was the only chance they had.

"What are we doing here?" Killean asked as Andre and Simone exited the other side of the car. Killean tracked their every step around the vehicle.

"We're here to crash a wedding," Joseph said and rubbed his hands together. "It's the happiest of occasions, for those who are invited and those who aren't."

He waved his hand at the Savages gathering around them with their chained hunters. About half of the Savages held yellow poles with two prongs on the end that looked like giant cattle prods; the others carried dart guns. These must be their other ways of controlling the hunters that Joseph mentioned.

Looking away from the Savages, Killean inspected the fifty or more vehicles in the lot that didn't belong to the Savages. There could easily be a hundred or more people inside.

"You plan to slaughter an entire wedding celebration?" he asked.

"Yes," Joseph said. "Or at least I plan for the hunters to slaughter them. We may get a taste, but this is *their* playground, Killean, and don't forget it. Everyone here knows not to sample the treats unless I say it's okay. Is that understood?"

"Yes," Killean replied. "But there are too many people here. How will you explain all the bodies? I doubt the hunters will make clean kills."

"Part of the fun is how brutal a starved vampire is." Joseph sighed and licked his lips. "It's almost as pleasurable to watch them kill as it is *to* kill. A tragic fire will explain the massacre. The arsonist blocked all the doors before setting the place ablaze. The police will have to come up with their own suspects and reasons for why no one escaped out the windows."

Andre stopped beside Joseph and yanked Simone to a halt when she attempted to keep walking. She jerked briefly against the chains before bowing her head. Her fingers picked at her hands in a nervous, jittery movement. Then she lifted her head, and he heard her sniffing at the air from behind the hood. Killean extended his hand for the chain; Andre smirked at him.

"Give him his toy, Andre," Joseph commanded.

Killean gave Andre a lethal stare, promising death as he took Simone's chain from him. Blood spilled from the skin she'd pulled back on her hands; the sweet scent of it caused Killean's nostrils to flare as a new emotion swirled within him, pity. He'd never pitied anyone before. He did not possess compassion for others, but hunter or not, Simone didn't deserve this, no one did.

"Let's go," Joseph said.

Killean almost balked as the last of his morality reared its head. So far, he hadn't killed anyone who hadn't at least somewhat deserved it, but the people in this building were innocents. He wouldn't kill anyone here, but passive or not, he would still be a part of the brutality about to unfold.

He glanced at the thirty plus Savages gathering closer and the twenty-five hunters they'd brought with them tonight. There were far too many for him to try running for it now with Simone. He would have to wait until the bloodlust was on all of them before he could chance an escape.

The only problem was, he didn't know what *he* would become once he entered that building and the massacre began.

"Make sure the other doors are blocked, the phone line is cut, and no one has slipped outside for some recreational fun," Joseph commanded five of the Savages before turning to Killean with a wicked smile. "It won't do us any good to leave witnesses or to let one of our meals run away."

"None at all," Killean murmured in agreement.

"Come, let's have some fun!"

CHAPTER TEN

Killean rested his hand on Simone's elbow, drawing her closer as Joseph led the way through the cars toward the building. Careful to make sure she didn't accidentally hurt herself, he guided her through the obstacles in their way. Her chains and those of the other captives rattled as they walked while the music played and the crickets chirruped.

He memorized the layout of the building and searched for exits, but he didn't see any options on this side other than the door and windows. He wouldn't have a better idea about more exits until they were inside and he could see the design of the structure more clearly. No matter what, all the other doors were being blocked and would be useless, so it would have to be a window or this door they used to escape.

"This place has no security system," Joseph said as he stepped onto the wheelchair ramp. Killean guided Simone onto the wooden walkway behind Joseph. "I had some of my men check it out a couple of days ago after I saw the couple's joyful announcement in the newspaper. I did some research online and discovered they have a guest list of over one hundred. People really do share too much about their lives nowadays."

"They do," Killean agreed as more silhouettes passed behind the curtains.

The newlywed couple was utterly oblivious that the happiest day of their lives was about to become their last. Life was all so fragile and uncertain, even for an immortal.

A few short weeks ago, he'd been set in his course and sure nothing could derail it. Now he was as far from that course as he could get and marching toward something that, if Simone weren't here, he would fight to the death to stop. But he'd done all this for her, and he would make sure she never had to bear the guilt of what was about to take place inside. That guilt would reside solely on his shoulders.

"The idea of ruining someone's most special day was too much for me to resist," Joseph said.

"I understand," Killean replied.

Joseph smiled at Killean over his shoulder as he rested his hand on the knob. "I knew you would. And now the party can start," Joseph said as he pushed open the door.

The annoying twangs of the Chicken Dance had Killean fantasizing about killing the DJ when he stepped inside with Simone. Laughter and music flowed freely around the large, open room. The revelers gathered in the middle of the dance floor stepped back to allow the bride and groom to take center stage when the song changed to something more romantic.

The bride's dress spun around her as the groom twirled her across the center of the dance floor. Her radiant smile made her glow while the groom beamed down at her. Killean moved stiffly out of the way to let the other Savages file in behind him. He felt torn between the surreal beauty of this moment and the temptation of the thundering beats of the hundred hearts pumping blood through all these veins.

So much blood, so much death, and so much *innocence* crowded this hall.

He wanted to tear them all apart and feast on them. He longed to scream at them to run and save them all.

The conflicting emotions battering him made it difficult to think. Death and power, he yearned for them with an intensity bordering on madness. But he'd stepped into the realm of lunacy when he walked away from the Alliance and willingly turned himself into a monster.

There is no saving the soul of a demon.

And that's what he was, a demon. As a vampire born to two vampires, he'd always been closer to the demon DNA that initially spawned the vampire and hunter lines. There was less human in him than a turned vampire, but he'd maintained some of his morality to fight the Savages for centuries.

If there's no saving the soul of a demon, then why fight it anymore?

His gaze fell on Simone, standing motionlessly at his side. Maybe he couldn't save himself, but he could and *would* save her. Keeping his eyes on her, Killean reined in some of his bloodlust, but he couldn't get his fangs to retract.

He could protect her, but how did he protect the people in this building?

He had no answer for that question.

When more Savages and their captives filed through the door behind him, they finally drew the attention of a couple of men standing near the edge of the dance floor. In short-sleeved dress shirts and slacks, two of the men wore loosened ties while the third had no tie and the top buttons of his shirt undone. Flushed with exertion and booze, their faces were red beneath the white lights encircling the wooden beams running across the cathedral ceiling of the hall.

The three men stood with their mouths gaping as they took in the spectacle of a group of men and women holding the chains of others in hoods. Then the tieless one nudged the others and said something to them.

"What about cell phones?" Killean whispered to Joseph. "They can easily call the police."

"There's not much cell service in this area, but we've jammed it just in case. They're not calling anyone."

Which meant Killean wasn't either. Not like there was anyone he could call. With no idea where they were, he couldn't give an address to Ronan, and calling the police would only bring more victims to the party.

Killean quickly took in his surroundings. There were over a dozen windows in the place; the ones behind him, six across the way, and more behind the bar that was to the left of the dance floor. The DJ had his equipment set up on a small stage at the far end of the hall, opposite the bar.

The three men shook themselves out of their stupor and started toward them. One of them pulled out his phone, but he didn't dial anything, probably because he was reluctant to draw the police to his friend's wedding.

Run you idiots, Killean thought as the men stopped before them.

"I'm sorry; this is a... uh... it's a private party," the tieless guy said as he stared at the hooded figures.

"Is it now?" Joseph purred.

One of the men took a small step back when the door closed behind the last Savage. Killean gazed over the crowd of vampire heads; most of them were in the building. A few remained outside, either looking for stragglers or keeping watch.

The three guys glanced nervously over the group, and the one with the cell punched a number into it. He lifted the device to his ear, frowned, and pulled it away to stare at the screen. When the men first approached, their eyes held the glassy sheen of alcohol, but now the fog was clearing as apprehension etched their features. The man with the phone hit some buttons again, held it to his ear, and paled before lowering it.

Killean refrained from shouting at them to bust out the windows and flee as Joseph turned toward him and handed out a key. "You'll need this."

He forgot about the humans as the key to Simone's freedom was slipped into his hand.

"It's time for you to go," the tieless guy said, but he didn't sound as confident.

"We don't plan to stay long," Joseph assured him, and the men exchanged a look.

Glancing over his shoulder, Joseph's eyes met Killean's before going to the other Savages.

"Turn them loose," Joseph commanded.

Before Killean could react, the hoods were removed, the chains unlocked, and the gags untied. Twenty-four of the twenty-five hunters sprang forth. The three men didn't have time to shout a warning before some of the starving hunters pounced on them. Inhuman snarls filled the air as muscle crunched beneath fangs and the men released garbled cries. With the humans to distract them, the hunters didn't turn on their captors but ran toward the people surrounding the dance floor and the bar to the left of it.

The music was so loud the celebrators didn't become aware something was wrong until three of the hunters launched onto the back of a woman standing near the dance floor. They tore at her flesh as they dragged her beneath them.

The woman's screams were drowned out by the music, but those closest to her staggered away from the blood spilling across the floor as the monsters bit at her arms and neck. The scent of blood permeating the room grew stronger than the alcohol and sweat that greeted them when they entered.

Simone twitched and whimpered beside him; her fingers flexed as fresh blood slid from the skin she'd torn from her hands. Her hunger beating against him only enflamed his until he felt as crazed as the Mad Hatter.

"Turn her loose, Killean."

So caught up in the massacre, and his growing thirst, Killean had forgotten about Joseph and the other Savages. When his gaze focused on Joseph, he saw the suspicion in the other's eyes while they surveyed him and Simone.

You have to let her go. But if he did, he'd never be able to save her.

Against his back, the heat of the other Savages pressed closer when he didn't immediately react to Joseph's command. Humans ran for a door marked stairs and another one behind the bar. Their shouts grew louder as they banged on both of the blocked doors. Some of them were so panicked, they ran for the door behind Killean, but the Savages blocked their exit.

Someone bashed a chair into one of the six windows lining the wall across from him. Glass shattered, but before the man could leap out, a hunter tackled him around his legs and brought him down on the broken shards. The scent of the man's blood spilling across the glass sent the hunter into a frenzy, and instead of using his fangs to feed, he tore at the man until he was licking the blood off his drenched hands.

The DJ fled, but dance music continued to blast from the speakers as the man bolted for a door behind his equipment. The Savages took him down before he could make it to the exit.

The blood, the killing, the screams, and pulsating music were combining until Killean's thoughts centered on one thing...

Death.

He set Simone free.

CHAPTER ELEVEN

Scents and sounds bombarded Simone from every direction, but the blood... oh, the blood. It was so tempting, and it was *everywhere*. The screams matched the beat of her heart as movement came from every direction. She didn't know where to go or what to do first as her head bounced back and forth.

She didn't see people, all she saw was an end to the fire scorching her veins. She wanted to sink her fangs into *every*thing.

She didn't realize she was running until her feet skidded out from under her and her ass hit the floor with a thump. Her breath exploded out of her and her teeth clacked together; she stared dazedly at the red coating the floor and her.

Then the scent of all that red hit her. Saliva pooled in her mouth, and strange sounds issued from her as she realized she'd fallen in a puddle of blood. Unable to stop herself, she brought her hands to her face and started licking the blood from her palms.

A shiver of delight raced down her spine when the delicious, warm taste of it hit her tongue and slid down her throat. She licked faster and faster, cleaning the blood from her skin as she turned her palms before her. *Finally,* she was getting the chance to feed, but the blood wasn't enough to ease the hunger shredding her insides.

Dropping her hands, her gaze locked on a man when he fell in front of her. His chin banged off the floor and blood spurted from his broken flesh. *Mine! Eat. Feed. Ease. STARVING!*

Killean couldn't tear his eyes away from Simone as she crawled through the blood toward the man two of her fellow hunters had taken down. *If she kills him, all of this will have been for nothing.*

"When do we feed?" one of the Savages asked Joseph.

Joseph's gaze flicked to the Savage, and his eyes deepened to a ruby color. "When *I* say you can," he sneered. "These people are for the hunters, and it still might not be enough to turn them. The hunters are stronger and resist becoming one of us more than most after they feed. Many of the other captured hunters were starved and set free to kill more than once before they finally broke."

Killean realized Joseph was talking to him when he felt the man's stare boring into the side of his head. He forced his gaze away from Simone. "Interesting," he murmured to Joseph, but not at all surprising. Since their creation, hunters had killed vampires; they would not easily succumb to the manipulations of these Savages no matter how much torture they endured.

"But they all eventually broke, and they're so worth it when they finally succumb," Joseph murmured as he surveyed the slaughter with obvious glee. "They're so much more powerful than a normal vampire turned Savage. Of course, they're not as strong as us purebreds, but they're still magnificent to watch."

Killean had seen the power of a turned hunter in Kadence and Nathan after they transitioned. Would Simone and the other hunters possess special abilities like Kadence and Nathan? Or were the twins unique?

And he would not call these hunters magnificent to watch. This was the worst of vampire nature, and it disgusted him how badly he wanted to take part in it.

He focused on Simone as he tried to calm his tumultuous emotions. She reached for the man who had fallen before her, lifted his arm, and sank her fangs into it.

No! The denial screaming through him was not only because he didn't want her to kill, but also because seeing her feed on a man twisted his insides into a ball. *She's mine!*

It was supposed to be *his* blood she drank, not some stranger's.

Killean didn't stop to think how irrational his thoughts were considering he planned to free her from here, return her to her people, and never see her again.

Joseph gestured some of the Savages forward. "Stop any humans from escaping out the windows, but no sampling," he ordered. "Anyone who takes even a nibble will be destroyed."

The Savages spread out through the room as more humans broke out windows, but those people were brought down by hunters or pushed back by Savages. The groom had backed the bride into a corner behind the bar and was using a stool to bash at the hunters closing in on them. On his next swing, a hunter ripped the stool from him and tossed it aside.

Joseph was focused on watching the Savages pushing and pulling the terrified humans back into the room. He smiled cruelly when one of his flunkies couldn't resist sinking his fangs into the throat of a young woman in a fluffy pink dress.

"Now, it's time for me to play," Joseph said and glided across the room toward the Savage.

Glancing behind him, Killean saw a few Savages with their gazes locked on him. He had no doubt they'd been ordered to keep an eye on him, but there weren't many hunters and Savages between him, Simone, and the windows.

Most of those sent to keep the humans inside were shoving their victims toward the hunters while a few stood in front of the other windows. Andre was one of those corralling the humans; he laughed as he pushed a screaming woman toward the hunters before kicking out the knee of a man. Joseph was near the bar feasting on the Savage who'd disobeyed him.

Eighty feet separated him from the tables and windows across the way. The once pristine, white cloths covering those tables were streaked with blood, as were the walls and floor but none of the tables blocked the windows.

If he could get to Simone...

He didn't think about what would happen to him or Simone if they caught him. The time for thinking was over; if he didn't stop her, she would help to kill that man, and if he didn't go now, he would lose his chance.

Killean sprinted across the dance floor, leapt over a table, and landed beside Simone. His feet skidded in the blood, but he caught his balance before he fell as a shout sounded from the Savages behind him. Though the screams of the humans were dwindling as more of them perished, the cries of the dying drowned out the alarm the Savages raised.

Bending, Killean wrapped his arm around Simone's waist and yanked her back. When he tore her fangs from the man's arm, she screeched, and her hands and legs flailed. Clasping her against his chest, he placed his hand on her forehead and pinned her head to his shoulder to suppress her.

"I'm trying to save you!" he hissed, but even with having fed, she was still too far gone in her hunger to understand him.

Ignoring her screams and the fingers tearing at his forearms, he ran for one of the broken windows. Andre darted in front of him and planted his feet like a football player about to make the block. The grin on Andre's face infuriated Killean.

Lowering his shoulder, Killean charged him but switched

course at the last second and barreled toward one of the unbroken windows. If he weren't holding Simone, he would have gone straight at Andre and destroyed the bastard, but he couldn't risk a fight with her in his arms. They only had one chance at freedom, and he couldn't risk her getting away from him.

Hunching over Simone, he used his body to protect hers when he hit the glass. There was a small hesitation before the window gave way beneath the impact of his body. Curling himself further around her, Killean sheltered her from the glass slicing across his arms and cheeks as the window blew outward.

The air rushing around him whipped at his hair and clothes as they fell fifteen feet before crashing into a shrub. Sticks jammed into his flesh; the bush bent before bouncing them away from the building. Killean's shoulder crashed onto the dirt road, and he rolled to get away from the window and the glass. As he moved, Killean kept his weight off Simone the best he could, but she grunted when he rolled again.

Fingers scraped down his back and tangled in his shirt. Killean rolled again and lashed out with a kick that snapped the Savage's head back. He didn't have time to stop and kill it though as shouts rang out from inside and figures appeared in the windows overhead. Killean kicked again and then once more until the Savage's face caved in and it released him.

Another one leapt out the window as Killean launched to his feet. Two more followed it.

Jarred and bouncing, Simone tried to process what was going on, but all she knew was someone had ripped her away from her delicious meal. Straining against the iron-clad grip on her waist and head, she tried to break free, but the hold was as imprisoning as the chains she'd been freed from.

I'm free! The thought burst through all the confusion muddling her brain and hope swelled forth before she recalled she wasn't free; someone still restrained her. She kicked and clawed at her captor, but they didn't relent as her feet dangled over the ground while air rushed around her.

"Stop struggling!" someone grunted in her ear.

The voice sounded familiar, but she couldn't quite place it. Then, it didn't matter as she scented her captor's blood on the air and her mouth watered.

Killean bolted across the dirt road and plunged into the woods with Simone clasped against his chest. The excited cries of the Savages followed him into the shadows of the forest. Branches and limbs slapped at him as his feet easily found their way through the debris littering the ground. The crunching of sticks and the grunts of his pursuers sounded behind him as he jumped over a downed tree before darting around a boulder.

Shifting his hold on Simone, he glanced over his shoulder to discover one of the Savages closing in on them. Killean grasped a tree branch and bent it back until it snapped off. He hefted it in his hand as Simone lunged against his arm locked around her waist. He struggled to keep his hold on her as her fingers clawed at his arm and she tried to lift herself free of his grasp.

"Be still!" he ordered, and spinning, he heaved the branch like a javelin thrower at the bastard pursuing them.

The branch struck the Savage in the chest. It was off the heart, but the Savage yelped as the impact lifted the creature off its feet and flung it backward. He heard the others crashing through the woods behind them, but Killean didn't see them through the trees, and they sounded as if they were still a good hundred feet away, if not more. He'd bought them some time.

Placing his hand on Simone's forehead again, he held her more securely against him as he poured on the speed. No moonlight penetrated the thick canopy of leaves overhead, but he saw well enough that he didn't worry about crashing into anything or tripping over something. Unfortunately, his pursuers could also see well, and they weren't carrying a pissed-off hunter.

"Stop!" he hissed when Simone kicked him in the shin and almost tripped him.

If he continued to run with her dangling against him, he would end up falling. Slowing only a little, he twisted her in his arms until her chest was flush against his.

"Wrap your legs around my waist," he commanded.

Either the urgency of the situation, the tone of his voice, or instinct finally pierced through her hunger as she lifted her legs. Her dress pushed back when she locked her legs around his waist. Killean cradled the back of her head and placed it in the hollow of his shoulder as he ran.

CHAPTER TWELVE

THE SCENT of resin and blood filled Simone's nostrils as she was embraced against a rock-hard surface that flowed with the grace of water against her. Something about the embrace and scent tickled her memory, but she couldn't quite place it as the blood singing through the veins of whoever held her occupied all her senses and thoughts.

Without thinking, she sank her fangs into flesh and groaned in ecstasy when blood slid down her throat. Unlike anything she'd ever tasted before, this blood flooded her body with renewed strength as it eased the burning in her veins far more than the meal she consumed earlier. She tried to recall what was happening around them, but she was too far gone in the blood filling her and the awakening sensations of her body to pull away.

As power filled her, a growing awareness spread through her body. Her nipples puckered and her body came alive in a way it had only once before. The scent and solid muscles holding her coalesced into a memory of standing on a beach while being kissed for the first time in her life.

That kiss and the tender stroking of his tongue had awakened her to passion. No matter how much she tried to forget him, and the way he'd made her feel, he'd haunted her dreams every night until her capture. And then he'd been in her nightmares too.

Now she knew it was him holding her and *him* feeding her.

Killean, she remembered as she rubbed harder against him and drank deeper.

When Simone locked her legs tighter around him and started grinding against him, Killean almost fell. Out of her mind with thirst, she didn't know what she was doing as she rode him; often blood and sex went hand in hand for a vampire.

Years ago, it had been the same for him too. Those were the days before age, time, and the death surrounding him battered him into something he barely recognized before stealing sexual gratification from him. Until Simone, he hadn't had an erection in years, and the few he did have before then were impossible to find any release from.

Killean gritted his teeth against his growing desire, but the feel of his mate in his arms, feeding on him, and taking satisfaction in his body was almost too much for him to resist. However, he had to resist if they were going to survive.

Killean smelled and heard the roaring river before spotting it through a break in the trees. Whitewater sprayed into the air when it crashed against the rocks jutting up from the fast-moving water. The rapid current would batter anyone caught in it against the rocks, smashing their bones before sweeping them away.

Killean didn't hesitate before plunging into the frigid water.

Water sprayed up around him, speckling his face and sticking Simone's dress to her back as he strode out to the center of the river. The river became a living entity, sucking at him and trying to pull him under, but though his legs ached, he resisted being pulled under by the powerful flow.

When he was away from the rocks and in the center of the river, he pressed his hand against Simone's back before lifting his feet and allowing the current to take them away. Their pursuers were still too far away to see him, and once they reached the river, it would take them time to figure out if he'd crossed to the other side, remained on their side, or entered the current.

The water would mask their scent, and though he had no idea where the current was taking them, it would get them there fast. He used his feet to push them away from the rocks the best he could and his body to protect Simone from the ones he couldn't avoid.

Spinning away from one of the rocks, he grunted when his back smashed up against another. Water flooded his mouth as the current pinned him to the rock digging into his spine. Simone seemed not to notice the river beating against her as she continued to feed while Killean used his elbow to maneuver them away from the rock in slow, jerking motions.

Finally away from the rock, they were thrown back out toward the center of the river. Killean threw out his foot to push away the next rock rushing at them. His foot collided with the boulder, his knee bent, and it took a herculean effort to thrust away again.

The water crashing over them washed away the blood and grime covering them. The raging river pounded in his ears and covered any sound of an approaching enemy, but it also hid any noises they might make and most of their bodies.

Killean was counting on most of the Savages remaining at the wedding to contain the hunters and clean up their mess, but enough would come after them that they would be a threat. And one of them would be Joseph, he was sure of it.

Simone whimpered when one of the rocks caught her arm, and her fingers dug deeper into his nape while she drank. His eyes drifted halfway closed as he briefly allowed himself to savor the feeling of having his mate feeding on him. She felt so amazing and right that he could almost forget the circumstances and her heritage.

He could feel her vitality returning and the strength of her hold on him increasing as his blood nourished her. The sounds she made ceased being the ones of an animal feeding and became those of one rutting as she ground against him.

He seized her hips to hold her still; Simone mewled in displeasure and bit harder. Out of her mind with bloodlust, she had no idea what she was doing, and he couldn't let it continue. Not only would she not be acting like this if she were rational, but the more steps they completed in the mating bond, the more difficult it would be for them to separate. He couldn't deny her his blood when she so obviously needed it, but he had to refuse her this.

For Simone, the mating instinct might be more difficult to deny after feeding on him. If she experienced the pull of the mating bond with him, her drinking from him would accelerate her necessity to complete it. However, there was a chance this little hunter wouldn't recognize him as her mate like he did her.

He knew how things worked with vampires when they encountered their mate, but the joining of hunters and vampires was something new. Kadence and Nathan had experienced a draw to their mates before their turning, but hunters could be like humans and capable of walking away from the connection. Or some hunters might be able to resist the lure of the bond like they withstood a vampire's power of persuasion.

He hoped hunters could resist; he didn't want Simone as his mate, but he would make sure she survived. When he put his foot out to push them away from a jagged boulder, his muscles trembled and his ankle almost gave out; she was taking too much. Still, he couldn't refuse her the blood she desperately required. He was strong enough to withstand this drain, and he would.

As the blood eased the discomfort in her veins, Simone

slowly became aware of her surroundings. Water tore at her clothes and battered her body while it dripped from her lashes and clogged her nostrils. Goose bumps covered her flesh, and she couldn't stop shivering.

She also became aware of the new sensations in her body as she hung onto the vampire who confused her more than all the mysteries of the universe. Her skin tingled with awareness while something built between her thighs and she thrust her hips against him.

What am I doing?

Simone recoiled when she realized she was rubbing against him like a cat in heat while drinking from him. However, she couldn't go far as Killean kept a firm hold on her.

For the first time since this whole mess started, her fangs retracted when she willed them to, and she turned her head away from the lure of his blood. She started to inhale a shuddery breath, but all she got was a mouthful of water as it sprayed her face. Sputtering and choking, Simone spit out the icy water.

"Easy," he murmured in a voice so low she barely heard him over the rush of the river. "They're still hunting us; stay calm."

Simone was anything but calm as her mind and body were a tumult with the confusing emotions battering it. What had she been doing to him? And why did she want to keep doing it?

Over the years, there had been times when she woke after a dream with a similar yearning between her thighs, but this was *far* more intense. On those nights, she'd lain awake, uncertain of what to do and unable to move because the feel of her sheets and nightgown rubbing against her only made it worse.

She hadn't known how to ease the needs of her body, and being the proper hunter she was raised to be, she *never* asked anyone about it. She knew how things worked between a man and woman, or how they were supposed to work, but her knowledge about sex was far from vast.

Instinctively, she knew Killean could answer her questions and satisfy her yearning. For some strange reason, she wanted this rude, confusing, *Savage* vampire to do it.

You're an idiot. Yes, she was. She had no idea where they were and could only recall vague impressions of what occurred tonight, but they were far from danger. If they didn't drown or freeze in the water, the Savages would still be after them, and if they caught them...

She hugged Killean closer when she realized they would take her back and finish what they started, but they would *destroy* him. And it wouldn't be a simple killing. No, they would make him pay for what he'd done, but exactly what had he done?

Her brain felt like it was trying to wade through mud as she pieced together bits and pieces of her imprisonment. Savages brought Killean in to where they were holding her captive and treated him as one of them. Was he one of them, or had it all been a ploy to save her and the other hunters?

Maybe it had been a ploy, but she didn't think anyone in the Alliance would agree to a vampire murdering innocents no matter what the cause. And there was no denying Killean had killed, as beneath his strong resin scent and the fresh water cascading over them, she detected the rot of a Savage.

It wasn't as strong as it was on the monsters who imprisoned her, and when she wasn't searching for the rot, his natural scent overpowered it, but there was no denying what that odor meant.

He was one of *them*, so why was he taking her away from them? Or was he taking her back to them? No, that made no sense. She couldn't remember much about tonight, but she knew they'd been with Joseph and the other Savages. They wouldn't be in this river if they weren't trying to escape her captors. Plus, Killean had said they were still hunting them, but maybe he didn't mean Joseph and his Savages, perhaps he meant Ronan. Maybe the Alliance had somehow found them.

And then she recalled the building, the blood, and being swept into a pair of arms and carried away from all the screams. The details remained fuzzy, but Killean had taken her from Joseph.

But why? And just who and what was this enigmatic vampire?

Simone frowned as Killean's eyes slid toward her and their gazes locked. In the tanned complexion of his harsh face, the golden color of his magnificent eyes stood out starkly. She read nothing in those eyes or his expression.

"Why did you take me from there?" she asked.

"Quiet," he replied gruffly.

Simone glowered at him. No one could annoy her the way this vampire did, but though she was tempted to do the exact opposite of what he commanded, she wanted to survive as a non-monster more than she wanted to annoy him too.

Drawing on the proper upbringing that propelled her through life, she buried her irritation and closed her mouth as she nestled closer to the warmth he radiated. The trees on the shoreline whipped by as the current swept them toward an uncertain destination. However, she preferred the unknown and the ice rattling her bones to what lurked behind them.

Killean tried to keep himself distanced from Simone, but when she trembled against him and her teeth chattered in his ear, he couldn't stop himself from rubbing her back to warm her. He studied the shifting shadows leaping through the trees in search of anyone hunting them, but he didn't see any sign of their enemies.

The current was fast, but if the Savages realized what he'd done, they would be able catch up to them. And it was only a matter of time before they figured it out.

He had to get them out of this water.

Kicking toward the shoreline, Killean suppressed a grunt

when the current caught him and smashed his back against a rock before shooting him into the middle of the river. It took him a couple more tries, but eventually, he succeeded in getting them to land.

His legs wobbled from blood loss when he staggered onto solid ground, but he managed to stay upright. If they were going to evade Joseph, he had to feed, and soon. Holding Simone in his arms gave him strength as he ran.

CHAPTER THIRTEEN

He hadn't run far before the rapids of the river became a lazy stream, and he came across a campground where, nestled on the shoreline of the river, more than a dozen RVs were set up. Most of the RVs were unlit, but outside of one, a group of campers sat around a dwindling fire. The scent of pot wafted to him as the handful of men gathered around the fire passed a joint while they sipped beer and spoke in low murmurs.

Killean needed to feed, but with the amount of blood Simone took from him, he'd end up drunk and high if he consumed their intoxicated blood. Turning away from the men, he didn't set Simone down as he slipped through the RVs parked along the river. Water dripped from them and his boots squished as he jogged onward.

"What is this place?" Simone whispered.

"A campground. Humans vacation at them."

Simone gazed in awe at the vehicles and people gathered beneath the trees. It was an odd thing to do, yet it was peaceful here and she could see the allure of it.

"Have you never seen one before?" Killean asked.

"No. I've rarely been outside a stronghold, and I never encountered anything like this when I was."

Killean clenched his teeth as he recalled how sheltered the hunter women were and how much of the world she'd been deprived of seeing. "Did you ever want to see more?" He was stunned to hear himself asking the question when he was determined not to get closer to her or learn more about her.

"Not really," she admitted. "I was curious about the outside world of course, but not overly so. Now I think it's strangely fascinating, maybe because I almost lost everything and still might if Joseph finds us."

"I'm going to make sure that doesn't happen," Killean vowed.

"Thank you," she whispered.

Killean frowned at her. "For what?"

"For taking me from there and keeping me safe. I don't know why you did it, but thank you. What they wanted to do to me—"

"There's no need to thank me," he said gruffly.

Simone was amazed to realize he was discomfited by her gratitude. "But—"

"No buts. Do *not* thank me."

Simone had no idea what else to say, and honestly, a simple thank you seemed insufficient for saving her life, but she had no idea what else to do or say to express her gratitude.

They encountered a few more humans outside their campers or tents, but most of them were drinking, and the ones who weren't were with others. If he'd been at full strength, he would have gone for the humans in groups, but he couldn't deplete himself further by bending them to his will and changing their memories.

Killean wound his way through the RVs and tents tucked between the thick pines, oaks, and maple trees. Where the stars peeked through the bowers overhead, they were bright in the night, but no moon graced the sky. Almost half the sites were empty, but it was still only mid-May, and Killean suspected there would be a lot more people here in the summer—wherever here was.

They crossed through a section made up mostly of tents where no one was awake. Stopping, he scented the air for the stench of a Savage, but he detected only the scent of pine and burning wood. He set Simone down beside a newer Dodge truck.

Stepping away from her, he inspected her to make sure she wasn't hurt. Her cheeks, which were so gaunt in captivity, had filled out now that she'd fed, and the dark circles under her eyes were almost gone. Her wrists had stopped bleeding, though they were still bruised and raw, as was the flesh she'd picked off her hands. A vampire as young as her shouldn't be capable of healing so fast, even after feeding, but because they were mates, his blood accelerated her healing abilities.

"I have to feed and find us a ride out of here," he said.

"You're going to feed on one of *these* people?"

"It's how I survive," he growled in response to the revulsion in her tone. "It's how *you* survive now too."

Simone couldn't stop herself from blushing as his words reminded her of the wanton way she acted while feeding on him. Out of habit, she almost apologized to him, but she clamped back the words. Unlike the hunter men she apologized to over the years for many numerous offenses, including something as small as taking up their time, Simone didn't think Killean would appreciate her apology. She had no reason to believe this, but her instincts told her it would only make him mad.

"Can't it wait?" she asked instead.

"No. You took a lot of blood out of me."

The fire in her cheeks spread down her nape and across her shoulders; she couldn't hold his gaze anymore.

"And I need to regain my strength if I'm going to fight off anyone who comes for us," Killean continued. "Stay here. If you hear or see anything abnormal, come and get me. Do *not* scream for me."

"Why not?" she asked, and her eyes flew up to his.

"Because if it's Savages you see, your scream will only draw humans and those Savages will have no problem killing them. They could decide to turn this place into another buffet for them to dine at."

A ripple of shock ran through her. She had no idea what to make of this mystery of a man. When he first kissed her, he was one of Ronan's men, a Defender, and part of what Nathan termed the Alliance. The next time she saw him, he was standing beside the monster who'd shattered her life and turned her into the enemy she always feared. And now he was trying to protect humans while smelling like a Savage and planning to feed on people.

What was going on here? Before she could ask him, he turned away and knelt next to the orange tent beside the truck.

"Please don't kill whoever's in there," she whispered.

Killean scowled at her. She had a right to be concerned and no reason to expect him to do anything other than kill the man he scented inside, but he *wanted* her to think better of him, which only pissed him off more.

Simone clasped her hands before her as she resisted going after Killean when he pulled the zipper back and disappeared inside.

Killean placed his hand over the mouth of the man sleeping within. He'd chosen this tent because the man was alone and he hadn't smelled any drugs or alcohol coming from within. This close to the human, he was pleased to learn his assessment was correct and the man had gone to sleep sober.

The man came awake with a jolt and bolted upright, but before he could yell against Killean's hand, Killean struck. When he sank his fangs into the man's neck, the man went rigid and his heartbeat skyrocketed.

Killean could have taken control of the human's mind and made this experience far less painful for him, but he was *so* depleted that he hadn't wanted to waste time and energy doing such a thing. However, as the man's agony beat against him, Killean realized more than hunger had propelled him into feeding on the man without preparing him first; if he couldn't kill him, then he would experience the man's suffering.

And he couldn't kill, not only because Simone had asked him not to, but also because now that she was free there was no longer a reason for him to do so. No matter how badly he wanted to experience the pleasure of life filling him, he would *not* give into the impulse.

However, with a sinking sensation in the pit of his stomach, Killean realized he needed to experience this man's pain as much as he needed his blood. The reality of what he was doing crashed over him, and Killean withdrew from his victim. As if all the bones were pulled from his body, the man whimpered and slumped forward.

"Don't move," Killean commanded. Now that the blood had replenished some of his strength, he felt more comfortable using his ability.

Sitting back, Killean studied the man as he sat with his head bent forward and his gaze focused on the air mattress he still sat on. Guilt tore at Killean as a broken air surrounded the innocent man.

Despite the fact they were some of the worst of humankind, Killean had made sure to take over the minds of his earliest victims and blocked their pain from them. When he hunted with Joseph, Killean couldn't block out the pain of his victims without drawing attention to himself, so he'd experienced the suffering of his victims. He hadn't felt bad about it as he'd done what was necessary to survive, and those humans weren't exactly upstanding citizens.

But this man was an innocent, one he didn't plan on killing and hadn't meant to harm. When he attacked this man, he'd been reacting to some new, brutal instinct—an instinct that marked him as more of a Savage than the deaths forever staining his soul could.

What was wrong with him?

You've made yourself into a monster.

He wanted to deny it, but it was true. He'd forged himself into this unfamiliar creature who feasted on blood and misery. He'd anticipated his increased appetite for blood, but he hadn't expected this intense craving to experience the pain of others too. Having to battle both needs was a war he wasn't prepared to wage, and he didn't know if he could.

CHAPTER FOURTEEN

Unwilling to get close enough to close the punctures on the man's neck with the healing agent in his saliva, Killean searched for another way to obscure his marks. He discovered a pocket knife next to the lantern beside the sleeping bag and opened it. Gripping the man's head, Killean kept him at arms-length as he placed his knife to the man's throat. The man flinched but didn't recoil when Killean carved a line connecting the two punctures, obscuring what they were.

He closed the knife and returned it. Taking a moment, he gathered his rattled composure before facing the man again. When his eyes fell on the blood trickling down the man's neck, his fangs pricked. Everything in him thirsted to drink all the blood from this man and experience the rush of life filling him with power.

No one would have to know if he killed this guy.

Simone glanced anxiously at the other tents as she watched the trees. No breeze stirred the air, and in this section of the campground, it was quiet as a tomb. From here, she couldn't see the groups of humans gathered around the fires or hear the rushing water of the river.

The occasional snore from someone in a nearby tent broke the hush. She supposed quiet was a good thing, but dread crept up her spine, as did the growing certainty something terrible was closing in on them.

Crouching, she leaned closer to the tent. "Killean?" she whispered.

Killean's head turned toward the flap when Simone's voice pierced the growing haze of bloodlust clouding his judgment. She'd asked him not to kill the man, and maybe she wouldn't know if he did, but *he* would know, and he wouldn't be able to look her in the eye again or live with himself.

"Is everything okay?" he asked.

"Yes. Are *you* okay?"

"I'll be out in a minute."

Killean edged further away from the man while he still could. He crossed the line when he killed before, but ending the life of this innocent man would make him no better than Joseph. It would forever sever any hope Killean had of somehow saving himself—if he wasn't already damned.

"Where are your truck keys?" Killean demanded.

"Under the pillow," the man replied in a wooden voice.

Leaning around him, Killean retrieved the keys from under the pillow. "You scratched your neck on a branch while hiking. You will remember none of this, and you will not report your truck stolen for two days. Understood?"

The man's eyes remained glazed as he nodded. "Go back to sleep and wake up tomorrow as if nothing happened."

The man was settling onto his mattress again when Killean pushed the flap aside and left the tent.

Simone scrambled back when Killean emerged. Her eyes shot behind him, but the flap fell into place before she could see whoever was within. The scent of fresh blood tickled her nostrils as her gaze raked Killean.

During his run to the campground, the breeze had mostly dried their clothes, but Killean's shirt and jeans hugged his lean frame as he towered a good seven inches over her five-eight frame. The scar on his face was whiter than usual and stood starkly out against his bronzed complexion. The lethal air surrounding him caused her to step further away.

"Are they...?" Her voice broke on the question as a tremor raced through her.

Did she really want to know if he'd killed the man or not? Killean was all that stood between her and the Savages and the only one she had to rely on, what would she do with the answer? Run from him? And go where?

She doubted Nathan and the hunters were still at the hotel where she last saw them, so how would she go about finding them? And what would they say or do if she found them? She was a vampire now; the hunters may have formed an Alliance with the vampires, but what would they do with her? Even if they took her back, she certainly couldn't just resume her old life.

But then, she had no idea what Killean intended for her. It couldn't be any worse than what Joseph planned, and because of that, she would follow him anywhere right now.

Then his crass words from when she was a prisoner drifted back across her mind and her blood ran cold. *"I knew her when she was a hunter, and the little bitch thought she was better than vampires. I think it's time she learns what it's like to have one between her thighs."*

Was all this because she'd broken their kiss on the beach? Had he come after her and taken her from Joseph just to punish her? She may not know him well, but she wanted to trust Killean, and if he took that trust and destroyed it, he may just ruin her too.

"What you said to Joseph about me in that place, is *that* why you came for me?" she blurted.

Killean frowned at her; he was still fighting against going back into the tent and finishing what he'd started, so he couldn't recall what she was talking about. "What did I say?"

"That I thought I was better than vampires and it was time to... to..." Her words trailed off as fire crept into her cheeks.

Killean almost groaned as he recalled his words; he'd known they would come back to haunt him. "To have one between your thighs?"

Simone couldn't look at him as she edged further away. Killean almost grabbed her and hugged her close, but he didn't think she would react well to such a thing right now. His fingers flexed as helplessness filled him.

"No, Simone, that is *not* why I came for you." Distrust and hope shimmered in her eyes when she finally lifted her head to look at him again. "You will *never* have to worry about me being a threat to you. *Ever*."

Simone gulped as his eyes burned with golden fire. She wanted to believe him, but she barely knew him. However, even though his vulgar words echoed in her mind, a part of her believed she could trust him. He may be one of the surliest and most distant men she'd ever encountered, but he'd saved her life, and she doubted he'd risk his own life to free her just so he could punish her for breaking their kiss.

"I mean it, Simone. I will *never* be a threat to you, and I will *never* force myself on you." Over the years, he'd been many things, but never had he pushed himself on a woman, and he never would.

"Then why did you say those things?" she asked.

"Because they were what Joseph wanted to hear."

"I see."

Killean knew she didn't, but they didn't have time for this. "We have to go."

He was right, but she had to know if he'd killed whoever was inside that tent. She'd spent her entire life locked behind walls and doing everything expected of her because one misstep might not make her a contender for Nathan's wife.

And all her obedience had gotten her was Nathan choosing another woman over her.

She was so unbelievably tired of being afraid of offending or annoying someone, even if it was a vampire who could easily break her neck.

"Is the person in that tent dead?" she asked with a lift of her chin.

"No," Killean replied in a clipped tone.

He brushed by her and stalked over to the truck. Unlocking it, he opened the passenger door and held it for her. Simone hesitated before walking over to the truck; there was no reason for him to lie to her, and even if he was lying, she had no choice but to go with him.

She was almost to the truck when Killean thrust out his arm, blocking her from the vehicle. Stunned by the action, she tilted her head to look up at him and froze when she saw the bright red color of his eyes and the firm set of his chin. He radiated violence as he searched the woods surrounding them.

"What is it?" she whispered.

"A Savage," he murmured as he scented the increasing stench of rot on the air. Then he spotted the shadow slipping through the trees a hundred feet away from them.

Simone's heart leapt into her throat as she glanced around in panic. Joseph had found them! They would take her back, return her to chains, and destroy Killean! *No!* She didn't care what happened, she would never return to that place alive.

"Let's go," she whispered and grasped his arm to tug on it.

"I think there's only one of them."

"So?"

"So, it has to die."

"No, Killean. We can go. We can drive away from here and never look back."

"If we do that, this one will alert the others to where we are and what we're driving. They'll be on us before we get ten miles down the road."

Simone bit back a moan as her terror escalated. She couldn't go back there, and if something happened to him...

She'd be done for. She knew nothing of the human world. She'd be as vulnerable to unsavory people as she was to the Savages. Not only that, but she didn't want anything bad to happen to Killean. There was no denying he was powerful, but if he went after this Savage, he could lose, and it would be her fault. She'd weakened him by taking his blood; he'd fed since then, but was it enough to get him through a fight?

CHAPTER FIFTEEN

"Killean—"

"Shh," he whispered.

He watched the Savage slipping through the trees, but kept his other senses attuned to his surroundings as he tried to ascertain if this one was a decoy while more slipped up on them. He heard no other sounds, and the scent on the air was only strong enough for one.

"Get in the truck and lock the door," Killean said.

Simone wanted to argue with him, but she couldn't do anything that might put him at risk. Lifting her dress, she was reaching for something to help her inside when Killean clasped her elbow and boosted her up. A small, electrical current ran from his hand and into her arm before he settled her inside and released her as if she'd burned him.

"Here are the keys." He shoved the keys into her hand. "Do *not* open these doors for anyone other than me. If I'm not back in three minutes, drive out of here."

She didn't get a chance to tell him she couldn't drive before he shut the door and stalked away. Simone locked the door while she watched Killean slip into the trees. Placing her hands in her lap, she wrung them nervously as she searched the shadows. She felt horribly exposed beneath the dim glow of the interior light, but she didn't dare take her eyes off Killean to search for a way to turn it off.

Like he was more shadow than man, Killean glided seamlessly in and out of the trees; if she looked away for even a second, she'd lose sight of him.

Then the light turned off, and she almost screamed as a figure surged up from behind Killean in the dark. She hadn't seen the Savage hiding behind a tree, but Killean must have as he turned when the creature lunged at him and seized it by the throat.

Simone had always shied away from violence, she hadn't even liked going near the male hunters while they were on the training field, but she was riveted on Killean. Leaning forward, she rested her fingers on the dashboard as Killean lifted the Savage like he weighed no more than a feather and smashed it against a tree.

Before the Savage could react, Killean drove his fist into the monster's chest. Simone gulped as she watched his wrist disappear into the creature's ribcage before Killean pulled his hand back. She thought she should be horrified by the heart Killean held in his hand, and the brutality he'd unleashed with such speed and zero remorse, but she didn't feel unsettled by it.

She was impressed and something more, something she couldn't quite put her finger on until Killean released the body. *Relief.* She was relieved he was safe, and not because she would be vulnerable without him, but because she didn't want anything bad to happen to the infuriating man. It made no sense to her. She barely knew him, but the idea of something happening to him scared her.

Killean dropped the Savage's heart on the ground and bent over the dead body. The enticing scent of the creature's blood teased Killean's nostrils, but he resisted its temptation as he searched the Savage's pockets. He didn't find a cell phone, which meant this bastard hadn't been able to get a call out to his fellow shitheads about where they were.

Lifting the body, Killean tossed it over his shoulder before reclaiming the heart and carrying it over to the truck. He dumped the body into the back and glanced at Simone who watched him with wide eyes.

He held up his index finger to her before returning to the kill site to make sure any spilled blood was obscured by debris. From an empty campsite, he gathered a piece of burnt wood still sitting in a firepit and ran the wood over the leaves and pine needles covering the blood to obscure the scent.

When he finished, he walked the thirty feet to the river to throw the wood into it and wash his hands while he searched for more Savages. He saw no sign of them, and he didn't detect their scent on the air.

Returning to the truck, his eyes met Simone's as he approached the vehicle. In the light of the stars, he could see her pale face as her eyes tracked his every move. When he reached the driver's side of the truck, he wondered if she would let him in or if he would have to break the window. Before his hand fell on the handle, she leaned over and unlocked the door. Killean opened it and climbed behind the wheel.

Simone watched as he started the truck. When the headlights flared on, he turned them off and shifted into reverse. She'd been in a few vehicles in her lifetime, but she'd never driven one, and she found herself fascinated by the mechanics of it. Tonight was no exception as Killean went through the process with ease. He pulled the truck out of the parking spot and onto the dirt road running through the campsites.

"Are you okay?" she asked.

"Fine," he replied.

He hadn't been hurt, but every muscle in his body was tensed as if he were prepared to attack again. However, she decided she was better off letting it drop. "What are you going to do with the body?"

"Drop it off somewhere no one will can find it before the sun takes care of the remains."

"Do you think there are others out there?"

"No. This one was alone."

"How can you be so sure?"

"Because I didn't sense them out there, and I would have detected them."

The confident way he said it buried some of her worry, but she still couldn't help feeling as if those monsters were closing in on them. Simone gazed out the window as they passed more campers before traveling by a large, log building. A sign outside the building read, *Guest Check-In & Mercantile.*

After they passed the building, Killean left the dirt road behind for a paved street leading away from the campground. She relaxed when the bumpy road gave way to the smooth hum of tires on asphalt. No streetlights illuminated the night, but she saw well enough to differentiate the pine, oak, and maple trees crowding the road. Given the size of their trunks, some of the trees had to be a couple of hundred years old.

When they'd traveled a couple of miles, Killean pulled over to the side of the road. The trees in this area were set further back from the road, which would allow more sunlight to spill onto the road in the morning. There were no nearby houses.

"I'll be right back," he said.

He left the truck running as he jumped out and walked around to the back to retrieve the body and heart. He carried the Savage over to a five-foot-deep embankment on the side of the road. It wasn't the ideal spot to discard a body, but the embankment would hide it from any travelers before the sun could do its job. He couldn't drive around with the body in the bed of the truck all night. If any Savages happened to be near the road, they would scent the blood, and he wasn't about to ring the dinner bell for them.

Killean returned to the truck and searched the bed for any blood. He pulled his shirt off and used it to wipe away the few drops that had spilled there before tugging it back on. Leaping out of the truck, he returned to the driver's seat and pulled away from the embankment.

Another mile down the road, he turned on the headlights. The beams hit the trees and only illuminated twenty feet of the windy road.

Simone spotted a few houses set back from the road, but no light shone from any of their windows. For a second, she had the unsettling feeling the world had ended and they were all that remained as they climbed hills before coasting back down them. Well, them and the Savages stalking them were all that remained.

She tore her attention away from the forest when her skin crawled and she became certain there were monsters out there, watching them from glowing red eyes. Her imagination had never been overly active. In fact, it had been rather *in*active for most of her life; now, it was making up for it with all sorts of horrible possibilities.

She held her breath and didn't dare look out the window beside her as she became convinced she would find Joseph loping beside the vehicle or running straight at her with his fangs extended and his red eyes blazing.

"Do you know what happened to my mom?" she asked. "I lost sight of her when they raided our compound, and she wasn't in that place with me."

"No, I don't," he said.

"Oh," she whispered, and her shoulders slumped.

"But I also don't know who your mom is," Killean said when he sensed the sorrow his words caused her.

His words helped to raise her spirits a little. If he didn't know her mom, then he couldn't know if she was alive or not. Until she learned differently, she would believe her mom was alive and safe with Nathan and the others.

"Where are we?" she asked.

"I don't know."

The crispness of his reply drew her attention to him. His knuckles had turned white on the steering wheel, and he sat so rigidly it seemed the next bump might shatter his bones. Her hearing and vision had remained the same after she transformed from a hunter into a monster, but she detected the steady beat of his heart now, whereas before she wouldn't have noticed it.

Did she notice his heartbeat now because blood was how she survived, or was it the man she noticed more about? She didn't know the answer, but she suspected it was the latter.

"Those things didn't tell you where they were taking us tonight?" she asked.

"They didn't tell me anything. They didn't trust me enough for that."

"Didn't you see—"

"They kept me blindfolded," he interjected. "And tonight was the first time I didn't have to ride in the trunk when I went somewhere with them."

"Why did they make you ride in the trunk?" she blurted.

His red eyes were the brightest thing about the night when they slid to her. "Because they didn't trust me."

The deliberate, enunciated way he said it caused her hackles to rise. Even when she'd still been a hunter, Killean had managed to infuriate her in ways no other ever had. As a hunter, she'd wanted to smack him; as a vampire, she imagined grabbing the back of his head and bouncing it off the steering wheel.

Instead, she smiled as she replied through her teeth, "I see."

Killean focused on the road again as it twisted deeper into the woods and rose higher until he didn't know if they would ever find their way out of here. Side streets broke off from the one they were on; he had no idea where they led, and more than a few times he was tempted to take one of them, but he decided to stay on the current one. For all he knew, one of those roads might loop back to the campground. This one had to lead somewhere eventually.

He glanced at the GPS screen in the center of the dash. He knew there was a way to look up nearby attractions, but he didn't want to mess with it right now, and he wasn't familiar enough with the things to have any confidence he could pull up the information he sought.

Then the road started to descend, and in the distance, he spotted the faintest hint of a light glimmering through the trees.

"Did Nathan send you to find us?" she asked.

Killean's grip tightened on the wheel at the mention of the hunter leader. He knew Nathan and Simone had been expected to marry, but was Simone in love with him? And what did he care if she was?

"Nathan," he snarled, "is a happily mated *vampire* now."

A jolt of surprise ran through Simone. Nathan had announced his intention to marry Vicky and become a vampire, but it still astounded her he'd actually gone *through* with it. She couldn't picture Nathan as a vampire, but she'd *never* imagined herself as one either.

"Mated?" she asked. "What does that mean?"

"It's an eternal, soul-deep bond between two vampires. When a vampire encounters their mate, they often complete the bond."

"How do they do that?"

"Through an exchange of blood and sex. If the mate is still

mortal, a vampire will have to make them immortal to complete the bond and protect them better. If a vampire loses their mate, they either go insane or die. Encountering their mate and completing the bond stabilizes a purebred vampire battling their darker urges."

Many vampires never found their mates and either battled the emptiness forever, turned Savage, or died. Killean expected death to be his saving grace as he'd die before claiming a hunter as his mate.

"And do a lot of purebred vampires have these darker urges?" she asked.

"All the male ones do."

"What are they?"

Killean shrugged. "It depends on the vampire. For some, they can't get enough sex or they seek out pain. Others can't get enough blood or are driven to kill. Some have a combination of one or two things, and the rare unlucky few have a combination of everything."

"And you battle one of these things?"

"Yes."

Simone didn't ask which one. She'd seen Killean in action tonight; every inch of him was a lethal killer.

"I see," she murmured. "Well, vampire or not, Nathan would still try to save us."

"He'd try to save you even though the hunters Joseph captured broke off from him because they didn't agree with his love of a vampire and his decision to combine forces with Ronan?"

"Yes," she said without hesitation.

Killean's teeth grated together at her unwavering certainty in her ex-intended. "Nathan didn't send me."

"Did Ronan?" Nathan would want to save his hunters, but it

would make more sense that Ronan sent Killean instead of Nathan. Simone didn't see Killean taking orders from Nathan.

A stab of guilt tore through him at the mention of Ronan. "No."

Simone stared at him as she tried to figure out why this man was sitting beside her. If he'd intended to stay with Joseph, then why did he pull her away from him? But if no one sent him, then why was here?

"Then you really planned to join Joseph and his group?" she asked.

His head snapped toward her, and before he could stop himself, he bared his fangs at her. "No!"

Simone recoiled against the door as anger emanated from him.

CHAPTER SIXTEEN

KILLEAN'S SHOULDERS hunched as he tried to regain control of the fury her words created. He was being an asshole, he knew it, but not killing the man in the tent, sitting this close to her, having her think he would actually *choose* Joseph over Ronan, and being reminded of what he'd become was too much for him right now.

"No," he said more calmly as he focused on the road. "I did not want to join Joseph."

Simone eased away from the window as some of his tension ebbed. She didn't think he would hurt her, but she didn't understand him. "Then why were you with Joseph, and why are you here now?"

"For you."

Simone blinked at his response. She wasn't sure she'd heard him correctly. Had he said, *for you*, or *will do*, or even *achoo*?

That was it! He must have sneezed, but he hadn't moved.

"Did you say... for you?" She had no reason to expect him to do anything for her and would feel like the biggest idiot if he had sneezed.

"Yes."

Simone stared at him, but he didn't look at her as he pulled up to a stop light on a cross-section of road.

Killean studied the smattering of stores lining the street. Most of them were dark, but a few had spotlights illuminating their signs. One was a fast food place, another a red barn converted into a gas station; there was also a barbeque restaurant and an antique store, but at this time of night they were all closed.

When the light turned green, Killean merged onto the four-lane road and headed west in search of a hotel. They were over forty miles from the campground, and with the many side roads he'd seen along the way, he felt confident the Savages wouldn't be able to trace their route and track them.

"So, no one sent you; you came on your own?" Simone asked.

He didn't know why she was so incessant on following this conversation, but he wished she'd let it go. "Yes."

"Because of me?" she croaked.

"*For* you," he muttered as he studied the buildings lining the road. There were more antique stores, restaurants, a doggy daycare, bait shop, and a few maple syrup stands.

"For me." She ran the words over in her mind, but she had no idea what to make of them, but guilt stabbed her as she recalled thinking that if anyone was going to join the monsters holding her, it was him. She had no idea why he'd come for her, but it was obvious he did *not* want to be a part of Joseph's group. "Why me?"

When the silence stretched on, Simone realized he didn't plan on answering her. "Killean—"

"I have my reasons, and you won't learn them. You're free, be content with that."

Her eyes narrowed on him. Simone had spent her entire life being seen and not heard; she'd accepted it, but she was tired of accepting things, and she did not want to accept them from *him*. The only problem was, she'd be arguing with a wall if she continued to push this, and there were other things she wished to discuss.

"When will we be going back for the other hunters?" she asked.

"Like our location tonight, I have no idea where they are."

Simone felt as if he'd kicked her in the chest as a sob lodged in her throat. *I have no idea where they are.* Those words were as condemning as the hangman's noose. "They can't be found?" she whispered.

"No."

"Could someone else in the Alliance find them?"

"No."

Turning away from him, Simone took a few moments to compose herself so she didn't burst into tears. He'd been uncomfortable around her gratitude; he'd probably open the door and fling himself out if she started crying. Besides, she wasn't ready to give up; there had to be some hope for them.

"We have to find them and get them out."

"That's not going to happen," Killean stated.

"What do you mean, that's not going to happen?"

"Unless you know where you were kept, then finding the others isn't going to happen."

"Those Savages knocked me out before they took me from the stronghold," she murmured. "I don't remember anything until I woke in that place."

"And I was stripped of my possessions, blindfolded, placed in a trunk, and driven around for hours before being taken to Joseph. I know as much about where they are as you do. I *might* be able to get back to the hall we escaped from, but I'm not taking you anywhere near those bastards again, and I doubt any of them are still there. The minute they captured those hunters, there was no saving them."

"But I was saved."

When his golden gaze swung toward her, the steeliness of it stole her breath. His arms had been warm and tender when he held her, but there was nothing tender about the ruthless man sitting beside her.

"Because I got lucky, and so did you," he said. "Do you want to push your luck?"

"They're my friends, my family..."

Her voice trailed off as she realized those hunters were as lost to her as the city of Atlantis, but she would grieve for them later, when she was alone and had time to give in to her emotions.

"Why did you take me from there and not one of them?" she asked.

Killean would not answer that question.

Simone waited, but when his lips remained compressed together, she realized he still would not reveal his reasons to her. *Stubborn, annoying vampire.*

"Will those hunters all become Savages?" she asked.

"If Joseph has his way," Killean replied.

Killean swung the truck into the parking lot of a small motel with an open vacancy sign. He pulled into a parking spot before the white building with pale blue shutters and put the truck in park.

"And are you a Savage?" Simone inquired.

Killean studied the motel before replying, "I'm more one of them than I'm not."

He admitted it to her, and for the first time, he admitted it to himself.

Simone was uncertain how to react to this admission. Maybe, as a normal vampire, he wasn't her mortal enemy, like she'd been raised to believe vampires were. But as a Savage, he was certainly a monster she was supposed to hate.

So why didn't she hate him? And why did she believe he was

far more than the brutal exterior and callous indifference he portrayed?

She was probably a fool for believing he wasn't as cruel as he sometimes acted, but she couldn't shake the instinctual feeling she was right.

"No matter what I am, I'll get you back to your people," Killean assured her.

She almost asked why, but she'd only find herself smacking into another wall of stony silence from him.

"Do you have any special abilities?" he asked, wondering if perhaps she possessed something that could help them out of this mess.

"Abilities?"

"Yes, abilities. The abilities Kadence and Nathan possessed as hunters were amplified when they became vampires."

"Oh, ah... I didn't know they had any kind of abilities."

"Now you do, so what about you? Do you have any special talents?"

"Not unless you include sewing faster than everyone in my class." Her smile slid away when he didn't look at all amused by her poor attempt at humor. "No," she said more seriously. "I didn't have any abilities as a hunter, and I don't now."

So, like humans and vampires, only a select few hunters had extrasensory abilities, Killean realized.

"What can Nathan and Kadence do?" Simone asked.

"Kadence can see pathways and knows things. Time slows for Nathan in a way that makes it easier for him to fight. Their powers can also combine to work together."

"Amazing," she breathed. "Being twins has always made them rare amongst our kind, and this makes them even more special."

And it did nothing to help them. "We need a room," Killean said.

Before Simone could reply, he opened the door and climbed out. He walked in front of the truck and around to open her door. Clasping her elbow, he helped her from the vehicle and drew her close against his side.

Killean studied the woods behind the building and the road they'd left as he scented the air. He didn't detect any nearby threat, but he wasn't willing to leave her alone out here. "Come on," he said and drew her toward the office.

Simone perched on the edge of the king-sized bed while Killean shoved a chair under the doorknob. The blockade wouldn't do much against a vampire trying to break in, but at least it was something. Each of his awkward movements was entirely unlike the fluid grace vampires and hunters possessed; there was something almost pained about him, but he would never reveal what it was to her.

Simone tore her attention away from him and back to the small, austere room. Scratches marred the surface of the rickety wood bureau across from her. A small, box television sat on top of the bureau, but it remained off. She'd watched very little TV in her life and had no interest in it now.

The wood panel walls held two pictures of mountains with streams, but one had a bear and the other a family of deer. The brown, industrial carpet didn't have any tears in it, and she didn't see a single speck of dust anywhere, but the color scheme made the room feel dreary.

This was the only bed in the room and had been the only room available. She'd stood by Killean's side and watched as he mesmerized the clerk into giving him the keys, forgetting what they looked like, and believing they paid enough to stay here for two days.

She'd known vampires could do such a thing, but witnessing it was something else entirely. Then it had dawned on her that she could do such a thing now too; the realization unsettled her. A couple of weeks ago, she'd been one person, and now she was someone entirely different.

Her head bowed as she stared at her clasped hands. Who and what was she now?

Not knowing the answer to that was like plunging over a cliff, entirely terrifying yet strangely freeing. She hoped she discovered the answer before she hit bottom.

After receiving the room key from the clerk, Killean gathered a stack of brochures from a rack beside the door in the office. Those glossy prints now sat beside her on the bed. *Welcome to the Green Mountains* was printed on more than a few of them, and as she flipped through the attractions, she realized they were in Vermont.

"Would you like a shower?" Killean asked.

Excitement shot through her before diminishing. "I don't have any other clothes to put on." And she didn't see the point of showering only to throw her grubby dress back on.

"There are bathrobes in the closet; you can wear one of those. We'll get new clothes tomorrow."

The idea of wearing only a robe around him caused a blush to stain her cheeks; she'd never been so indecently dressed around a man before. However, the allure of a shower won out over her sense of modesty. Rising, she walked over to the closet, removed one of the two bathrobes within, strolled into the bathroom, and closed the door. She couldn't wait to scrub the feel of that place off her.

She turned the water as hot as she could stand it and undressed. Looking at her soiled underclothes made her cringe. She'd have to wear the dress again, but there was *no* way she could let those filthy things touch her body again.

She tossed her underclothes into the trash and stepped beneath the pounding stream of water. She scrubbed at herself until her skin turned red and continued until it was raw. No hot water remained, yet she lingered until she couldn't tolerate the cold anymore.

CHAPTER SEVENTEEN

When she climbed from the shower, she felt more refreshed and cleaner, but she hadn't succeeded in scrubbing away the memories of what the Savages did to her. With a sinking heart, she realized she would never be free of those memories, and she didn't want to be. The hunters who remained there deserved for her to remember and to do what she could to stop it. What that was, she had no idea, but she wouldn't let Joseph and those other bastards get away with destroying her kind.

She may not have rid herself of the memories, but at least she smelled of soap instead of the rank body odor, garbage, and mildew aroma of that place. Standing before the steam-covered mirror, she worked the tangles from her hair with her fingers before wiping away the steam to inspect herself.

Simone blinked at the image staring back at her. She hadn't known what she expected to find in the glass, but discovering she looked the same caused her hand to tremble. She'd been through so much and she was no longer mortal, yet that was her pale skin, deep auburn hair, and though she'd been raised not to be conceited, she was aware many considered her pretty if not beautiful.

There were minor differences, such as her cheekbones were more noticeable and she'd lost some weight, but she suspected those differences were more noticeable before she fed from Killean.

Darn it, there was that blush again as the memory returned of his blood filling her mouth while she did things she'd never thought herself capable of doing to him. Refusing to delve into why she'd acted in such a way, she shoved the memory aside and turned away from the mirror. She picked up the robe, slid it on, and belted it around her waist.

She was relieved to find that, with the belt tied, the thick robe was as modest as some of her dresses. Gripping the neck, she held it close together, and after opening the door, she kept one hand on the belt while she exited the bathroom. Killean sat at the foot of the bed with his elbows on his thighs. His dark brown hair stood on end as he ran his fingers through it and tugged at the strands in a way that must be painful.

Sensing something explosive about him, Simone stopped in the doorway. "Are you okay?" she whispered.

Killean couldn't look at her; not after he'd spent the entire time she was in the shower fantasizing about what it would be like to join her. He'd lick every bead of water from her silken flesh before dipping his head between her thighs. Killean almost groaned when his cock stiffened at the image. He hoped she hadn't left him any hot water. Shoving himself off the bed, he walked awkwardly toward the closet.

"I'm fine," he said. She edged out of the way when he approached, and her hand gripped the robe against her neck. He couldn't stop himself from scowling at her. "I'm not going to attack you."

"I... I know," she stammered. But did she?

"I'm not going to try and see your breasts either," he said and flicked a pointed glance at her white-knuckled grip on the robe.

"I... I..." Simone's voice trailed off; she had no idea how to respond to him. She should apologize, it was what she did after all, but before she could get the words out, he was speaking again.

"Did they do something to you in there?" he demanded.

Joseph had told Killean the hunters remained chained almost all the time and were off limits, but was that just for him? Joseph was the one who changed her, had he violated her at the same time?

A haze of red shaded Killean's vision at the possibility. She would never be his, but the idea of such a thing happening to her made his blood boil. *No* one should ever have to endure being violated, but especially not Simone, who was practically a babe in this world. He wanted to draw her into his arms and shelter her; at the same time, he itched to tear the life from something and batter it into a million pieces.

"They did plenty to me in there," Simone replied slowly, wary of his red eyes and the violence his tensed muscles, clenched jaw, and the throbbing vein in the center of his forehead radiated. "They chained me, they turned me into a vampire, they starved me, they—"

"Did they rape you?" he interrupted sharply. When Simone's heartbeat skyrocketed, he realized he'd better rein in his temper; he was scaring her.

"I... uh..." Simone grappled to fit more pieces of her memory into place as she contemplated Killean's question. She recalled Joseph forcing his blood on her and the agony of the change afterward. And when it was over, she'd woken to find herself chained with the others, but he hadn't done anything else to her. "No, he didn't."

"Did anyone molest you in *any* way?"

"Other than what I've already stated?"

"Yes."

Looking at him, she decided it was probably best to keep from him the time she tried to escape and the Savages who caught her fondled her breasts. She had no fear he would hurt her, but he looked ready to go on a rampage, and she had no idea what he would do to anyone he encountered.

"No. They mostly left me alone." It wasn't entirely a lie, she'd said *mostly*. "Even when they took me to the bathroom, they would chain me in there and leave me alone."

Killean's shoulders relaxed as some of his bloodlust eased. "Good. While you're with me, you will *never* have to fear that I will try to rape you." He'd already assured her of this, but it seemed she hadn't believed him.

"I didn't think you would," she admitted.

He glanced pointedly at her hand on her throat again.

"I've... I've never..." She *despised* this blush she couldn't control. "It's not because I think you'll do something!" she blurted. "I've never been so scantily dressed around a man before."

"I assure you, Simone, you are more than properly covered. All I can see is your feet and your face; you don't have to worry about exposing too much around me."

"Ah, yeah," she muttered.

"I'm going to leave the door to the bathroom cracked. If you hear anything unusual, scream, and I'll be out here in an instant," he told her.

"I will," Simone promised.

CHAPTER EIGHTEEN

KILLEAN DIDN'T FALL asleep until after the sun rose and the risk of Savages being out lessened. Before lying down, he'd considered calling Ronan but decided to hold off. He may not have a lot to tell Ronan that could help in their fight against Joseph, but he had to share the info he did have. However, he wasn't ready to face the disappointment and distrust he knew he would receive, and deserved, from his mentor and friend yet.

Beside him, Simone had lain rigidly at the very edge of the bed. The covers were tucked up to her chin and only her face was exposed like she was a turtle. She'd remained that way until sleep claimed her an hour before sunrise. Then she'd relaxed enough for a hand to emerge over the covers.

After she slept, he'd rolled over from staring at the ceiling to watch her. Her face relaxed in sleep, and her soft breaths exhaled over her luscious lips. He found himself thinking less about Joseph finding them and more about what it would be like to run his hands over her enticing curves. He fell asleep with those happy imaginings in mind.

When he woke later in the day, he discovered his arm draped

protectively around Simone's waist and her back tucked against his chest. Her thick hair tickled his nose and lips as he inhaled the hotel shampoo and eucalyptus aroma she emitted. Somehow, his hand had slid beneath her robe to cup her breast, and her puckered nipple burned his palm.

He'd never been so hard in his life, and her ass rubbing against his dick did not help. And then, the enticing scent of her blood hit him, and saliva filled his mouth. He longed to sink his fangs into her while he parted her thighs and buried himself inside her.

She's a hunter. But that reminder didn't dim his lust. However, he'd promised her he wouldn't do anything inappropriate with her, and he meant it. The lowest forms of life were the ones who took advantage of those weaker than them. He was about to pull his hand away when Simone shifted, so her breast filled his palm.

It was then he realized she was awake. Killean froze as he waited for her to tell him to get away, but she didn't speak as her breath came a little faster. Killean rubbed her nipple and relished the sensation of it hardening beneath his touch. Larger than his hand, her breast spilled over his palm while he caressed her.

When Simone first woke to find his hand on her breast, she hadn't known what to do, but she'd felt no apprehension. She'd only experienced a sense of rightness in his arms. She didn't understand the feeling, but instead of pulling away from him, she'd remained where she was as she listened to his breathing while he slept.

Then he'd awoken, and she'd barely contained her excitement when instead of pulling away, he continued to hold her. Her head spun as Killean's touch seared her flesh. She shouldn't allow this; she was meant to be a hunter bride. It was the role she'd been born and trained for, and hunter brides were only supposed to know the touch of their husbands. But how many hunters would take a vampire as their bride?

Not many. Probably not any.

And how many of them could set her on fire the way Killean did? Most of the time, she wasn't sure she liked this man. He was angry, distant, and sometimes cruel, but something about him called to her in a way no other had. Her attraction to him had been strong and surprising as a hunter, but now it was almost consuming.

Did vampires feel things more acutely than mortals, or was this something else entirely?

She found herself not caring about the answer as the next stroke of his thumb electrified her body. That awful aching was back between her thighs, and she found herself squirming against the rigid evidence of his arousal pressing against her butt.

When his hand slid from one breast to the other, Simone instinctively arched into his touch. Not only was the ache growing, but wetness spread between her legs when he leaned closer and his warm breath tickled her skin.

Killean slid his tongue over her ear before drawing it between his teeth and nipping it. "You are a walking temptation." Rolling her nipple between his thumb and forefinger, he tugged on it, and she moaned in response. "Do you like this, Simone?"

Embarrassment clogged her throat at his titillating words; she had no idea how to respond to him.

"Or do you like this more?"

Releasing her breast, Killean skimmed his fingers down the curve of her side, over her rounded hip, and down between her legs. When his fingers slid through her nest of curls, Simone went still as stone against him and her thighs clamped shut.

Killean froze when he realized what he was doing. This woman was a *hunter*! What would his family think if they could see him now? They would consider him weak and despise him for his weakness.

But not only was Simone a hunter, she was also an innocent. One who deserved better than a Savage's touch, and one she would be bound to forever if he let things progress between them.

Jerking his hand back, he rolled away and launched to his feet. He tried to adjust his robe to cover his erection, but it was impossible. Unable to look at her again, he stalked into the bathroom and almost slammed the door before recalling he had to hear her over the water if something went wrong.

His shower couldn't have been any colder if he added ice to it, but it did nothing to dampen his lust for her, and he didn't bother trying to jerk off to ease his erection. It had been years since he was successful in the endeavor, and though he was aroused to the point of pain, it would only infuriate him if he tried to masturbate and still couldn't find any release. Instead, between the icy water and his willpower, he eventually got his erection to soften.

Turning the shower off, he climbed from the tub and toweled himself dry as he stared at the door. He had to get away from her before something like that happened again, but where did he take her?

He didn't know if Ronan and the others were still at the compound or if they moved after he left them. If they hadn't moved, they wouldn't let him step foot on their property again, not with what he was now.

He would have to call and hope Ronan still had the same number so he could arrange a way to give Simone back. He didn't know what he'd do after he was free of her. He didn't trust himself to be around hunters or humans anymore; he might never be capable of being around them again.

With what he was now, he couldn't return to his old life, but what was his new one? Would it forever be this hideous in-between of fighting against becoming a monster and battling his conscience?

He'd chosen this path, but he'd battled bloodlust his entire life and felt confident he could handle what would happen to him after he killed. That was before the bloodlust became a living entity pulsing through his veins. With every one of those pulses, the demon part of him begged for him to kill.

And he certainly hadn't anticipated how enticing the idea of keeping the hunter in the next room would be. *Remember what she is.* But the hatred he'd felt for hunters most of his life didn't boil to the surface as he recalled the feel of her soft body molded against his.

He ran a hand through his tousled hair before slipping the robe back on. He was ravenous. Usually, he could go a couple of days between feedings, but not anymore. He required blood soon.

He nudged the door further open, and his gaze fell on Simone. Her shoulders tensed when he reemerged, and she hunched forward on the edge of the bed. Her head was bent, so her cascade of long hair shielded her delicate features from him.

Staring at her profile, he felt like a bigger asshole. She may be a hunter, but as such, she'd led the most sheltered of lives until she was taken from her stronghold. *Don't get closer and don't understand her; she's going back!*

Still, he found himself saying, "I'm sorry. That shouldn't have happened."

Simone cursed the fire burning her cheeks. She couldn't bring herself to look at him, so she gazed at the carpet.

"It won't happen again," Killean stated.

And a part of her inwardly cried at his statement. She should stay as far from this complicated vampire as possible, but she *yearned* for it to happen again. She wished it hadn't stopped in the first place. Yes, it had frightened her when he tried to touch between her legs, but it also excited her. She'd felt perched on the edge of finally learning what her body craved so badly.

"Are you hungry?" he asked.

Simone shook her head; it was the best she could do.

Killean walked over and retrieved his filthy, discarded clothes. He tugged his jeans on under the robe before removing it to pull on his shirt. "We'll go out and buy some clothes from the nearby stores," he said.

When she still wouldn't look at him, Killean tried to keep his temper under control. "I really am sorry."

Simone cringed. "It's fine," she managed to choke out. "Really. Don't apologize."

Killean had no idea how to proceed; he'd never been in a situation like this with a woman. But he'd upset her, and he had to try to fix it. "I realize you don't have a lot of experience with men, and I shouldn't have—"

"Stop," she groaned, unable to handle anything else he might say. She was sure she would spontaneously combust if he kept trying to apologize.

Killean closed his mouth. He didn't know how to deal with women. It had been years since he'd had any close interaction with one, and his past interactions consisted of a tumble in and out of their beds.

The last woman he'd been close with was his mother, and she died when he was seven. He'd spent the four hundred forty-five years of his life since her death avoiding getting close to anyone. He planned to remove Simone from his life, but he still felt like the biggest piece of shit. What had he been thinking to touch her in such a way? She was responsive in the beginning, but she'd had no idea where it all could lead.

"I took advantage, and I shouldn't have," he said.

Simone dropped her head into her hands and tried not to scream. Why did he have to keep going with this?

"And for that, I am sorry," he said.

"Stop!" she cried, and dropping her hands, she turned to face him. Looking at him was far less mortifying than his continued apologies. "I didn't... I wanted... I said it's *fine*!"

Her eyes burned a brilliant white-blue as she shouted the last word at him. The wildness of that color brought his dick back to life, and he shifted as his jeans became uncomfortable.

"You wanted what?" he asked.

Simone resisted slapping her hands on the bed; she had no idea how to deal with this man. He was so much *more* than anyone she'd ever met.

"Simone?" he pressed when she didn't speak.

"Stop being such a... a... jerk, and let it go!"

CHAPTER NINETEEN

Killean would have laughed at the fact her best insult was jerk, but he was far too irritated by their circumstances to find anything amusing.

"We're going to teach you how to swear, dolly," he muttered.

When Simone glowered at him, he found he far preferred her anger to the distress and humiliation she exuded seconds ago.

"I am not a *dolly*," she retorted.

Killean enjoyed this spirited side of Simone and wanted to see more of it, but fire was spreading through his parched veins. He needed to feed, and to do so they had to leave this room. "Unless you want me to pick out your clothes, I suggest you dress so we can go shopping."

"We can't wear those clothes in public, people will stare at us."

"Who cares?" he asked. "Would you prefer we go out in the robes or naked?"

"Of course not!"

"Then get dressed and let people stare. You've already spent far too much of your life worried about what others think of you."

Simone opened her mouth to argue, but how could she argue against the truth. Shoving herself to her feet, she snatched her dress off the chair in the corner. Even though it was ruined, she'd neatly folded it and set it there after showering last night. She glared at him as she stalked past him to the bathroom and closed the door.

She tried not to cringe as she pulled the filthy dress on, but the smell and feel of it made her skin crawl. When they got back, she would scrub herself all over again. She also tried not to think about the fact she was nude beneath the dress. For some reason, it made her feel more scandalous than just wearing the robe had.

She ran her fingers through her hair and almost fell over when she lifted her head to gaze into the mirror. The startling, white-blue color of her eyes robbed her breath, and her stomach plummeted into her toes. *What's wrong with me?*

She'd prefer not to speak with Killean again, but she had no idea what to make of this alarming development. Cracking the door open, she peered out to discover him leaning against the wall next to the exit. His eyes were closed and his head bowed, but she sensed a wealth of stress beneath his calm exterior.

"What's wrong with my eyes?" she asked and was amazed her voice didn't tremble.

Killean opened his eyes and lifted his head. "Instead of red, that's the color a hunter's eyes become after they turn. The same thing happened to Kadence and Nathan. When you calm down, they'll return to their normal color."

Simone stepped back into the bathroom and closed the door. She rested her forehead against the cool wood as her mind spun. Turned, she was *turned*. She'd known that, of course, but seeing her eyes and hearing him say those words made it *real*.

Nothing would ever be the same again. Her life as she'd always known it was gone. She didn't fit in anywhere anymore.

Her entire life had been about becoming a hunter wife and mother, but now she could be *anything*!

Her momentary elation deflated as reality descended. What exactly could she be with her limited education, training, and newly acquired vampire status? She didn't fit in with the human world, and even if she'd still been mortal, she knew nothing about people and had zero interest in fitting in with them.

So what did she do now? Her mind spun as she tried to figure it out, but she didn't have any ideas. The possibilities were so vast yet so limited that it made her head pound.

It didn't matter, she decided, she could figure it out later; Kadence and Nathan would help her. Her future would never be what she'd anticipated, but they would help her get through this, and with an eternity ahead of her, she had plenty of time to sort through everything.

Without having to get married and take care of her husband, she could delve deeper into all the things that interested her, like gardening. She enjoyed digging her hands into the earth, planting things, and watching them grow, but she'd never explored the interest further than what was necessary for her to know as a wife and mother.

Mother. Tears pricked her eyes as her thoughts turned to her mom. *She's okay*. She had to be because Simone couldn't think about the possibility she was dead, not with everything else going on.

Simone splashed cold water on her face and took calming breaths while she willed her eyes back to their natural color. Gradually they returned to normal, and she found herself gawking at her reflection in the mirror. It was as amazing as it was unnerving to watch.

Gathering her courage, she threw the door open and stepped into the room. Her hands fisted when Killean smirked at her. She had no idea how he did it, but half an hour ago, he'd had her desperate for more of his touch, and now she was contemplating smacking him.

Killean savored the beauty of her clover-colored eyes and the flush of healthy color in her cheeks. In his many years, he'd seen countless beautiful women, but none of them had affected him as she did. And looking at her, he couldn't recall a single one of those women.

Moving away from the wall, he opened the door and walked outside to stand under the blue overhang shadowing the sidewalk in front of the rooms. He inhaled the crisp air as he gazed at the mountains on the other side of the road. Their high peaks seemed to touch the white clouds drifting around them.

The parking lot of the hotel had a few other cars in it, but no one was moving about, and the peaceful day was a balm to the tumult rolling through him. He waited for Simone to exit the room before closing the door and taking her elbow.

She stiffened against him but didn't try to pull away when he led her toward the passenger door of the truck. Stepping out from the overhang, he recoiled when the sun hit his exposed skin and blisters broke out. Smoke rose in tendrils from him while the scent of cooking flesh filled his nostrils.

Killean pulled Simone back into the safety of the shadows as the blisters on his hands broke, and the ones on his face oozed over his cheeks. Cursing his stupidity, he hurried her back to the room as he checked to make sure no one witnessed what happened. The day remained clear of anyone in the parking lot, and the road free of travelers.

Unlocking the door to their room, Killean led Simone inside and closed it behind them. Leaning against the door, he tried to gain control over the volatile sway of his emotions while smoke continued to curl up from his skin.

CHAPTER TWENTY

SIMONE TRIED NOT to gawk at the smoke wafting from Killean or the blisters swelling on his flesh. She forgot her earlier irritation with him as the anguish twisting his face into a grimace caused his scar to stand starkly out against the red hue of his skin.

"Fucking idiot," he snarled as he stepped away from the door.

"What happened?" she asked as he stormed over to the bathroom and turned on the light.

Killean stood and stared at his burnt flesh while self-hatred coiled through him. The blisters on his hands and face would heal soon, and would do so faster if he fed, but the oozing wounds didn't matter. What mattered was he hadn't seen this coming. He'd expected the sun to have a stronger effect on him after he killed, but he hadn't expected it to be *this* severe.

His burnt flesh was one more sign he was further gone into his Savagery than he'd anticipated becoming or realized he was.

Gazing down at the popped blisters on his hands, he watched as blood welled forth and dripped off them. Killean turned the faucet on and plunged his hands under the cold water to rid himself of the blood, but it wouldn't wash away.

Gripped by confusion, Killean scrubbed at his hands until his peeling skin fell into the sink and the blood flowed freely.

Simone watched in dismay as Killean tore at his hands like a wild animal trying to free its leg from a trap. She had no idea what he was doing or how to stop this, but she wanted to go to him and hold him close. Despite the desperation he emanated, she sensed he needed comfort.

"The blood," he muttered.

She didn't think he was aware he spoke, but she didn't see any blood, not yet anyway. If he kept at his hands like that, there would be plenty of it soon. And how could he keep scouring his burnt skin that way? It had to be excruciating for him, yet he showed no sign of stopping.

"Killean?" she whispered.

He didn't react to her as his skin broke apart and the first drops of blood dripped into the sink. Horror filled her as she watched the pink swirling down the drain.

"Killean, stop."

Without thinking, she rested her hand on the sleeve of his shirt. When he twisted toward her, his eyes were redder than the ripest strawberry, yet he didn't seem to see her. Simone's hand slid down his arm when she recoiled from the madness oozing from him. She hadn't meant to touch his ruined flesh, but her fingers fell on his hand.

Hungry for blood, Killean almost dragged her against him and sank his fangs into her throat, but when her fingers touched his skin, a sense of calm spread over him, and he came back to his senses. He glanced down at his hands, but instead of the copious amounts of blood he'd seen coating them, only trickles of it spilled from the flesh he'd split open with his vigorous scrubbing. Those wounds were already healing as were the blisters on his face.

Ashamed and uncertain of what she'd witnessed from him,

Killean couldn't meet her eyes again. He went to turn off the water before realizing his hands trembled and his fangs throbbed with every pulse of his blood. He pulled his hands back before she could see the shaking in them.

Get it together! Lifting his head, he gazed with loathing at the image staring back at him. There had been plenty of times in his life when he hated himself, but none so much as right now.

Not killing was causing him to unravel, but he shouldn't be losing control in front of *her*.

Killean wanted to step away from Simone, but he didn't trust himself to break contact with her calming touch yet.

"Are you okay?" she whispered.

"I'm fine," he bit out.

"You said, *the blood*. What did you mean by that?"

How did he explain to her the blood he'd seen drenching his hands? How did he explain he was losing his mind and he suspected it was because he hadn't killed anyone recently? They'd always known Savages maintained their intelligence and didn't become mindless animals once they gave in to their bloodlust, but did they go insane if they tried to resist their compulsion to kill?

If that was true, then there were only two options left to him—give in to the darkness lurking beneath his surface for centuries or death. Out of those two, he knew which one he'd prefer.

He had to get Simone away from him and somewhere safe before he lost himself to whatever madness this was.

"I didn't mean anything by it," he said.

Simone didn't believe him, but she didn't see any good in pushing him on it when he was so unstable. "What happened outside? Why did you burn like that? I've seen you in the sun before." She didn't like bringing up their encounter on the beach, but Killean had stood in the sun's rays then.

"I've killed enough that the sun affects me like it does other

Savages now," he said bluntly. "Maybe not as bad as some, but bad enough that I cannot walk freely in it again."

Simone gulped. Beneath his natural, woodsy scent, she detected the rot of a Savage on him, but it was nowhere near as bad as the monsters who held her prisoner, and his outdoorsy scent masked the odor unless she was searching for it. There was no masking the scent seeping from Joseph and his followers.

"You really did kill innocents to get in there," she murmured as the reality of what he'd done sank in.

She didn't know why it had taken her this long to realize it. Maybe it was because most of their time together had been spent running for their lives, or because he was so different from Joseph and the others that she hadn't believed it. Or maybe it was because, even with knowing what he'd done, she still wanted to draw him close and kiss him while she held and comforted him.

"What do you think I did to get in there, *hug* people?" he spat.

Simone didn't back away from his fury. He wouldn't hurt her; he may kill anyone else, but he wouldn't harm her. He'd given up and risked too much to rescue her only to hurt her now. Besides, if he wanted her dead or a monster, he could have killed her or left her with Joseph.

Nausea twisted in her belly as a new thought occurred to her. "Those people you killed are dead because of me."

"No," Killean said. He loathed the idea of her carrying any guilt for his actions. "They are dead because of *me*. I chose to murder them, and I did it for *me*. Don't feel sorry for them; they were all pieces of shit and some of the worst of the human race. Each of them was either a rapist or child molester. Their deaths mean someone else won't suffer at their hands."

"I don't understand why you did it though," she whispered around the lump in her throat. "Why give up what you knew and everything you were, for *me*?"

Killean turned off the water and grabbed the hand towel from the rack. He patted the blisters on his hands before shoving past her and into the bedroom.

"Killean?" she inquired.

"Because I couldn't let you stay there," he said as he lifted the phone from the nightstand beside the bed. He dialed the front desk.

"Why not?" Simone demanded.

"Hello," a voice on the other end of the line said.

"We need towels in room twelve, send someone," Killean commanded.

"Right away," the voice replied and disconnected.

"What are you doing?" Simone asked.

"If I can't go out for breakfast, then I'll order in," Killean replied as he hung up the phone.

Simone looked from him to the phone and back again. "You plan to feed on whoever comes here?"

"Vamps require blood to survive, dolly."

Simone fisted her hands as he called her that again. He'd also called her a dolly on the beach; she hadn't liked it then, but she hated it now! After everything she'd endured, she was as far from a dolly, or the Simone who'd stood on that beach, as she could get. Then, before she lost her temper with him, she realized he was baiting her into an argument so she wouldn't pursue her line of questioning.

"Why did you come for me?" she asked.

Killean lifted his head to stare at her. "Because I did."

For the first time in her life, Simone stomped her foot as her temper frayed. "That's not an answer!"

"It's the only one you're getting."

Before she could decide if she wanted to shout at him or kick him in the shin, a knock sounded on the door.

"Housekeeping!" a voice called from the other side.

Killean strode around the bed and opened the door. "I have your towels," the woman said and lifted a stack of them.

"Come in," Killean said and stepped back to let her enter.

The middle-aged woman gazed warily at the fading burns on his face and his scar before edging inside the door. Her shoulders relaxed when she spotted Simone. "Hello," she greeted. "I'll put these in the bathroom."

Before she could walk away, Killean took possession of her mind and bent his head to feed on her.

Simone blinked at the speed with which he'd done it, but then jealousy tore through her with an intensity that left her shaken. She'd never experienced such an overwhelming surge of the emotion before, and she hadn't expected it, but his dark head bent over the woman's pale throat made her want to scream.

It was the most irrational feeling she'd ever experienced; she had no claim over him and no reason to feel jealous because he was doing what he must to survive, but she couldn't rid herself of it. She focused on the wall and tried not to think about what he was doing with another woman.

What is wrong with me? She didn't know the answer, but she couldn't deny that she yearned for it to stop as she resisted clapping her hands over her ears to block out the sounds of his feeding.

Killean resisted tearing the woman's throat out and draining the last of her blood as he retracted his fangs from her. He used the healing agent in his saliva to close the punctures before clasping the woman's chin. His vision blurred as he struggled to keep himself controlled while the demon within him screamed for death.

Simone. Her name became the only source of light in the darkness trying to drag him into its alluring depths.

Lifting his head, he focused on Simone. The muscles in her

neck stood out as she scowled at the wall across from her. He'd never expected it from her, but she practically vibrated with fury.

"Simone?" he inquired, uncertain as to why she looked so livid.

"Are you done?" she demanded.

"Yes. Would you like to feed on her?"

"No." In the mood she was in, Simone might do something she regretted if she went anywhere near him or the woman.

Unable to deal with whatever was bothering Simone right now, Killean focused on the woman again. "You will do some shopping for us." He proceeded to give her a rundown on the clothes they required before speaking to Simone. "What size are you?"

Simone forced herself to look at him again, but when her eyes fell on his hand clutching the woman's chin, she glanced away. "Size?" she asked.

"Yes, what size clothes do you wear?"

"I don't know," she muttered.

"What do you mean, you don't know?"

"I've made my clothes since I was old enough to use a sewing machine. I have no idea about *sizes*. I know my *measurements*."

"That's not going to help us," he murmured as his gaze ran appraisingly over her, but he had no idea about women's sizes either. "What size would you guess she is?" he asked the woman.

Simone was certain they could hear her teeth grinding together as the woman's gaze ran over her.

"I'd guess a six or eight jeans; medium or large shirt," the woman replied in a flat voice.

The odd numbers confused Simone.

"Good," Killean said. "Bring us back those sizes and a few different bra and underwear sizes that you think will fit her."

Simone's face colored at the idea of Killean ordering bras and underwear for this woman to pick out for her. She didn't know how to respond, so instead she said the only other thing she could think of. "I don't wear jeans."

"Bring back some dresses too," Killean said and released the woman.

"How is she going to pay for all that?" Simone asked.

"Do you have a credit card?" Killean asked the woman.

"Yes," she replied.

"Good. Use that to pay."

He'd planned to use his mind control to get clothes for them when they went out, but he had to use this woman to do it for them now. He doubted any of the stores would still be open by the time he could leave this room, and he wanted to hit the road as soon as night fell. Besides, it would be better if only a few people saw him and Simone while they were in town. He hadn't planned this, but it worked better for them.

"And if anyone asks why you're buying these things, say it's for charity," he instructed.

He suspected many of the locals knew each other and would find it weird she was buying clothes that wouldn't fit her as she was more voluptuous than Simone. And if she didn't have a boyfriend, buying men's clothes could raise suspicions.

"Go now," he commanded, and the woman left the room.

Killean stepped into the doorway she'd left open and watched as she strode across the parking lot and climbed behind the wheel of a new sedan. She sat stiffly in the seat as she pulled out of the parking lot and onto the main road.

When Killean closed the door and slid the chain into place, he noticed the back of his hand was almost healed, and his face no longer felt like someone had taken a blowtorch to it. He turned to Simone, and when her white-blue eyes met his, they called to the most primitive part of him as he recalled how uninhibited she'd been while she fed on him.

The shift in Killean's stance drew Simone's gaze to the

outline of his arousal in his jeans. She bit her lip as her body involuntarily responded to him by taking a step closer.

He should go in the bathroom and take another cold shower, but Killean found his feet frozen to the floor. If he couldn't kill, he could at least enjoy having his mate feed from him again. She'd already drank from him once, feeding from him again wouldn't progress their bond any further. Until they parted ways, when she required nourishment, he would give it to her.

"Are you sure you don't want to feed, Simone?" he inquired. "From me?"

CHAPTER TWENTY-ONE

The idea of feeding on the woman hadn't been at all appealing, but the idea of his blood sliding down her throat had her on the verge of launching herself onto him. As if he were the magnet she couldn't resist, Simone found herself taking three more steps forward before coming to her senses and stopping.

Killean's heart thundered in his chest when she halted in the center of the room and licked her lips. When she seemed unable to take another step forward, he strode away from the door and stopped in front of her.

Simone's head tipped back as he stood over her. The harshness of his face and his scar made him appear far more intimidating than he was. She didn't recall giving her hand the command to move, but her fingers suddenly rested against his chest. She should refuse to drink from him again until she knew what was going on with him and why he'd come for her, but she could no more turn away from him than the sun could refuse to rise.

Killean flattened her hand against his chest as he enveloped her neck with his other hand and drew her forward. Having fed from him last night, she shouldn't have to feed again so soon, but she'd been starved, and her hunger was palpable on the air. When her delicate pink tongue flicked out to wet her full lips, Killean groaned and pulled her against him.

Rising onto her toes, the rush of his blood pumping through his veins teased her nostrils more than the pancakes and sausages her mother cooked on Sunday mornings. When Killean guided her to his throat, she didn't resist. Needing to taste him, Simone ran her tongue over his salty flesh before sinking her fangs into his neck.

The warmth and sweetness of his blood filling her mouth overwhelmed her, and she mewled as her fingers gripped his shoulders. Of its own volition, her body pressed against his until a piece of paper couldn't fit between them. When his hand gripped her ass, she didn't try to pull away.

Her dress hiked up around her knees when he lifted her off the ground and she slid her legs around his waist. Then she felt his arousal between her legs, but this time, instead of being mindlessly unaware of what she was doing, she was very aware of it as she started to rock against him.

Simone bit harder as something instinctive rose inside her. In Killean's arms she felt as if she were flying free of the cage that housed her for far too long.

"Shit," Killean hissed when Simone rose and fell against him with increasing urgency. She hadn't been this abandoned when she'd been starved and mindless in the woods. Though he'd meant to keep his distance from her and maintain control, he staggered back until his knees caught the edge of the bed and he sat on it.

He settled his hand in the small of her back as her fingers clawed at his shirt until the material gave way. Beneath the prim and proper exterior she exhibited was a hellion seeking to break free, and Killean so badly wanted to free her.

When Simone's hands fell on Killean's bare flesh, her palms heated until she was certain she'd branded her prints onto him. And with a shock, she realized she *yearned* to brand him and mark him as hers. She didn't know where the urge came from, but it wedged deeper and deeper until she was filled with the impulse to etch herself onto *every* one of his cells.

Retracting her fangs from his neck, she leaned back to gaze at his magnificent body. Beneath her palms his flesh was supple and his muscles as unbending as steel; the wiry brown hairs spreading across his upper torso tickled her fingers. She couldn't get enough of exploring him and learning all the differences between their bodies.

Wrapping his hand around the back of her head, he pulled her down to him and claimed her mouth in a kiss that left her breathless. His lips burned into hers as his tongue stroked her mouth before slipping inside. Simone's fingers curled into his shoulders as his tongue explored her mouth before entangling with hers.

His kiss on the beach had been an awakening experience for her; this one was soul shattering.

Gripping her ass, Killean lifted and flipped her until she was pinned beneath him on the bed. He broke the kiss to gaze down at the feral color of her eyes as she gazed breathlessly up at him.

Tugging at her dress, he pulled it up until it was a tangled mess around her hips. The auburn curls between her thighs glistened with her desire for him, and he found himself unable to resist stroking his fingers over her.

"If you tell me to stop, I will," he said when she went to close her legs. They couldn't have sex, it would only make the mating bond tougher to resist, but he could do so much more to her. "At any point in time, tell me no, Simone, and I will stop whatever I'm doing, but I'm asking you to let me pleasure you."

Let me pleasure you. Those words caused Simone's heart to

skip a beat. There was so much promise in them and so much uncertainty; she wanted to know what he meant so badly she could taste it. She relaxed and shivered when he spread her legs wider and his gaze locked between her thighs. He looked like a starving man being escorted into a feast, and it only heightened her desire for him.

Killean relished the silken feel of her. Grasping the top of her dress, he pulled it down until her lush breasts spilled free to bounce over the neckline. Her nipples stood out from her strawberry areolas, and he bent his head to tug one into his mouth while he spread her wetness over her clit before fingering her entrance.

Simone whimpered and squirmed beneath him when he released her nipple and sat back to relish the sight of her. Her glossy auburn hair was a stark contrast to the white sheets, and for a second, she reminded him of an angel sitting on a bank of clouds.

And he was something worse than the devil, something that shouldn't be allowed to touch someone as wondrous as her, yet he couldn't stop himself from slipping his finger inside her. When the muscles of her sheath clenched around it, his dick jumped in anticipation of the decadence to come, but it would have to get used to disappointment.

With his thumb, he rubbed her clit again and enjoyed the small sounds of delight she emitted. So tight, so wet, and so enticing, he couldn't resist edging back on the bed and bending his head to lick her clit.

She instinctively tried to close her legs as her eyes flew open to discover his head between her thighs. She clutched his hair to pull him away, but when he licked her and drove his finger into her at the same time, she pulled him closer. Men should *not* do this to women, but she couldn't bring herself to pull away from him when it felt so *good*.

This is it, she realized.

This was what she'd been missing on those nights when she woke after her strange, barely remembered dreams. Killean was the answer to solving the ever-elusive mystery of what her body sought on those nights. When his next stroke caused her eyes to roll back, she gave herself over to him.

Killean removed his finger from inside her and climbed off the bed to kneel before her. When she moaned in disappointment, he grasped her ass to pull her closer to the edge of the bed. Placing his hands on her thighs, he pushed them further apart as he bent his head to her sweet recesses once more.

Satisfaction filled him when her hips began to rise and fall in rhythm with his thrusting tongue. She may have been uncertain about what he intended, but he'd melted her reservations, and now she eagerly met his pace.

It had been years since he tasted a woman, and over those years he couldn't recall what they tasted like, but he would always remember the honeyed flavor of Simone.

His cock swelled further as her movements became more demanding and he sensed her impending release. Unable to take the pressure anymore, he reached down with one hand, undid his jeans, and grasped his shaft. His hand was a poor substitute for being inside her, but he stroked himself while feasting on her and fingering her clit with his free hand.

Simone didn't understand the tension building in her body, but she felt like she was on the cusp of something. Then Killean's finger did something while his tongue moved within her and waves of ecstasy swept from the center of her body, down to her toes, and up to her scalp.

Her back arched off the bed, and her fingers dug into the sheets as cries she'd never heard before issued from *her*. Never had she imagined anything could feel as wonderful as this, and she never wanted it to end.

Simone collapsed onto the bed as Killean licked the last of her release away. The taste of her orgasm heightened his pleasure, and he gave himself one more stroke before clutching his dick against his stomach and coming with a low groan.

Reluctantly, he withdrew from the exquisite heat of her and bent his head to rest it on the bed. It took him a second to fully comprehend what the semen on his stomach meant; for the first time in nearly a century, he'd successfully jerked off.

He lifted his head to gaze down the length of Simone's enticing, lithe body. Her full breasts, still free of their confines, swayed with every one of her inhalations as she struggled to catch her breath. Her thighs remained open; her modesty forgotten.

When her eyes met his, they were still that enticing white-blue color, and a sultry smile curved her mouth.

CHAPTER TWENTY-TWO

"That was... amazing," Simone breathed as she gazed into Killean's golden eyes.

When Killean found himself growing aroused by the sight and scent of her again, he wiped his stomach on the sheet and rose to his feet. He could *not* allow himself to be swept up in her again; he didn't think he could stop himself from taking her if he did.

Simone gasped when she saw his penis. It was the first human one she'd ever seen outside of art pictures in books. It was far different than what she'd imagined it would look like. She also realized what he'd been doing with it while he was kissing her down *there.*

She should be mortified by the knowledge of what he'd done and what they'd shared; she was only intrigued. She'd never known such a thing could happen, but she found herself desperate to learn more about what a man and woman could do together. And she wanted Killean to be the one to teach her.

She doubted any hunter would take her as a bride now, and

she didn't want them to, so she saw no reason to keep playing by their rules of the perfect, virginal bride.

For the first time in her life, she realized she was sick of trying to be perfect. She'd never considered that the hunter way of life would become something she resented, but suddenly, she did. All her life she'd been molded into what others wanted her to be, but now she could discover who she was without any expectations, and it made her more brazen than she ever would have been before.

"Can I see it?" she asked as she sat up on the bed.

"See what?" Killean asked before he realized her gaze was latched onto his dick.

"You," Simone said, and for the first time since this started between them, a blush crept into her cheeks. She was ready to begin discovering herself, but she still wasn't comfortable with her new, bolder attitude.

In all his life, few things had rattled Killean so much as that one simple word. Unable to resist her request, he stepped closer to the bed. Simone bit her lip as she inspected his shaft, which lengthened beneath her curious gaze.

"Can I touch it?" she asked.

He tried to tell her she could do anything she wanted to it, but words failed him, and all he managed was a nod.

Simone stretched her hand toward the length of him and grazed the soft tip. In response, his penis jumped slightly, and Simone almost laughed out loud, but she didn't think he would appreciate it if she did. Gliding her fingers down him, Simone took note of how hard he was beneath his taut skin. This part of the male anatomy was larger and thicker than she'd expected, but nowhere near as frightening as she'd assumed it would be.

"Amazing," she murmured and enclosed her hand around it.

His breath sucked in through his teeth, and her eyes flew up to his reddening ones. She couldn't help but smile when she realized pleasure and not pain caused his reaction. A thrill went through her, and for the first time, she felt in control of her life as she literally held this powerful man in the palm of her hand.

He may be an abrasive jerk most of the time, but he captivated her, and it pleased her to learn that she affected him as much as he did her.

Killean reached for her hand to show her how to please him, but a knock on the door halted his movement. Instead of running Simone's hand over the length of him, he pulled it away and gripped her arms to haul her to her feet. Her breasts, still free of her dress, burned his flesh as he held her against his chest and scented the air for a threat. He caught a whiff of lemon cleaner and bleach.

"It's the housekeeper," he said and relaxed against Simone.

Releasing his grip on her arms, he stepped away from her. Her skin had paled at the knock, but the rosy hue of satisfaction still colored her cheeks as her hair tumbled around her shoulders and back. He couldn't stop himself from tracing her full bottom lip with his thumb; she was beautiful.

He lowered his hand from her face, and his fingers skimmed her breasts as he gently pulled up her dress and settled it into place before forcing his recalcitrant cock back into his jeans. When he was sure she was covered, he strode over to the door. He checked the peephole to make sure the woman was alone before opening the door and stepping aside.

The woman walked woodenly inside. She didn't look at him or Simone as she set the bags she carried on the floor.

"Is she okay?" Simone whispered.

"She's fine," Killean assured her. He instructed the woman to recall handing them their towels before taking a break to do some shopping. "You put all the clothes you bought in a donation bin and returned to work after finishing."

The woman's mouth had slackened while he spoke, and her

eyes remained glazed. Killean escorted her to the door and opened it to nudge her outside. "Resume your day as if everything is normal."

Killean closed the door behind her and slid the chain into place. Stepping over to the window, he pulled back the curtain to watch as the woman walked a few doors down, pulled out a keycard, unlocked the door, and stepped inside. A couple of minutes later, she emerged with a cart loaded with cleaning supplies and rolled it over to another room.

Sure the woman was doing as he commanded, Killean released the curtain and turned to face Simone.

"Can I control people too?" she asked.

"Not as strongly or as convincingly," he said. "You can tweak some memories and take control of someone's mind, but it will take age and power to twist their memories for so long, or to get them to do something so elaborate."

"I'm okay with that," she murmured. "I don't think I'd be comfortable with so much power."

"You adjust and grow with it."

"There are some who use it for evil."

"For as long as the world turns, there will always be those who abuse their power, but there will also always be those who seek to stop them."

Killean picked up the bags and set them on the bed. He opened the ones containing Simone's clothes and laid them out first.

Her nose wrinkled when she spotted the jeans, and her eyes widened at the vibrant colors of the short dresses. "I can't wear..." Her voice trailed off.

She'd been about to say she couldn't wear those; it was against the rules to wear something so colorful or short, but the hunter rules didn't apply to her anymore. However, she would *not* feel comfortable in dresses above the knee. She was willing to start exploring the world and herself further, but she wasn't ready for that leap.

She lifted a couple of pairs of jeans and two black shirts from the bed before scooping up the underwear and bras and heading into the bathroom to see what fit best.

SIMONE GAZED out the passenger window as the scenery flashed by in a blur of green trees speckled with farmhouses. Through the night pressing against the windows, she could make out the shapes of horses and cows sleeping in their pastures. Their headlights were the only thing illuminating the gloomy ribbon of road as they wound around curves and up and down hills.

She glanced at the hands she'd folded in her lap. Despite her initial apprehension about wearing jeans, she found them comfortable and didn't mind them. The strange sizes irritated her, but she discovered the ones marked eight fit her best; she was most comfortable in the baggier, large shirts and 36 C bras, though the clothes she made for herself fit far better. However, she would learn how to make jeans in the future.

She didn't know where they were going, and she didn't ask. They hadn't talked about what they'd shared earlier, but she found she didn't want to discuss it. She was afraid it would ruin things for her if they talked about it; so for now, she was content to sit beside Killean and listen to the strange music drifting from the radio.

Having only listened to classical musicians during her training and at home, this faster-paced, more chaotic music took some getting used to. At first, it made her head ache, but a few different songs had her tapping her foot along with the beat. She was also starting to like the idea of words accompanying the melodies.

"Who sings this?" she asked when one especially catchy song caught her attention.

"Queen," Killean replied without looking at her.

"That's funny."

"What is?"

"It sounds like a guy singing."

Killean surprised himself by almost laughing. He couldn't remember the last time something had amused him enough to make him want to laugh, but then there were many things he couldn't remember doing before Simone walked into his life. "It *is* a male band."

"Then why would they name themselves after a position a woman holds?"

"I don't know. Perhaps they thought the name would be memorable."

"And are they memorable?"

"Most know who they are. Didn't the hunters let you listen to music?"

"Oh, yes; I am well versed in classical music, and though it was never my best instrument, I can play Chopin's Piano Concerto No. 1 rather well on the piano."

Killean had been alive when Chopin was, but he had no idea what song she was referring to. "Impressive."

Simone shrugged. "Not really. It's what I was bred and raised to do. I can also play the violin better than the piano. I can design and sew a shirt and pants for my husband in mere hours, and I am well read in classic literature. I play chess, cribbage, and would learn any other game that interested my husband. I was also the best cook in my class."

Certain he detected a hint of bitterness in her tone, he glanced at her and noted the slump of her shoulders. "And none of those things please you?"

"What good does any of it do me anymore? No hunter would take me as a bride given what I am now."

Killean nearly ripped the wheel from the truck at the possibility of her marrying another, sharing a bed with another, and bearing their children. "And would you take them as your husband?" he grated through his teeth.

"Just last week the answer would have been yes."

"And now?"

"It's not what I want from my life anymore."

The rigid set of his shoulders eased as he focused on the lonely stretch of road once more. They could have taken the highway, but he'd decided to stay on routes where they were less likely to be spotted. He had no idea how vast or strong Joseph's resources were, and he couldn't risk showing up on some camera at a toll booth, gas station, or highway that Joseph might be able to monitor. These back roads were less likely to have that kind of technology.

"And what do you want from your life, Simone?" Killean didn't know why he asked the question. The less he knew about her, the better, but he couldn't deny his curiosity.

"I have *no* idea," she admitted. "At first, going from knowing exactly how my life would unfold to not having a clue was terrifying and freeing; I don't find it so scary anymore. What about you, Killean, what do you want from your life?"

Blood, death, you. But if he said any of those things to her, she'd probably jump out of the vehicle and run screaming into the woods. "To return home."

"Can you go home with what you've done?"

"I don't know."

Simone studied the severe edge of his profile. When he wasn't an angry, intimidating buffoon, he was rather handsome. The scar added to his menacing air, but something about the mark was so entirely Killean that she couldn't picture him without it. And whereas others might have found the scar detracted from his looks, she believed it added to them.

How did he get it? She almost asked the question, but she bit her tongue to keep herself from doing so. It really wasn't any of her business how he received it, and despite what transpired between them in the hotel, she suspected it might be something he didn't want to share with her.

Besides, there was something else she wished to learn the answer to more.

"Why did you come for me?" she asked again.

CHAPTER TWENTY-THREE

KILLEAN HAD HOPED she'd forgotten that question or decided to drop it; he should have known better. "Would you have preferred I left you there?"

"Of course not," she replied. "I'm just trying to understand why you didn't leave me there when, after we kissed on the beach, you acted like I disgusted you."

She didn't like recalling that day; between him and Nathan, it had been humiliating. She'd considered it the worst day of her life until she was taken, and then the degradation Joseph put her through made that day seem like a day in the park.

"So why did you come after me?" she asked.

"Because I didn't want you to become one of them."

"But why? Was it because we kissed?"

"That's the only answer I'm going to give you, so let it go and be happy you're not there with the others."

Simone didn't think he'd rescued her because he cared for her. They didn't know each other well enough for that, and she didn't see Killean as the type to become emotionally attached to anyone, but she wasn't going to give up until she learned the truth. Continuing to press him now though would get her nowhere. She'd just have to keep hammering at his walls until she finally found a weak spot that caused them to collapse.

"Fair enough," she murmured and turned to look out the window again.

Silence stretched between them as the tires hummed over the pavement. A few vehicles passed them going the other way, but they had the road mostly to themselves. When she glanced at the clock, she and saw it was nearly nine.

"Have you ever heard of any other hunters becoming a vampire?" Killean asked when he recalled the being he encountered in the bunker. "I mean besides Kadence, Nathan, and you. It wouldn't have happened recently, but probably occurred millennia ago."

Simone bit her lip as she shook her head. "I studied our history, but I never heard of such a thing happening. They might not have taught it to us though."

"Might not have taught it to all the hunters or just the women?"

"I would like to say all, but probably just the women."

"Hmm," he grunted. "While you were a prisoner, did you see a vampire who was over seven feet tall, but had the white-blue eyes of a hunter?"

For some reason, his description of this creature made her skin crawl. "No, but after the first couple of days, I didn't register much beyond the hunger. You saw this thing?"

"Yes."

"And you think it was another turned hunter?"

"I don't know what else it could be, not with those eyes. And judging by the power it emitted, it was ancient."

"How much power?" she asked in a hoarse voice.

"More than I've ever encountered before."

Her breath caught at this revelation. She'd felt the aura of power surrounding Ronan, and if this thing was even more powerful than that...

She shuddered and rubbed at her arms when goose bumps broke out on them.

"How old are you?" she asked to distract herself from the horrible possibilities of what something so ancient and evil could unleash on them.

"I fully matured and stopped aging at twenty-four, so I will forever look that age. I'm four hundred fifty-two now."

"Wow," she breathed.

"And how old are you?"

"Twenty-three, but I'll be twenty-four July first." As if that would somehow make a dent in their age difference.

"And I will be four hundred and fifty-three on November sixteenth."

"You'll officially be ancient then," she replied.

Killean released a small bark of laughter; it had been so long since he laughed that it sounded rusty to him. Simone didn't seem to notice as she smiled at him. He found himself momentarily dazed by the loveliness of that smile and the twinkle in her eyes.

Simone relished the sound of his laugh. It wasn't carefree or loud, but it was deep and vibrated his chest. "And what's your last name, ancient?" she teased.

"Claymore and yours?"

"Baker."

Simone had hundreds of more questions for him, but some might irritate him or get him to clam up again, and she was enjoying this more carefree side of Killean. Just minutes ago, she never would have suspected it existed; she didn't want to scare it away.

They traversed another fifty miles in silence before Killean pulled into a gas station that looked like it was last updated in the fifties. The old-style pumps would make antique hunters drool. Chimes went off when Killean drove over a black strip and parked next to one of the pumps. A young man in his twenties jogged outside and was at Killean's door before he could turn off the truck.

"What can I get for you?" the kid inquired when Killean rolled down his window.

"Fill it up," Killean said as he pushed a button to open the gas tank.

The kid nodded before turning away.

"I need to use the restroom," Simone said, and opening her door, she jumped out into the brisk air.

"Not alone," Killean replied.

He flung his door open and hurried around the front of the truck to join her. Her fierce frown didn't deter him when he stopped at her side.

"I've been going alone most of my life. I think I can handle it now," she said.

"Not alone," he repeated as he clasped her elbow. "Where's the bathroom?" he asked the kid.

"My dad has the key inside," the kid replied without taking his gaze off the rising numbers on the pump. "He'll tell you where it is."

Killean led Simone across the pavement and into the small convenience store. The middle-aged man behind the counter didn't look up from his newspaper when the bell over the door rang.

"Keys to the bathroom?" Killean asked him.

Without looking, the man pulled a spoon from the wall and plopped it on the counter before turning the page. "Outside to the left," the man said.

Simone grabbed the spoon before Killean could. "Thank you."

They walked outside and around the side of the building to the metal bathroom door. Simone used the key, slipped inside, and locked the door behind her. Crossing his arms over his chest, Killean leaned against the wall while he studied the road. Crickets chirruped and frogs croaked in the nearby fields. He smelled horses, but he couldn't see them in the fenced-in paddock across the way. Overhead, thousands of stars lit the black tapestry of the night while a crescent moon hung in the sky.

On the distant horizon, a set of headlights soared over a small hill. They vanished into a dip in the road before reappearing. Killean stepped away from the wall as the vehicle neared. Despite the calm of the night, a looming sense of doom built in his chest. He had no reason to suspect being discovered, but the sooner they were away from this place, the happier he would be.

The car was almost to the gas station when Simone emerged from the bathroom. "Do you need to use it?" she inquired.

Killean didn't look at her as the car swung into the gas station and parked near the door of the store; more headlights loomed on the horizon. They'd passed other vehicles on their way here, and for all he knew this was the only gas station around for miles, so it was a big draw for the locals, but he still didn't like seeing so many vehicles on the road.

"Killean?"

"Shh," he whispered, and clasping Simone's arm, he slid further into the shadows of the building as the kid pumping the gas turned to look at the idling sedan.

A beat-up truck pulled in and parked next to the car. Three young guys jumped out, waved to the kid pumping gas, and sauntered into the store. A woman climbed out of the sedan with her baby and followed the guys inside.

Killean relaxed, and taking the spoon from Simone, he strode with her back to the store, put the spoon on the counter, and they returned to the truck. Opening the passenger door, he helped her into the truck before walking around to the other side and climbing behind the wheel. Killean closed the door and studied the quiet night.

"That will be seventy-five dollars," the kid said as he returned to Killean's window. "Would you like me to check your oil and wash your windshield too?"

"No," Killean said as he took control of the kid's mind. "And I already paid you."

"You're all set, sir," the kid said and tapped the window frame. "Have a good night."

The kid stepped away from the truck when Killean started it and pulled away from the pump.

Simone turned to stare out the back window as the gas station vanished from view. "Do you think Joseph and his followers could find us?" she asked, knowing that was the source behind Killean's strange uneasiness at the gas station.

"I'm not taking any chances."

Killean drove faster to put more distance between them and the gas station. The truck surged forward as it rose over hills before coasting down them. They were heading into a dip in the road when he spotted headlights coming toward them. The lights momentarily vanished from view before he spotted them again.

Simone's fingers dug into the armrest of the door as the headlights approached. A sense of foreboding built in her stomach though she had no idea why. She suspected Killean's agitation was catching as there was nothing unusual about this vehicle.

The car was almost to them when it suddenly swerved into their lane and came at them head-on. Simone gasped and slammed her feet into the floor as if that could somehow stop them from barreling toward the vehicle.

"Hold on!" Killean shouted and jerked the wheel to the left.

For a second, it seemed as if they were going to miss the car entirely, but the car outmaneuvered the truck and came back toward them. Simone could only sit and watch helplessly as the car homed in on them like a shark on a seal. It was so close, she could see the vicious grin of the driver as he hunched over the wheel.

Simone cried out when the front ends collided with a screech of metal. Golden sparks flew over the hood of the truck and peppered the windshield. Pushed away by the truck, the car turned and its dented bumper scraped along the passenger side as the car slid by her. Simone found herself looking down into the hate-filled, red eyes of a Savage as the car went past her.

Killean yanked the wheel to correct the truck before the impact sent it careening off the side of the road and into an embankment. The ass end of the truck fishtailed and the tires squealed when he stomped on the gas. In the rearview mirror, he watched as the car spun in the middle of the road and started after them.

"Are you okay?" he demanded of Simone.

"Ye-yes," she stammered.

"Hold on."

In the front, a rattling sound increased from the damaged bumper when he accelerated. If the bumper had been shoved into the tire, it was only a matter of time before the tire popped, but he didn't dare slow down as the car steadily gained on them.

The speedometer climbed from sixty to seventy to eighty. They were at ninety when a piece of the bumper broke off; it smashed into the side of the truck before spiraling away and crashing into the middle of the road. The bumper broke apart when it bounced over the pavement. Forced to swerve around it, the car lost some of its momentum and fell back a little.

They were up to over a hundred when the rattling grew loud enough to drowned out the radio. "Put on your seat belt," he said to Simone.

She fumbled for the belt and tugged it over her shoulder

before clicking it into place as the car closed the distance between them to twenty feet. When the truck soared over the next hill, the wheels came off the ground, and for a second they flew over the earth until gravity won out. Simone's teeth clacked together when they hit the ground, and the truck released an ominous groan.

Simone's nails dug into the armrest as the truck made an awful noise she believed meant it was about to burst into a million pieces. Somehow all the nuts and bolts managed to stay in place, but the rattling grew louder.

Killean could no longer see the headlights of the car as it was nearly on their ass. With the damage to the truck and the fact the car was simply faster, they would never outrun it, and he couldn't allow them to get the upper hand. He had to do whatever was necessary to keep Simone safe and free from Joseph.

"Brace yourself," he said.

"For what?" Simone asked.

"Impact."

Simone didn't have a chance to respond before Killean threw his arm out and pressed it against her chest; he shoved her back in the seat. The truck tires squealed, and smoke plumed up around the windows as he stomped on the brakes. Another loud squeal came from behind him, but his stop was so sudden that the car didn't have time to avoid plowing into the ass end of the truck.

Metal crunched as the tailgate bent in, and the bed of the truck bowed up from the force of the car being driven into it. The back window shattered, and glass rained down around them. When the airbags exploded, Killean released the wheel to tear away the one in front of him before ripping Simone's out of the way.

The truck shifted to the side when the passenger side tires gave way; the rotors digging into the asphalt tore up chunks of pavement and sent more sparks over the hood. They were shoved another fifty feet forward before the hideous screeching and twisting of metal came to an end and the truck stopped sliding.

Lowering his arm, Killean turned to Simone as she slumped in the seat. The pallor of her face terrified him as he rested his hand on her shoulder. "Are you okay?" he demanded.

"Yes," she said.

"Are you sure you're not hurt?"

She lifted her head to reveal her quivering lower lip. "I'm not hurt."

Realizing it was fear and not pain that had her so rattled, Killean wanted to stay and comfort her, but lingering would only give those bastards a chance to close in on them.

"Stay here," he commanded before flinging his door open and plunging into the night.

Steam poured from the crunched-in hood of the car as he ran toward it. The nose of the car was buried in the bed of the truck, but all the Savages had survived the crash. The driver beat at the steering wheel pinned against his chest as he tried to free himself, but the wheel was lodged in the Savage's diaphragm, making his chest nearly concave. He wouldn't get free anytime soon, but another Savage was already climbing out of the back seat.

Seizing the door the Savage had opened, Killean smashed it into the vampire and pinned the creature between the door and the car. The vamp grunted, its hands flailed, and it beat at Killean when he put more of his weight against the door. When the door started cutting into its chest, the Savage changed tactics; instead of beating at Killean, the vampire gripped the edge of the door and attempted to push it away.

Lowering his shoulder, Killean pressed it against the door to keep the Savage trapped while freeing his hand. He delivered a series of three consecutive blows to the Savage's face. Its nose and cheekbone gave way as the other back door and the passenger side door of the car opened. When two more vamps emerged,

Killean realized he didn't have time to mess around with this Savage anymore.

Jumping back, Killean leapt away from the door and jerked it open. He swung his hand forward as the Savage staggered toward him. The ribs Killean had crunched in the door gave way beneath the force of his fist as he plunged it into the Savage's chest. The beat of the Savage's heart tickled his fingertips before Killean clenched the organ in his hand and tore it free.

The vamp staggered forward before collapsing to his knees and falling face-first onto the road. Killean released the heart and looked over the car at the Savages on the other side. Red filled his vision when he saw one of them was Andre, and they were heading for Simone.

CHAPTER TWENTY-FOUR

KILLEAN RACED around the back of the car towards the bastards. Seizing Andre, Killean lifted him and threw him into the mangled bed of the truck. He didn't stop to kill Andre as the other Savage neared the passenger side of the truck and *Simone*. The need to destroy coursed through him until every beat of his heart repeatedly hammered one word—*kill*.

Before the Savage could grab the door, Simone opened it and shoved it into the creature's chest. The force of the blow caused the vampire to stumble back a few feet, and Killean dove at him. Wrapping his arms around the Savage's waist, Killean tackled him.

The creature grunted when they hit the ground and tumbled across the asphalt; in an attempt to dislodge Killean, its hands flailed behind its head. Killean ignored the blows landing against the side of his head and sank his fangs into the Savage's throat.

The creature howled as its blood burst into Killean's mouth. Jerking backward, Killean tore the Savage's throat out and spat away the chunk of flesh before twisting its head to the side. Sinew and bone gave way beneath his hands as Killean tore the head from the Savage's shoulders.

When something crunched behind him, he gripped the Savage's hair and turned to find Andre only ten feet away and sprinting toward him. A look of murderous rage blazed from Andre's eyes, and a Joker-style grin twisted his features as he closed the distance between the two of them.

Killean threw the head at him, and though it caught Andre in the chest, it did nothing to deter the Savage. Before Killean could regain his feet, Andre crashed into him.

Simone gawked as the vampire barreled into Killean, and they both somersaulted into the middle of the road. Panic tore through her when they stopped rolling with the Savage on top of Killean.

No! The scream echoed in her head as the Savage pulled back his arm and battered Killean's face. The scent of Killean's blood filled her nostrils, her throat went dry, and helplessness filled her as she watched them fight.

She'd resented the self-defense classes Nathan decided the women in the stronghold should take. Those classes were breaking from their ways, and the first time she'd been reluctant to learn anything she was supposed to. Now, she wished she'd paid more attention as Killean's fingers dug into the Savage's throat while the beast continued to pummel him.

She may have no idea what to do, but she couldn't sit here and watch Killean being beaten. Her legs wobbled when she leapt out of the truck, but she managed to steady them beneath her as the vamp pulled back his arm to punch Killean again. Simone forgot all about her hesitation and terror when she spotted Killean's blood glistening on the Savage's knuckles.

She had no idea what she would do as she sprinted across the road toward them, but she had to stop this. There was no time to think as she launched herself onto the Savage's back, gripped a handful of his hair, and ripped his head back.

She didn't realize her fangs were extended until she sank them into the Savage's throat and a wash of hot, rancid blood filled her mouth. Killean may be more Savage than anything else, but his blood didn't taste rotten as this thing's did.

She'd prefer to spit his blood out, but she didn't release her hold on him. The monster reared back and battered the side of her skull with one, beefy hand. Stars burst against the back of Simone's closed lids as a ringing erupted in her ears. Thick fingers entwined in her hair and though the vampire's movements were growing sluggish, he yanked so cruelly she was sure he tore a handful of hair from her head.

Wrath unlike any Killean had ever known tore through him when Andre hit Simone. Blood pooled in his right eye from a cut above it as he lifted himself onto his elbows and drove his head forward. Andre howled when Killean bashed his forehead into the Savage's nose, flattening it beneath the impact.

He wanted to shove the prick off him, but he didn't dare risk doing so with Simone clinging to his back; Andre would injure her if he fell on her. Seeming to realize the same thing, Andre suddenly lunged backward and flipped himself toward the pavement.

Simone cried out when she realized the vampire's intent and released him. She tried to leap off his back, but she wasn't fast enough and found her arm pinned beneath him. She bit her bottom lip to keep from crying out.

Then Killean was rising over them. She'd never seen anything like the wrathful look on Killean's face as his eyes burned hotter than the fires of Hell and his fangs slicing his bottom lip caused rivulets of blood to slide down his chin.

She *almost* felt sorry for the creature on top of her.

Grabbing Andre's throat, Killean plucked him off her and

dangled him over the ground with one hand. Andre's feet kicked in the air as he issued strangled cries of terror. He tore at Killean's hand when Killean dug his fingers into his throat. Blood poured down the sides of the wounds Killean inflicted on him and splashed onto the ground around his feet.

Through the thick muscle of Andre's neck, Killean's fingers touched, and he released an inhuman snarl before he tore Andre's throat out. Andre's head lulled back on his spine before Killean gripped the top of his head and pulled it free.

He stared into Andre's unseeing eyes before he dropped the head and focused on Simone. Killean knelt at her side and started to reach for her, but the blood dripping from his hands stopped him before he could touch her. The sight of that blood brought him back to the motel room as he scrubbed the blood from his blistered hands. However, this time the blood was real, and he felt more in control of himself than he had in that moment.

Killing sates the beast. But then, for him, killing had always kept the demon part of him at bay. Yet, as he gazed at the bodies surrounding them, he felt as if something were missing as the demon part of him hungrily sought out something more than this death.

Then he realized that he wanted to do more than deliver death to his victims. Killing wasn't enough for him anymore, he also wanted to experience the suffering of those he slaughtered, and he hadn't done that with these three.

Killean lowered his hand and rested it on the ground before her. "Are you okay?" he asked.

"Yes. Are you?" she asked and stretched a shaky hand out to caress his battered face. His right eye was nearly swelled shut, and blood spilled from a nasty gash above it that revealed a gleaming piece of his skull.

"I'm fine," Killean said and turned away from the gentle prodding of her fingers. "I'll heal when I feed. I have to clean up this mess, and we have to get out of here before someone comes across us."

Killean gazed at his hands before wiping them on the front of his shirt. Blood already splattered it; adding more didn't matter. Taking the elbow of the arm Simone wasn't cradling against her chest, he helped her rise before gripping the wrist of her injured arm.

"Do you think it's broken?" he asked as he tenderly examined it.

"I think he just squished it."

"It will heal fast."

He released her arm and lifted his eyes to meet hers. Unable to resist, he clasped her chin and ran his thumb over her lips to wipe away the blood staining them. It bothered him she'd fed from another, *he* should be her primary source until they were separated, but the lethalness she'd exhibited excited him. There was far more to this little hunter than he'd ever realized.

"Stay here while I clean this mess up," he said.

"I'll help you."

"No," Killean said. "I don't want you touching these things."

"Killean—"

"You're injured, Simone. Just let me take care of it."

Simone stepped back, and he turned to gather Andre's head and body.

"How did they find us?" she asked as he worked.

"I don't know," he said.

"Do you think there were more of them at the campground, and they saw us leave?"

"No. I would have sensed them if there were, and they would have found us sooner if they knew what vehicle we were driving. They could be patrolling all the roads and simply got lucky."

He didn't believe that, but he didn't know how else the

Savages could have stumbled across them. There hadn't been any other vampires at that campground; he was sure of that.

Killean carried the remains of Andre over to the car, opened the passenger door, and heaved him inside. The Savage pinned behind the wheel made a gurgled sound and jerked harder at the column keeping him in place. Killean leaned over to examine the Savage more closely and realized the wheel was fusing into the vampire's skin as it healed.

"You should be afraid," Killean assured him before closing the door on Andre's body.

Simone stood behind the truck while he gathered the rest of the bodies and tossed them into the back seat of the car.

"Go stand by the front of the truck," he said to her when he shut the door on the last of the remains.

Simone flexed the fingers of her injured arm. They tingled with the feeling returning to them, but it didn't hurt when she twisted her arm to the side. "Why?"

"Because I'm going to kill him."

She glanced pointedly at the blood splattering the street around her. "I already saw you kill *all* the others."

"Yes, but I'm going to drain this one dry," Killean replied unapologetically. He would not make excuses for who or what he was now, and he had to feed. These deaths hadn't completely satisfied his bloodlust the way drinking the life from someone would.

Simone stared at him as she tried to process what he was telling her. This last kill would not be as merciful as the others. No, this one would be an unleashing of the Savage he'd become. She should be repulsed; instead, all she felt was a level of understanding she'd never expected to experience for a being who thrived on killing.

In the glow of the one remaining headlight on the car, Killean watched her turn away before he walked around to the driver's side door, pulled it open, and bent down to meet the eyes of the Savage within. The vamp's eyes rolled in his head, his distressed sounds increased as he beat his hands uselessly against the wheel.

Killean tore the steering wheel off its mount and out of the pinned Savage's chest. The wounded vamp couldn't put up much of a fight, but Killean wasn't so far gone that he would kill a defenseless man.

Hauling the Savage from the car, Killean barely acknowledged the blow the creature delivered to his cheek before he sank his fangs into the Savage's throat. The monster hit and kicked him for a good thirty seconds before the agony of having its blood unwillingly drawn overwhelmed it. Its fingers dug into Killean's forearms as its body went rigid in his grasp.

Killean savored the vampire's suffering as it flooded his system and eased the demon's craving for this pain-filled, bloody end. The last of the Savage's blood slipping down his throat didn't bring with it the rush of power the life of an innocent did, but he still felt sated when he released his bite.

Lowering the dead Savage, he met Simone's gaze over the roof of the car. He didn't know how long she'd been standing there, but it had been long enough to see at least some of what he'd done. He braced himself for her revulsion, but he saw no disgust or loathing in her eyes; instead, there was only a strange caring he didn't understand, and it unnerved him.

He didn't want her understanding or to care what she thought of him, but with a sinking feeling, he realized he did care. However, she *would* be going back.

Killean shoved the Savage into the car and bent down to pull the latch for the trunk. When it popped open, he stalked behind the vehicle to examine the contents of the trunk before pulling out a lug wrench. Taking the wrench, he walked over to where the gas lid was located and slammed the wrench into the side of the car until he found, and punctured the gas tank.

Gas poured onto the roadway as he tossed the wrench into the trunk and returned to the truck. He searched the vehicle for anything he could use to start a fire and discovered a disposable lighter in the glovebox. He removed their bags of clothes from behind the seat before returning to the car and taking off his shirt. After dipping his shirt into the gas, he flicked the lighter to set it on fire before tossing the cloth onto the spreading puddle of gasoline under the car.

He'd returned to Simone and was already running with her across a field of cows when the car erupted into a ball of fire.

CHAPTER TWENTY-FIVE

Tendrils of pink spread across the horizon when Killean opened the door of the motel room he'd confiscated from a bleary-eyed clerk. They were getting inside with time to spare, but the hair on his nape rose when he glanced warily at the sky. He didn't know if he'd ever walk in the sun the same as he had before, but it was as much a peril to him now as Joseph.

Killean stepped into the room behind Simone and closed the door. He tossed the bags of clothes onto the bed and pulled back the curtain to peer out the window. It could have been pure luck those Savages stumbled across them last night, or it could have been something more.

Neither of them had a tracking device on them, they would have discovered it by now; he was certain of that. And besides there had never been a time when Joseph or one of his flunkies could have installed one on him.

He suspected Joseph had more eyes out there than he'd initially believed, but where did that leave them? After fleeing the fire, they'd run through numerous fields and yards before he discovered a car with keys still in it. Taking the car, he'd driven another fifty miles before coming across this town.

He'd taken the car out of town and ditched it in a pond ten miles away before they doubled back on foot to this motel. Stores and restaurants lined the main road outside of the motel, and the area was already busy as cars drove up and down the street. Joseph may be attacking large groups like the wedding party, but he wouldn't be so ballsy as to attack them here with so many witnesses.

He didn't think Joseph could have tracked them here, but he'd believed they were relatively safe before, and he had no idea how many other towns were in this area. For all he knew, this was the only town near where they encountered the Savages on the road, or there were ten others in the vicinity. If the owner of the car reported it stolen and it was discovered in the pond, it would be a lot easier to track them down, but there was nothing Killean could do about that now. He was stuck here for the day.

Turning away from the window, his eyes fell on the phone sitting on the stand in the middle of the twin beds. He'd been putting off calling Ronan, but he had to get a warning out while he still could. Ronan had to know the little he'd learned about Joseph and his operation.

Walking over, he sat on the edge of the bed and lifted the phone from its cradle. Simone sat across from him as he dialed the last number he had for Ronan. Placing the phone against his ear, he listened as an automated message came on to say the number wasn't in use.

"Shit," he muttered and hung up.

Simone clasped her hands before her as Killean glowered at the phone. Over the course of the night, the cut over his eye had healed to a scratch and the swelling was gone. She knew vampires healed fast, but this was incredible.

"Who are you trying to call?" she asked as she stretched her wounded arm. It was still a little sore, but she hadn't been anywhere near as injured as Killean.

"Ronan." Picking the phone back up, he punched in the number he had for Saxon. He couldn't handle Declan's strange insight right now, and Lucien would probably hang up on him.

The phone rang four times before a groggy voice answered, "Better be good, I was dreaming about unicorns."

"It's not good," Killean said.

"*Killean*?"

Saxon sounded like he'd be less surprised to receive a call from God, but Killean didn't blame him. They'd probably never expected to see or hear from him again unless it was in a battle where they stood on opposite sides. That would never happen, but he couldn't kid himself into believing he was the same vampire who walked away from them.

He flexed the hand in his lap. Blood no longer stained it, but he clearly recalled the blood flowing over his flesh and sliding down his throat while he killed those Savages. And he already longed to be covered in, and tasting, that blood again. Fisting his hand, he dug his nails into his palm and used the pain it created to keep focused on the conversation.

"It's not Santa Claus," he muttered.

"Is it the Krampus?"

Killean snorted. "It could be."

For the first time since he'd known him, Saxon was speechless as he didn't say another word.

"I tried calling Ronan first," Killean said, "but his phone's not in use."

"It broke during a fight a couple of days ago; he has a new one."

"I see." So Ronan hadn't abandoned his phone because of him; he guessed that was a good sign.

"What have you done?" Saxon blurted.

"What had to be done. I have Simone."

"*Simone* is your mate?"

"Yes," Killean grated. "Do you know her?" One thing Saxon loved was beautiful women. Killean had no doubt Simone would have spurned any advances Saxon might have made toward her, but he didn't like the idea of the notorious playboy looking at Simone with any kind of interest.

"Not personally, but I know she's Kadence's friend and was supposed to be the intended bride for Nathan."

"And now you know something else about her. Say hello." Killean handed the phone out to Simone.

Simone's eyebrows rose at this statement and the strain pouring off him. She couldn't hear what was being said on the other end of the line, and didn't know who Killean was talking to, but the scar on his face was more visible, and the fisted hand on his lap was white. She wished she knew what was going on inside his head, but she'd have a better chance of solving the mystery of life than puzzling out this man.

Her gaze traveled to his chest, and her head tilted to the side when she spotted a faint white scar over his heart. Simone had no idea how she hadn't noticed it yesterday, but she'd been so swept up in him, she wouldn't have noticed a tornado coming through and tossing them into Kansas.

Simone leaned forward and pressed her ear to the phone. "Hello."

"Simone?" a voice she didn't recognize inquired.

"Yes."

Killean pulled the phone away and rested it against his ear. "See, she's free."

"Is she a Savage?" Saxon asked.

"No, they turned her, but I got her out of there before she became a Savage. The hunters captured with her are all well on their way to becoming one though. I couldn't get any of them out, and I don't know where they are."

Almost a full minute passed before Saxon replied. "Are *you* a Savage?"

"I got her back," Killean said instead of answering. It didn't matter what he was anymore.

"That's important."

"It's *the* most important thing," Killean stated.

"What are you going to do with her?" Saxon inquired.

"Get her out of this state, if I can."

"That sounds... intriguing. Which state would that be?"

Killean filled him in on everything he'd learned while with Joseph and what they'd gone through since escaping him. It wasn't much, but it was more than the Alliance had known about Joseph before.

"You think they're in a bunker in Vermont?" Saxon asked when he finished.

"I got the impression we were underground and of being inside a bunker. If it's in Vermont or not, I don't know. It could be in New Hampshire, Maine, maybe even Mass, New York, or Canada for all I know. I believe the wedding was in Vermont, *we're* in Vermont, but as for the location of the bunker, your guess is as good as mine."

"I'm not much of a guesser."

"Neither am I," Killean said.

"What are they bunkering down against?"

"I have no idea."

"This creature you saw while in there, you really think it's another turned hunter who became a Savage?"

"I do. And it's ancient."

"Interesting," Saxon murmured. "Have you asked your little hunter about it?"

"Yes. She doesn't know anything, but that doesn't mean Nathan won't."

"I'll look into it. It sounds like you could use some help—"

"I think it's best if you and everyone else stays away. I'm not sure how they found us last night, and it's a bad idea to risk anyone else." He wanted Simone somewhere safe more than he wanted his next breath, but they couldn't risk losing anyone else in the battle against Joseph when there was no guarantee they could save her. "No matter what becomes of us, Joseph must be stopped."

"He will be," Saxon said. "I'll talk with the others about this thing, tell them what we've discussed, and get back to you."

"This is a motel phone, and we might be forced to leave. If that happens, I'll call you again. Don't lose your phone."

Before Saxon could reply, Killean hung up.

CHAPTER TWENTY-SIX

Saxon tossed aside the sheets and climbed out of bed. He pulled on a pair of sweats before stalking out of the room. Walking down the hall, Saxon cheerfully knocked on the doors he passed as he called for a meeting in a loud, singsong voice. It would piss them all off, which only made his smile widen.

When he reached the end of the hall, he turned back, leaned against the stair banister and crossed his arms over his chest while he waited for his friends to emerge. Doors creaked open, and Lucien stuck his head out to heave a boot at him.

"Fuck your meeting!" Lucien snapped as Saxon sidestepped the boot that went soaring over the rail.

"What couldn't have waited until tonight?" Ronan demanded as he stepped halfway into the hall. Declan emerged from his room, and stretching his back, he yawned loudly.

"Killean called," Saxon said and was pleased to note they looked as stunned as he'd felt when he first heard Killean's voice on the other end of the line. "We need to speak with Nathan. I'll be waiting for all of you in the bar."

He didn't wait for a reply before descending the stairs to the foyer below; he had no doubt their curiosity would win over their exhaustion. His steps were soundless on the marble as he made his way across the foyer and into the bar.

Despite the smirk reflecting at him in the glass behind the liquor bottles lining the shelves behind the bar, his hand shook when he lifted a bottle of Scotch, and his hazel eyes were troubled. His dark blond hair, still tousled from sleep, stood up in spikes around his face. He didn't bother to try to tame it before grabbing a glass.

He'd never expected to speak to Killean again unless it was in a fight, but though his friend hadn't denied being a Savage, Killean had sounded relatively normal on the phone. There had been tension in his voice, but who wouldn't be stressed after what he'd gone through? Then why was he so rattled by the conversation?

Was it the fact Killean still sounded so normal when he'd obviously infiltrated Joseph's inner circle to free his mate? Or was it that Killean had, in a roundabout way, confirmed he'd become a killer and therefore an enemy?

They'd all suspected he'd fallen, of course, Killean had as much as said he planned to become a Savage in the note he left, but Saxon had held out hope that Killean wouldn't follow through with his plan.

That hope was gone, but now he had bigger questions. Killean had fallen, but was he a Savage, or was he something else? What would he do now? And could he be saved?

That was the biggest question of all, Saxon decided as he swallowed his Scotch. The burning liquor didn't ease the tumult of emotions battering him.

When Joseph turned Savage, it hadn't overly surprised him. There was always something about the vamp he hadn't liked, and that was saying a lot as he wasn't that discerning when it came to others, especially women. But Killean...

Well, he'd never seen Killean's desertion coming; Killean had always been distant but loyal. He'd never shown any indication he might waver from his mission or his allegiance to Ronan. However, since Killean walked away, Saxon had harbored the fear that if Killean could fall, any of them could.

And Killean had done it for a woman; that was the most astonishing thing of all considering he'd shown as much interest in women over the years as he had frogs.

Saxon refilled his glass and took another long drink. He may be a Savage, but it appeared Killean's loyalty to Ronan remained unshakeable; otherwise, he wouldn't have called to report what he'd learned. Unless, the call was part of a trap devised by Killean and Joseph, but Saxon preferred to believe their fallen brother would make his way back to them.

Lowering the glass, Saxon wiped his mouth with the back of his hand as Lucien and Declan glided into the room. A few minutes later, he heard the front door open before Ronan and Kadence joined them followed by Nathan and Vicky. Everyone either settled into either the leather chairs or the stools in front of the bar.

"What did Killean have to say?" Ronan inquired.

Leaving his empty glass behind, Saxon claimed the bottle and walked around the bar to settle onto one of the stools lining it. He set the bottle on the bar and fiddled with the label as he told them what Killean revealed to him.

"Do we believe him?" Lucien asked when Saxon finished. Lucien's onyx eyes were like chips of black ice when they met Saxon's. "Or is he feeding us false information?"

"I believe him," Saxon said.

"Why?" Ronan asked.

Peeling away a piece of the label, Saxon laid it neatly on the bar as he spoke. "Because he doesn't want our help."

"That doesn't mean anything. Killean might not want our

help because he's safely ensconced with Joseph three miles from here and is simply waiting to attack," Lucien retorted.

"Then why call in the first place?" Declan asked as he twisted a lollipop stick between his fingers. A strand of his dark auburn hair had fallen into one of his troubled, silvery-gray eyes.

"To learn what we're doing," Nathan said.

"He didn't ask about any of us," Saxon replied. "He didn't ask if we were still here or if we moved after he left."

"Because he might already know we didn't move," Lucien said.

Lucien could be right, but Saxon refused to let his pessimism deter him. "He called to give me the information he has in case they don't make it out of Vermont."

"He really has *Simone*?" Kadence whispered.

"Yes," Saxon said. "I spoke briefly with her. They turned her, but Killean said she's not a Savage. He freed her before that could happen."

"And he could be lying about that too," Lucien said.

"Is *he* a Savage?" Nathan asked.

"I'm not sure what he is. I don't think he's one of them, not entirely, but he's not the same man who left here." That was easy to discern by talking to him. "How different he is, I don't know."

"What about the other hunters Joseph took?" Nathan inquired.

"Killean couldn't save them."

Vicky rested her hand on Nathan's arm when his shoulders slumped and sadness filled his blue eyes.

"Killean told me to look into a wedding reception in Vermont," Saxon said. He told them about the reception Killean and Simone fled from. "He's not sure of the location, but he thinks it ended in a fire with no survivors."

"That shouldn't be hard to find. I'll get my computer." Declan rose and left the room. He returned a minute later with a laptop and settled into his chair. Opening the computer, he tapped rapidly at the keys.

"Were there other hunters turned into vampires in the past?" Ronan asked Nathan.

"No," Nathan replied. "I know our history, and that was *never* mentioned before."

"Could they have kept it a secret?"

"If anyone knew about such a thing, it would be my line as we've always been in charge. Kadence was the first to make the transformation."

"If it did happen, could your ancestors have buried it to keep it hidden?" Ronan asked.

"I'm sure they wouldn't want that dirty little secret getting out," Lucien muttered.

Nathan looked about to deny it, but then he held his hands up before him and shrugged. "They may have wanted to keep such a thing hidden, but I think they would have preferred us prepared if we ever came across something like that."

"They might have been ashamed or refused to believe it themselves and decided to hide it," Vicky said.

"I'll ask Roland and the other elders if they've ever heard of such a thing to make sure, but I doubt they'll know anything either. If this is a hunter turned vampire, then it is most likely someone the other hunters believed dead all these years, but who was instead turned and has been in hiding."

"That's a frightening thought," Kadence said. "But maybe Killean was mistaken about what he saw in there."

"Or maybe he's feeding us lies," Lucien said.

"That's possible," Ronan murmured as he draped his arm around Kadence's shoulder and drew her against his side.

"What does he plan to do with Simone?" Nathan asked.

"He's trying to get her away from them," Saxon said. "After that, I don't know."

"I can't believe Simone is his mate," Nathan muttered as he ran a hand through his black hair. "That won't end well."

"Why not?" Vicky demanded. "It's worked out well enough for you and Kadence."

"It did," Nathan agreed as he took her hand. "But Simone is so proper, and Killean is so..."

"Rude," Declan supplied when Nathan's words trailed off.

"Yes."

"Opposites do attract," Vicky said. "And now that she's a vampire, she'll feel the pull of the mating bond more intensely than you and Kadence did while you were hunters."

"And it was still strong for us," Kadence said. "We have to help them."

"He wouldn't tell me where they are," Saxon said.

"Convenient," Lucien muttered.

"I've got it," Declan said as he rose from his chair and walked over to the bar. He set the computer on the bar and turned it to face everyone. "Ninety-five dead in a fire in Norton, Vermont. The police say all exits were blocked and they're looking for who could have started it. There are no witnesses. Due to the extent of the fire, identification will take a while, but they believe all wedding guests, including the bride and groom, perished in the blaze."

"Okay, so he was telling the truth about that, so what?" Lucien asked.

"So, it gives us an idea of the things Joseph is targeting. Remote areas and groups of people who aren't huge but aren't small either. If we keep an eye out for more fires or accidents matching those criteria, we might get a better idea of where Joseph is centered," Ronan replied. "Where in Vermont is Norton located?"

"Near the border of Canada and New Hampshire. Not much of a population," Declan said.

"And Joseph took the hunters from a stronghold in New Hampshire," Kadence murmured.

"Declan, do a search of Vermont, New Hampshire, and Maine for anything similar to what happened at this wedding," Ronan commanded. "Check back three months, and if you find things that match, go back further."

"He's changing his MO," Nathan said. "Before he was using the sewers and the homeless to create Savages, but once we discovered that he changed things."

"He might have been doing this all along," Ronan said. "But since it doesn't fit the normal criteria of what we expect from a Savage, which is to hunt clubs, bars, and the homeless, we weren't looking for it. We were also expecting smaller-scale attacks and not ones of this magnitude."

Declan's fingers flew across the keys before he stopped typing and lifted his head. "I've got three fires and two gas explosions that have gone unexplained with no known perpetrators throughout those states in the past three months. Fifteen people died in the first fire, twenty in the second, thirty-five in a gas explosion, thirty-seven in the next explosion, and sixty-two in the last fire."

"So, the death toll is going up as he's gathering and creating more Savages," Ronan said.

"Shit," Lucien muttered.

"If Joseph and Killean were working together, Joseph wouldn't willingly let Killean feed us this info about the wedding," Saxon said. "He'd know we would discover these other incidents once we learned about the wedding."

"Maybe," Ronan murmured. "If you pinpoint the locations of those events on a map, are they centered around anything?"

Declan worked at the computer for a minute before replying. "No, they're all scattered across different states and towns."

"But we know the pattern to look for now because of Killean," Saxon said.

He had no idea why he was pushing so much for them to trust Killean on this. The two of them were Defenders together for a century and a half, there was a bond there, but he knew very little about Killean. Still, they'd saved each other's lives more times than he could count, and Killean deserved some faith because of that.

But he didn't think that was the reason he was pulling so staunchly for Killean. No, he could admit it was because he *needed* someone to come back from the line Killean crossed because he was so damn close to going over it himself.

Saxon lifted the bottle and drank half of it. When he lowered the bottle, he found Declan staring at him in that maddeningly penetrating way of his. Saxon grinned at him as he set the bottle on the bar.

"So what do I tell Killean?" Saxon asked.

"I'd like to speak with him," Ronan said.

CHAPTER TWENTY-SEVEN

Simone watched Killean as he ran a hand through his brown hair and tugged on the ends of it. When he released it, it fell in a tussled wave about his handsome face. Her fingers twitched with the impulse to run her finger over the sharp blade of his cheekbone before pressing her lips to his.

"Who was that?" she inquired to distract herself from the idea of kissing him.

"Saxon. He's going to speak with the others."

She almost asked if they would take him back, but the question died in her throat. She doubted he knew the answer.

After everything he'd done for her, they *had* to take him back.

Her gaze fell to the faint, white scar on his chest again, and without thinking, she leaned across the distance separating them. "Where did you get this?"

Killean recoiled and threw his hand up to knock her fingers away the second they brushed across the circular mark. Memories of that hideous night crashed through him, a snarl curled his lip before he launched to his feet. Only one man had ever asked him about the events surrounding his acquisition of it. That man was dead.

"That's not for little dollies to know," he growled as he stalked over to the bags at the end of the bed. Opening one of the bags, he dug through the clothes and pulled out a maroon T-shirt.

Simone's hand remained hanging in the space between them before she lowered it. He hadn't bruised her when he knocked her hand aside, but the volatility of his reaction stunned her.

She watched as he tugged on a shirt with jerky movements so different than the fluid grace he usually possessed. She had no idea what she'd done, but once her shock over his reaction wore off, anger replaced it.

"Stop calling me dolly. I'm not a fragile, breakable thing. I survived what many wouldn't, and I have suffered!" Simone somehow managed to hide her astonishment over her raised voice. She'd *never* done that before.

Killean lifted his head to glare at her. "You endured two weeks of Hell, but I've been roasting in the pits for over four hundred years."

"Oh, you poor, tormented vampire, you. *Every*one endures adversity, some more than others, but the strong ones choose not to let it turn them into miserable..." she tried to think of the best way to describe him before blurting, "jerks!"

"We really have to teach you how to swear, dolly."

Simone lost the composure she always carefully maintained as she launched to her feet. "Just because I'm not some classless barbarian like you, doesn't make me a doll!"

"Barbarian, you're upping your word game with that one."

Her fingers hooked into claws as she contemplated tearing his face to shreds. "Maybe I've led a sheltered life and haven't endured the suffering you claim you have, but at least I'm not a coward hiding behind my misfortune to keep from getting close to others like *you*!"

She knew she'd struck a nerve when his eyes flared red and a vein in his forehead throbbed to life. The murderous look on his face should have petrified her; instead, she found her back straightening while she held his infuriated gaze.

Killean stalked toward her until they stood toe to toe. Simone lifted her chin, and her white-blue eyes blazed with defiance when they met his. She infuriated him, but he enjoyed this sign of strength from her.

"I can handle anything you or anyone else throws at me," she said.

"Can you, dolly?"

"Yes!" she practically shouted and almost kicked him in the shin. "I'm not fragile, and I've seen the worst of what the evil in this world has to offer!"

"You haven't scratched the surface of the evil in this world. It's not just vampires who are capable of committing atrocities."

"I know that!"

"Do you?" He lowered his head until their noses were almost touching. "Do you think it's only vampires and humans?"

An uneasy chill slid down Simone's spine as she stared into his red eyes. He wasn't just angry, and not just being cruel; there was something else in his gaze, something so lost and damaged it made her yearn to hug him as much as it frightened her. But she also didn't understand who else he could be talking about.

Then she recalled his wrath toward her on the beach, his aversion of her kind, and she decided she didn't want to hear anything else he had to say. But only a dolly would hide from the cold truths of their world; she refused to be a sheltered, frightened woman anymore.

Besides, she already knew that before hunters learned not all vampires were evil, hunters had indiscriminately killed them. It wasn't something the hunters were proud of, but they hadn't known the truth.

"I know my kind killed innocents in the past when they didn't know any better!" she retorted.

"And some hunters are going against Nathan and probably continue to do so while knowing the truth."

She couldn't argue with that.

"I've watched countless vampires die at the hands of your kind over the years. My entire family was slaughtered by *your* kind. My mother, my father, my two little sisters, and my older brother were all killed in one night, and I was left with this!" He pointed to the scar on his face. "The only reason I still have an eye is because they wanted me to see everything they did to my loved ones; the man who cut me laughed as he told me this."

He tore his shirt open to reveal the circle near his heart. "When they decided I'd seen enough, they plunged a stake into me. They missed my heart by centimeters but assumed I was dead. That is the *only* reason I'm standing before you now. I was able to leave the Defenders, the only family I've known these past four hundred years, to find you because your ancestors *fucked up* and failed to kill me when I was seven years old!"

Killean pulled away from her as the knowledge of what he'd revealed rocked him back a step. For centuries, he'd kept the details of that night to himself. When his uncle asked him what happened, Killean revealed most of it, but his uncle was dead.

"Compared to that, yes, you are a little doll," he continued with less vehemence as the devastated look on her face robbed him of some of his antagonism. "One who has been sheltered for her entire life. There are things about me, and things I've done, that you could *never* comprehend. So much blood has stained my hands that it's seeped into my soul and become a part of me, especially the innocent blood I've shed. If you think you're strong enough to handle that, then welcome to the dark side, dolly; it only gets more twisted from here."

They tortured him, she realized with sick dread. Hunters

weren't perfect, but they'd tortured a child and taken joy in it. She wanted to deny his words, but looking into his anguished face, she knew she could never deny the truth.

"But hunters didn't know vampires could have children until recently," she said. "Why would they attack you?"

Killean shrugged. "Maybe they believed my parents changed us to create some sort of demented family. Whatever they believed, they didn't care that we were only children when they attacked."

Simone's gaze returned to the scar on his chest. Now that she knew who caused it, she could tell a stake made it, and it had been *so* close! If it was a little further over, he wouldn't be standing before her. That knowledge caused a chasm to open in her heart as the idea of a world without Killean left her cold.

She also understood his intense dislike of hunters. Understood the disgust she saw on his face after he kissed her and the hostility he emanated every time he said the word hunter. But she didn't understand one thing...

"Why did you come for me?" she inquired.

Killean hadn't known what to expect from her, but it wasn't that. "I told you—"

"You've told me nothing!" she interrupted. "And I want an answer. Hunters killed your family, and it's obvious you despise my kind, so why did you come for *me*?"

"I wasn't going to leave you there."

"Why not? You left all the others there. Why not me? What is so special about *me*?"

What isn't special about you? He wondered as she kept her shoulders back and refused to step away from him.

"Are you going to refuse to tell me and continue to be the coward who uses his past as a shield against others?" Simone demanded when he didn't reply. "Your family died over four hundred years ago; it's time to move on! You can't continue using them as an excuse to keep from opening up to others."

Killean didn't know if he wanted to kiss her or throttle her more. "I am not a coward."

"Maybe not physically, but emotionally you are!" she insisted. "My father was killed by a vampire when I was seven too, and Savages tortured my friends and me for two weeks, but I don't hold that against you or other vampires. Yet you continue to hate hunters for something that happened *centuries* ago!"

"You don't hold that against vampires? You fled a safe stronghold to escape the Alliance," he retorted, "and ended up being a prisoner because of your dislike of vampires."

"I fled to escape my embarrassment over being tossed aside by Nathan for another woman!" she snapped.

"Oh, did he break your heart?" Killean taunted, but his hands fisting as he braced himself for her reply. He didn't know how he would react if she said yes.

"No!" she cried. "I was never in love with Nathan. But the life I'd been expecting to live was ripped away from me in an instant, and it was humiliating. *Everyone* expected us to marry, but I was publicly thrown aside for another, so excuse me for needing to escape!"

"So, the dolly ran like a coward."

Simone didn't think before her hand flew up and connected with his face in a resonating blow that echoed through the room. With lightning speed, Killean snatched her wrist and held it between them. Simone gawked at her hand before her eyes slid to him. She expected to see rage in his gaze; there was only disbelief.

She braced herself for him to explode, but he only continued to stare at her as if she were an alien life-form. A trickle of shame ran through her at her actions; she *never* should have hit him, but she wouldn't apologize for it either.

She was done with hiding her emotions and apologizing for things.

"I. Am. Not. A. Doll," she enunciated clearly.

"You have no concept of the real world," he growled. "Or the creatures stalking it. Creatures like *me*."

Simone refused to rise to his baiting anymore as she knew he was trying to draw her away from the subject he wanted to avoid. "Why did you come for me?"

Killean tugged on the wrist he held to draw her a step closer, but she didn't try to pull away as he'd anticipated. He couldn't believe that, not only had she hit him, she refused to be intimidated by him. The woman was completely baffling and infuriating.

"Why did you come for me?" she asked.

"Do you really want to know?" he growled as his control over his temper started to fray.

"Yes."

"Because you're *my* mate."

And somehow, deep inside, she'd already known that was the reason. "What does that mean?" she asked.

"It means, whether we like it or not, we're at least partially tied to each other for the rest of our lives."

"So, because of what I am to you, you gave up everything that meant anything to you, even though you don't know me, not really?"

"Yes, but you have one thing wrong."

"And what is that?" she asked.

"I didn't become what I am now because of you; I did it *for* you. And I would do it again."

Simone's breath rushed out at those words. She never would have believed anything remotely sweet could come out of Killean's mouth, but she'd been mistaken.

"So we'll be mates now?" she asked, uncertain how she felt

about that. No one could make her feel as alive as he did, but the whole mate thing was a pretty *big* commitment and he could be a pretty *big* jerk. They might kill each other if they were forced to live together for an eternity.

"Our bond won't ever be completed," he stated.

"Why not?" she demanded and realized her emotions were completely out of control. He'd thrown her off completely with all his revelations, and she had no idea how to react to all of them.

"Because I won't condemn you by binding you to the thing I've become. You've consumed my blood, and if you're feeling any pull from the mating bond, it will make things difficult for you to not have me in your life, but it's best for you if I'm not."

"I'm capable of handling more than you give me credit for."

"Are you capable of handling the darkness I possess now that I've killed humans?"

"Yes."

"Really?"

"Yes!" she insisted.

Even as she said this, a part of her screamed, *No! What are you, an idiot? This man is dangerous. He's bordering on the edge of losing control and becoming more Savage than not; he'll steal your heart and tear it out if he loses control.*

And he could so easily steal her heart; he already owned a piece of it for sacrificing himself to save her. Never had she imagined someone like Killean becoming a part of her life. Every image she ever had of her future husband was of someone who was kind, considerate, and a hunter.

Killean was the exact opposite of everything she'd dreamed of in her life, but she wanted him more than she'd ever wanted anything else. Maybe it was the mating bond at work, or maybe it was that no matter his harsh exterior, she knew a kind man lurked beneath; one who'd denied himself love since the death of his family but who so badly needed it.

"Then you must know that when I kill now, all I want is to feel the suffering of those I feed on," Killean said and held her gaze as he revealed the worst part of himself to her. When he was done, she would never again consider taking him as her mate, which was what he wanted. *Liar.* But Killean didn't stop.

"You should also know that when I'm not imagining all the things I want to do to you in bed, I'm thinking about how many different ways I can kill and feast on someone. Since reaching maturity, I've been obsessed with killing, but I managed to keep myself restrained from destroying any innocents. Now that I've finally given in to my darkest impulses, my need to kill has become this ever-constant *thing* gnawing at my insides, and all it craves is *more* blood, death, and pain."

Simone inwardly cringed at his words, but years of wearing a demure mask came in handy as she held his gaze. "I can handle anything." Before her capture, she wouldn't have been at all certain of this; she was now. "I'm not saying let's complete the bond, but you won't scare me off either."

Killean released a snort of laughter. "You have no idea the things I'm capable of doing."

"And you have no idea what I'm capable of handling."

The jarring ring of the phone silenced his reply as his gaze went to the nightstand. Releasing her wrist, he stepped around her and lifted the phone from the receiver. "Yeah," he said.

"Killean?"

Ronan's voice deflated his anger. "Yes," he said.

The relief in Killean's voice drew Simone's attention. When he sank onto the bed, he looked more relaxed than she'd seen him in a while. He also looked almost happy.

"How are you?" Ronan asked.

"Been better," Killean admitted. "Saxon spoke with you?"

"Yes, and we've talked with the others. Nathan has never heard of another turned hunter before Kadence. He's spoken with the elders, and the other hunter factions he's still in touch with, but none of them have ever heard of such a thing happening before either."

"I know what I saw."

Killean's gaze fell to his hands, and an uneasy feeling crept into his gut. *Did* he know what he saw in the bunker? He'd seen blood drenching his hands that was never there too.

No, he'd seen that creature before the hallucinations started; it was *real*.

"It could be something else, it could be the hunters weren't told about such a thing happening, or it could be a hunter they all assumed dead until now," Ronan said.

"It's really powerful, and I believe it's older than you."

"And it can still die," Ronan said.

"Yes, it can."

Killean's gaze slid to Simone as she watched him with compressed lips and narrowed eyes. The composed, pristine doll he'd first encountered on the beach was gone. The woman standing there resembled a banshee with her hair flowing about her shoulders and a wild gleam in her normally tranquil eyes.

He liked this side of her; he liked *her*.

The realization hit him like an arrow between the eyes. All this time, he'd considered her a passive creation of the hunter's archaic ways, but free of their hold, she was defiant, stubborn, and stronger than he would have believed her capable of being. He'd been confident her captivity would destroy her, or if not destroy her, make her meeker, but like a phoenix, she'd risen from the ashes of her old life and spread her wings to become something stronger.

She was amazing.

"How is Simone?" Ronan asked.

It took him a minute to find his voice to respond. "She's a fighter."

Simone quirked an eyebrow. Was he talking about *her*? Could dollies fight? The question left a bitter taste in her mouth, and she found herself scowling at him again. To her utter annoyance, he smiled at her.

"Kadence would like to speak with her," Ronan said.

"Here she is," he held the phone out to Simone who turned her glare on it. "Kadence is asking for you."

She snatched the phone from his hand. "Hello."

"Simone," Kadence breathed. "Are you okay?"

Her irritation fell away at the sound of her best friend's voice. "Yes, I'm fine," Simone assured her.

"What about Killean? Are you scared of him? Is he treating you okay? Is he dangerous?"

"Not at all. Yes. And not to me," she answered each rapidly fired question honestly. What Killean would be like around others, she didn't know, but he would never be a threat to her even if she slapped him a hundred more times. The reminder of what she'd done and the complete loss of her temper caused her cheeks to flush.

"Can he be trusted?" Kadence asked.

"Yes." Killean may doubt that, but she didn't.

"It's so good to hear your voice."

"Yours also. My mom? Is she okay? I lost sight of her after I was captured, and she wasn't with us in that place."

"She's fine," Kadence said. "She's worried about you, but I'll let her know we talked."

"Oh, that's wonderful." Tears of joy filled Simone's eyes. "Please tell her I love and miss her."

"I will."

They spoke for a few minutes more before she handed the phone back to Killean who talked with Ronan and hung up.

When his gaze returned to her, her shoulders went back. She didn't want to fight with him anymore, but she was prepared to battle him until he got it through his thick skull that she wasn't fragile. The silence extended into minutes while they gazed at each other.

"I can handle the darkness, Killean," Simone finally said, "but I'm not sure you can handle letting go of your past enough to walk out of the shadows."

With that, she turned away, gathered some clothes from one of the bags, and strode into the bathroom.

CHAPTER TWENTY-EIGHT

KILLEAN STARED at the ceiling as he lay on the bed with his hands propped behind his head while he listened to Simone's soft breaths. Rolling over, he gazed across the distance separating the two beds and at the curve of her back. They'd removed their socks and shoes, but both still wore their clothes in case they had to flee from here.

The last words she'd spoken to him ran on a constant loop in his mind. *"I can handle the darkness, Killean, but I'm not sure you can handle letting go of your past enough to walk out of the shadows."*

What had she meant by that? How could he just walk away from the events that forged him into the man he was?

Suddenly, she rolled over and he found himself staring into her striking eyes. And just looking at her, for the first time in his life, he considered letting go of his past to embrace a future with her.

But how could he bind her to someone such as himself?

She was far too good for him. He'd been broken before he

reached maturity and found himself seeking death; he was worse now.

"I know the stake missed your heart, but at seven you hadn't fully matured yet, so how did you not bleed out?" Simone asked.

Simone braced herself for him to tell her to mind her own business, call her a dolly, or some other incensed reaction. Instead, he merely lay there, staring at her in a way that made her feel cherished though she had no reason to believe he would ever treasure her.

Killean debated answering her, but he'd already told her more than he'd intended, so he saw no reason not to reveal more.

"My uncle found me before I bled out," Killean finally said. "He lived on the estate next to ours in England. And by next to ours, I mean his manor was an hour ride away by horseback. When my father didn't arrive for their weekly card game, he came to check on us. He found me, barely clinging to life, and gave me his blood to save me."

"What became of him?"

"Hunters killed him fifty years later. He was the last of my family."

Simone held back the tears burning her eyes. His entire family had been wiped out in such a short amount of time, and by her kind. "I understand why you've hated my kind for so long, and what they did to you and your family was unforgivable, but things are changing between our sides. Those hunters didn't know there were good vampires in the world and believed you were all evil."

"The things those hunters did to my family, and me, makes some Savages look kind.

I wasn't the only one they cut. They tortured us for hours."

"Hunters don't do those things." Simone regretted the words as soon as they were out of her mouth; she felt a snapping in him from across the three feet separating them, and her denial was childish. He still bore the scars of what those hunters did to him, and they were only the ones she could see. She suspected his inner scars ran far deeper than the ones he wore for the world to see.

Killean sat up on the bed and set his feet on the floor. "You said you could handle the dark side, dolly, yet you're denying what I'm telling you."

Simone sat up too. "I can handle it. It's just that hunters... we're not... we're..."

"What?" Killean asked when her voice trailed off. "You're not evil? You're the good guys? Perhaps, like vampires, many hunters mean well, but some of them are vicious bastards who hide behind the killing of vampires to unleash the rot inside their souls." Lifting his hand, he ran his fingers along the scar on his face. "I still bear this, and the one on my chest, because I was so young the scars were forever etched onto me."

"I see," Simone said. "What else did they do?"

She didn't want to learn anymore about what was done to him as a boy, but she suspected that if she backed away now there would be no hope of anything more developing between them. He would drop her off somewhere and walk away, and she didn't want that. She *would* understand him better, and she believed he needed to get this out. What happened that night had eaten at his soul for centuries; it was time to set it free.

Killean couldn't look at her as the memories of that distant night replayed in his mind. No matter how much time passed, he could still recall every detail as if it happened only yesterday. But he'd replayed that night thousands of times and found countless ways he could have saved his family if he'd just done *something* differently.

"There were twelve of them against two adult vampires and four children; it wasn't much of a fight, but my father managed to kill two hunters and my mother one, before they brought us down. My parents fought so hard to save us, and they loved us so much, but it wasn't enough. When they were dead, the hunters focused all their attention on me and my siblings," he said.

The screams of his younger sisters resonated in his ears as his brother yelled and swore and struggled. While three men kept him pinned to the ground, Killean watched his siblings fall. After he succeeded in biting the hunter who cut his face, the man announced they would save him for last, so he could watch everything they did to the others and see what they would eventually do to him.

When he looked at Simone again, the helpless rage filling him that night boiled to the surface. "I've never understood why I survived when my family perished. They were all better than me, kinder and stronger."

"Oh, Killean," she breathed when she saw the raw guilt he'd been living with all these centuries. "That's not true."

"It is. Would you like to know what else your ancestors did to us?"

Killean heard the challenge in his voice, but Simone had grown increasingly pale while he spoke, and he kept waiting for her to tell him to stop. He kept waiting for her to run from him as any sane woman would, and when she ran, she would confirm this could never be between them.

She absolutely did *not* want to know, but she found herself saying, "Yes. If you're willing to tell me."

Launching to his feet, Killean stalked away from her and over to the plate glass window with the curtains covering it. That was *not* the response he expected.

"Killean?" she whispered.

He turned back toward her, but when he saw the frightened, nearly pleading look on her face, his words died away. *Simone* wasn't there that night; he was punishing her for sins she'd never committed and would *never* commit. Some of the hunters were murderous, hideous bastards, but Simone was not one of them, and neither was Nathan and Kadence.

"Killean?"

Running a hand through his hair, he tugged at the ends of it as he tried to bury his memories. The torment, degradation, and sorrow of that night burned like acid in his chest. His fangs throbbed to sink into someone and destroy them as the innocence of the boy he'd been was destroyed that night. He needed to feast on the pain of others and let it course through him until it buried his past.

"Killean?"

Killean forced himself to focus on Simone again. "Some things are better left in the past."

He paced over to the door and glowered at the sun creeping around the edges of it. He couldn't go out to kill until night descended, but he didn't know if he could handle being caged in this room much longer.

Simone didn't know what propelled her to her feet. Before she could fully comprehend what she was doing, she was standing beside him with her hand on his arm. She almost released him and backed away when his reddened eyes swung toward her. She'd never seen him look so volatile, so ruthless, so... *lost*.

Her heart ached in a way she hadn't experienced before as her hand tightened on his arm. This powerful, lethal man was broken, and he needed her. There was so little in her life she was sure of any more, but she was sure of this, and she was sure she needed him too. No matter how disturbing his past, no matter the things he did, she would not walk away from him.

"I have to go out," he said. "I *have* to feed."

"You have to kill, you mean."

Surprisingly, he was the one who flinched at her words.

"I saw what you did to that vampire, and I didn't run away. I won't now either." She may not want to hear what else he had to say, but she would listen to it all because he *had* to say it. "I know what you need, Killean. I know what you are, and I'm still here. What else did those hunters do to you?"

Killean shook his head, not to disregard her words but to shake off the past cleaving to him like a second skin—a skin threatening to choke him with every passing second.

"*Tell me*," she said quietly, but with an authority she hadn't known she possessed.

Killean focused on the far wall as screams echoed in his head and the scent of centuries-old terror and blood permeated his nostrils. It was as if he were in that house again, pinned down and helpless.

"They raped them," he murmured. "My brother and my sisters. They raped them for hours and tortured them before killing them."

Simone's breath caught as bile swelled up her throat. Denials screamed through her head, but she saw the horrible truth in his slack face that looked far younger than it usually did. Staring at him, she caught a glimpse of the boy he'd been. The one who was loved by his parents and the one forever altered in a night. She almost wept for him, but Killean would leave here if she cried.

"And what did they do to you?" she whispered.

Killean tore his gaze away from the wall to focus on her. When he gazed at her, he could keep himself in the present. "I was not spared."

He thought it would shame him to admit this to her, to anyone, as he'd kept it from his uncle too. Though he was sure his uncle had known the truth. But Killean experienced no shame. Instead, it felt as if a weight were lifted from his shoulders. The horrible truth was out there, and it hadn't made him weaker, and she wasn't gazing at him as if he were repugnant.

"Oh, Killean," she breathed. "I am so sorry."

Killean pulled her hand away from his arm. "You weren't there. Don't apologize for it, and don't feel sorry for me."

Tears welled in her eyes as he turned away from her and paced over to the window. He pulled a corner of the curtain aside to peer out. Though she'd glimpsed the boy he'd been, he was stealing himself into a ruthless man again, but then he would have had to become hardened to survive what was done to him.

They were only children and *hunters*, the ones she'd always considered the *good* guys, had done unspeakable things to them. She didn't doubt Savages inflicted the same abuse on other innocents, but hunters were supposed to be above that.

Her tears dried up as rage swelled forth. If it had been possible for those hunters to still be alive, she would have killed them herself for doing such a thing to those children, and to *her* Killean. Her fangs pricked at the idea of him enduring that abuse, and suddenly, she had an overwhelming urge to kill something too.

Then she recalled his words after he'd scrubbed at the blisters on his hands and understanding dawned. *"Don't feel sorry for them; they were all pieces of shit and some of the worst of the human race. Each of them was either a rapist or child molester. Their deaths mean someone else won't suffer at their hands."*

"*This* is why you only killed rapists and child molesters," she breathed as understanding dawned. It was also why he'd seemed so upset when he asked her if Joseph or anyone else had violated her. He knew how horrible such a thing was, and he didn't want anyone else to have to suffer through the same thing he had.

Killean didn't reply, but she knew she was right.

"You were only children," she said.

"We were *nothing* to them, and they let us know it."

"No wonder you hate that I'm your mate so much."

And her heart broke as she realized he might never be able to let go of his past and see her as anything more than a hunter—a thing he despised.

Killean's attention shifted to her, and the tears shimmering in her eyes caused his hand to fall away from the curtain.

"But I don't hate it," he said. "Yes, in the beginning, I was *infuriated* by it and believed it the cruelest twist of fate. I vowed to let you rot with Joseph, but I found myself unable to leave you there. Then I vowed to get you free, take you back to your kind, and never see you again. Now I know you're much more than I thought you were, and I'm such a miserable, selfish prick that I don't want to let you go."

Admitting that to her terrified him more than admitting his past did.

Simone didn't know how to feel about that. The wildness she sensed in Killean frightened her; she didn't know what he would do, how well he could control himself, or if he would ultimately lose himself as Joseph and the other Savages had, but Simone knew she could ease the turmoil churning through him.

"You gave up everything for me; that's far from selfish, Killean. And whether you believe it or not, you deserve to be here; you deserve to have lived."

"I have to feed," he said again.

She brushed her hair off her neck as she closed the distance between them. "You don't have to go out to feed; I'm right here."

CHAPTER TWENTY-NINE

Saliva rushed into Killean's mouth as he gazed at the tempting curve of her delicate neck. A single, brown freckle just below her ear was the only thing marring the perfection of her ivory skin. He rested his fingers against her throat to feel her steady pulse. Such an enticing beat; such an alluring woman. She lured him like no other, but if he fed on her...

It would be one step closer to completing the mating bond, one step closer to Simone never being free of Savages for he held out little hope for himself anymore.

"Killean—"

"If I drink from you, it will only further the mate bond between us." His fingers traced her throat while he spoke. "Drinking from each other and sex will seal it."

"I'm not offering you my body, Killean, only my blood."

"It will still make it more difficult for us to resist each other, and you have to be able to walk away from me."

"Why?" she demanded.

Killean blinked at her. Didn't she see him for what he was?

"Because you deserve better than me, and I am not the man I was before."

"Well, that man kissed me and told me to get back to the hotel," she reminded him. "My memories of him aren't overly fond ones." Though she would forever remember the searing heat of her first kiss and the passion it awakened in her.

"And the man before you is a monster."

She clasped his hand against her throat and held it there. "The man before me saved my life and can be whatever he chooses to make himself."

"You don't know the things I want... the things I *need* now."

"No, but I know what I can give you to help ease your need. Allow me to do it."

A stronger man would have stepped away from her; two weeks ago, *he* would have stepped away from her, but his gaze remained fastened on her neck as his need to kill became replaced by a compulsion to taste her.

When his hunger beat against her, Simone released his hand and lowered hers. His fingers caressed her skin before sliding around to cup her nape. Those exquisite tiger's eyes and his touch burned into her flesh until she felt consumed by the power of him. She played with fire by allowing him to do this, but she found herself throwing open her arms and plunging into the blaze.

Her life had been tossed into a tailspin when she was taken and turned; since then, this was the first thing to happen that she *knew* was right.

Simone held her breath when he bent his head, and his warm breath tickled her throat. His fangs scraped her flesh, and she braced herself for the agony to follow, but she would handle the pain, as he'd managed it when she fed on him.

Then his fangs sank into her flesh, and Simone stiffened as she fought her instinct to shove him away.

The first drop of her potent blood hit his tongue when he felt Simone's resistance building against him and a sliver of her pain teased his mind. He craved the misery of others, but not *Simone*. Retracting his fangs, he pulled away from her.

"What... what's wrong?" she stammered.

Killean caressed her nape as he gazed at her pale face and upturned chin. "I won't hurt you."

"But it always hurts."

He mentally kicked himself for being an idiot. Her only experience with having someone take her blood had been a brutal one. Yet, having endured Joseph's vicious assault on her, she still willingly offered him her throat all while expecting to have to suffer again.

After everything he'd said and done to her, she still wanted to help him. His life had been brutal, what happened to him as a child forever altered him, but she'd experienced her own horror. She'd watched many she loved die, while others were twisted into something else entirely, yet the beauty of her soul remained untarnished. He'd called her a dolly, but he was the one broken by his past, while hers strengthened her.

He'd never hated himself more. Simone was *his* mate, and she deserved so much better than him. He'd never wanted to be a better man before, but he did now, for her.

"I underestimated you," he murmured as he bent to kiss her forehead then the tip of her nose. "You're no doll; you're a warrior and a stronger one than me."

Simone didn't know if he was playing with her or not, and if he were playing with her, she would hit him again. "I'm no fighter. I don't even know how to throw a proper punch."

His thumb ran over her full bottom lip as he held her gaze. "Not all warriors are fighters," he murmured. "Some warriors never back down and give much of themselves to help others while making the world a better place. You are *that* kind of warrior, Simone. Though I *am* going to teach you how to protect yourself better."

"I plan to learn."

"You deserve better than me as your mate."

Simone frowned at him. "Give yourself some credit, Killean. Many wouldn't have come for me; many wouldn't have been brave enough or strong enough to do what was necessary to get in there and back out again. I'm here because of you, and I'm offering my blood to you. I'll endure the pain like you did when I fed on you."

His smile robbed her of her breath as it lit his eyes, and she caught a glimpse of the happier man he might have been if not for that horrific night of his childhood. But she didn't want him to be a different man; she wanted this dark and twisted soldier.

"I experienced only ecstasy when you fed on me," he told her. "You're a young vampire and didn't allow yourself to open to my feelings, but if you had, you would have discovered that having you drink from me is one of the greatest joys of my life. The other is knowing the honeyed taste of your orgasm."

Her cheeks burned, but whether it was from his blunt words or the desire they awakened, she didn't know.

"That day on the beach was the first time I felt desire for a woman in nearly a hundred years," he continued.

"How is that possible?" she blurted.

"When a purebred vampire reaches maturity, they begin to hunger for something so incessantly it starts to take them over. For me, all I wanted was death. Eventually, it eclipsed my desire for women and anything else, until you. A mate can curb the appetites of a pureblood while bringing that vampire back to life in many ways, which is what you have done for me."

Simone opened her mouth to respond, but no words came out.

"When I drink from you, it doesn't have to be painful; in fact, it can be very stimulating." His finger ran over the curve of her cheekbone before dipping down to the collar of her shirt. Fresh color spread across her flesh when he stroked her exposed chest bone with his knuckles. "Don't resist my bite, and you will know only pleasure from it."

All her nerve endings tingled from the exquisite promise of his words. Killean lowered his hand to her hip before drawing her closer to him. His other hand clasped her neck as he bent his head; his lips teased hers in a caress lighter than a spring breeze. Then his tongue briefly brushed her mouth before he nipped at her bottom lip.

Simone sighed when his fang pricked her flesh; he licked away the bead of blood he created. He nipped her again, and though the smallest pinprick of discomfort followed, she experienced none of the bone-shattering, complete immobility that arrested her when Joseph feasted from her. The following hours and what felt like weeks of torture gripping her throughout her transition faded away as Killean's tongue teased her lips until she opened her mouth to let him taste her.

She'd said she was only offering him her blood and not her body, but his kiss made her want to throw those words out the window. The clothing that had been so comfortable was suddenly abrasive against her skin.

His hand on her hip slid around to cup her ass. Drawing her closer, he lifted her until she was flush against the hard evidence of his arousal. She rocked against him while he deepened the kiss.

Killean had only meant to taste her, but he should have known he would crave more of her; he'd been unable to resist her from the beginning. All his life he'd taken what he wanted, and Killean wanted her more than the revenge he'd sought on the hunters who slaughtered his family. He'd never been able to find those bastards, but he could have *her*.

His mouth slid away from hers and across her cheek before

dipping to her neck. She tensed when he licked her flesh but eased against him as she recalled the ecstasy his tongue had given her yesterday.

"Don't resist my bite, and you will know only pleasure from it." His words ran through her mind as his fangs grazed her skin. He wouldn't lie to her about this when the truth would be so easy to discern.

Then his fangs pierced her skin, slightly above the marks he already created on her. The pinch was fleeting, but Simone's breath still caught. *Don't resist; don't resist.* It became a mantra in her head until she realized he was drawing her blood, and she didn't feel like shrieking to the heavens to make it stop.

When she felt his next pull, something inside her melted as a wetness spread between her legs. She'd felt his torment earlier and his compulsion to destroy, but now all she experienced was his joy. When he bit deeper, Simone reacted like she'd grabbed a live wire as her body jerked toward him.

Killean growled as her potent blood filled his mouth and slid down his throat; it was an ambrosia he'd never get enough of tasting. More power than the lives he'd taken slithered through him as her blood filled him.

With his hand on her ass, he lifted her, and she wrapped her legs around his waist. As she rose and fell against his erection, her fingers dug into his nape, and her head fell forward as a growing pressure built within her. She sought the release he'd given her yesterday, but she also wanted more of him as the rush of his pulse filled her ears. Without thinking, she sank her fangs into his throat, and his hot blood filled her mouth.

Killean's self-restraint vanished when Simone's hunger surged forth to blend with his. In two strides, he covered the distance to one of the beds, and without breaking his bite on her, he laid her down and settled over the top of her.

CHAPTER THIRTY

Feeling completely out of control with his blood filling her and her growing need for more of him, Simone's hands dropped to the bottom of his shirt, and she tugged it up. She had to feel more of him, but when his lower back was exposed and she felt his chiseled muscles against her fingers, she realized it wasn't enough.

Unwilling to release her bite on him to pull the shirt over his head, her fingers gripped the material, and she yanked it apart impatiently. She had no idea where her years of proper breeding went, and she didn't care as the shirt fell away and her hands rested on his back. However, it still wasn't enough of him.

Releasing his bite on her, Killean gripped the sides of Simone's shirt and pulled it apart. Buttons rattled around the room as they rolled into the shadowy recesses. When she was bared to him, his hands splayed across her ribcage before moving down to her concave belly. She wiggled beneath him as his fingers found the button of her jeans and pulling it free. Then he tugged the zipper down.

He traced the contours of her hip bones as he tugged her

jeans and underwear lower. Her fingers eased their grip on his back when he shifted, and she retracted her fangs. He pulled her clothes the rest of the way off and tossed them aside.

Running his hands over her shapely calves and up her thighs, he relished her silky skin while he massaged her flesh. The intoxicating scent of her arousal excited him further as he explored her hips before lifting her into a seated position and pulling off her ruined shirt.

Simone nuzzled the hollow of his throat while removing the remains of his tattered shirt. With the taste of his blood lingering on her tongue, she found herself yearning for more of it as he unhooked her bra and tossed it aside.

Cool air rushed over her bare flesh, and she realized that for the first time in her life, she was naked in front of a man. Instead of trying to cover her nudity, she enjoyed it when his eyes ran hungrily over her. She'd grown up with the rules their skirts must be ankle length, their blouses loose-fitting, and their colors respectful, but she relished being exposed to a man who so obviously desired her.

I'm free! She almost laughed out loud at the realization, but she was far too caught up in Killean to laugh.

Killean stiffened when her fingers traced the scar on his chest, but he didn't knock her hand away this time. Instead, he let her explore him as the healing warmth of her touch seeped through his skin and into his soul. He should stop this and take her back, leave her with those who would protect her, and vanish from her life before he destroyed her, but he couldn't.

He'd been a selfish bastard his whole life, and he still was. Unless she stopped him, he would claim her.

Simone was enraptured with Killean's body as she ran her fingers down the line cutting down the center of his abs and through the hair traveling from his navel to the waistband of his jeans. His skin, pulled taut over the lean muscles carving his torso, was supple.

Killean couldn't tear his eyes away from her rapt expression as she explored his body. No one had ever looked at him like that; it was as if she couldn't get enough of him. With everything she knew about him, she should be revolted by him, but she remained fascinated.

Then her hands fell to the button of his jeans, and she slid it free before tugging the zipper down. When his rigid cock sprang free, she caressed the head of it with her thumb. The small smile curving her lips was more a mystery to him than the one Mona Lisa wore.

When he clasped her neck, her eyes came back to his. He stared at her before bending his head to claim her lips. Her fingers curled into his chest, her lips parted, and he tasted his blood on her. He was already inside her, and she him, but he wanted more.

Reaching down with his free hand, he pulled his jeans further down his hips as she enclosed her fingers loosely around his shaft and gave a tentative stroke. Grasping her hand, he encircled it more firmly around him and guided her down before up again. Simone didn't try to pull away; instead, she followed his guidance and grew more confident in her touch while he kissed her.

His fingers grazed the tops of her lush breasts before he cupped one and ran his thumb over her nipple. It puckered beneath his ministrations, and he gave it a small pinch she reacted to with a delicious moan. Killean groaned when her thumb sliding over his head spread his precum.

Breaking the kiss, Killean gently pulled her hand away from him before grasping his jeans and shoving them the rest of the way off.

"Stop me," he said as he kissed her silken hair and cupped her cheeks to lift her face to his. "At any point in time, tell me this isn't what you want, and I'll walk away."

His words came out as more of a plea than a command, and she realized she had to stop him because he couldn't do it himself. And no matter how far this progressed, he would stop the second she told him to.

And if she didn't stop this, she knew what it would mean. She'd be linked to this tormented man for the rest of their lives as only death would separate them. Being bound to Killean in such a way would be the most challenging thing she'd ever endure in her life. Was finally satisfying the needs of her body and learning what he could teach her worth that?

Yes, she believed it was as she *craved* being bound to him. Maybe it was because she was a vampire seeking her mate, but she suspected it was because this man infuriated and stimulated her more than any other. She relished the excitement and uncertainty he brought to a life that was nothing but dull and certain before he walked into it.

There was no love between them, but there was trust and growing mutual respect, which could bloom into love if they allowed it. And she didn't doubt that though being bound to him would be difficult, it would be completely worth it. He was abrasive and ruthless, but he was also proud, strong, and a man deserving of love and goodness in his life, even if he didn't see that yet.

Think, Simone. This can't be undone.

But she'd been thinking her whole life. It was all she'd been raised to do. For once in her life, she wanted only to feel and experience things, and no one could make her feel as much, or as profoundly, as Killean.

Though his thighs straddled hers, Simone pulled herself up a little higher to press her lips against his. This kiss was the most irrational, condemning thing she'd ever done in her life, and she found herself smiling as she clasped the back of his head to draw him closer.

He was *hers,* and he would be forever. No matter what the rocky road ahead of them entailed, and it would be rocky, she would traverse it with him.

A pang of trepidation went through her over what was to come, but excitement took over when he pushed her down onto the bed. Propping himself up with one hand, Killean leaned over her until his skin was sliding against hers in the most erotic of ways. Simone squirmed beneath him when his other hand ran over her hip before dipping between her legs.

She instinctively rose to meet his touch when he stroked her sex, and Killean growled against her mouth when he discovered how wet she was for him. *My mate.* The words played on a loop in his head while the recently released Savage part of him thundered through his veins.

That more volatile part of him wanted to take her right now and seal the bond before she could change her mind. He fought the growing impulse as he slid a finger into her sheath and nipped at her lip when her muscles gripped him.

No matter what the worst of him clamored for, he had to make it as easy as possible for her when he took her. There would be no way for her to entirely avoid the pain, but he wouldn't inflict any unnecessarily on her to satisfy his carnal urges and the demon within him.

Simone gasped when he slid another finger into her, stretching her further. The sensation wasn't unpleasant, and she found herself rocking against his hand as she rapidly approached the release he'd given her before. Breaking the kiss, Simone turned her head to the side, and her body arched as she splintered apart. Her fingers dug into his back as she cried out in ecstasy.

Killean watched the bliss playing over her features as her muscles contracted around his fingers. Slowly, he removed them from her and, grasping his dick, guided it to her entrance. It throbbed in his hand, and if he weren't careful, he'd spill the second he settled inside her.

Panting for breath, Simone gradually came back to her body when she felt something hard prodding against her once more. Her haze of euphoria slid away as she met Killean's vibrant red eyes. With his jaw set, his scar was more visible as his skin pulled taut over his cheekbones. She sensed the savagery within him as he held himself above her, but instead of being afraid of it, she rested her hand against his cheek and spread her legs wider.

When the tight muscles of her sheath enveloped the head of his cock, Killean couldn't stop himself from surging forward. Simone yelped when he buried himself inside her, and her fingers clawed his back. Some of the madness clamoring at his veins eased as he gathered her in his arms.

"I'm sorry," he murmured as he kissed her ear. "Give it a little bit, and the pain will fade. Do you want me to stop?"

As much as it hurt, the last thing she wanted was for this to end. Maybe it wasn't as pleasant as it had been before, but she relished the feel of his arms around her. "No."

Simone buried her face in the hollow of his throat while she tried to adjust to the feel of him inside her. Compared to what Joseph had done to her, this pain was nothing, but she'd still been thrown off by it after such enjoyment. Then Killean withdrew partially from her before slipping back in. Simone wanted to pull away at the same time she found herself melting further into him.

Killean somehow managed to restrain himself from thrusting into her until he found his release. It had been so long since he'd been with a woman that he felt like an untried youth. Except those women had meant nothing to him, and now he held his mate in his arms. His excitement and his rising need to complete the bond was making it difficult to maintain his control.

When her legs slid around his waist, and her fangs scraped

his flesh, he pulled her hair back to expose the creamy expanse of her throat. He sank his fangs into her, and her blood filled him while he filled her. Her lips skimmed back, and Killean nearly came when her fangs pierced his flesh.

Joined, her thoughts coalesced with his as the mating bond encompassed them. There would be no escape from this, but he didn't want to escape.

Overwhelmed by the beauty of the moment and everything happening between them, tears slid down her face as she gave herself over to the emotions Killean emitted. His hunger, desperation, and brutality battered her, but so did his awe over what was transpiring between them. She hadn't realized how far into the darkness he'd slipped, or how much he needed death, and *her*.

She vowed to do whatever it took to get him through this battle he waged. Her hands slid into his hair, and she cradled him as he thrust forward and shuddered against her. Deep inside her, she felt the pulsations of his release binding her further to him.

CHAPTER THIRTY-ONE

Killean caressed Simone's back as she lay against his chest. Her hair, spread out like a fan around them, tickled his skin as she slept soundly. Her breasts against his flesh were a temptation he gritted his teeth against succumbing to. After their first time, when he'd been unable to stop himself from finding his release inside her before she orgasmed, he'd waited a bit before taking her again and making sure she came before him.

Turning his head, he gazed at the light filtering around the edge of the drapes. It would still be some time before the sunset, but he would have to feed soon. Simone's blood and the mate bond helped calm his incessant need for death, but he'd unleashed the demon when he started killing humans, and it wouldn't be completely caged again.

Before, the idea of spending the rest of his life battling the beast would have been daunting, but with Simone at his side, it didn't seem like such an impossible task. It was one he could and would conquer.

Simone whimpered and nestled closer. Her fingers twitched

on his chest before she settled down again. When she woke, would she regret what they'd done?

The demon within him reared its ugly head at the possibility, but nothing could undo what was done. He was a bastard for taking her and completing the bond, but he'd give her the best life he could. He would keep her safe, and he wouldn't let the worst of himself taint her.

Simone stirred again as boots sounded on the walkway outside. Killean's fangs lengthened, but the boots passed by and went to the room next door. He heard a knock before a murmur of voices.

"Killean?" Simone whispered.

"Hmm?" he asked as he turned his attention back to her.

"Are we going to get out of this?"

"I *will* get you to safety," he vowed.

"And then what will we do?"

"I have no idea," he admitted. "I don't think Ronan will take me back, and I don't blame him if he doesn't. I'm a killer; he shouldn't trust me." *I don't trust me.*

"I trust you," Simone said.

He smiled as he kissed the top of her head. "That's because you might be crazier than me."

Simone chuckled. "Not likely."

"I own some properties we can retreat to if it becomes necessary, but I don't want to back away from the war with the Savages."

Simone had known she was binding herself to a warrior when she gave herself to him, but she hated the idea of him out there, fighting Savages while he teetered on the edge of becoming one.

"Can you handle fighting that war?" she asked.

Killean wanted to assure her he could handle anything, but she'd fed from him, they were bound to each other, and she would learn the truth if he tried to keep it from her. Besides, he couldn't bring himself to lie to his mate. "I'm not sure, but I have to try."

"I can't lose you."

"You won't," he vowed. "If it becomes too much for me, I will back away, but you will *never* lose me, Simone."

Despite the reassurance of his promise, dread churned in her belly. "Things have changed so much in the past couple of weeks. I never expected my life to take this direction."

"Do you regret what happened between us?" he asked and braced himself for her answer.

"No! I don't even regret being captured and changed. I'm freer now than I've ever been."

"Yet you just sealed your life to mine."

"And I'm still freer," she said. "I was so good at being perfect. I was the best student, the best seamstress, the best cook, and the best future wife there ever was amongst the hunters. I was so obsessed with being this perfect automaton that I never stopped to question if any of it was what *I* wanted for my life."

"And was it?"

"No. Marriage to Nathan, or any other hunter, was a duty I would have carried out to the best of my ability, and I never would have stopped to think about me."

"So, what do you want for your life?"

"Now, once we're free of this mess, I want to explore *our* future together. I want to learn to protect myself and help you against the Savages. I want to avenge my friends and the hunters Joseph has destroyed. I *will* help put a stop to the evil Joseph is trying to spread through the world."

Killean gritted his teeth at the terrifying thought of his mate fighting Savages, but she'd been denied so much in her life that he didn't have the heart to deny her this too. "Fighting a Savage takes a lot of training," he said.

"It's a good thing I'm immortal and have a lot of time then. I *am* going to learn to fight, Killean."

"Yes, you are," he agreed. He hated the idea of Simone battling a Savage, but she would learn how to defend herself better. "But it could be years before you're good enough at it to take on a Savage."

"Then it's a good thing I have plenty of time."

"And some vampires never become capable of doing such a thing; they just don't have the talent."

"I'll be good at it," she stated. "I'm a fast learner, and I'm good at everything I'm determined to learn because I never give up, and I practice until I'm close to perfect at it."

He did not doubt that.

"I won't be the dutiful wife or mate," she said. "I don't have to cook for you, but I'm not sewing for you either."

The definitive way she said it made Killean smile. "I won't ask you to."

"I want more from my life than being your mate and the mother of your children. Though I'm looking forward to both those things; I want to find something for me too."

Killean's hand stilled on her back. He'd spilled in her twice. Their child could be forming inside her now, but while the possibility excited him, it also terrified him. What kind of father could he be while walking the thin line between monster and man? He'd have to make sure he didn't come inside her again until they were free of Joseph and not until Killean knew what he would become.

"And what do you want for you?" he asked.

She lifted her head to smile at him. "I don't know. I haven't found it yet, and the unknowing is so freeing."

She was about to lean down and kiss him when a loud bang from the room next door yanked her back. Killean sat upright and tossed the sheet aside before rising to his feet in a move so fluid she barely saw it.

A muscle throbbed to life in his jaw when he strode toward the wall separating their room from the one next door. Another loud bang sounded, and the landscape picture on the wall beside the door rattled.

Killean caught the coppery tang of blood on the air before the door separating the two rooms burst apart in a shower of wood splinters. Killean blocked one of the shards from burying itself in his eye as a burly man tumbled into the room.

Fisting his hands together, Killean lifted them and hammered them onto the man's back before the man crashed into him. Air exploded out of the man's lungs in a loud grunt before he crumpled to the ground. Putting his hands beneath him, the human tried to rise, but Killean planted his foot on the man's spine and pushed him down before turning his attention to the other room.

A human with a blackening eye poked her head around the shattered remains of the door. The woman's lower lip trembled when she gazed at the man before her eyes slid to Killean.

Rage blistered through Simone at the lascivious look in the woman's gaze when it raked over Killean's nude form and the woman smiled. Keeping the sheet clasped against her chest, Simone glowered at the woman as she rose from the bed. Killean's head turned toward her, and his eyes flared red.

"Get dressed," he commanded.

"*You* get dressed!" Simone retorted as the woman's attention remained on him.

"I can't let this guy up. Get dressed, Simone."

"I'm not leaving you alone with her!"

Her jealous and defiant nature would have amused Killean if he didn't sense something wrong with this situation. "I'll be fine," he said. "Go on."

Simone turned her scowl from him to the woman and back again.

Simone go, he sent the thought into her mind. *Hurry.*

The urgency she sensed in his words pushed aside her anger; she hated leaving him out here with *her,* but something wasn't right. Simone gathered the sheet closer against her, grabbed the bags of clothes, and stalked into the bathroom.

CHAPTER THIRTY-TWO

"What's going on here?" Killean asked the woman. The man tried to rise again, but Killean kept him down.

"It was just a little fight," the woman said.

"The bitch cheated on me!" the man spat. "Her lover just came to the door."

The hair on Killean's nape rose as he recalled the boots clunking down the walk earlier. "And just where is this lover?" he inquired.

"Gone," the man said. "I scared him off!"

Why hadn't he heard that part of this argument? Killean wondered as he tried to see past the woman and into the room, but all he saw was a piece of a bureau. He scented the air, but he didn't detect the rot of a Savage on it. However, his instincts were screaming at him that something was wrong here, and he never ignored his instincts.

The woman's eyes narrowed on the man, and stepping into the doorway, she planted her hands on her hips. "Oh, and you aren't banging that waitress from Tilly's?" she demanded.

"I'm a man; I've got needs."

"And I've got needs too, ones you aren't fulfilling!"

"Slut!"

"Two pump chump!"

The man jerked beneath him again; this time Killean almost let him go. He didn't care if they killed each other, but he couldn't shake a sense of wrongness here, and he might need them.

He glanced at where his jeans lay in a heap on the floor. He didn't care who saw him nude, but running around naked wouldn't keep him off the radar of Joseph's followers. The door to the bathroom opened, and Simone stepped out in a pair of jeans and a gray T-shirt.

"Can you get me my jeans?" he asked her.

"Gladly." She hurried over and snatched them off the floor before handing them to him.

When Killean lifted his foot off the man, he went to rise, but Killean shoved him down again. "I'd stay down if I were you," Killean warned. "I'm not in the mood, and if you don't kill each other, I'll gladly kill you both."

The woman chuckled, but a sliver of dread ran through Simone. Killean was dead serious. He lifted his foot and again the man tried to rise. When Killean shoved him down, his chin and nose bounced off the floor and blood spilled from the split skin of his chin.

"Hey now! Don't hurt him!" the woman cried, and the man grunted.

The woman stepped further into their room as Killean tugged his jeans on and returned his foot to the man's back.

"Simone, come here," he said and extended his hand to her.

She almost balked against the commanding tone of his voice, but the desperation in his eyes froze her. Killean was too wound up for her to fight him on this; he might completely unravel if she did. When she clasped his hand, he pulled her against his side before releasing her.

"You," he said to the woman. "Come here."

Killean sent his power out to trap the woman's mind but her eyes didn't glaze over and she remained defiant.

"I'm not listening to you!" she retorted.

"Shit," he muttered as he looked from Simone to the man at his feet to the sunlight filtering around the edges of the curtain.

"What is it?" Simone whispered.

"Someone already has control of their minds. Most likely it's a Savage who works for Joseph and who hasn't killed enough that the sun affects him and who might not have the stench of rot yet."

"No one has control over my mind," the man said.

"Shut up," Killean hissed as he strained to hear anything beyond the room, but he only detected the hum of tires on the road outside and the song of the birds in the nearby trees.

"Let Waldo up!" the woman cried.

Simone stepped toward the woman when the look Killean sent her promised death. "She's not in control of herself," Simone said.

"I don't give a fuck," Killean grated through his teeth. "She's putting you at risk."

Kneeling, Killean settled his knee in the middle of Waldo's back. "Who sent you in here?"

The man's pudgy face flushed as sweat beaded his brow. "I... I don't know what you're talking about," Waldo stammered. "We were fighting, and I fell into the door. Look, mister, I'm sorry, and if you let me up, we won't bother you again."

Killean sent his power forward and tried to wiggle his way into Waldo's mind, but he came up against a wall of resistance. This couple might be the happiest couple in the world under normal circumstances, but someone had either implanted new memories in their heads or provoked them into this fight.

Rising, he gazed at the covered window before glancing at Simone; he had to get her out of here.

"Killean, what is going on?" Simone asked.

"One of Joseph's cronies sent them in here to drive us out." He'd believed it to be a remote possibility Joseph would find them; he'd been wrong.

Simone's blood ran cold at the mention of Joseph. "How do you know it was one of them and not some other vampire?"

"Because even if Ronan and the others ignored my instructions to stay away, they would have come to us and wouldn't be playing these games. And that's exactly what this is, a game. Joseph's puppet could have sent this couple in here with a straightforward message to leave now, but instead, they created a fight to throw us off and to make me work to discover that their minds were manipulated. They did this with the intent of unnerving us."

And they succeeded, Simone thought as she gazed at the couple.

"We're sorry we interrupted your day," the woman said. "But this is between me and Waldo. Let him up, and we'll leave you be."

Killean ignored her as he took his foot off Waldo's back and delivered a knockout blow to his cheek. Grasping Simone's hand, Killean pulled her toward the broken door.

"No!" the woman moaned. "Why did you do that?"

Killean didn't answer as he stalked toward her. The woman stumbled back as she retreated into her room, and Killean followed with Simone. His gaze darted over the king-sized bed the woman plopped onto before taking in the small bureau and the TV hanging on the wall above it. He didn't detect anyone else in the room; whoever wore the boots must have retreated during the commotion.

"What did you do to Waldo?" the woman practically shrieked at him.

"Where are your car keys?" Killean demanded of her.

Taking their vehicle was the least ideal prospect; whoever was controlling this couple probably knew which car belonged to them, but with his inability to tolerate the sun, Killean didn't have any other choices. He couldn't walk around the parking lot looking for a car to steal, and if he started knocking on the doors of the other rooms in search of someone to control so he could have their keys, whoever was watching them would still know which vehicle they were in when they left.

Besides, taking a different car would only draw more human attention to himself. He didn't want to do what he believed they were being herded into doing, but more Savages would come for them if they remained here.

The Savages didn't want to attack them here where there could be numerous human witnesses, so they were using this couple to try to drive them out. If they stayed though, Joseph would find a way to flush them out, most likely a fire. If Killean and Simone remained, the humans here would become casualties, and the two of them would be trapped. At least on the road, they would have some options.

Like a volcano simmering toward eruption, the tension in him was escalating toward a breaking point. He labored to keep the demon leashed while his body clamored to set it free and let it tear apart anyone who came near Simone. His head buzzed like a swarm of bees filled it, and he found himself teetering on the edge of madness.

"Car keys?" Killean demanded of her again and, to him, his voice sounded as if it were coming through a thick fog.

"I'm not telling you!" the woman spat at him.

Reacting on instinct, Killean clamped his hand over the

woman's mouth and sank his fangs into her throat. Unable to take control of her mind to suppress it, the woman's pain blasted against him at the same time Simone's shock rippled through their bond. The woman's hands pushed feebly against his chest before they froze, and her endless, voiceless scream echoed in his head.

A rush of excitement filled him as her blood slid down his throat. He'd needed to feed before this started, and as her agony battered him, the demon part of him purred like a contented cat as Killean fed it the misery and power it craved.

"Killean," Simone whispered.

She knew the strangeness of this situation had him on edge, but she hadn't expected *this*. However, she should have suspected this breaking point was coming. Not only was he a vampire, but Killean was far more volatile than the other vamps in the Alliance. He wasn't the same as the Savages who imprisoned and tortured her, but he was stuck somewhere in the middle, and that middle made him unpredictable.

"Killean." When Simone rested her hand on his arm, the sound he released reminded her of a wolf guarding its dinner.

Before she could pull away, he twisted his arm and his fingers clutched hers. Everything in her wanted to jerk her hand away and condemn him for this brutal act as pain twisted the woman's features, but she couldn't turn away from him when he needed her. She'd told him she could handle the darkness inside him, and she would.

However, this could *not* be a constant thing. She would not tolerate him killing innocent people, and she'd go mad if she had to continue watching him feed on other women. No matter what he was to her, no matter what he'd done for her, she would not let him destroy others and trample her feelings to satisfy himself.

When the woman's heartbeat slowed, excitement pulsed through Killean; he was *so* close.

"Killean, don't," Simone whispered when she detected the decrease in the woman's pulse. "Stop. She doesn't deserve this."

On the brink of feeling the rush of power that came with the end of life, Killean almost finished the woman, but Simone's growing distress stopped him. She was his mate, and she didn't approve of this.

Retracting his fangs, Killean stepped back from the woman and wiped the blood off his mouth with the back of his arm. The woman's dazed eyes briefly met his before they rolled back in her head and she slumped onto the bed.

Killean watched the steady rise and fall of her chest before turning to Simone. Shame coiled through him when he saw the displeasure in her eyes. He shouldn't have lost control in front of her, but there was nothing he could do to take it back.

"She's going to be okay," Killean assured her.

Simone pursed her mouth as she stared at him. His lips were redder from the blood, vitality emanated from his pores, he was more in control, and the woman would be fine, but she was still angry at him. However, her anger could wait until they were away from this place.

"We have to go," he said.

"Yes," she murmured.

Killean released her hand and walked around the room in search of the car keys. He found the woman's purse in the bottom of the nightstand, pulled it out, and dumped the contents on the bed. He shifted through the tampons, wallet, a bag of white powder that looked like cocaine, and another bag of mushrooms, before finding the car keys and a phone.

"You're going to have to drive until the sun sets," he said to Simone as he held the keys out to her.

"I don't know how to drive. The hunters didn't believe it was necessary for the women to learn."

"They didn't believe it was necessary?" he asked in disbelief.

"Until Kadence, women never left the stronghold. And Kadence only knew how to drive because Nathan couldn't say no to his sister, so he taught her. One day, I'd like to learn how to do it."

Killean lowered the keys. "I'll teach you when this is over."

Simone gave him a half-hearted smile. She admired his optimism, but they had no idea what they faced outside this room.

"I'll be right back," Killean said.

He walked into their room before returning with only a single bag of what remained of their clothes. Digging into the bag, he removed a black, long-sleeved shirt and pulled it on before donning his socks and sneakers. Killean handed her the bag before rolling the woman over and stripping the comforter from the bed.

When he finished, he went into the bathroom and emerged with white towels he wrapped around his hands until only his fingers were exposed. He then draped a towel over his head before sliding the comforter around his shoulders. By the time he was done, he looked more like a mummy than a man and would draw attention, but not as much as the smoking man running across the parking lot would.

"Let's hope they're parked close," Killean said.

Simone's heart ached as she watched him. At one time, he'd walked as freely in the sun as she did, and now all she saw of his skin was his face and fingers. It still wouldn't be enough to keep him protected.

CHAPTER THIRTY-THREE

Smoke wafted from Killean's fingers as he merged the car onto the highway. When they'd had the truck, he avoided the main roads, but now he saw them as his savior. Joseph may be able to monitor them on the highways better than the back roads, but he wouldn't come after them if there were too many witnesses. He would wait until Killean was somewhere remote, so he had to avoid those places if he could.

Killean removed his smoking hand from the wheel and replaced it with his other one. Blisters immediately broke out on his flesh. After only a few minutes on the road, he'd discarded the towels when they nearly caught fire, and now his hands were fully exposed to the UV light.

Some of the other drivers gave him strange looks when they passed, but he ignored them. He may look odd in his shroud, but he would look odder with flames shooting out of his head.

Simone gazed worriedly at Killean as the flesh on his fingers peeled back to reveal his sinew and then the tips of his bones. The set of his jaw and a muscle twitching in the corner of his right eye were the only indications he gave of pain.

"Maybe I can try driving," she offered as he switched hands again.

"Not on the highway," he murmured. "Not for your first time."

Thankfully, he'd discovered sunglasses in the car, but his eyes still stung behind the dark lenses, and he kept blinking against the light. It was a good thing he'd fed on the woman as he weakened every time his body healed the burns it sustained. After a while, his healing ability couldn't keep up with the burns, and his skin stopped completely repairing itself before he had to switch hands again.

He glanced at the GPS in the center of the dash. He'd programmed it to avoid tollbooths; he may be able to change the memories of the collector, but he couldn't alter what was on the cameras monitoring those tolls.

In the rearview mirror, he searched for someone following them, but he hadn't seen any of the same cars since leaving the motel. But whoever had been at the motel wouldn't have to follow them; they could monitor the car's GPS from afar. They needed a new ride, but he couldn't get out of this one until nightfall; he hoped the constant healing wouldn't have him too exhausted to do what was necessary when that time came.

He also hoped the couple they'd left behind would remain undiscovered and tied up until they acquired a new car. They couldn't risk being stopped by the police while driving a stolen car. Unable to change the woman's memories, he'd made a slit in her neck to hide his bite and left it to their booted stalker to do what was necessary to cover their tracks. And if their stalker decided not to do it, the drugs Killean left in plain view would explain whatever tales the couple spun to whoever found them.

Killean switched hands again. "Can you get the phone?"

Simone opened the glove box to pull out the woman's phone. "There are a dozen missed calls," she murmured as she gazed at it. She wasn't familiar with the things, but that's what the words on the screen said.

"I didn't hear it ring. Is it on silent?"

Simone turned it over in her hand before hitting a button that lit up the screen, but it didn't reveal anything. "I... I'm not sure. Maybe."

"The hunters didn't teach you about cell phones either?" he asked.

"They were starting to before I left Nathan's stronghold; I chose not to learn," she admitted.

Killean extended his charred fingers toward her. "Let me see it."

Simone winced at his brutalized skin, but she handed the phone over before she accidentally broke it.

Killean frowned when he saw the missed calls were all from the same number and all within the past hour. For every call, there was a voice mail. Whoever was calling wasn't a contact of the woman's as the phone didn't reveal a name, only a number. He glanced at the road before turning his attention back to the phone as it lit up in his hand with another incoming call. The phone made no noise, but the same number displayed on the screen.

Killean waited for voice mail to pick up and the call to end before scrolling through to listen to the first message. He hit speaker and set the phone in the cup holder as he switched hands.

"Hello, Killean." His grip tightened on the steering wheel, and his charred skin broke apart when Joseph's voice filled the car. "I see you."

The message ended when Joseph hung up. Beside him, Simone's hands gripped her thighs, and her lower lip trembled. She cast him a fearful glance before gazing around the car.

"Hit delete," Killean instructed her.

Simone gulped, found the delete button, and pushed it.

"Now hit the arrow in the middle," Killean said.

When Simone did, Joseph's voice came over the speaker again. "Peek-a-boo."

The sick feeling in her stomach grew as she deleted it before moving onto the next message. "I seeeeee you."

Then the next one. "She sure is a purty one, Killean. I always was a sucker for a beautiful lady myself, but I think there's something more between you, isn't there?"

"I'm going to kill him," Killean muttered.

Simone went through the rest of the taunting messages and deleted the last one before the phone started ringing again. Before Simone could figure out what to do, Killean hit the green button on the screen. The ringing stopped, but he didn't speak.

"Well, hellllllooo," Joseph purred. "I was wondering when you'd answer."

"Joseph," he greeted dryly.

"Killean."

The silence stretched until Simone's fingers became cramped from clenching her legs so fiercely. She glanced between Killean, the phone, and back again. She swore some of the smoke wafting from Killean had nothing to do with the sun and everything to do with the fury he exuded.

"Do you really think you're going to get away from me, Killean?" Joseph asked.

"I already have."

"Ahh, but you haven't gotten far at all. You're only about a hundred miles from where you started. Quite a pathetic escape attempt in all honesty."

Killean didn't respond as he switched lanes to pass a Mac truck. Pressing on the gas, he surged past the truck and over in front of it. Unwilling to risk being pulled over and caught on the camera in a police car, Killean had kept his speed down, but now he wanted to floor it all the way to the state border.

Instead, he eased off the gas as he struggled to rein in the Savage side of him seeking to be freed.

"And where are you going to go?" Joseph inquired. "We both know Ronan won't take you back; you're too far gone. All enshrouded against the sun—"

Killean hung up when Simone gasped. She stared at the screen in horror before her gaze swung to him. "He *is* watching us!"

"He had someone at the motel who saw us leave," Killean said. "And this car has GPS; he's probably tracking our every move."

"What do we do?"

"We wait until night, and then we switch vehicles."

"But if he's tracking this vehicle, won't he know when we stop? And won't he know which vehicle we switch into."

Killean had been hoping she wouldn't think of that; he didn't want her to worry any more than necessary. "It's a possibility."

"Killean..." Her words trailed off when the screen lit up again. Killean hit the red button, and it went black.

"He's going to kill us," she whispered.

"I'm going to keep you safe," he vowed. He didn't tell her they would probably prefer death if Joseph got his hands on them.

The screen lit up again, and Killean hit the decline button. This went on for the next five minutes before the screen lit up with words instead of a number.

"What is that?" she asked.

"Text message," Killean replied. "Read it to me."

Simone lifted the phone from the cup holder. "It says... *It's not Joseph. Answer the phone.*"

She had no idea why, but a chill ran down her spine at the

cryptic words. Unlike Kadence and Nathan, she didn't have any gifts, but her instincts screamed a warning at her now.

"You have to answer when it rings," she said.

The distress in her voice drew Killean's attention. Somehow, he knew the creature in the bunker was the one who sent the message, and so did Simone. The screen lit up to reveal the same number once more. Simone stared at it while the seconds ticked by and the screen continued to glow.

"Please, Killean," she whispered.

He hit the green button.

"Killean."

The unfamiliar, ancient voice made him think of cobwebbed crypts and sandstorms blowing across desert roads. Killean rested a blackened hand briefly on Simone's knee when she started rapidly tapping her foot.

"That would be me," he said.

There was a brief pause before the creature spoke again. "I'm going to make you a one-time offer. I'll let you keep the girl. I'll even let you keep her as she is and not turn her into a Savage if you return to me now."

"And why would you make such an offer?" Killean asked.

"Because it's *you* I want. The girl is a nonentity."

Simone's back straightened as resentment boiled within her. She'd lived most of her life as a *nonentity*, and she refused to be considered one by this *thing*.

"I'd prefer not to kill you, but I will," the creature continued.

"And what would Joseph prefer?" he asked.

"Whatever I say he does."

So this thing *was* the brain behind Joseph's operation, but what was that brain plotting? Killean pulled his hands off the wheel and propped his knee against the bottom to steer for a little bit.

"And what do you want me for?" Killean inquired.

"You can bring Ronan to my side."

Killean almost laughed at the notion this thing believed *that* could be a possibility. However, he suspected laughing might bring the full wrath of this creature down on them. It may prefer him alive, but it would also splatter him like a bug on a windshield, and it knew where they were.

"I see," Killean murmured.

"And if you can't bring him to my side, then you've at least been with him for a while, and I suspect you know more of his weaknesses than Joseph does."

Killean opened his mouth to tell it Ronan had no weaknesses, but he wouldn't reveal anything about Ronan to this creature. Besides, it would have been a lie, and he suspected this creature already knew that Ronan had one very *big* weakness in the form of his mate.

Killean glanced at Simone as she glared at the phone. He had one huge weakness now too.

"Plus," the creature said, "you're an extremely powerful vampire, Killean. I sensed it when we passed in the hall. If the girl is your mate, then you'll be even more powerful, and I like power. You can keep the girl, as she is if you come to me before tonight."

Killean stared at the road as he contemplated a response that wouldn't get them killed in the next hour. "And where would I go to find you?"

Simone shot him a look.

"I'll call back with a location; answer when I do."

The phone went dead, and only the hum of the tires punctuated the silence.

"I'd rather be dead than have either of us under that *thing's* control," Simone finally said.

Killean winced at the mention of her death, but he wasn't sure how to prevent it from happening. They were under a microscope right now. If he turned himself in, he would be handing himself over to become a monster, but they would keep Simone alive if only because they could use her to control him. To have her under the control of such a thing was unthinkable, but even more unthinkable was her death.

"Killean," she said when he didn't reply. She knew he didn't want to be a puppet against Ronan, but he would do what he believed necessary to keep her alive. "I mean it, Killean."

He shifted his knee and reclaimed the wheel with one of his barely healed hands. Even with the woman's blood so fresh in him, he was weakening fast. When that thing came after them later, and it would, he wouldn't be able to put up much of a fight against it.

"If you turn yourself over because of me, I'll never forgive you, and I'll blame myself," she said. "Besides, it won't let me stay as I am, and we both know it."

She was right. If he turned himself over, they would be allowed to live, but the vampires they were now would cease to exist. Though he would lay down his life for her, he couldn't let them destroy her in such a way.

"Killean," she said when he lifted the phone and punched in another number.

"I'm not calling them," he assured her.

"Speak," Saxon said after the third ring.

"It's me, and we've got a problem." Killean proceeded to fill him in on everything that had happened since they last spoke.

"Shit," Saxon muttered when Killean finished. "Do you know the license plate number of that car?"

"Can you look in the glove box for the registration?" he asked Simone.

When she stared at him in confusion, he inwardly cursed the hunters for making her so vulnerable and asked her to pull the papers out. He spotted the registration as she sorted through everything. He had her hold it so he could read the plate number to Saxon.

"Maybe Declan can do something with it," Saxon said. "Call you back at this number?"

"Yeah, and if you don't hear from me again, it's because we're dead."

Killean hung up before Saxon could reply and leaned back in his seat. The sun was sinking behind the horizon and his skin was burning at a slower rate, but this knowledge didn't ease the turmoil churning within him.

Simone rested her hand on his knee and squeezed it.

CHAPTER THIRTY-FOUR

When Saxon's number appeared on the screen again, Killean answered the phone. "Saxon," he greeted.

"Sorry to disappoint, but this is your friendly, vampire, computer guru," Declan said. "And like Mighty Mouse, I'm here to save the day."

Killean almost rolled his eyes, but he was glad to hear Declan's jovial tone no matter how out of place it was. "And how do you plan to do that?"

"With a few strokes of my magic fingers."

"I see," Killean murmured.

"And I see that in two miles you'll be coming up on exit thirteen," Declan replied.

Killean glanced at the GPS screen. "Yes."

"You're going to stay on the highway when you get to that exit, but your GPS is going to show you taking it and following a new route along some back roads. In other words, your navigation system will be useless to you soon. I'm going to keep rerouting the car's GPS through different back roads, so stay to the highway as much as possible. We can't have your route accidentally intersecting with the GPS. When we hang up, throw out the phone, and you'll be off their radar for a little while. They'll eventually figure it out, but hopefully, you'll have a new car by then. Good luck."

Declan hung up before Killean could reply. Snatching up the phone, Killean rolled down his window and waited until they were almost to exit thirteen before heaving it out. In the side mirror, he watched it shatter and spin across the highway.

They should have at least an hour before Joseph and that thing figured out something was off; they might have even more time, but he was only going to give himself an hour to come up with a new plan.

Killean searched for cameras monitoring the parking area and the brick building in the center as he drove around the perimeter of the lot, but the only cameras he saw were focused on the building. He had no intention of going anywhere near it.

Driving around to the back of the lot, he took the road marked for trucks instead of cars. Turning off his headlights, he maneuvered through the dozen or so large trucks parked in the lot. Some still had their running lights on, but others were completely dark.

"What now?" Simone asked.

"Now, we catch a ride."

He parked between two of the idling trucks and turned off the car. When he flexed his knuckles, the fresh skin on the back of them broke open, but no blood spilled free, and the blisters were healed. He removed the blanket from his shoulders and tossed it into the back seat. By now, Joseph and that thing probably had Savages scouring the highway and video feeds for this car, but hopefully, they would be far from here before they were detected.

Opening his door, Killean climbed out. The chilly night air soothed his burnt skin as it flowed over him. He watched the back of the brick building, which was five hundred feet away, while he walked around to Simone's side of the car. A few people lounged outside of the bathrooms, but most scurried back and forth to their cars. None of them looked at all suspicious, and he didn't smell a Savage on the air.

Killean opened Simone's door and took her hand to help her out. She stretched her back while she gazed at the building. When he squeezed her hand, he drew her gaze and nodded to one of the idling trucks before leading her over to it. Climbing onto the step of the truck, he released her hand and banged on the window.

From within, he heard the drone of voices from a TV or radio, but no movement. He banged more loudly on the window and was rewarded with a muffled curse. The cab of the truck shifted when someone stirred inside.

A minute later, a craggy face appeared in the window and then the door was shoved open. If he'd been human, Killean would have been knocked on his ass by the door, but he was quick enough to avoid it as he hopped onto the pavement.

"What do you want?" the woman who opened the door demanded.

Not at all what he'd expected, Killean gazed up at the petite black woman who glowered at him from eyes the color of a doe's. Gray hair created a curly cloud around her wrinkled face. Though her hair was gray, her skin was remarkably unaged except for the frown lines marring her forehead. She wore a baggy T-shirt and a pair of sweatpants that looked more like pajamas.

"We need a ride." Killean ignored the gun in her hand as he sent his power forward.

"And I'm supposed to care?"

"You're going to give us one," he commanded as he took control of her mind.

For a second, she rebelled against the command, and then her eyes glazed over and her face grew slack.

"Let us in," he said.

The woman shifted back, and Killean helped Simone climb inside. Simone slipped into the sleeping area with a single twin mattress and a tiny TV playing an old sitcom at the back of the cab. A half-eaten sub and a bag of chips sat beside the TV.

The woman remained kneeling on the driver's seat as Killean climbed into the truck. He slipped into the back with Simone before crawling out again to sit in the passenger seat. He studied the shifter and the numerous buttons on the dash before focusing on the woman.

"Close the door," he commanded. "And sit down."

She shut the door and settled behind the wheel where she sat with her hands in her lap and a blank expression on her face. As much as he disliked humans, he didn't enjoy the emptiness that came over them while they were under the control of a vampire.

"You're going to take us to the Mass border," he said.

He didn't know where they'd go from there, but he would figure that out when they arrived. Until then, they had a driver and the perfect cover from any cameras or tolls in this truck. He didn't expect it to last as eventually the Savages would discover the car and realize what he'd done, but they'd make it to Massachusetts first.

CHAPTER THIRTY-FIVE

Less than an hour after crossing into Massachusetts, Killean ordered the woman to pull over on the side of the highway where he was sure there were no cameras. If the Savages discovered which truck they'd taken, he didn't want them to learn where they rode the truck to, but then he wasn't entirely sure of their destination.

He had no idea where Ronan and the others were anymore, but he had to find a safe location for Simone. Even if the Defenders didn't take him back, they would take her, and he would get her to them.

Climbing out of the truck, he clasped Simone's hand and helped her down. He instructed the woman to forget everything that happened and return to what she was supposed to be doing before closing the door and leading Simone into the woods.

He'd instructed the woman to let them off near an exit with signs for food and lodging and bordering on the edge of a forest. They made their way through the woods and into what turned out to be a busy town with cars idling at stoplights and neon signs broadcasting everything a traveler or local could want.

Killean avoided anywhere cameras might be located on traffic lights or buildings as the predawn travelers drove down the road.

"Where are we going?" Simone inquired and stifled a yawn.

"We'll find somewhere to stay before sunrise and figure out our next move."

He led her to the closest motel and used his mind control to procure a room at the back of the building.

"Are there cameras here?" he asked the clerk.

"Two out front and two in the back," the man replied.

"Closed circuit or do they feed into somewhere?"

"Closed circuit."

"Let me see the video."

The clerk led him to the recording equipment. Killean removed the tape and destroyed it before shutting off the TV and turning off the cameras. When he finished, Killean took the key card from the clerk. He led Simone out of the office, down the walkway, and around the corner to their room where he opened the door to reveal a dingy room with tan walls, brown carpeting, and a king-sized bed.

Simone couldn't stop her nose from wrinkling at the hideous, flower-patterned comforter on the bed. She'd never seen anything so ugly as that blanket or so wondrous as the bed beneath it. The events of this day had left her drained; she wanted to crawl onto the bed, place her head on those pillows, and sleep for a week.

But the Savages might be coming for them.

"Could they track us here?" she whispered.

Killean wished he could assure her they were safe here, but he couldn't. He didn't know how Joseph located them in the truck, the motel had probably been easier, but Killean still hadn't been expecting them. He couldn't shake the notion Joseph and that other bastard were toying with them and following their every move. They were the mice trapped between the paws of the cat, and it was only a matter of time before the cat delivered its killing blow.

"I'm not sure," he admitted. "But I think we've lost them."

Simone slumped onto the bed and dropped her head into her hands.

"The Alliance will take you back," he said.

It took a few seconds for his words to sink in. When they did, she lifted her head to stare at him. "And what about you?" she demanded.

"I might not be welcome there."

"I'm not going back without you."

"Simone—"

"No, we're bound together. I was well aware of what a life with you might entail when I allowed it to happen. Besides, we can't be separated."

"We can," he said. "It won't be easy on either of us, but we can live separately and see each other when we can."

She forgot her exhaustion when anger rolled through her. "And you would be okay with only seeing me when you can?"

"I didn't say I'd be okay with it, but I'll do whatever's necessary to keep you safe."

The reasonable tone of his voice only infuriated her more. "And you know what would be best for me?"

"On this, yes."

That was it! All her years of proper behavior vanished as a haze of red shrouded her eyes. Her fingernails bit into her palm until they pierced her flesh as she rose to stand before him.

"Everyone in my life has always believed they knew what was best for me, and they've all been wrong." The calm tone of her voice amazed her, considering she wanted to claw his eyes out. "And you're wrong too."

Fury radiated from her like a beacon from a lighthouse.

Killean hadn't expected her to be capable of exhibiting so much of it, but his little hunter was full of surprises.

"When it comes to keeping you safe, I will do whatever is necessary," he said.

"All while you remain somewhere unsafe?"

"I'll minimize my risk of death."

"You'll minimize your risk of death," she murmured in disbelief. "You are such a... a... moron!"

Killean couldn't stop himself from smiling. "We really have to teach you to swear."

That was it! The red shading her eyes became so sharp she could barely see him as the blood rushing through her veins thundered in her temples.

"I will not be locked away again!" The calm tone of her voice vanished, and she sounded like the shrew who needed taming, but she didn't care. "I am not a dolly! I am not the perfect, little obedient woman I was born and raised to be! I won't be that woman for the hunters, and I certainly won't be it for you!"

"I'm not asking you to be."

There was that reasonable tone again. She didn't think he had any idea how maddening it was, or he'd be guarding the privates she was contemplating kicking into his throat.

"No, you're asking me to be caged again, and it won't happen," she said.

"Being caged is better than being dead."

"Is it?"

Killean started to tell her of course it was, but the words died on his tongue. Was it?

"You wouldn't be caged with Ronan and the others," he said instead.

"I'm not going back without you, and even with you, I won't be what I once was. I'm in this fight now, a part of it, and I'm going to stay that way."

"You don't know how to fight!" he snapped as his composure started to unravel. The most important thing to him was keeping her safe, and she was making it more difficult than it had to be.

"And that will be remedied as will my lack of driving skills. It's *my* life to live, and you have no say over it."

"I am your mate; I *will* keep you safe," he grated through his teeth.

"You are my *partner,* and you will share in my life, not control it. Also, there will be no more feeding on other women in front of me, and you can't hurt people like you did with that woman! I don't like it, and I won't tolerate it."

Killean blinked at her. "You're laying down rules for *me* to follow?"

"Yes."

He didn't know how to respond. What happened to the meek little hunter he first encountered on the beach? He hadn't liked that woman, far preferred the feistier one she'd become, but this was absurd.

"Then you will also follow *my* rules," he said.

"If I agree with a rule you set forth, I will follow it, but I will *not* blindly follow anything anymore."

"Then I will continue to feed on women."

"Not in front of me! There's no reason for it."

He opened his mouth to protest; no one had *ever* told him what he could and couldn't do, not even Ronan, but the words died as Killean recalled the look on her face after he fed on the woman from housekeeping. Simone hadn't been his mate then, but she'd radiated a fury he hadn't expected from her.

She was his mate when he fed on that woman earlier, and he recalled her displeasure with him afterward. He hadn't liked watching her bite Andre, and that had been an attack. If the roles were reversed and he had to stand by and watch her feeding on a man, he would shred the man in a fit of jealousy. He felt like the moron she'd accused him of being for not seeing earlier that such a thing bothered her. He was over four hundred years old, and he was clueless about so many things, especially women.

"I'm sorry. I never meant to upset you. I didn't think when I fed on that woman earlier; it was an impulse I couldn't control, and I'm not used to being out of control." He despised admitting this, but Simone already knew exactly how close to unraveling he was. "It won't happen again unless it's necessary to protect you."

"I understand what you are, Killean. Understand you're stuck somewhere in the middle of being what you once were and this new creature who's not entirely Savage but certainly isn't merciful."

"Make no mistake, Simone, I was never merciful."

"Maybe not," she said. "But you were never purposely cruel to those you fed on either."

"I am now. It is something I try to keep suppressed, but sometimes it slips free like it did with that woman earlier. You would be better off with Ronan and the others."

"I'm better off with you, and that's final."

Physically stronger, he could force her back to Ronan's, but what good would it do him? She'd hate him if he did, and being bound to a mate who despised him for the rest of their lives sounded like the worst kind of fate. "Simone—"

"This is not a negotiation, Killean. I accept everything about you, and we will *not* be separated."

Before he could reply, she stomped past him and into the bathroom where she slammed the door behind her. Never in her life had she slammed a door, but it felt good. Simone found herself smiling as she stepped in front of the mirror to wash her face and regain some of her composure.

When she emerged, Killean sat on the edge of the bed looking a little shell-shocked. She would have felt sorry for him if she wasn't still annoyed with him. It must be difficult for a vamp of Killean's age to adapt to anything new, and Killean had given up the existence he'd known for centuries with Ronan, become someone he wasn't quite sure of, and acquired a mate all within a week's time.

He'd also expected her to be more of a pushover, but then, so had she.

Lifting his head, his golden eyes locked on hers as he held his hand out to her. "Come here."

Simone hesitated; she longed to take his hand, but she didn't want him thinking she was giving into him.

"We'll stay together," he said. "For as long as we can, but there might come a time when you *have* to go somewhere safer, and you'll go because if something happens to you, Simone..."

His voice trailed off as the possibility of losing her threatened to choke him. He'd never wanted a mate, and certainly not one who was a hunter, but now that he had her, he would do anything to keep her, even if it meant she ended up hating him at some point. For now, he could give her the assurance they wouldn't be separated.

Some of Simone's resistance melted, and she took his hand; he pulled her forward until she stood between his legs. Taking her other hand, he clasped them both behind her back and smiled at her. The last of her irritation melted when that breathtaking smile lit his eyes.

"To tell the truth, I'm glad you don't like me feeding on other women," he said.

Simone was uncertain how to take that when his eyes were gleaming mischievously. "Why?"

He kept her wrists clasped behind her with one hand while he rested his palm on her hip and gave her a small shake. "Because it means I make you as crazy as you make me."

Simone grinned at him and tugged one hand free to brush back a strand of dark brown hair falling across his forehead. Her fingers lingered on his temple before sliding down to trace his scar. He stiffened a little but didn't knock her hand away, and though the smile slid from his lips, his eyes still twinkled.

"You drive me insane," she told him.

"You have to be a little insane to be with me," he murmured as he clasped his thighs against her sides and his hand rested on her ass.

"I agree. I was perfectly poised, well-mannered, and rational before you, but you make me throw out all my training in an instant."

"I like you ill-mannered and ill-tempered," he teased.

"You're incorrigible." Simone's fingers stilled on his cheek when his smile returned.

"Come now, dear hunter, you know I much prefer you wild and improper; I think you prefer yourself that way too."

"I do," she admitted to him, and to herself. "I really do."

Releasing her wrists, Killean rose in one fluid motion to stand before her. Simone would have taken a step back from the abrupt movement, but his hand cupping her butt kept her from doing so.

Lowering his mouth, his lips brushed hers as he spoke. "I think it's time to unleash some of your wildness now."

CHAPTER THIRTY-SIX

He spun her around and, catching her, drew her against his chest. Simone didn't have time to react before his hand slid around her waist and locked her in place. His lips nuzzled her ear as his other hand skimmed her breasts. Her legs went weak when he cupped one breast while he nipped at her ear.

She had no idea how he could make her go from wanting to choke him to wanting to shred his clothes from him so fast. He really had made her a little insane, but she relished the insanity as she never felt more alive than when she was in his arms.

Releasing her breast, his hand ran down the front of her shirt before slipping between her legs. He cupped her there before rubbing his fingers and palm against her in a way that had her hips finding the rhythm of his touch.

Killean nipped at her ear again before running his tongue over the outer edge of it. Grasping the button of her jeans, he tugged them open before pushing the zipper down. He dipped his hand inside her underwear and groaned when it slid through her wet curls. His mate was the most enticing woman he'd ever encountered; Simone had yet to learn how irresistible she was, but she would, and he'd be in deep shit when she did.

He couldn't wait.

Simone gasped when the tip of Killean's finger entered her. The heady evidence of his arousal pressed against her back as his fangs skimmed her neck. Reaching over her shoulder, she clasped the back of his head and guided it to her throat.

Simone cried out when he bit her; she gripped his wrist and rode his hand as she neared release. Then his hand was retreating, and she was left aching for more as his fangs retracted from her throat.

"Not yet, my sweet," he murmured.

Before she could voice her disappointment, he propelled her across the room to face the wall. Killean grasped her hands and placed them on the wall.

"Keep your hands right here," he commanded before tugging her jeans and underwear down her toned thighs and over her shapely calves. He lifted one foot to slide off one side before removing her pants.

Kneeling behind her, he ran his hands over her calves and smiled when she shivered in response. He massaged his way further up her legs, spreading them apart as he worked over her thighs and between them. Her legs nearly gave out when he gave her sex a long, slow lick before cupping her ass and slipping his hands inside her shirt.

"Lift your arms," he said.

Simone removed her hands from the wall and lifted them so he could pull the shirt over her head. He released her shirt before unhooking her bra and tossing it aside. His erection throbbed as his gaze ran hungrily over her shapely backside. She was exquisite.

Simone turned her head to watch as he simply stood and

stared at her. She was completely exposed to him, yet instead of feeling weak, she felt cherished.

"You're beautiful," he murmured.

When she began to turn toward him, he gripped her hips to keep her facing the wall.

"Don't move," he said.

Curiosity over what he intended gripped her, and she discovered she didn't mind obeying this command as he released her to shed his clothes. She hadn't known it was possible to undress so fast, but he was naked behind her before she could do more than blink.

A smile curved her mouth when he stepped closer. "What's so funny, minx?" he inquired.

"I didn't know anyone could strip so fast."

His chest brushed her back as he settled one hand on her hip and gripped his shaft with the other. "That's only the first of many things you're going to learn is quite possible when it comes to the two of us."

He slid his cock between her thighs and teased her entrance with its head.

"I look forward to them all," Simone said when he slid partially inside her before burying himself to the hilt.

Instead of beginning to thrust and putting them both out of their misery, he remained still within her. Their breathing fell into a matching rhythm as Killean clasped her hands and lifted them to place them on the wall with his fingers entwined in hers. Unable to stand this torment any longer, Simone pushed her hips back.

His warm breath tickled her ear when he spoke. "Don't move."

"Killean!" she protested, but it died when he pulled one of her hands from the wall and brought it to his mouth.

Sucking her finger into his mouth, he ran his tongue over it.

When her head fell back to rest on his shoulder and her hips pushed back, he nipped her finger and growled a warning. He pulled her finger from his mouth and planted her palm on the wall.

"Don't move again, Simone, or I'll leave you aching all night."

She tried to protest his words, but it came out as a whimper. He leaned slightly back, and his tongue left a trail of heated kisses across her shoulder. Moving her hair aside, he kissed her nape before cupping her ass in his palms.

Simone panted for air as everywhere he touched became electrified until her entire body felt like a live wire. Her head fell forward until her forehead rested against the wall. It took all she had not to shove demandingly against him and plead with him to end her torment, but she didn't want it to end. She was caught in a purgatory between pleasure and pain; one she enthusiastically embraced as his hands explored her backside before slipping around to her front.

Killean was torturing himself as much as her, but the more he explored her, the more he enjoyed prolonging their release. He caressed her nipples before sinking his fangs into her shoulder. She moaned in response as the muscles of her sheath clenched around his shaft.

Releasing her breasts, he skimmed his knuckles down her flat stomach and over the curve of her hip before sliding a hand between her legs. Simone wiggled against him when he stroked her clit.

"Don't move," he whispered.

"Killean." She was unable to hold back a protest.

"Don't. Move."

Blood trickled from the punctures she put in her bottom lip when she bit it. So lost to his torment, she hadn't realized her fangs had extended.

The scent of her blood on the air tantalized his nostrils; he clasped her chin and turned her head toward him. When the white-blue color of her eyes met his, something more than the emotions of lust and possessiveness tore through him. This beautiful woman had willfully bound her life to his, and in doing so, she'd made his lonely and tormented existence fade away as if it never existed.

Leaning forward, he licked away the drops of her blood before claiming her mouth in a kiss. Her legs wobbled, and for a second, he thought she would collapse as he pulled his shaft out of her before sliding in again.

Simone's fangs latched onto his lip, and she clasped the back of his head as she instinctively found the pace of his tongue and body. Something within her came undone as she drank deeper from him. She wanted more—no, she *needed* more.

But what more did she need?

Then, Killean grasped her hands and returned them to the wall. When his movements became harder and more demanding, she eagerly met each of them. He was far more forceful with her than he'd been before, but she yearned for this complete loss of control.

Then he was pulling away from her, and before Simone could respond, spinning her around. He gripped her hips and lifted her. Simone wrapped her legs around his waist as he sank himself inside her and clasped her wrists against the wall.

She gazed into the fiery color of his eyes while he remained unmoving inside her. The power he exuded crackled against her skin. He could snap her as easily as she could break a toothpick, but she felt no fear of this formidable man who battled to keep himself restrained from attacking others. He could be a threat to so many, but never to her.

Killean savored the beauty of her swollen lips, flushed face, and heaving breasts. The proper hunter he first encountered was gone, and in her place was a vampire who craved her mate.

Killean held her eyes as he slowly began to thrust into her again.

Simone watched his muscles flexing against her while he moved with fluid grace. His body fascinated her; *he* fascinated her, and she wanted to experience more of him. She jerked against his restraining hold on her wrists.

"Let me touch you," she said, and Killean released her.

Her hands settled on his shoulders before sliding down the front of his chest. She grazed her nails over his flesh as his eyes burned into hers.

"Harder," he commanded.

For a second, she didn't understand, but then he grasped her hand and scraped her nails down his chest. Her nails left reddened streaks on his flesh.

"Harder, Simone."

She hated the idea of harming him, but something inside her couldn't resist the hoarseness of his voice or the excitement she sensed building within him. She scratched him again, but not enough to draw blood.

Killean shuddered as pain and ecstasy mingled together until the Savage part of him was slowly relaxing. Apparently, it didn't matter to the demon who felt the pain as long as it experienced some.

"Harder," he commanded. He expected her to balk, but Simone licked her lips and obeyed him.

This time, her nails drew blood, and Killean released a sound of bliss that made her half crazed. Then she realized what she'd done to *Killean.* She had only a second to be disturbed about it before he clasped the back of her head and drew her mouth to the ruby rivulets trailing down his chest.

"Yes," he groaned when she licked the blood away before sinking her fangs into him.

Killean thrust harder into her as he felt himself spiraling out of control. Her pulse quickened as her muscles gripped his cock tighter, and through their bond, her need for release battered him like a hurricane battered the shore. Sinking his fangs into her throat, he plunged into her once more and was unable to stop himself from coming when the intensity of her orgasm tore his release from him.

CHAPTER THIRTY-SEVEN

Killean lay in bed, staring at the ceiling as Simone slept soundly beside him. So exhausted by what they'd exchanged, she hadn't stirred in hours, but he didn't dare sleep; not while they were still vulnerable.

He inhaled the mingling scents of sex and blood on the air as he tried to sort through his tumultuous thoughts. What they'd exchanged earlier was something he'd never experienced before. He'd never gotten off on pain before; he was not one of the purebreds who sought it out after fully maturing. He'd always preferred blood and death.

But now, this new, twisted creature he'd become sought to experience the suffering of others, but also thrived on it being inflicted on him too. And though there had been some hesitation in the beginning, Simone had grown more comfortable giving him what he asked for when he took her again.

Would she regret what they'd done when she woke? Would his need get worse as time progressed or would it ease if he refrained from killing humans? And if it did worsen, would Simone eventually balk and run screaming from him when his demands went from drawing his blood to something more extreme?

She'd yet to back away from anything thrown at her, but he couldn't expect her to keep following him down this rabbit hole of increasing depravity.

Resting his hand on her hip, he gazed at her beautiful face, slack in sleep and so innocent. She was more a tigress than the timid kitten he initially believed her to be. Her proper demeanor had hidden a passionate woman who would have remained hidden if she'd continued her sheltered existence inside the hunter stronghold. Now that it was unleashed, she was more than willing to embrace it and explore it further.

Her openness was one of the things he loved about her.

The realization startled him as he stared at the woman in his arms. A woman he'd initially despised because of the circumstances of her birth. And now he wouldn't trade her for anyone or anything; hunter or not, she was the best thing that ever happened to him.

He'd spent the years since the death of his family wondering why he survived when they died. They'd all been better than him. Animals followed his sister Betty around like she was the Pied Piper. She'd possessed an affinity with all things four-legged, and the only time she wasn't holding something furry was when she was sleeping.

His other sister was the most loving vampire he'd ever encountered and would run across fields to hug someone. He'd never met anyone who possessed the amount of compassion she had. His brother had been so strong, and someone Killean followed like a puppy as he tried to emulate everything his brother did. And his parents, so in love with each other and so happy. The rare times they raised their voices at one of them was when they'd done something wrong, but their patience was something Killean never possessed.

But, after all these years, he realized why he survived—for her. The events of that night forged him into the man he was—one capable of doing whatever was necessary to save and protect her. Killean would never again question why he wasn't dead too or wish that he'd died with them; he finally had a reason for living other than death.

He *would* be the man she deserved.

He ran his finger briefly over her lower lip before kissing her, releasing her, and rolling carefully away. Setting his feet on the ground, he stared at the sun poking around the edges of the tan drapes covering the window.

After burning and healing so many times yesterday, he needed to feed again. Because he was her primary source of nourishment, Simone's blood wasn't enough to ease his hunger.

Scowling at the sun, he rose and padded naked over to the window. Pulling back a sliver of the curtain, he avoided the sun's rays as he peered out at the town. Cars packed the busy streets, while people strolled the sidewalks. There was an endless supply of food out there, but it did him little good in the daytime.

He could call the office to order dinner again, but if a woman arrived, he couldn't feed on her. Releasing the curtain, he stepped away from the window and glanced at Simone before walking into the bathroom. He turned on the light and slipped inside.

He left the door cracked open to hear any noise as he turned on the shower and stepped beneath the spray of water. When he finished, he toweled off, redressed, and returned to the bedroom. Simone remained sleeping while he paced from one side of the room to the other while his hunger grew with every passing second.

~

Simone woke and stretched her hand for Killean, but she knew he was gone before her hand fell on the cold spot beside her on the bed. The sound of running water drifted to her, and when she turned, she saw the bathroom door cracked open, but she didn't see Killean.

Killean. She smiled as she rolled back to gaze at the covered window. Her body felt sated and well used in the most pleasant of ways. She'd never imagined things could be like this between a woman and a man or that she would enjoy being with a man so much.

She recalled the blood she spilled sliding down his tantalizing skin and the sounds of ecstasy he emitted as he demanded more and more from her. Realizing he not only craved her body and blood, but also something more twisted from her would have made the well-bred hunter she'd been run screaming.

The vampire she'd become thrived on every second of it.

She had no idea what that said about her, but she couldn't deny Killean wasn't the only one who had some darkness within them. Maybe hers had always been there, buried beneath the years of striving to be perfect. Maybe the torture she'd endured at the hands of Joseph unleashed it, or perhaps Killean unleashed it, but it was there.

And if she really contemplated it, she suspected it was always there. She'd never chafed against her role in the hunter society like Kadence, but a tiny part of her had longed for more than the position she was allotted. She'd successfully buried that small rebellious part years ago, but now it was spreading its wings.

She frowned when she realized the water was still running but it didn't sound like a shower. Rolling over, she gazed at the bathroom door. All she could see was a sliver of light around the edges, but was that muttering?

Tossing the sheet aside, she rose from the bed and strode over to the bathroom door. "Killean?" she inquired as she rested her hand on the door. "Are you okay?"

Her only response was the running water and mumbled words she couldn't quite make out. Taking a deep breath, Simone pushed the door open and bit back a gasp when she spotted Killean, hunched over the sink while he washed his hands beneath the flow of steaming water. She had no idea how long he'd been doing this, but the water ran red with his blood as it spilled down the drain. She had a flashback to him standing over the sink in the other motel room, doing the same thing.

"The blood," he muttered. "The blood is everywhere."

Simone broke free of the paralysis gripping her as she shoved the door open and rushed to his side. "Stop," she whispered and rested her hand on his forearm.

"There's so much blood; I can't wash it away. It will never go away."

"It's *your* blood, Killean. If you stop, it will go away."

"It will never go away."

When his reddened his eyes met hers, her heart plummeted into her stomach with a sickening lurch. It was as if he didn't see her and was caught in some horror she couldn't begin to contemplate; she had no idea how to free him.

"Killean?" she whispered. She couldn't lose him; she just couldn't.

"It's everywhere," he said though he still didn't seem to see her. "It's on my hands, on my arms, it's inside me; it's stained my soul. It won't stop flowing."

"We can stop it." She turned off the water. She wanted to tell him the blood hadn't stained his soul, but it obviously had. Clasping his cheeks, she forced his dazed eyes to look at her. "Together, we can do anything, Killean."

Releasing him, she removed the hand towel from its hanger next to the sink and carefully wiped away the blood to expose the flesh he'd peeled away to reveal the muscle and bone beneath. Tears burned her eyes when she saw the extent of the damage he'd inflicted on himself, but she blinked them away. When she finished, she used another towel to cover his hands and the blood still oozing from his wounds.

"No more blood," she said as she brushed back a strand of hair curling against the corner of his eye. "Killean?"

She ran her finger down the curve of his cheek and across his scar. His eyes closed, and he turned his cheek into her palm before stepping away.

"I'm fine," he said abruptly.

Self-hatred coiled in his belly when he realized Simone had once again seen him gripped by the strange hallucinations that seemed to be haunting him.

CHAPTER THIRTY-EIGHT

SIMONE GAZED after Killean's back when he stepped around her and left the room. She exited the bathroom as he stopped by the battered TV on its wheeled TV stand. He stared at the carpet like its presence there baffled him.

"Killean, what is going on?" she asked.

His gaze dropped to the towel enveloping his hands. He didn't want to take it off as he wasn't sure what seeing his blood would do to him. His mind spun as he tried to recall what had driven him into the bathroom earlier.

One second, he was pacing the room with his appetite mounting, and the next he'd felt something warm trickling across his hands. When he looked at them, he discovered blood seeping down his arms and spilling onto the carpet, but no blood stained the carpet now.

However, he'd been convinced the blood was there, and it had propelled him into the bathroom to scrub it from his flesh. *None of it was real. It was all another hallucination.*

Killean's lip curled in self-loathing as he tore away the towel. Blood still seeped from some of his self-inflicted wounds, but they were mostly healed. The sight of his blood didn't send him spiraling into madness, but then he hadn't been bleeding when the compulsion to wash the blood away gripped him.

"Killean, *talk* to me."

He set the towel on the TV stand and turned to face Simone. Worry creased her brow and shone from her eyes. Her distress beat at him through their bond. Her apprehension only made his self-hatred grow; the last thing he wanted was to upset her.

He'd vowed to be the man she deserved, and he was already failing. He owed her an explanation, but he didn't know how to explain what was happening to him because *he* didn't know what was happening to him.

"This is the second time I've seen you like this," Simone said.

"I don't know what's going on," he admitted. "It's the second time I've been certain there was blood on my hands I couldn't wash away. It's not there, but when I see it, it feels as real as if it *is* there."

He lifted his hands before him, but all he saw were the wounds he'd inflicted on himself. Lowering his hands, Killean met her gaze. "I'm hallucinating it."

Simone gulped at his admission. He was a vampire on edge and experiencing hallucinations. So much could go wrong with that scenario, and worst of all, it could go wrong with *her* Killean. "Why?"

"Because I've killed innocents. It's unnatural to me, and I'm trying to stop, or at least I think that's why. Many vampires who turn Savage choose it for themselves and embrace it, but the Savages Joseph is creating aren't choosing for themselves and have a harder time with it. Joseph told me some of the hunters fight becoming a Savage so much they sometimes have to starve and set them free a few times before they give in and embrace their new nature.

"We've always assumed the Savages Joseph created remained

Savage because after a while they stopped caring about killing innocents and lost their morality. And maybe, for many that is true, but I'm beginning to think that part of what keeps a vampire a Savage is if they try to stop killing, they're driven nearly mad when they deny their hunger."

And suddenly, the horrible clarity of at least some of what was happening to him hit her. He was going through this because of what he'd done to rescue her. The Savage part of him, the one that craved the pain of others and having it inflicted on himself, didn't care about the blood it had spilled to free her. However, the vampire, the Defender, the *man* was haunted by the lives of the humans he'd taken and desperate to purge the guilt from his body, but he never could.

She had no idea why his anguish over what he'd done only emerged sometimes, and in this way, but it didn't matter. All that mattered was saving him from being trapped in this hideous pit of self-hatred and self-mutilation. He'd saved her, and she would save him too.

"Are they nearly driven mad because they deny their hunger or their urge to kill?" she asked.

"I'm not sure," Killean admitted as he leaned against the wall. "But both times it happened to me, my hunger was almost out of control."

"You were hungry earlier?"

"I still am, though I feel more in control again. I don't know how long that will last. I have to feed more regularly now, and the burning and healing took a lot out of me yesterday."

"Then why didn't you wake me?" she demanded, annoyed he'd denied himself when he didn't have to. "You could have fed on me!"

"No, I couldn't. I've been feeding and supplying you; the two of us exchanging blood isn't enough to nourish us both, especially not me with my increased need for blood."

"Oh." Simone's shoulders slumped as her irritation deflated. "Then we'll find someone else."

Killean nodded toward the window. "Sun's still out, and I did enough crisp frying yesterday to last me a lifetime."

He'd hoped to sound teasing, but her distress didn't ease as she gnawed her bottom lip while staring at the covered window.

"We'll call the office and have them send someone," she said. "Like you did before." She didn't like the idea of setting someone up in such a way, but Killean came first, and he needed this.

"And if it's a woman?"

Simone opened her mouth to respond before realization set in. "You already thought about doing that and discarded the idea because of what I requested of you earlier."

"I rejected the idea because no matter what madness resides in me, I will *not* hurt you."

"No madness resides in you," she whispered.

"Something does, Simone. I'm not the man I once was; we both know it. But what I am now, neither of us knows, and you cannot deny that."

"If you feed on a regular basis, you will hold these hallucinations at bay."

"You're so certain?"

"Yes." And she was sure of it because she had to be. The idea of losing him to something she couldn't stop petrified her, and if she dwelled on the possibility, it would make her insane too. "And if you stop killing, you'll one day be able to walk in the sun again, and you'll beat back this... this..." she fumbled for the right word, "darkness inside you."

Killean tilted his head to study her. "And until then?"

"Until then, I will help you get through this, no matter what it takes, and we will walk in the darkness together."

Simone didn't have a chance to blink before he stood in front of her. Clasping her chin loosely in his fingers, he lifted her face until she was gazing into the stunning, golden pools of his eyes.

"You did not sign up for this insanity when you bound yourself to me," he murmured.

"I signed up for you, Killean, and if you think I was foolish enough to believe it was going to be an easy journey, then you're an idiot. I knew it would be difficult, and I did it anyway. Not only that, but I would do it again."

Killean had never felt so humbled or lost to someone in his life. "No matter what happens, from here on out, you have to know something."

Simone gulped as she braced herself for whatever bombshell he would drop on her next. "What?" she croaked.

"I am fucking in love with you. In all my years, I've never met another woman like you and haven't loved another; I never considered myself capable of it, but you have proven me wrong yet again. You continuously amaze me, and I will love you until the day I die, Simone."

That was the biggest bombshell of all as her muscles turned to jelly. Before she could reply, he kissed her. Tears burned her eyes as her hands encircled his forearms.

He loved her. She'd spent her entire life preparing to be the wife of another, but she never prepared herself for love. She hadn't expected to have a husband who loved her. She'd hoped for it, but it was possible such an emotion would never develop between them.

She had love from her mate though. Even if she was wrong and she lost Killean to this madness, she would forever be grateful to have had him in her life.

"Don't cry," Killean whispered as he wiped the tears from Simone's cheeks. He was aware they weren't tears of sadness as her joy radiated against him, but he still didn't like seeing them.

Simone smiled as she shook her head. "You're a mess, and

we're a mess together, but you've made me happier than I ever dreamed I could be. I love you too."

He smiled at her before kissing her again. Simone was beginning to lose herself to him when she recalled the events that brought them to this place. She pulled reluctantly away from him and clasped his wrists. "You have to feed."

"Simone—"

"We'll call the office, and if it's a woman, *I* will feed on her, and then you can feed on me. Will that be enough to supply you?"

"Yes, but I won't ask you to do that."

"You didn't ask me."

"Simone—"

"I'll call now." She pulled away from him and hurried over to the phone.

She dialed the number for the office and requested more towels. When she hung up, neither of them spoke as they dressed and waited for the knock on the door; it came five minutes later.

"If it's a woman, I'll take control of her mind if you prefer," Killean said. "So you don't have to do it."

"Yeah, okay," Simone muttered. She was nervous enough about the idea of having to feed on someone other than Killean; she couldn't deal with the mind manipulation thing too.

Killean opened the door to reveal a pretty woman in her twenties on the other side. Her eyes widened on him, and the scent of her desire filled the air.

"Come in," he said, and she stepped into the room.

Simone's eyes narrowed on the woman as her eyes followed Killean's every move like a tracker pursuing their prey. Her fangs lengthened, and her hands fisted when the woman glanced dismissively at her before focusing on Killean again.

"I brought your towels," the woman said and handed them out to him with a flirtatious smile.

Bloodlust thrummed through Killean's veins when he took the towels from her and set them on the bed. His gaze fell on the pulse in her throat before darting away. No matter how badly the demon part of his DNA clamored to get at this woman, he would keep it leashed. He turned his attention to Simone as he wrangled his Savage nature into submission. Seeing her helped calm him, but not enough that he was confident he could resist the call of the woman's blood for long.

They had to do this fast.

Turning back to the woman, she jumped when he grasped her chin between his fingers. "You will not move, and you have nothing to fear."

The woman's gaze became increasingly glassy while he spoke until she stood slack-jawed and unmoving before him. Killean released her and stepped away while Simone approached. "You don't have to do this," he said to her.

"I know I don't, but I'm going to."

Apprehension stole through Simone as she gazed at the expressionless woman. She'd fed on Killean, but she had no idea how to go about doing this. *He needs you.*

Settling her hands on the woman's shoulders, she stepped closer. The blood pulsing through the woman's neck caused Simone's mouth to water, but she couldn't bring herself to lean forward and settle her mouth against the woman's throat.

Killean grasped the woman's wrist and lifted it before her. "It may be easier for you to feed on her wrist. You don't have to get as up close and personal."

Simone's gaze fastened on the pale wrist; yes, it was a better option. She didn't touch the woman's hand but instead gripped Killean's wrist as she brought the vein to her mouth. Her eyes met and held his before she bit deep.

The fresh blood filling her mouth was far different than Killean's. It was sweeter but nowhere near as potent, and she felt no emotional response from the woman who did no more than give a tiny flinch when Simone's fangs pierced her flesh. Simone's eyes drifted closed as the blood filled her system.

Killean tore his eyes away from Simone. It was a woman she fed on and he still disliked having anyone, other than *him*, sustaining her. His teeth ground together as he waited for her to finish.

"That's enough," he said after a minute, and Simone released her bite on the woman.

Stepping away, Simone used the back of her hand to wipe the woman's blood from her mouth and watched as Killean gave the woman a set of new memories before practically shoving her out the door. His eyes burned like hot coals when he leaned against the door and stared at her.

"Come here," he said in a hoarse voice.

Simone went eagerly into his arms.

CHAPTER THIRTY-NINE

KILLEAN NAVIGATED the car he stole from a young woman at the hotel down the bumpy dirt road. He'd chosen the vehicle because it was an older Ford without the GPS of the newer cars. Even with instructing the woman not to report it stolen for a couple of days, he didn't want to be inside anything that could be tracked by outside sources.

Overgrown trees crowded the sides of the road; their limbs sounded like skeletal fingers scraping the mirrors, windshield, and roof as he drove beneath them. The forest was so thick along the sides of the road that the headlights barely penetrated more than ten feet in front of them. They'd been on the road for a few miles already with no end in view.

"Where are we going?" Simone asked as she gripped the door handle to keep from bouncing in her seat over the potholes.

"I'm not sure."

Ronan often bought properties to use as emergency retreats and investments. Killean had a few such properties himself, but he'd never been here before. However, he'd gotten the address and directions from Ronan when they spoke earlier.

After another few miles, the road suddenly dead-ended in front of an old brick building that looked as if it had crawled out of the pages of a horror novel. As he gazed at the bars covering the windows—some of which were broken—the arched front door, and the austere, uninviting brick exterior, he suspected this place was once an asylum. To the left of him, an SUV and pickup truck were parked, but he didn't see anyone inside them or walking around the building.

"WHAT IS THIS PLACE?" Simone whispered; something about it gave her chills.

She leaned forward and craned her head to take in all three floors of the structure. The vines climbing up the side of the building were ivy, but though the plant should be green and flourishing this time of year, its thick brown vines were bare of any leaves and peeling off the bricks. The only thing thriving here was the dense underbrush crowding the structure and probably the rats.

When the front door opened, Ronan stepped out and climbed down the three wooden steps that looked as if they'd been newly erected; Nathan followed him. Simone's heart leapt when she spotted Nathan. She'd never been in love with him, she didn't want to return to her past, but he was a familiar, comforting face.

When Kadence elbowed her way past her brother to stand beside Ronan, Simone almost threw her door open and plunged into the night to hug her, but she held herself back. Simone didn't know what they planned for Killean or her, and until she knew they would both be safe, she had to be careful.

She glanced over at Killean when he rested his hand on her knee. "Let's get this over with," he said.

Simone nodded, and Killean turned his attention back to the

group standing at the bottom of the steps. They wouldn't jump him or try to kill him; he may not be one of them anymore, but Ronan would give him the benefit of the doubt until he had no reason to. And then, although he wouldn't like doing it, Ronan would slaughter him if he deemed it necessary.

"Wait for me," Killean said, and opening his door, he stepped into the night.

Declan exited the building behind the others, but Killean didn't see Saxon and Lucien anywhere. He suspected they were in the woods, probably with some hunters, watching to make sure he'd come alone. Killean didn't blame them for their distrust; he would be just as suspicious if one of the other Defenders fell and tried to return.

Killean walked around the car, and opening the door, he held his hand out to Simone. She clasped it and slid from the car to stand beside him with her chin raised and her shoulders back. Nathan and Kadence's eyebrows rose at this sign of defiance.

Simone stepped closer to Killean as he led her toward the others. She studied the four vampires before glancing at the ominous woods. The hair on her nape rose when she felt eyes following her from the thick shadows. How many were out there watching, waiting for some sign to bring down Killean?

She'd kill anyone who tried. The possessive, murderous impulse didn't surprise her. Before being captured, she'd never considered taking the life of another, but now she would do whatever it took to protect him. Her fingers entwined with his as they stopped in front of the others.

"Ronan," Killean greeted.

"Killean."

A tense silence followed their crisp greeting until Simone wanted to scream to break it.

"I'd get a refund on your new cologne if I were you, Killean," Declan said, and everyone shot him a look. "Too soon?" When they all continued to glare at him, Declan shrugged before pulling a lollipop out of his pocket; he unwrapped it and stuck it in his mouth. "Tough crowd tonight."

"Are you okay, Simone?" Kadence asked.

Simone smiled at her. "Yes. I *really* am."

Kadence stared at her before glancing nervously at Killean.

"Did anyone follow you here?" Ronan asked.

"Not that I'm aware of," Killean replied. "I think we successfully lost Joseph and that thing in Vermont."

Ronan's gaze went beyond him to the road. "Then let's discuss this inside."

Inwardly, Simone cringed at the idea of entering the building, but she followed Killean as Declan turned and strolled inside. Ronan, Kadence, and Nathan hung back until they passed and fell into step behind them. Simone glanced back at them; she didn't like having them behind Killean, but Killean never looked back.

It's okay, Killean whispered into her mind and squeezed her hand. *If they wanted me dead, I would be already.*

That didn't overly reassure her, but he was right. Simone turned her attention away from the three behind them as they stepped inside. Her mouth almost dropped when they stepped into the elegant foyer. She glanced behind her to make sure the outside world remained the same and she hadn't stepped through some cupboard leading to a magical world.

The overgrown outside remained the same, but it definitely didn't match the white marble floors and wide stairs leading to the second floor. A flashlight set on the newel with its beam pointed at the ceiling illuminated the polished oak railing of the stairs.

"What is this place?" she asked as she examined the exposed wires dangling from the ceiling.

"It was an asylum," Ronan answered as he clasped Kadence's

hand and pulled her against his side while Nathan closed the door. "Now it's a barely started project of mine. This way," Ronan said and led them into another room.

The room they entered was stripped down to the beams in the walls, and the plywood floor thudded beneath their feet as they walked toward the table and chairs in the middle of the room. Another flashlight sat on the table with its beam pointed toward more wires hanging from the beamed ceiling.

Ronan pulled out a chair for Kadence to sit, and Killean did the same for her. Simone hesitated before sliding onto the chair while the men remained standing.

"Where are Saxon and Lucien?" Killean inquired.

"They'll be here soon," Ronan said.

Killean rested his hands on the back of Simone's chair. He wouldn't sit until Declan did, but Declan had wandered over to gaze out one of the barred windows. From the other room, the front door creaked open, and footsteps thudded across the foyer. Lucien and Saxon glided into the room with two hunters Killean recognized as Logan and Asher.

When she saw them, Simone started to rise, but Killean rested his hands on her shoulders to keep her in place. Her uneasiness rippled across their bond as she eyed the hunters like she might take them out herself. Killean was less than thrilled to be in a room with so many hunters; he may have taken one as his mate, and he understood the necessity of the Alliance, but he still didn't trust them.

Lucien's sandy blond hair stood on end as if he'd been running his hands through it, and his eyes were chips of black ice when they scanned Killean; Killean gazed impassively back at him. Out of all the Defenders, Killean knew Lucien would be the least forgiving; it just wasn't his nature.

Saxon stopped next to Killean and clapped him on the shoulder. His hazel eyes exuded warmth when they met Killean's. "It's good to see you," Saxon said.

"You also," Killean replied.

Saxon strode over to one of the chairs, pulled it out, sat down, and smiled at everyone. He seemed not to notice the tension in the room as he pulled out another chair and kicked it toward Asher.

"Take a load off," Saxon said cheerfully.

Asher glanced at Nathan before perching on the chair as if it were Old Sparky. Killean would have laughed at the hunter's obvious discomfort if hunger wasn't mounting in his veins. He was becoming increasingly worried he might have made a bad choice by bringing Simone here. He should have put her somewhere safe and come alone, but where would have been safe for her? And being apart from her would have made him more volatile.

She wasn't like him; he reminded himself. If they killed him, they would hand her a death sentence too, but if they locked him away, they would keep her safe.

CHAPTER FORTY

Turning away from the window, Declan's boots thumped across the floor as he strode over to the table and sat. Pulling the lollipop from his mouth, he removed the wrapper from his pocket and enclosed the end of it. He set the remains on the table and clasped his hands before him.

"Sit," Ronan said to Lucien.

Lucien shot Killean a suspicious glance, but he settled onto another chair, and Logan sat beside him. Eventually, they all sat.

From across the table, Ronan's reddish-brown eyes were more red than brown when they met Killean's. Ronan's dark brown hair curled at the collar of his shirt as he sat back in his chair. "Tell us everything from the beginning," Ronan said.

Killean had already told them most of it, but he did so again. He suspected Ronan wanted to make sure his story remained the same and to see him as he told it. Killean didn't blame him, but the realization he'd lost Ronan's trust weighed heavily on his shoulders. He would earn it back.

However, he didn't fault anyone for distrusting him when he wasn't sure of himself anymore. Although Simone maintained a resolute trust in him that was both humbling and empowering. He wouldn't break her faith in him no matter how appealing sinking into the pits of blood and death continued to be.

A couple of times, the others interrupted him to ask questions, most of which he didn't know the answers to, but for the most part, they remained silent while he spoke.

"Joseph and his cronies most likely found you the first time in Vermont because even if that guy waited to report his truck stolen, they could have gotten into the camp's database and accessed the vehicle information there. Most camps require the campers to register their vehicles while there," Declan said.

"Wouldn't it have taken them a while to pinpoint the truck?" Saxon asked.

"Not if they have someone as talented as me with computers," Declan replied. "If they don't, once they discovered the camp, they could have taken control of one of the workers and made them get the info. It doesn't sound like there was much else along this river...?"

His voice trailed off as he looked questioningly at Killean. "The camp was the first thing we came across other than woods," Killean answered.

"And one Savage had already found you there, so it was only a matter of time before more of them stumbled across it. They most likely assumed you stole a ride from the camp. Once they had the info about the vehicles registered there, they could search the campsites to discover which ones were missing. Once they discovered the vehicle you took, they locked onto its GPS and, viola, they located you."

No one spoke for a minute, and then Lucien snorted. "I hate technology."

"It's endlessly useful and as endlessly dangerous, it just depends on who's wielding its power," Declan said and wiggled his fingers at Lucien who scowled back at him. Declan's silvery-gray eyes shimmered with amusement, and his auburn hair appeared almost black in the dim light. "Though I'm not sure how they found you in the hotel," Declan said.

"We put some distance between us and the accident scene, but for all I know that was the only hotel in a hundred mile radius of where they found us the first time," Killean said.

"Or someone working for Joseph could have spotted and reported you," Saxon said. "We have no idea how many humans and vampires he has working for him."

"That too," Killean said.

"What about the car you drove here?" Nathan asked. "Will they be able to figure out you stole it and track it?"

"The newest things in that car are its crank windows," Killean replied. "I made sure of it."

"Good," Ronan said.

"How many people did you have to kill for Joseph to accept you?" Lucien inquired with open hostility.

Killean's head turned toward him, and their gazes locked. Under the table, Simone rested her hand on his knee and squeezed it as she glowered at Lucien.

"Ten of the worst humans I could find. They were rapists, child molesters, drug dealers, and so on," Killean said.

"How restrained of you in your role as God," Lucien drawled.

An uneasy silence descended over the room, and then Killean gave Lucien a smile that could have frozen fire. "I'd kill a hundred more of them to set her free again. Perhaps, one day, you'll understand why."

"And have you stopped killing?" Declan asked.

"Yes," Killean said and tore his eyes away from Lucien to focus on Declan.

"And you plan not to murder humans anymore?" Nathan asked.

Killean tried not to feel annoyed as he met the blue eyes of the hunter leader. Not so long ago, the only ones with any right to question him and his actions were the Defenders, but things were different now, and these hunters hadn't slaughtered his family.

Despite his relationship with Simone, he had to remind himself of this. Times were changing, but he still wasn't ready to completely trust these hunters. It would come in time, but old habits died hard.

"I have no intention of killing humans anymore," he answered. "I will continue to kill vampires."

"So you haven't had any problems since you stopped killing?" Logan's pine green eyes were doubtful as he asked this question.

"I didn't say that," Killean replied. "Not killing has been difficult at times."

"But you believe you can keep yourself under control?" Nathan inquired.

Simone's fingers tightened on his leg, and when she leaned closer to him, she drew the eyes of everyone at the table. Killean rested his hand possessively in the small of her back.

"Yes, I do," he said firmly, and they all looked from Simone to him. Bracing himself for what he would reveal next, he held Ronan's gaze as he spoke. "There's something you should know about Savages. I believe it's not only bloodlust that drives some of them to continue killing after they start."

"What else then?" Ronan inquired.

"Hallucinations," Killean said and told them about the ones he'd experienced. "If I feed daily, I can keep them at bay, and my bond to Simone helps keep me grounded, but most vampires don't have a mate to help them. If all Savages experience the same kind of hallucinations when they try to stop killing, it could explain why those who would never choose to be killers eventually turn into a Savage.

"Joseph said some of the hunters take longer to fall in line and have to be starved and allowed to kill more than once before they break. However, it could be the hallucinations that break them and not the bloodlust. I suspect if I gave in and started killing again, the hallucinations would stop."

No one spoke as they absorbed his words with incredulous looks.

"Those poor bastards," Asher finally said.

"It was horrible in there; you have no idea," Simone said. "The torture, the humiliation, the terror..."

Her voice trailed off as her fingers bit into his knee.

"I'm glad you're with us," Kadence said. Her silvery blonde hair fell forward to brush against the table as her azure eyes shimmered with tears. "At least one of you was saved."

Simone smiled at her, grateful to have Kadence's support in this room filled with antagonistic men. She didn't get any outright hostile vibes from them—well, maybe Lucien—but she also didn't feel overly welcome.

"If we can find them, maybe we can save some of the others who were taken," Nathan said.

"By now those hunters have killed more than I did, and they don't have a mate to pull them back from the madness. I only see blood on my hands that won't come off; what they see could be a hundred times worse. Saving them is worth a try if they can be located, but there might not be anything left to save," Killean said. "But I don't think they can be located."

"Maybe not, but Joseph will turn them loose one day, and if we can capture some of them, we can try to save them," Nathan replied.

"We'll deal with that if and when the time comes." Ronan leaned forward and pinned Killean with his unrelenting stare. "Why didn't you come to me before taking this course of action to find her?"

"Because you would have tried to stop me," Killean said.

"And I couldn't have that. There was no other way to find her. We were *there*, and we still have no idea where Joseph's hiding place is. You would have done the same for Kadence."

Ronan couldn't argue that, and Killean knew it. There wasn't anything Ronan wouldn't do to save his mate.

"I believe what you're saying, but you have to know I can't let you live with the hunters and us," Ronan said. "There are children and others who aren't trained in fighting with us. I can't put their lives at risk should you falter."

"I understand," Killean said. He'd expected as much.

Anger and sadness rose in Simone as she gazed back and forth between Killean and Ronan. Killean tried to hide it, but through their connection she felt his twinge of distress. "That's not fair!" she blurted.

"Simone—"

"No!" she interrupted Killean before facing Ronan. "He sacrificed himself and everything that meant so much to him to rescue *me*! If not for Killean, I'd probably be one of those *things* by now. You have no idea what it was like in there or what they did to us. It could have gotten so much worse for me, but Killean came for me. You can't punish him for that!"

Nathan and Kadence sat with their jaws hanging open while Logan and Asher looked as if she'd spoken some alien language they couldn't begin to comprehend. They'd expected her to come back as a docile vampire, but she would never be docile again.

Ronan's eyebrows were in his hairline, but the corner of his mouth quirked in amusement, which only annoyed her more. He could kill her before she rose from this table, and she doubted many who dared defy him survived, but she didn't care. Killean deserved better than this. The other vampires looked either amused or as if she were a bug stuck to the bottom of their shoe.

"I knew the consequences when I left, Simone," Killean said. "It's not a punishment; it's the way things must be."

When she spun on him, the color was high in her cheeks, and her clover-colored eyes burned with indignation. He loved this fiery hunter with her protective and loving nature.

"But—" she started to protest.

"It's okay," he said as he clasped her hand on his knee and lifted it to place it on the table. "I made a choice, and I would do it again."

A sob lodged in her throat. Because of what he'd done for her, he lost everything that meant so much to him, yet he still wouldn't change anything. She hadn't considered it possible, but she fell more in love with him.

I'm sorry, she whispered into his mind.

I'm not, he said without hesitation.

She rested her head on his shoulder. The others continued to stare at her as if they didn't know who she was, but that was okay. She was very aware of who and what she was now.

Sitting up, she threw her shoulders back as she gazed at each of them before focusing on Ronan when he started speaking again.

"I'm not saying you're not still one of us," Ronan said to Killean. "But until we and *you* know for certain you can be trusted around others, this is what must happen."

Simone ground her teeth but refrained from commenting. No matter how much she disliked it, Ronan was right. She completely trusted Killean, but he had to prove himself to them again, and she understood their protective nature. There were children involved, and hunters such as herself, who couldn't defend themselves against vampires. Given some time, it would all work out, she was sure of it.

"Do you have somewhere safe to stay?" Ronan asked.

"Nowhere close by," Killean said.

"You can stay here, or if you would prefer, the house behind the prison is available."

Killean had been to the prison Ronan purchased and modified to hold Savages and purebreds. He'd seen the house behind the prison; it was small, but at least it wasn't a construction zone like this place. He glanced toward the window and noted the lightening of the sky on the horizon. It didn't matter; he wouldn't be going anywhere anytime soon.

"The sun is rising," he said.

Ronan glanced at the window and his brow furrowed in confusion before smoothing as understanding dawned. "I'll keep the workers away, so they won't bother you," he said.

"Thank you," Killean replied. "And Simone—"

"I'm not leaving you," she interrupted.

He turned to face her. "It's safer if you go with them."

"We already discussed this; I'm not leaving you."

Killean contemplated forcing her to go with them, but he couldn't make her do something he wouldn't do himself.

"Fine," he said before turning to Ronan who was failing at his attempt to hide a smile. Declan didn't bother trying to hide it; he smirked. Killean contemplated choking them, but that would only make him look like more of a Savage. "I'll also need a vehicle."

Ronan's smile grew at the clipped tone of his voice. "I'll have one brought over later and the car removed."

"Thank you," Killean said. "And if you have blood bags to spare, I'll take them. I think it's best if I stop feeding on humans for a while."

He'd never been a fan of using a bag to feed and the feel of plastic against his fangs, but avoiding the temptation of a throat, and all that delectable pain, was best until he got himself under control. *If* he ever got himself under control.

"We have plenty to spare," Ronan said.

CHAPTER FORTY-ONE

Killean had assumed they would move to the prison after their first day in the asylum, but when Declan and Saxon dropped off a truck with a mattress, enough blood to keep them supplied for a month, and clothes later that first day, he and Simone never discussed leaving and settled into a rhythm in the old asylum.

While the workers were kept away, some of their tools and building materials remained. Unsure of what to do with himself during the day, Killean started repairing the room where they initially met with the others. What supplies he didn't have, he ordered, and someone brought them to him as most stores closed by the time the sun set enough for him to go anywhere.

Simone helped him with the remodeling, but she spent a lot of time during the day bringing the gardens outside back to life. Often, he'd watch her from the windows as she pruned the overgrown plants into submission. The ones she couldn't save, she dug out and threw into the woods.

He and Simone spent their second day exploring the asylum, and while some rooms could be the staging for horror movies, he saw the beauty in the old place and itched to bring it back to life. As time passed, he finished remodeling the first room and two others on the first floor of the sprawling place; all they needed was a coat of paint, and the rooms would be complete.

Their days fell into the natural flow of fixing the place up, teaching Simone how to defend herself, and taking breaks to make love. As she predicted, she was a fast learner, and her determination to perfect the moves he taught her never wavered. With time, she would be a lethal adversary.

At night they walked the grounds, or Simone practiced driving before they curled up together on the mattress still located in the first room.

Over the month he spent away from the battle against Savages and the threat of Joseph, Killean grew calmer with every passing day. He experienced a few more hallucinations, but feeding once or twice a day kept them at bay. It was more often than he fed before he became a killer, but he was acclimating every day. He'd grown accustomed to the bags though he far preferred Simone's vein. He was impatient to put an end to Joseph, but he recognized this break was necessary to retain his sanity.

Dreams of blood and death haunted his nights, but when he woke to find Simone at his side, he was able to retract his fangs, and his bloodlust ebbed after a few minutes. He suspected the vivid images of tearing someone's throat out was one more thing that kept some vampires Savage.

He told Ronan and the others about the dreams when they came to "visit" as Declan put it, but they all knew they were checking on him. He was fine with it, he understood their reasons, and even if he couldn't hunt with them, he missed his friends, which was something he wouldn't have believed possible before he left them.

He'd known that, as a Defender, he was part of something

and they were his friends and family, but Killean didn't think he'd formed any attachments he couldn't handle losing. He'd been wrong.

Simone's mother also came to visit them once a week. Awkward was a feeling he'd been completely unfamiliar with until the petite woman with graying auburn hair and piercing green eyes walked through the door.

It took her some time to warm up to him, but she'd been unfailingly polite. On her last visit, they discussed more than the weather by debating if a good pruning might save the pear tree in the garden. He figured it was progress.

He glanced over at Simone as she dipped her roller into the tray of paint before slapping it against the wall. Yellow paint speckled her nose, cheeks, and the bandana she'd tied around her hair. The baggy coveralls she wore hid most of her lush figure, but the sight of her warmed a heart he believed deadened before her.

He'd spent the years following the death of his family as nothing more than a walking zombie until she entered his life. Now, even with his constant battle against his more sinister urges, he'd never felt more alive or loved.

Setting his brush on the tray, he walked over and wrapped his arms around her waist before drawing her against his chest.

"You're going to make a mess!" Simone laughed when he ran his finger over the roller in her hand before streaking paint down her delicate nose.

"That's the point," he told her as he turned her in his arms and started peeling the coveralls from her. He proceeded to use the paint to emphasize the beautiful dips and hollows of her body while she painted his.

It was almost nightfall before Simone dragged herself from Killean's arms. When she stretched her arms over her head, the dry paint coating her skin cracked yet felt strangely pleasant.

Killean propped his head on his hand as he watched her with love shining in his eyes.

"You're beautiful," he said.

"I'm filthy, thanks to you," she replied.

"I didn't hear you complaining."

"And you won't next time either." She bent to kiss his forehead and danced back when he tried to grab her. "I'm going to take a shower."

"Minx!" he called after her.

"You're incorrigible!" she shot back as she strolled from the room.

"You wouldn't have me any other way!"

No, she wouldn't. Leaving the wood floors Killean had laid down in what she'd come to consider their room, she entered the foyer. The marble was cold beneath her bare feet as she padded across to the hall on the other side. They'd been here for a month now, but she still experienced a chill every time she entered a shadowed corridor. Simone swore she felt the eyes of those long gone from this residence staring at her from the shadows as she walked, but when she spun to face them, she never saw anything.

"You're an idiot. There's no such thing as ghosts," she muttered. And though she believed this to be true and had yet to experience any sign of the paranormal within the old building, the hair on her neck rose.

She'd learned enough history to know when this place was functioning it hadn't been one of joy for those residing here. The residents had suffered here, and not just from whatever ailment landed them here, but also at the hands of those seeking to cure them. Maybe those with the supposed cure meant well, but in some cases, they'd done more harm than good, and she felt that lingering suffering in these corridors.

Thankfully, the one remodeled bathroom was the second door off the hall, and she didn't have to be in the shadows for long. Stepping into the bathroom Killean remodeled, she flicked on the switch to illuminate the crème walls, black marble counters around the sink, and the tan tiles of the shower stall. She stepped into the shower, slid the door closed, and scrubbed the paint from her skin before exiting.

Opening the cabinets beneath the sink, she removed two towels and wrapped one around her hair and the other around herself before emerging from the bathroom. A cloud of steam followed her out the door.

When she walked back into their temporary bedroom, she discovered Killean standing by the nearly floor-to-ceiling windows he recently installed. The original windows had been much smaller, but Killean had knocked out more wall space to make room for these. Now that it was dark out, he'd thrown open the heavy drapes to welcome the night.

In the glass, his reflection was almost serene. She stopped to savor his lean, well-muscled body splattered with paint and bathed in moonlight. She'd come to love this brazen, harsh, powerful, tender man more than she ever believed it was possible to love someone.

The scar on his face and the one on his chest had faded a little, something he attributed to their bond, but they would never disappear entirely. He received them too early in life for them to vanish entirely, but unlike his outer scars, Simone knew Killean's emotional scars healed with every passing day.

Killean's head turned toward her, and he smiled. Once so rare, those smiles were becoming a daily occurrence that brightened her life far more than the sun could.

Eventually, his old life with Ronan and the others would resume, but she hated the idea of anything intruding on the reprieve from the real world they'd been granted in this lonely place. And she wouldn't let him return until he was ready. She didn't want to risk him returning to the war too soon and losing all the progress he'd made in coming to terms with his past and the actions he'd taken to save her.

"It's a good night for a walk," he said as he stepped away from the window.

"It is," she agreed.

She dressed while he went to shower, and when he returned, he pulled on some clothes, looped his arm through hers, and led her out the door. They wandered into the gardens that had become a labor of love for her. Before being taken, she was learning to grow food that could be harvested for her husband's dinner. Now she worked in the garden because she enjoyed plunging her hands into the earth and getting them dirty.

When he discovered her growing love of plants and her interest in learning more about them, Killean ordered her books on plant ID and care. She was enjoying studying those books to learn more about the different species and the proper way to prune and care for them. She had a talent for bringing plants on the edge of death back to life, and she took pride in her developing skill. Under her hands, the garden was flourishing again.

Simone rested her head on Killean's shoulder while they strolled the path she'd cleared this week. Orange daylilies and red roses lined it. Behind them, and staggered throughout the landscape, was a various assortment of plants, some of which were in bloom. The full moon illuminated the cracked and uneven bricks beneath their feet and the owl watching them from the branches of an oak tree.

"It looks amazing," Killean said. "You've done wonders here."

"I think I'll be able to save the magnolia tree and those azaleas," she replied as she pointed to the struggling bushes that had been buried beneath vines until today. "I'm not sure about that cluster of rhododendrons, the bittersweet was deeply entangled in them."

"If anyone can bring them back to life, it's you," Killean murmured as he kissed her temple.

Pleased by his confidence in her, Simone squeezed his arm. "I know our time here is only temporary, but I don't want it to end."

"Neither do I," Killean admitted, but the end would come.

CHAPTER FORTY-TWO

"I've brought more blood," Declan announced when Killean opened the door for him. He hefted two cotton bags in the air to show he meant what he said.

Killean scowled at him as he remained behind the door, hidden in the shadows while the early morning sun streamed across the foyer. "Do you know what time it is?"

"Time to get your lazy ass out of bed," Declan replied as he sauntered into the foyer with Saxon following him.

"We just finished a patrol," Saxon said. "And we've received word some of the hunters spotted Joseph last night."

Killean's irritation over them arriving so early vanished. The end of his and Simone's reprieve was coming sooner than he expected. "Where?"

"At a bar in Plymouth," Saxon said.

"Are they sure?"

"Yes."

"Shit." Killean closed the door behind Saxon and leaned against it. "Were any of the turned hunters with him?"

Declan set the bags on the ground before facing him. "They

only saw Joseph, and they lost him before they could learn if anyone else was with him."

"Shit," Killean said again.

"That about sums it up," Declan agreed.

"I *need* back in the fight."

"Not our decision to make."

Declan strolled over to the stairs and settled onto one. Drawing his knees up, he propped his elbows on them while he studied Killean.

"What?" Killean asked, annoyed by Declan's scrutiny.

He'd long been aware Declan possessed an ability none of them did. What that ability was precisely, he didn't know, and he didn't care when Declan focused it on someone else. However, he didn't like Declan's piercing attention directed at him.

"You are happier and calmer," Declan said. "It's good to see."

"That's because he's finally getting some action," Saxon said.

"Don't talk about her like that!" Killean snarled as he took a threatening step toward Saxon.

Saxon had stood by him the most throughout all of this, but he wouldn't tolerate anyone speaking about Simone with anything less than complete respect.

Saxon held up his hands. "Sorry. Momentary lapse of sanity; I forgot how cranky you mated vamps get."

Some of Killean's irritation waned when he smelled Simone approaching before she appeared in the doorway. She stared at Saxon and Declan before looking questioningly at him.

"Some hunters spotted Joseph last night," he told her.

The color drained from her face. "Can he find us?"

"Not likely," Saxon said.

"But it's not impossible?" she pressed.

"It's not impossible," Killean admitted.

"What do we do?" she asked.

"I'm not sure," Killean said. "I have to speak with Ronan."

"He's on his way here now," Declan replied

Stepping away from the door, Killean walked over to stand beside Simone.

"I'm not leaving you," she stated as if she'd been reading his mind.

"We'll discuss it after we speak with Ronan," he said.

"There's nothing to discuss," Simone bit out.

The crunch of tires on the road saved him from getting into this argument with her. He'd relented to her desires before, but if Joseph was appearing again, then things were different now, and he would do whatever it took to keep her safe. He walked back toward the door but stayed out of the sun when Saxon opened it. Declan rose from the stairs and leaned against the railing as Ronan, Nathan, and Lucien came through the door.

Ronan's eyes were a fiery red color, and beside him, Nathan's normally blue eyes were a striking white-blue. Bloodlust slithered up from the depths of Killean's soul in response to the barely leashed violence they radiated. The need to have Joseph's blood staining his hands and spilling down his throat thundered through his veins. His fangs lengthened, and for the first time since arriving here, he felt on the verge of losing control again.

Killean focused on Simone as he worked to contain his rising need for death. She gazed at him from troubled eyes as her love and confidence in him shimmered across their bond. Looking at her and feeling her unwavering faith in him helped him regain control.

"What happened?" Declan inquired of Ronan. The knuckles of his hand on the banister were white as he gazed at Nathan and Ronan.

"A bar caught on fire last night in Plymouth. All seventy-two people inside died," Lucien said.

"That fire is no coincidence following a Joseph sighting so close to it," Saxon said.

"No, it's not," Ronan grated, and his eyes latched onto Killean. "Do you think you're ready to return to the fight?"

When Simone's apprehension rippled through his mind, Killean returned to her side and took her hand. "I am," he said.

Ronan's gaze ran appraisingly over him. "If you think you might require more time, you can have it."

"I don't need more time," Killean said firmly. "I want that fucking prick dead more than you do."

He glanced pointedly at Simone, whose lips were nearly white as she pressed them together. More than her terror for him was bothering her now, but also her terror of Joseph and what would happen if he found her. Killean would make sure Joseph paid for what he'd done to her and that she *never* had to fear him finding her again.

Killean looked back at Ronan. "I haven't had any hallucinations in over a week, and Simone, as well as feeding every day, keeps my more lethal impulses at bay. I'm ready for this."

Ronan glanced between him and Simone before replying. "I believe you, but I still can't have you in the compound."

When Simone's breath hissed out, Ronan held up a silencing hand. "If it were only us, I would have allowed him back weeks ago, but the hunters are nervous," Ronan said.

"They need more time," Nathan explained to Simone. "You saw how well some of them handled it when I made my announcement about the Alliance and my decision to transition into a vampire. Even those who chose to stay with me after I became a vampire don't like the idea of having a vamp who has killed innocents living amongst them and their children."

Simone closed her mouth; she couldn't start spouting off about how they should get over it when she left after Nathan's announcement about the Alliance. The hunters who remained with Nathan were more accepting of his decision than her, and she couldn't condemn them for balking against this when she would have done the same.

"They will come around," Nathan continued, "and Killean fighting with us again will help them do so."

"I understand," Simone murmured. She didn't like it, but she did understand.

"If I hunt with you tonight, Simone can't stay here alone," Killean said.

Her hand crushed the bones in his together when she squeezed it. "Killean—"

"You have to be somewhere safe when I'm not here," he interjected before she could argue with him.

Killean still didn't know if Ronan and the hunters had remained on the same property after he left or if they'd moved, but she would be safe wherever they were now. Though he was curious about their current location, he hadn't asked, and he wouldn't; they would tell him when they were ready.

"I'll send men to pick her up before the sun sets and bring her to the compound," Ronan said. "Or I can have some trainees come here to watch her."

"I'll stay," Simone said at the same time Killean said, "She'll go to the compound."

"Killean—" Simone started.

"There is no discussion about this. I'm not entrusting your life to trainees. You'll be safer at the compound, and you'll be with Kadence and your mother," Killean said. "You can return here afterward."

CHAPTER FORTY-THREE

Over the next few days, two vampires and a hunter arrived to pick Simone up before sunset; the same three brought her back to Killean before dawn. They didn't blindfold her as they drove her to the compound the vampires and hunters shared, but she doubted she'd be able to find the place again if she tried. She was too busy taking in all the things to see along the way to notice the route they took to get back and forth.

She spent most of her life behind the walls of a hunter stronghold. She'd been knocked out when Joseph took her, and too focused on fleeing with Killean to really absorb much of the human world. Now she took the time to notice how strangely fascinating they were.

She marveled at the various colors of their vehicles, homes, stores, and clothes. She couldn't get enough of watching them walk the streets with their strollers and dogs. They watered their lawns while talking with their neighbors and ran or rode their bikes down the sidewalks and roads.

The humans were everywhere and so oblivious to the battle brewing under their noses that it amazed her. She almost envied them their peaceful oblivion and mundane lives, but not quite. If they were unable to stop whatever Joseph planned, the simple lives of these people might forever be altered, and they would never see it coming.

Every time they pulled through the gates of the compound, Simone couldn't help feeling a little shocked when the mansion where the vampires resided came into view. Imposing was an understatement for the gothic estate with its peaks and turrets. The gargoyles on the peaks and outside the doorways looked about to come to life, and she had to stop herself from gulping whenever she saw them.

On the other side of the compound, some of the hunters resided in a beautiful mansion, but many hunters, including her mother, resided in the trailers parked on the lawn of the hunter estate. Some of the hunters, mostly the elders, had moved from the trailers and into the homes being erected on the large, grassy lawn. Eventually, every hunter family would have their own home, and the trailers would be gone.

Every night when they arrived, the hunter children were running around and playing with what she'd come to learn were human children rescued from Joseph. Those children and their caretakers, Duncan and Sister June, had been brought here to live under the protection of the hunters and vampires. After exiting the vehicle, Simone would stop to listen to the children laugh and squeal in delight while they chased each other during their games.

She was able to watch them because a large section of the wall originally dividing the two properties, had been torn down to combine the estates. She'd been to the hunter side a couple of times, but though her visits were brief, she couldn't deny a more relaxed air encompassed the hunters. Most of the women had forsaken the dull gray, black, and white clothing they'd always worn in favor of the cheerier colors Nathan's mate, Vicky, brought into their lives.

She'd never expected anything to ever change for the hunters. Seeing so many changes at once was a little overwhelming for her at first, but they were good changes and ones the hunters all seemed to be embracing.

She found those hunters who weren't too afraid to speak to her—now that she was a vampire and mated to the "killer," as she'd heard some of them whisper after she passed—were happier.

Kadence had informed her they would also have to build more homes on the vampire side of the property for the growing number of vampire recruits they were gathering. They still had a lot to do, but the hunters and vampires had coalesced into a finely tuned army Simone never would have imagined possible when Nathan first made his announcement to combine forces.

While here, she spent her nights with her mother and Kadence. One night, Vicky also joined them. Her pregnancy still wasn't showing, but Vicky glowed with happiness as she revealed the maternity clothes the hunter women made for her. The vivid colors and designs were beautiful and would be flattering on her.

Simone mostly wore jeans now, but though she loved the colors of the clothes the others wore, she still preferred black and gray for her shirts. However, she had started wearing more dark blues and greens over the past couple of weeks. Maybe one day she'd feel comfortable enough to don the vibrant reds, yellows, oranges, and purples Vicky and Kadence wore, but Simone wasn't going to rush it.

Her first night away from Killean, Simone chewed her nails down to the nubs; something she'd never done before, but her terror for him mounted with every hour they spent apart. Would he be okay amid all the blood and death if he ended up in a fight again? What if the hallucinations came back while he was out there? What if the temptation to kill an innocent became too much and he lost control? Would the others forgive him if he did? Would she be enough to bring him back if the darkness trying to claim his soul overtook him?

Even though she could feel Killean's strength and reassuring presence through their bond, that first night apart was the longest of her life. When she climbed back into the SUV, and her protectors drove her off the grounds, she spent most of the ride mentally urging them to go faster.

When they arrived at the asylum, she hadn't waited for the vehicle to stop before throwing open the door and running into Killean's waiting arms. She'd been so focused on him, she barely noticed Declan and Saxon slipping away to their waiting vehicle.

The more time passed though, the less she worried Killean wouldn't be able to handle returning to his old life, but she still *loathed* being separated from him.

"THEY NEVER SWITCHED locations after I left them to find you," Killean said after he'd been working with the Alliance again for a week.

Simone lay in his arms, staring at the ceiling as he ran his fingers through her hair.

"I don't know if they did or not," she admitted. "I never asked."

"Ronan told me last night they never relocated."

Simone craned her head to peer up at him. "What does that mean?"

"I think it means that no matter what I did, they still trusted me not to reveal their location to Joseph."

The note of awe and hope in his voice made her heart ache as she realized he still didn't have confidence in himself. "You're not a monster, Killean. You never were no matter what you believe."

"I believe no one as amazing as you could ever love a monster."

"I'd love you no matter what you did or became. We're in this together for eternity."

Killean pulled her close and kissed her forehead more roughly than he'd intended. "We are, but you will never have to love a monster, Simone. I promise you that."

She listened to the reassuring thump of his heart beneath her ear as she nestled closer to him.

"It also means," he said after a few minutes. "That they're confident the compound is strong enough to withstand an attack from Joseph."

"It looks like it is," she said. "I don't know all the security they have there, but I know it's vast, and they work like an army together."

"They've become more comfortable with each other in the field too and more lethal."

"That's good. Did you encounter any Savages tonight?"

"Yes."

His pulse raced as he recalled the rush of battle and the thrill of the kill. He'd always excelled at dealing out death, but now he thrived on ending the life of another as it helped keep the darkness at bay by satisfying his more brutal impulses. He could never go back to the man he'd been before killing innocents, but Killean was learning to embrace the man he was becoming. He was a more lethal fighter yet, because of Simone, he was also kinder.

"Are you still doing okay?" she asked.

He hated the nervousness in her voice and the broken fingernails marring her delicate hands. She tried to hide those bitten nails, but he saw them. "I'm fine, love. Having you is all I need to bring me back should I ever feel myself teetering, and I have yet to feel that way."

Her fingers bit into his skin, and though his craving for pain lessened when he returned to killing Savages, his cock stirred in response.

"Good," she said. "Would you let me know if you did?"

"Yes. I wouldn't keep something like that from you; we're in this together."

"And don't forget it."

Rolling her over, he nudged her thighs apart and settled between them. "I never could," he assured her.

He brushed the hair back from her face as he kissed her while slowly entering her.

CHAPTER FORTY-FOUR

Simone gazed eagerly out the window as the vehicle bounced over the ruts in the road leading to the asylum. The two vampires in the front seats and the hunter beside her in the back were loudly debating the use of a designated hitter, whatever that was. She'd mostly tuned them out as what they were discussing sounded absurd.

The first time they picked her up from the asylum, the vamps had introduced themselves as Felipe and Edgar; Felipe was driving. The hunter was Sully, a young man of about twenty-five, who she'd known before leaving the stronghold. He was new to being allowed out on the patrols with the other hunters and vampires, but he'd been training since childhood to kill Savages.

Resting her head against the window, she gazed at the woods crowding the sides of the vehicle. They'd only been apart for eight hours, but the closer she got to Killean the more butterflies of excitement fluttered in her stomach. Some of Killean's friends would be waiting with him; they usually stayed until she arrived.

They rounded a corner, and though Felipe was busy waving his hand in the air as he declared the other two idiots, he still braked when someone stepped out of the woods two hundred feet in front of them. Simone didn't have time to brace herself against the lurch of the vehicle's tires coming to an abrupt halt. The seat belt caught and pulled her back before she smacked her face off the seat in front of her.

"Who is that?" Edgar muttered.

Simone leaned over to stare between the two seats and out the windshield. Three hundred feet in front of them, an imposing figure blocked the road. They were on a straightaway in the road, but the spill of headlights barely reached the figure and cast shadows over its face. Ice replaced the blood pumping through her veins when she realized who it was.

"It's Joseph," she breathed as the hair on her nape rose.

A sense of impending doom descended on her like an avalanche bearing down on an unsuspecting skier. She loathed tearing her gaze away from the powerful vampire standing in the middle of the road, but she couldn't deny the sensation of eyes boring into the back of her head. Stealing her nerves, Simone slowly turned to gaze out the back window.

Standing behind the vehicle, with their faces against the glass, stood three more Savages. The blazing red eyes of two of them were joined by the white-blue eyes of a turned hunter. The worst part was, she recognized the hunter.

"Dallas," she breathed.

"Shit," Sully muttered.

Dallas, the hunter who established his own stronghold in New Hampshire, the one she'd followed to get away from Nathan's leadership, leered at her as he tapped his forefinger against the glass.

"Hello, Simone." His fangs distorted Dallas's words, but they were still intelligible.

"Floor it," Edgar said.

"I don't think that prick is going to get out of our way," Felipe replied.

"There are more Savages in the woods," Sully said. "And they're closing in on us. If we don't move now, they're going to surround us."

"*Floor it*!" Edgar commanded.

Felipe slammed his foot down on the gas pedal. Dirt and stones clattered and banged off the underside of the vehicle as the tires spun on the road before catching. When the SUV lurched forward, Simone was thrown back against her seat.

The pitted road had kept their speed to ten miles per hour, but now the speedometer climbed steadily toward twenty and on to thirty. Simone bounced in her seat, and her teeth clattered together as they crashed in and out of the potholes while their speed crept toward forty.

Despite the vehicle rocketing toward him with increasing speed, Joseph didn't move. Instead, in the beams of the bouncing headlights, his smile widened, and an evil smugness radiated from him. Simone had the feeling they were playing right into his hands, but they had no other choice. They couldn't just sit and wait to be surrounded by his followers.

The SUV closed the distance from three hundred feet to two hundred to one hundred. When they hit a rut at fifty miles per hour, all four tires left the earth, and the vehicle soared for a few feet before crashing down with a grinding screech. Simone waited for the tires to explode or pop, but somehow they remained intact.

"Oh, shit!" Felipe cried.

Felipe stomped on the brake and gripped the wheel until he was rising out of his seat at an almost half-standing position behind the wheel. Plumes of smoke shot up from the tires, and the rancid stench of something burning filled the air as the backend of the vehicle swung to the side.

Everything seemed to move in slow motion as the following scene emblazoned on Simone's mind in vivid detail. From within some of the potholes, metal glinted in the headlights and the SUV continued its slide toward holes as Felipe jerked the wheel to try to avoid them. With the backend of the vehicle almost even with the front, Simone watched the jagged edges of metal drew closer.

When she rested her fingers against the glass, she realized she'd done so in a subconscious gesture to push the metal away, but there was no stopping the inevitable. The SUV lurched to the side as the passenger side tires slid into the potholes first and then loud pops resonated through the air.

The vehicle sagged further as air left the tires, and Simone realized what was coming before the ground rushed up to smash against the window beside her. When the window shattered, she threw her arms up to protect herself from the beads of glass raining over her.

The inexplicable sensation of time slowing abruptly ended as the SUV rolled across the ground at a perilous velocity. The seat belt dug into her shoulder and lap while her head bounced back and forth. The roof dented in with a screech of metal before the vehicle went airborne once more.

A scream lodged in her throat as one echoed endlessly in her head.

Killean!

Leaning against the front doorframe of the asylum, Killean searched the road for an approaching vehicle. The road was so long he never saw them coming until they were only a couple of hundred feet away. And even then, he heard the engine before he saw the lights.

Lucien walked out the open door and halfway across the porch Killean had almost finished building. The newly built porch ran the entire front of the building and had a beamed roof. It would also have a railing running around all of it, but he hadn't gotten that far yet. When he finished with it, he planned to hang a hammock and porch swing from the beams.

Declan sat on the steps with his hands propped behind him while he studied the sky already turning more gray than black as the stars faded from view. A few feet away from Killean, Saxon leaned against the brick wall with his legs crossed and his chin resting on his chest as if he were sleeping.

"Have you had any more hallucinations?" Lucien asked Killean.

An undercurrent of hostility still tinted Lucien's tone when they spoke, but his animosity had eased.

"Not in a couple of weeks," Killean replied. "Feeding regularly, killing Savages, and, mostly, Simone keep them at bay."

"What about the sun? Does it still bother you?" Saxon asked.

"Yes," Killean said. Everything else may have eased, but the effect of the sun remained the same.

"That will get better too," Declan said.

"And what makes you such an expert?" Lucien demanded.

Declan shrugged. "It's the way of the world; given enough time, everything changes."

"Hmm," Lucien grunted.

"Besides, in case you haven't heard, I'm a genius," Declan said.

Lucien scowled when Declan grinned at him. Killean knew they were here because they didn't like leaving him alone until Simone arrived. Some nights, Ronan sat with them too, and on other nights there would only be one or two who stayed with him. He didn't know if they stayed because they didn't trust him or if they were offering him support, but he welcomed their company even if they were babysitting him.

Killean glanced impatiently at his watch as a strange sense of unease gripped him. Simone and her guards weren't late, but something didn't feel right. Killean prowled toward the steps and strained to hear while he studied the woods.

"What is it?" Declan asked.

"I don't know," he muttered. "Something doesn't feel right."

"Are you like Declan now and getting feelings?" Lucien inquired.

"Maybe if you showed some feelings you'd get laid more often," Saxon retorted.

"Enough," Killean growled as the uneasiness in his stomach spread into his chest and lodged in his throat.

Declan rose and looked to Lucien. "Call Ronan."

"And say what, Killean has developed *feelings*?" Lucien demanded.

"Call him!" Declan commanded.

Lucien's eyes narrowed, but he pulled a phone from his pocket and dialed a number. Declan rarely raised his voice, but when he did, they listened to him.

Killean! The scream, issued from Simone, burst into his head with so much force it rocked him back a step. Her terror battered him like a tornado tearing apart a home before he cut it off. If he didn't sever their mental connection, he would become trapped in her fear and wouldn't be able to react.

A cloud of red descended over his vision, and a snarl erupted from him. He still felt her through their bond, and he followed that connection as he leapt off the porch. The trees blurred when he raced by them with far more speed than he'd ever exhibited before. If the others followed him, he'd left them far behind.

With every step, his driving need to get to her propelled him faster, but he didn't think it would be enough to save her.

CHAPTER FORTY-FIVE

The vehicle skidded a few feet before finally coming to a halt on its crumpled roof. Hanging against the seat belt, Simone studied her surroundings as she fumbled for the release. A tree had dented in the side and wedged itself against the space between the front and back passenger seats. It blocked part of the window, but if she could get free, she'd be able to climb out the window. The driver's side of the vehicle faced the road and remained on it, but her side faced the woods and was partially off the road.

The dented roof was only an inch or two above her head, all the passenger side windows and the back had shattered, but the windshield remained intact. Beside her, Sully grunted as he twisted in his seat. Edgar and Felipe hung in front of her; they were both gripping stakes while trying to unfasten their seat belts.

From out of the shadows, something metal glinted in the headlights before it smashed into the windshield. Spiderweb cracks spread out across the glass, but it held firm. The metal was yanked away and then swung forward again to batter the cracked glass. Simone instinctively jerked back when the glass fell apart and maniacal laughter sounded from outside.

The laughter continued as feet ran across the front of the vehicle and past Felipe and Sully. Like children playing a game of tag, she realized these creatures were toying with them and loving every second of it.

What was going to happen when they got tired of playing? She didn't want to know the answer to that question, but she had no doubt she would learn it.

Beside her, Sully braced one hand against the roof as he undid his seat belt and toppled from his seat. Kneeling in the middle of the glass-covered roof, Sully bent to peer out the windows. In the front seats, Felipe and Edgar freed themselves and landed soundlessly on the roof. Simone jerked at the button as she tried to get it to unlatch.

"Easy," Sully said as he crawled over to her.

Simone stopped yanking at the belt and took a deep breath to calm herself. Panicking now wouldn't do them any good.

"Brace yourself," Sully said.

Simone placed both her hands on the roof, and a second later, the seat belt released. Sully darted out of the way when her legs swung down, and she found herself kneeling on the roof. She rotated her shoulder to ease the discomfort from the belt digging into her skin.

"Do you see them?" Felipe asked as he craned his head to peer out the driver's side window.

"No. What was in the road that we hit?" Edgar demanded.

"A road spike, I think," Felipe said. "They set a trap for us."

"Assholes," Sully said.

A piercing screech suddenly filled the air. Simone almost covered her ears with her hands to block out the nails on chalkboard sound, but deafening one of her senses would be a horrible idea right now.

As the hideous noise continued, feet began to circle the vehicle as if the Savages were the monkey chasing the weasel around the mulberry bush. She realized the Savages were using their fingernails or branches and rocks to scrape along the SUV as they walked and some actually *skipped* around the vehicle.

It's a game; it's all a game, and we're the prizes.

Beads of sweat dotted Simone's forehead as she glanced at the others. When would these monsters stop playing and launch their attack? It had to be soon as these things must realize Killean and the others were nearby, and they wouldn't have much time to play these games before help arrived.

Then a horrifying possibility occurred to Simone; what if these monsters did have time to play these games? Killean and the others were always at the asylum before she arrived; what if these things had already launched an attack against them?

The panic she'd recently restrained flared back to life. She tried to mentally communicate with Killean but got no response. Her pulse raced through her veins, and her throat became dry as she struggled to retain her composure.

He's okay; you would know if he wasn't!

Taking a deep breath, Simone talked herself back from the edge of panic. She may not be able to communicate with him right now, but she could still feel him out there, somewhere.

And right now, she had to stay focused on the threat only feet away from her. Maybe these things didn't know Killean and the others were close by, but she didn't think that was true. She suspected this game was intended to torment them while these Savages waited for Killean and the others to arrive. And then when they came, the Savages would have the four of them trapped in this vehicle and would use them as a weapon against Killean, or at least they would use *her*.

She had to get out of this SUV.

Simone edged toward the window she'd sat beside. The

broken pieces of glass stuck to her palms and knees but only a few nicked her flesh. She was almost to the window when Dallas's head appeared beside the tree. Simone recoiled so fast from him that she almost fell on her ass.

"Boo," he taunted before vanishing.

Simone blinked at where he'd been as the awful screeching stopped and their awful laughter replaced it.

"I hate these bastards," Edgar muttered.

"We have to get out of here," Felipe said.

Simone gazed out the window as feet danced and twirled by it. She realized they weren't the mulberry bush; no, they were the sacrifice, and these things were devil worshippers dancing to satisfy their pagan God before slaughtering them.

She held her hand out to Sully. "Give me one of your stakes."

He did a double take. "Do you know how to use it?"

Though the question annoyed her, she couldn't blame him for asking it. When she resided in the stronghold, she'd never been a fighter. "Yes."

Sully hesitated before reaching into his windbreaker and pulling a stake free; he slid it into her hand.

"You're not going out there," Edgar said to her.

"We can't stay in here," she replied. "Killean will come, and if we're trapped in here, these things will use us against him when he does."

"*We* can't stay in here, but *you* can."

Simone glared at him, but before she could respond, a strange look descended over Edgar's face, and he was yanked backward. With his legs ripped out from under him, he crashed onto the roof. Felipe dove toward his friend, but his hands fell on the metal roof as Edgar was pulled out the broken front windshield.

Simone's pulse thundered in her ears as she gawked at the place Edgar had been and silence descended. Then a scream pierced the air before abruptly cutting off. The coppery scent of blood filled her nostrils, before Edgar's head landed on the ground in front of the SUV. It rocked back and forth before coming to a stop with its dead eyes and gaping mouth facing them.

Simone's hand flew to her lips as bile rushed up her throat. Beside her, the warmth of Sully's body did nothing to ease the ice permeating her bones. She didn't have time to process what had happened to Edgar before Sully lurched awkwardly forward and released a garbled shout.

Thrown off by the sudden movement, the weight of his body shoved her back as his chest hit the ground and his breath rushed out of him. Simone lurched for him when he was dragged backward a few feet, but she missed grabbing his wrists.

Sully threw his hands out and gripped the edges of the window to stop himself from being pulled out of the vehicle. Simone and Felipe lunged forward; Simone gripped Sully's forearms as she braced her feet against the SUV. Felipe wrapped his fingers around Sully's wrist before letting out an oomph and collapsing onto the roof.

Felipe's mouth formed an O as his fingers scrambled for purchase on the roof. His nails left gouges in its metal surface as he was pulled out of the vehicle. Simone's grasp on Sully tightened as she used her legs to try to pull him back inside the SUV.

She hadn't moved him an inch before Sully started screaming as if someone were eating him alive. She shuddered when she realized they actually *could* be feasting on him.

Sully's scream cut off, and his dazed eyes rolled toward her. She felt his life slipping away as his grip on the window eased, but she was helpless to stop it. From outside, slurping sounds reached her as they consumed his blood. She spotted half a dozen Savages kneeling beside Sully while they fed.

Sully's fingers uncurled, and his hands fell. When the Savages pulled him back, Simone kept her legs braced, but she was helpless to stop him from being pulled from her grip. When he disappeared, she found herself clinging to handfuls of his tattered shirt.

Tears burned her eyes, and a sob lodged in her throat as she released the pieces of cloth. She scrambled into the center of the roof and huddled there as she tried to figure out some way out of this mess, but all she thought about was the certainty of death in Sully's eyes before he vanished.

Get it together, or you'll be next, and they won't just kill you. They'll use you against Killean and turn you into one of them.

Gathering her courage, Simone leaned toward the stake she released when she lunged after Sully. She waited for something to reach in and grasp her hand when she snatched it up, but it was eerily quiet out there and she didn't see any more feet.

More of their twisted game. They were trying to break her mentally, but they would fail.

With the stake clutched against her chest, she remained kneeling in the center of the roof as the first of the feet returned. *Come after me, and I'll make you regret it.*

She tried to watch all the feet as the circling began again, but there were too many windows, too many ways in, and she couldn't monitor them all.

"Boo!"

Simone almost shrieked when an unfamiliar face appeared in the broken window Sully was pulled through before the Savage withdrew.

"Boo!" someone declared from behind her.

She spun but whoever said it was already gone.

"Boo!"

She turned again, but no one was there. Shifting her grip on the stake, she wiped her sweaty palms on her jeans. The weapon wouldn't do her any good if she couldn't keep ahold of it. Her heart thudded so forcefully she thought it might burst out of her chest, but beneath her terror was a rising swell of rage.

"Boo!"

This time, she didn't try to turn and see whoever shouted at her. If they yanked her out of the vehicle, so be it, but she wasn't playing anymore.

"Boo!"

The face appeared next to her, and reacting on instinct, she swung the stake out and straight into the Savage's eye. Nausea twisted in her stomach when the weapon plunged into the spongy organ. She clung to the stake when the vampire howled and reeled backward to tear itself free of the weapon.

Despite her disgust, satisfaction slithered through her. That would teach them to mess with her! But then the Savage's cries ceased, and all the feet stopped moving in unison.

Simone gulped as she realized the game was over; they were coming for her.

CHAPTER FORTY-SIX

Killean had traversed three miles when he rounded a bend in the road and spotted the SUV on its roof. At least a dozen Savages circled the vehicle, and he spotted more sliding through the woods. With this many Savages present, the stench of them rivaled a landfill in July.

The coppery tang of blood permeated the air. Not Simone's blood, he knew the sweet scent of that well, but he guessed it was the blood of those who'd been with her. Judging by the Savage's surrounding the vehicle, he suspected Simone was still inside.

The red shading his eyes became more intense as the darkness he'd kept at bay burst free. He didn't care what it did to him, he would destroy every one of these bastards to free Simone.

Killean bounded across the ground, grabbed the head of the Savage closest to him and yanked it to the side. The snap of the Savage's neck paralyzed him instantly. When the vamp dropped to the ground, Killean's gaze clashed with Joseph's over the wreckage of the SUV.

A sly smile spread across Joseph's lips. "There you are," he purred. "We've been waiting for you."

Killean glowered at him. He almost leapt onto the undercarriage and charged across the vehicle at Joseph, but first, he had to get Simone out of the SUV. While she remained in there, any or all these things could slip inside and capture her.

"Take him alive," Joseph commanded. "Our friend intends to play with him."

When the two Savages closest to him dove at him, Killean jumped back to avoid them. Clasping his hands together, he hammered them onto the back of one vamp before swinging an uppercut into the chin of the other. The second one's head snapped back, and teeth shattered as he fell into the SUV. The first one hit the ground, and Killean slammed his foot onto its back, breaking its spine.

None of the Savages he'd attacked were dead yet, but he didn't have time to end them. He had to stay free and incapacitate them enough to get Simone out of the SUV. If he could hold the Savages off long enough, it would give the others time to arrive and even out the odds a little. Then the killing could begin, and he would relish their screams.

Simone knew Killean had arrived before Savages started littering the ground outside the vehicles. She'd detected his scent, but more, she felt his presence in every fiber of her being. And she couldn't stay trapped in here. It would be too easy for the Savages to get their hands on her, and she needed to help Killean.

The Savages Killean had taken down remained on the ground, but some of them were regaining the use of their arms and legs. She had to move now.

Keeping the stake in hand, Simone scrambled toward the front window as Killean headed in that direction. The feet of two more Savages ran at him, and above her, something crashed onto the SUV. Simone hunched down when footsteps thudded over her head; the vehicle groaned as it was pushed further into the earth.

Then the footsteps stopped, and when Killean grunted and staggered to the side, she realized the Savage had launched themselves off the SUV and onto him. Another set of legs materialized next to Killean's, but these dangled from the ground as whoever leapt onto Killean hung off his back.

Simone ignored the glass digging into her palms and knees as she scurried forward to help him. Gripping the edges of the windshield, she started to pull herself out when fingers locked around her ankle in a vise-like grip. Simone bit back a cry as she was yanked backward; any sound she made would distract Killean and might get him killed.

Simone kicked at her captor but connected with empty air. Twisting to look behind her, she discovered a Savage leering at her while it wormed backward with her in its grasp. She didn't bother trying to grab something to stop her momentum; there was nothing to grab.

Gritting her teeth, Simone lashed out and plunged the stake into the Savage's forearm. The vamp hissed, and its fangs snapped at her hand as she twisted the stake until it hit bone. When the vampire ripped its arm away, it took her weapon with it, but released her ankle.

Simone didn't look back as she clambered forward and threw herself out the broken windshield. She had no idea what she was plunging into, but she refused to give anything else a chance to seize her and use her against Killean.

When feet swung by her head, she ducked back against the vehicle to avoid a kick to the face. She looked up in time to see a Savage crash onto the shredded remains of the driver's side tire. The Savage looked as if it were snapped in half as its body bowed at a completely unnatural angle.

Killean's back was to her as he battled the three Savages closing in on him. His shirt hung off his shoulders in tatters and blood streaked his flesh. Her fangs lengthened, and her fingers dug into the dirt road when she spotted that blood. These monsters had hurt him, and if they had their way, they would unleash far worse.

When the SUV shook and rattled behind her, she realized more Savages were running across it toward them.

"Killean!" she screamed. "Behind you!"

He turned as three Savages launched off the vehicle and onto him. He staggered beneath the impact of their bodies and nearly went to his knees.

No! She wouldn't allow anything to happen to him. Scrambling to her feet, Simone bolted forward as Killean spun to dislodge the Savages clinging to him.

Her fingers snagged the shirt of one of the vamps, and she jerked at it. Material tore beneath her hand, but the shirt collar caught and dug into the Savage's neck. A head twisted toward her; Simone almost released the vamp when its white-blue eyes clashed with hers.

Another broken hunter.

She didn't let her brain process who it was as she drew back her arm like Killean taught her and smashed her fist into the vamp's face. Blood shot out and spilled over them both when she bashed his lips into his fangs.

She was preparing to punch him again when hands grasped her arms. Inhuman sounds issued from her as she struggled against the vampires pulling her backward, but it was like pitting a lamb against a lion.

"No!" she cried when they lifted her and carried her away.

Killean spun when he heard Simone's cry, but he couldn't see much through the Savages holding onto him. "Simone!"

A blow against his temple staggered him to the side. His ears rang, and his vision blurred, but he retained his balance until he stumbled into a hole. When his right ankle rolled over, the weight of the Savages made it impossible for him to stay upright.

His knees buckled, and he hit the ground. Excited chatter filled his ears as one of the Savages yanked his wrist behind his back. Killean surged forward to break free of the imprisoning hold, but another Savage thrust their knee into his back and shoved him forward.

His chin smacked off the ground; dirt billowed up to clog his mouth and nose, but through the dust, he saw more feet rushing toward him. Then his gaze fell on Simone as she battled to break free of the Savages restraining her. When she succeeded in tearing one of her arms free, another vamp grasped her hair and yanked her head back; she yelped and kicked at her captors.

The sight of her being mistreated caused his muscles to swell in a way he'd never experienced before as fresh adrenaline flooded his system. His other hand had fallen before him when they pushed him down, and while he watched, a reddish black color crept from his fingertips to his knuckles before spreading out to his hand.

The two colors pulsed and swirled together until he could barely differentiate one from the other. He knew such a thing could happen to a purebred vampire when they were enraged, or their mate was threatened, but he'd never experienced it before. Now, power swelled like a tsunami inside him as the color spread up his arm to his elbow.

Feeling stronger than he ever had, Killean dug his toes into the dirt and lunged forward. The movement threw the four Savages pinning him down off balance. He managed to dislodge one, but the other three cleaved to him. When the fourth fell on the ground before him, Killean seized its throat and tore out its windpipe.

The vamp gurgled and clawed at its bloody throat as power swelled through Killean's thighs and legs until all his veins and muscles bulged with strength. Killean launched upward and threw back his arms to shake the remaining Savages from him like a dog throwing off water.

Simone's struggles against her captors ceased when her gaze fell on Killean. Her mouth dropped as she took in the reddish-black color churning throughout his flesh; she'd never seen anything like it before. A streak of red slashed across his left cheek, nose, and slid lower to encompass his chin while black surrounded both sides of it. His scar was a vivid red strip down his face.

The colors filled his neck and arms, and from what she could see of his chest through the remains of his shirt, it was also covered in red and black. The fury emanating from him battered her through their bond while his power vibrated the air around him. The Savages closest to him gawked at him while they scrambled backward.

Simone's mind spun as she tried to process what she was seeing, but it seemed the Killean she loved so much had been replaced by a demon straight from the deepest bowels of Hell. And given that the hunter and vampire lines originated from demons, maybe Killean was tapping into some more profound and primitive power.

What is he becoming? And how can I ever bring him back from whatever this is? The fact she had no answers to either of those questions terrified her more than Joseph.

When the Savage holding her hair stepped away from Killean, he tugged her head further back and caused her to gasp. In response, Killean released a roar that would have made a T-Rex pee itself and charged at them.

CHAPTER FORTY-SEVEN

The Savage pulling her hair, and one of the vamps holding her arms, squealed before releasing her and fleeing. But the other one was frozen in place as Killean's steps vibrated the ground. She didn't have a chance to blink before the Savage vanished from beside her.

She expected to have her arm jerked or pulled to the side when Killean yanked the Savage away, but all she felt was a breeze when the man left her side. Then she realized she felt the pressure of fingers still gripping her bicep. It took her a few seconds to gather the courage to glance down.

She nearly screeched when she realized Killean had somehow managed to sever the man's arm at the elbow, yet it still grasped her. The suspended arm flopped against her side. Bile lodged in her throat as she gripped the severed appendage and tossed it aside. Skin crawling, Simone wiped frantically at where the fingers had left bruises on her flesh.

"Easy," the word came from beside her.

Still feeling slightly hysterical by what she'd seen, Simone pulled back her hand and spun to punch whoever spoke. She stopped herself from launching a fist into Declan's face. His silvery-gray eyes were filled with concern as he glanced between her and Killean who had already dispatched the armless Savage and was now rending the head from another.

On the other side of the SUV, Saxon and Lucien emerged from the woods to battle the Savages there. The cavalry had arrived, but would they be in time to save Killean, and would they be enough to destroy the Savages who seemed to be multiplying like cockroaches as they glided through the woods?

Simone gulped as her mind spun with the horror unfolding around her. The sounds of fists hitting flesh, the cries of the dying, and the stench of blood permeated the air. Killean left a trail of mutilated and dead bodies behind him as he carved a path through the Savages toward Joseph. She'd never imagined such carnage could exist, and the horrible sounds filling the night would haunt her nightmares for the rest of her life.

The red of Killean's skin blended with the blood soaking his hair, skin, and clothes. Though Joseph seemed unfazed by Killean's steady approach toward him, he did watch Killean with the keen interest of Dr. Frankenstein waiting to see if his monster would come to life.

A sick feeling settled in the pit of her stomach. With the power and ruthlessness Killean displayed now, she understood why he intrigued Joseph so much, but Joseph's interest could only spell horrible things if he got his hands on Killean.

Joseph turned to the Savages closest to him and flicked his hand at Killean. "Suppress him; then bring him and the girl to me. I want them alive." Raising a hand, he waved it forward until a couple dozen Savages emerged from the woods to gather behind him. "If you can, bring at least one more of Ronan's men to me alive; the rest are expendable. Go!"

Some of the Savages wavered while the others plunged toward Killean. Joseph stared at the hesitators in a way that made it clear he would kill them if they didn't move. After they jumped into the fray, Joseph remained on the edge of the woods with his arms folded over his chest. He smirked as he leaned against an oak tree.

Hatred for the sick, twisted freak coiled in her belly. "Coward!" she hissed.

"Yes," Declan agreed and rested the tips of his fingers on her arm. He quickly moved his hand away when she turned her attention to him. "You have to stay out of this as much as possible. Stay away from the Savages, and most of all, keep away from Joseph."

She searched the woods behind her but didn't see any shadows slinking through the trees from Savages who might be creeping closer. It seemed Joseph's raised hand had drawn all the Savages to him.

Still, she wasn't about to take any chances, and if Killean needed help, she would give it. "Give me a weapon."

Declan's auburn eyebrows drew together over the bridge of his nose. "You have to stay *out* of this. The more jeopardy you're in, the more out of control Killean will get. If something happens to you, he'll completely lose it. With the state he's in, there might be *no* stopping him then."

Simone's skin prickled against his commanding tone, but though she was better trained at defending herself, she was *not* prepared for a battle of this magnitude, and she wouldn't do anything to put Killean in danger.

"I'll stay out of it," she said through her teeth, "but I need something to defend myself in case someone comes after me. Killean's been teaching me to fight, and I will do whatever is necessary to keep us both safe."

Declan studied her before giving a brisk nod. "Yes, you'll need a weapon."

He dipped a hand inside his shirt and pulled a stake free as

Saxon let out a muffled shout. She turned as Saxon yanked a stake from his chest. Judging by the blood spreading across his shirt, the stake had been a couple inches off his heart. Saxon spun the stake in his hand before plunging it into the heart of the Savage who'd stabbed him.

"Stay close to us," Declan said as he shoved the stake into her hand. "We'll keep them away from you."

Simone gripped the stake as he ran to help his friends while more Savages spilled from the trees behind Joseph. The Savages were still on the other side of the road, but there was little distance separating her from them as she edged toward Declan and the others. The Defenders were working to hold back the horde of Savages who had split away from Killean to come for her.

Killean was only thirty feet away from her, but it seemed like an infinite distance as she barely recognized him. None of the Savages could stop him as he tore the head from one and the heart from another before using a third as a battering ram against the others. When those Savages fell back, Killean bashed the Savage he held against a tree until nothing remained of its head.

This Killean who appeared to be more monster than the man she loved, should petrify her, but no matter what he became, she would never fear him. However, she was petrified something would happen to him, and she had no idea how to help. If she tried to jump into the fray and was captured, they would have control over him, and if she were killed, he would be lost.

She hated standing here, watching as the Savages surrounded Killean and swarmed toward his friends. From the other side of the SUV, she locked gazes with the reddened eyes of a Savage. Its lips skimmed back to reveal the saliva dripping from its fangs.

Placing its hands on the bottom of the SUV, the Savage vaulted onto it and raced toward her. Simone drew on the training Killean had given her over the past month; he'd drilled it into her head that staying calm while under attack was the most important thing.

The Savage leapt off the SUV with its arms out to grab her. Simone waited until he was almost on top of her before darting out of the way at the last second. She swung her hand down, catching the back of its head with her fist and the stake. The vamp grunted when it crashed face-first onto the ground.

Pride over taking this thing down shot through her; this thing had assumed she was an easy target and been wrong. Before the Savage could rise, she knelt and drove the stake through its back and into its heart. It was the first time she'd ever killed anything, and though she knew it was necessary, she couldn't stop a twinge of regret. She would have to get used to the feeling though if she were going to help Killean and the Alliance stop the flood of evil Joseph was trying to unleash on the world.

And she *would* help them end this.

She forgot her guilt when leaves rustled behind her. Pulling the stake free, she spun to take on her next adversary.

Instead, Nathan emerged from of the trees. His white-blue eyes clashed with hers before traveling to the Savage at her feet.

"Are you okay?" Nathan asked her as Kadence and Ronan stepped out of the woods to stand beside him.

Relief filled Simone when she spotted more vampires and hunters slipping through the trees to stand behind Nathan and Ronan. Now things would be more even. "Yes," Simone said.

Ronan's gaze raked over the battle before he focused on Kadence. "You and Simone are to stay close to me, but out of this as much as possible," Ronan said before turning to the others. "Kill them all," he commanded.

The vampires and hunters were silent as they glided from the trees to hunt with ruthless intent. Some of the Savages, unprepared for their arrival, were taken down before they realized the Alliance had arrived. When the other Savages became aware they were being hunted, they rushed forward with little regard for their lives.

Ronan sprinted forward to take down one of the six Savages surrounding Declan and the others. Blood poured from a gash on Declan's cheek, and a vivid smear of it stained Saxon's shirt. Lucien's shirt was gone, and blood spilled from the three large cuts marring his chest.

Simone ran beside Kadence as they followed Ronan while Nathan broke off to work with Asher and Logan. The three of them started cutting through the horde of monsters protecting Joseph and trying to take down Killean.

Killean's pulse thundered in his ears as he narrowed in on Joseph who continued to wear that hideous smirk. *Kill. Destroy. Murder. Feels soooo good. Kill. Kill. Kill.*

The words became an endless litany in his mind as the aroma of blood clogged his nostrils and his body became coated with the sticky substance. The cries of the dying were sweet music he relished.

However, no matter how much death he delivered, he craved more, and he especially wanted the end of one.

His gaze remained locked on Joseph as he homed in on him. He would tear Joseph's heart out and bathe in his blood by the time this was over.

Despite the murderous intent taking him over, Killean kept his senses attuned to Simone as he hacked through his enemies. Through their bond, he monitored her distress and uncertainty while knowing her exact location. He'd almost given up his pursuit of Joseph when the Savage went after her, but she'd taken the creature down before he could divert from his course.

Killean grasped the throat of the next Savage who lunged at him while another jumped onto his back. Before Killean could react, the one on his back sank its fangs into his throat.

Pain burst through his body, but instead of immobilizing him, he channeled the agony into his body and turned it into something he could *thrive* on as his skin deepened in hue. An almost brutal glee descended over Killean as he enclosed his arm around the Savage's head.

When Killean squeezed it like a nut in a nutcracker, the Savage's skull gave way with a crunch of bone before he ripped the creature over his shoulder and threw him on the ground. The vamp barely had time to recover before Killean seized its shoulders, lifted him, and sank his fangs into the Savage's throat.

The vamp's fingers tore at Killean's face before it stilled in his grasp. Keeping the vamp's back against his chest, Killean fed on it as he used the Savage's body to batter back the others. When the last of the vamp's life flooded his veins, Killean threw aside the Savage and ran at Joseph.

Joseph's eyes went beyond him, and for the first time, Killean saw uneasiness on his face as his smirk vanished. Killean didn't have to look to know the sun had reached the horizon, he'd become acutely attuned to it since its rays became lethal to him. Killean was almost to Joseph when the bastard turned and glided into the trees.

"No," Killean snarled as he poured on the speed.

CHAPTER FORTY-EIGHT

Killean barreled through the remaining Savages in his way and was almost on top of Joseph when Nathan burst out of the woods to the left of him. Killean spotted Ronan charging at them from the right with Kadence and Simone running behind him.

From somewhere within his coat, Joseph produced a crossbow and fired it at Nathan when the hunter was only three feet away from him.

"Nathan!" Kadence screamed when the bolt pierced through her brother's chest, lifted him off his feet, and knocked him on his ass. She broke away from Simone to rush to her brother.

Killean spotted more Savages gliding through the trees and closing in on Ronan. "Ronan, behind you!" he shouted.

Ronan turned as two of the creatures launched at him. Simone skidded to a halt to avoid running into Ronan when the weight of the Savages knocked him to the ground. Ronan gripped the shoulder of one and threw it away as he rolled to pin the other beneath him. Killean was closing in on Joseph and about to jump on his back when another Savage loomed up behind Simone.

"No!" Killean bellowed and switched course.

He closed the ten feet separating them in less than a second, and swinging his fist forward, he plunged it into the vamp's chest cavity. His fingers clinched around the creature's pulsating heart, and he tore it free. Simone gazed at him with wide eyes as he released the heart and the Savage toppled to the ground between them.

"Killean?" Simone whispered.

She barely recognized the blood-drenched man before her as his fangs hung low over his bottom lip and his skin continued to pulse with those colors. Then gold flickered through the ruby color of his eyes and she once again saw the man she loved. Red swallowed the gold again, but she'd seen enough to know that Killean was still there.

He almost touched her, but the blood dripping from his fingers stopped him from doing so. "It's okay."

Simone didn't know if that meant he would be okay or not, but his love for her shimmered across their bond. And then Killean's attention was drawn away from her and to Nathan, who had regained his feet and was closing in on Joseph.

Lunging forward, Nathan clamped his arms around Joseph's waist. Joseph twisted in an attempt to throw him off, but Nathan clung tenaciously as Kadence jumped onto Joseph's back, seized his hair, and ripped his head back. She delivered three, bone-crushing blows to his face before Joseph reeled backward and bashed her against a tree trunk.

Kadence cried out, and when Joseph staggered away from the tree, she released her hold on him and hit the ground. Ronan, having fought off the other two Savages raced over to kneel beside her as Nathan, still hanging off Joseph's waist, gripped Joseph's crotch and twisted his hand. Joseph howled as his dick and balls were almost ripped from him; he lifted his hand and swung it back to deliver a crushing blow that snapped Nathan's neck to the side and caved in the left side of his face.

"Stay here," Killean commanded Simone.

He ran through the trees at Joseph, and as the Savage freed himself from Nathan, Killean lowered his shoulder and drove it into Joseph's back. The Savage was thrown ten feet forward and hit the ground with enough force that the earth and trees shook. Killean didn't give him a chance to regain his feet before he closed the distance between them and slammed his foot onto Joseph's back to pin him to the ground.

Joseph rolled faster than Killean anticipated, and before he could pull his foot away, Joseph grabbed it and jerked him off his feet. When Killean's back crashed onto the ground, his breath wheezed out of him as Joseph rose into a seated position. When Joseph leaned toward him, Killean gripped his head and shoved it down as he lifted his knee and smashed it into Joseph's nose.

A whistling sound issued from Joseph's crumpled nose as he lurched forward to grasp Killean's shoulders. His fingers shredded Killean's flesh as Killean drew his knees up and wedged them between their bodies.

He shoved up with his feet but couldn't fully dislodge Joseph. A purebred vampire who was trained by Ronan and had killed countless innocents since turning Savage, Joseph was far more powerful than the other Savages Killean slaughtered.

Instead of trying to shake him free, Killean gripped his shoulders and rolled him over. He had only a second on top before Joseph rolled him again. Killean dug his fingers into Joseph's shoulders and tore away chunks of flesh and muscle before smashing his fist into Joseph's face.

Lifting his knee, Joseph rammed it into Killean's crotch. Killean grunted as pain lanced throughout his body. His distraction gave Joseph a chance to release a rapid series of punches into Killean's stomach. The blows left him nearly as breathless as his aching balls, but as the agony spread through him, his body absorbed and twisted it into a strength that fed him.

"Your little mate was the best thing I ever tasted," Joseph taunted.

Killean thought he'd experienced rage before, but those words pushed him into an entirely different state of it. A sound, more monster than man, issued from him as, grabbing Joseph's hair, he rolled with him again. There was no reason left to him as a yawning pit of darkness rose up to engulf him. He tore and beat at Joseph with the intensity of a rat burrowing through the earth to escape a fire.

Simone gawked as Killean's skin became almost entirely pitch-black. It was so deep a black, it looked like tar coating him as an inhuman sound she would associate more with a demon than a man issued from him.

Simone's hand went to her throat as Killean and Joseph pummeled each other. Joseph had appeared to have the upper hand in the beginning, but Killean had turned the tables and Joseph's blood now drenched him.

"What's happening to him?" Simone whispered out loud.

She'd thought she was alone and didn't realized Kadence stood beside her until her friend replied, "It happens to pure-breds when they're enraged, or their mate is threatened. He'll be... he'll be okay."

Kadence's words would have been more reassuring if she hadn't sounded so uncertain. Simone glanced behind her to find Ronan and Nathan battling more Savages. When she turned back, she discovered that Joseph and Killean were rolling toward the edge of a clearing. The sun streaming through the trees spilled across the leaf-strewn ground only feet away from them.

"Killean!" Simone screamed as she ran toward him, but they were rolling again.

Killean feasted on the pain of Joseph's fingers digging into his throat as the Savage sought to kill him.

"You're going to fucking die," Killean promised as he drove

the heel of his hand up under Joseph's nose and snapped his head back.

Gripping Joseph's shoulders again, the distant sound of screams barely pierced the bloodlust thundering through his veins as he once more rolled with Joseph. Agony blazed down his spine, the sound of crackling flesh filled his ears, and it took him a second to realize that he'd rolled them into sunlight.

CHAPTER FORTY-NINE

Simone watched in horror as Killean rolled into the clearing with Joseph and smoke coiled from both vampires. "No!" she cried.

Simone, her name was a cry of longing in Killean's head. What had he done? He couldn't leave her; he had to survive this or else she would be lost too. Focusing on the memory of her scent, her smell, her laughter and love, Killean gathered his dwindling strength to roll Joseph on top of him.

"Killean!" Ronan shouted.

Flames erupted from Joseph's clothes and crackled in the air. Holding Joseph above him, Killean turned his face away when fire shot down toward him. Joseph bellowed as he rained punches down on Killean's face. Pulling his hand back, Joseph aimed it over Killean's ribs and directly above his heart. When he drove it downward, Killean captured his wrist before Joseph could sink it into his ribcage.

Killean struggled against the weakness seeping through his sun-ravaged body; his arms shook as he held Joseph's wrist over his chest while Joseph bore his weight down on him. "Fuck you," Killean gritted through his teeth.

His eyes clashed with Joseph's red ones until flames burst from Joseph's eye sockets and licked his hairline. Joseph was far from done though as he lifted his other hand and delivered a staggering blow to Killean's temple. Like a spastic caterpillar, Joseph began to jerk and squirm to break free of Killean's hold.

Killean clung to Joseph as the sun seared away the flesh and muscles of his hands before spreading up his arms and crackling over his chest. Not having killed as much as Joseph, he was better able to withstand the sun's rays, but Joseph's flames were fueling his.

Killean closed his eyes when fire seared over them, but he didn't know if the flames were coming from him or Joseph anymore. Pain no longer fueled him as flames seared his nerve endings. He only knew the fire was still devouring him because of the stench of burning flesh.

"Let go of him, asshole!" Simone shouted.

Killean's eyes flew open when Simone's words pierced through the roaring fire. Despite his growing certainty that he was going to die, he felt a trickle of amusement as she planted her foot against Joseph's side. Simone's shoving against him did nothing to dislodge the burning Savage as Joseph's muscles were locked tight. Reaching through the flames, Ronan seized Joseph's shoulders, lifted him, and tossed him aside.

Nathan and Kadence sprinted out of the woods and stopped beside Joseph. Nathan pulled a stake free of the holster strapped to his side, and gripping it with both hands, he lifted the weapon. Ignoring the flames consuming Joseph's spasming body, Nathan sank the stake through Joseph's back and into his heart. When fire shot up around his wrists, Kadence used her shirt to help beat them out.

Ronan plucked Killean off the ground, draped him over his

shoulder, and raced into the shadows of the woods with Simone following. When Ronan set Killean on the ground, she fell beside him and, uncaring of the fire searing her skin, beat at the flames.

When her hands and clothes proved not to be enough to douse the fire, she threw herself on top of Killean to smother the worst of the blaze. Ronan stripped out of his burnt shirt and used it to put out more of the flames while Simone continued to beat at them with her badly burnt hands.

Smoke and fire clogged her nose and throat while her skin blistered and peeled away. The inferno seared her lungs with every breath she took, but she ignored the pain of the flames eating through her clothes and searing her chest and legs as she worked to save Killean.

When Ronan smothered the last of the blaze, Simone bent her head and strands of her charred hair fell forward. Her scorched throat and nose made breathing difficult as tears pooled in her eyes while she gazed at Killean.

The only skin remaining on him was on his feet where his boots protected him more than his clothes, but the boots had eventually burned away too, and the flesh on his toes was blistered and raw. All his hair, including his eyebrows, was gone. His lips, or what remained of them, had burned away to reveal his fangs; his nose and ears were only small nubs.

"Killean," she breathed and barely recognized her voice as emotion and smoke choked it.

His lips pulled back further, and she realized he was trying to smile though his golden eyes were dazed. His lashes and part of his lids were also gone, but the spark of recognition in his eyes eased some of her tension.

"You swore," he said in a voice that belonged to a corpse rather than the man she loved.

Then his eyes rolled back in his head, and he went completely still.

CHAPTER FIFTY

"KILLEAN?" she gasped. She wanted to grab his cheeks and attempt to shake him awake, but she couldn't get her fingers to do what she willed them to do. "Killean!"

"It's okay, he's alive," Ronan said. "We have to get him inside."

Simone tried to peel herself away from Killean before realizing some of their skin had melted and fused together. She still didn't feel any pain, but she suspected that would come when she started healing.

"Easy," Ronan said and knelt to help pull her free.

For a second, she feared she would pass out too, but she gritted her teeth and forced herself to stay awake while they were separated.

"You have to save him," she croaked, and her head rolled on her neck when she tilted it back to look at Ronan.

Ronan rested a finger on top of a barely burnt patch of flesh on the back of her hand. "I will," he vowed.

The crack of a branch behind Simone caused her to turn as Nathan and Kadence came forward. Nathan had his arm draped around his sister's shoulders as she led him forward. The bolt Joseph fired into him had been removed from his chest, but judging by the amount of blood staining his shirt, he'd lost a lot of it before the hole started to close.

"Simone!" Kadence gasped before her gaze fell on Killean. "Is he going to be okay?"

"Yes," Ronan said brusquely. "I have to get him inside, and he needs blood."

"Simone?" Kadence whispered questioningly.

"I'm fine." Simone coughed and then winced when the motion sent a rush of pain over her.

Her nerve endings were coming back to life, and she was feeling every one of them. Killean was so much worse than she was though. She went to grasp his arm but pulled her hand back. There was nowhere on him she dared to touch without fear of hurting him, but he was so far gone, he probably didn't feel anything anymore.

Don't leave me, she whispered to him and prayed he heard her.

Ronan slid his arms under Killean and lifted him off the ground. Unwilling to let him out of her sight, Simone staggered to her feet and nearly collapsed when agony radiated through her and her burnt flesh cracked.

"Simone!" Kadence cried.

Ronan shifted his hold on Killean to cup her elbow and steady her. "Declan, help her," he commanded.

She hadn't realized the others were there until Declan glided toward her. Bruises marred his face, blood splattered his clothes and skin, and gashes streaked his face and chest, but he seemed undaunted by any of it. Bloodied and battered, Saxon was propped against a tree while Lucien rested his hand on the trunk of another one. Logan and Asher leaned heavily against one another. Hunters and vampires stood around them; most were battered, and others carried some, but they were alive. Although, she had no idea how many were lost.

When many of them glanced nervously away from her, she looked down and realized the front of her clothes were gone. Only tattered remains adhered to her blackened flesh. Before, she would have been mortified over being exposed like this, even if she was so badly burnt she looked more like a charred chicken leg than a woman. Now all she cared about was getting Killean somewhere safe.

"The remaining Savages?" Ronan inquired.

"They've fled into the woods," Lucien said.

"Good," Ronan said. "Hopefully the sun will destroy more of them too. We have to go."

"I'm going to pick you up," Declan cautioned her.

Simone was in no condition to argue with him. She bit her lip to keep from crying out when he lifted her into his arms and followed Ronan through the woods at a dead run. Every step jarred her reawakening nerves, but Simone didn't make a sound as she gripped Declan's shoulders and did her best to remain still. She heard the footsteps of the others behind them, but she couldn't see them over Declan's shoulder, and she didn't dare move to look.

Smoke trailed from Killean again when Ronan sprinted across the open area separating the woods from the asylum. Ronan hunched over Killean, shielding him the best he could, but more flames erupted across Killean's chest. Throwing his shoulder down, Ronan smashed through the front door and ran inside.

Simone couldn't tear her gaze away from them as Declan followed. Ronan carefully set Killean on the floor near the stairs and away from the sun's rays. Kneeling beside Killean, Ronan smothered the flames with his hands before lifting his wrist to his mouth and biting deep. He held his wrist to Killean's lips so the blood went down his throat.

"Ronan?" Kadence asked; the shock evident in her voice.

The others all stopped on the threshold, and Declan's arms briefly constricted around her as disbelief rippled through him.

Ronan didn't look up as he replied. "He needs blood, and mine is the strongest here. Simone's would probably help him more, but she's in no condition to give right now."

"Put me down," Simone whispered to Declan.

He strode closer to Killean before setting her on her feet. Ignoring her cracking skin and the agony of her healing nerves, Simone fell to her knees on the other side of Killean. Ronan's eyes were a vivid shade of red when he glanced at her, and she saw the anguish in them. Even if Ronan understood why, he hadn't been happy with what Killean did to rescue her. However, he still cared for Killean; that much was evident in the set of his jaw and the lines of sorrow etching his eyes and mouth.

Tearing her gaze away from Ronan, Simone focused on Killean. "Please don't leave me," she pleaded as she rested her hand against the side of his face. Afraid she would hurt him, she barely touched him, but the small contact caused his eyes to flicker.

"Lucien, bring me some blood bags," Ronan ordered.

Before sunset, they carefully enshrouded Killean in blankets and transferred him into the back of a van. The blankets covered all of him, but the idea of bringing him into the sun again terrified her. However, Ronan wanted to move him before nightfall to avoid any Savages who might return, and Simone couldn't argue with that logic.

After supplying Killean with blood, Ronan and the others

spent most of the day disposing of bodies and cleaning up the mess created by the attack last night. She and Kadence kept vigilant watch over Killean, giving him blood on an hourly basis.

Simone also fed a lot more than usual, and the blood had accelerated her healing, but her red and blistered skin still cracked every time she moved. Her mending nerves felt like someone had taken sandpaper and rubbed every last one of them raw.

Simone climbed into the van to sit beside Killean and clasped his hand in hers. Blisters still marred his mottled, red, and charred skin, yet his lips were filling out, and his lids completely covered his eyes again. He still hadn't regained consciousness, but he was getting better. She cleaved to that knowledge as he remained shut off from her.

His skin was growing back in patches over his exposed muscle and bone, but the returning flesh held none of the strange colors that filled it before. When she and Kadence talked about it earlier, her friend said the same thing happened to Ronan when she was threatened, and he was fine. Kadence was sure Killean wouldn't suffer any ill effects from his strange transformation.

Simone scanned the road behind Ronan as he stood in the doorway of the van with Nathan and Kadence beside him. Nathan, looking much better than he had earlier, leaned against one of the doors.

"Do you think the Savages will return now that Joseph is dead?" Simone asked Ronan.

"There's no way of knowing what they'll do," Ronan answered. All his burns were already healed. "Joseph led them out here, but it sounds as if the creature you and Killean encountered is the one pulling the strings. We don't know what its next move will be; either way, it's not safe here anymore."

She knew it was true, but she hated leaving the place where she and Killean were cocooned in so much happiness for such a short time. Killean would never get the chance to bring this place back to beautiful life, and she would never see her garden again.

"Where will we go?" she whispered.

"You're coming to the compound," Ronan said.

"But the hunters—"

"Killean almost sacrificed himself to bring down Joseph. The hunters will have to accept him." Ronan shot Nathan a pointed look as he said this. "Despite what he's done, Killean's proven he's still one of us this past month and especially last night."

Simone couldn't argue with that, and if any hunter had an issue with this decision, they would have to come through her to get at Killean. "How do you think they found us?"

Ronan's jaw clenched before he spoke again. "I don't know. We should go."

Simone curled up beside Killean and draped her arm tenderly around him while Ronan and Nathan shut the back doors. If anyone tried to harm him while he was in such a vulnerable state, she'd tear off their heads.

CHAPTER FIFTY-ONE

Simone lifted her head when Killean stirred beside her. This small movement was the most life he'd shown in the past two days. Hope surged through her as she sat up to stare at his face. His hair, eyelashes, and eyebrows were still gone, but the rest of his skin had healed enough that all his muscles were covered. The scar running down the center of his cheek remained, but no marks blemished his skin from the burns.

Behind his closed lids, his eyes darted side to side. She rested her fingers against his cheek as she leaned closer to him. "Killean?" she whispered.

When his eyes opened, she found herself gazing into them. It was then she realized she'd feared never seeing those beautiful, golden eyes again. "Killean," she breathed.

Gripping her shoulders to push her back, he bolted upright, and his gaze flashed around the room where Ronan placed them. Ronan had said this was Killean's room when he was here before, but it seemed to take Killean a couple of seconds to recognize it as his body remained tensed beside her. Then his shoulders slumped, he released her, and a ragged breath issued from him.

"We're at the compound," he said.

"Yes."

His gaze raked her from head to toe. "Are you okay?"

"I'm fine," she assured him with a smile. "Completely healed and much better now that you're awake."

He grasped the ends of her sleek auburn hair, now cut to just beneath her ears.

"It was badly singed, and Kadence had to cut it," she said. "But I kind of like this." She gave her head a small shake. "It's much cooler and easier to take care of."

"You look beautiful," he said. The short cut emphasized the loveliness of her sculpted features, porcelain skin, and green eyes.

She rubbed his bald head. "It's much better than yours."

Killean reached up and laughed when he felt the smooth skin against his palm. "Much better," he agreed. "Ronan brought us here?"

"Yes. He said you've more than proved yourself, and the hunters would have to accept his decision. I agree."

"And have the hunters accepted it?"

Simone shrugged. "I haven't left the room since we got here, but everything seems okay; Ronan hasn't mentioned any unrest when he comes to visit, but he probably wouldn't tell me if there was."

"Probably not," Killean agreed.

"But the hunters won't pull out of this Alliance, not anymore. They're committed."

"They are. What happened to Joseph?"

"He's dead. Nathan finished what you started." Simone bit her lip as she studied him. She'd just gotten him back, but still... "You shouldn't have done that! You could have died!"

Killean clasped her hand, and lifting it to his mouth, he kissed the back of it. "I'm sorry I scared you, but it wasn't planned. I'm never going to leave you."

"You can't say that! We have no idea what the future holds for us."

"Simone—"

"You were so *badly* burned." Tears filled her eyes as she recalled the terror of the past couple of days.

"Shh," he whispered and drew her close to kiss her forehead. He despised the tremor in her body as she bowed her head and her fingers encircled his forearms. "I'm okay, and Joseph is dead. He'll never hurt you again."

"Dead," she whispered and for the first time allowed herself to savor that wonderful knowledge. They still had that other thing and plenty of Savages to contend with, but that murderous, sick *monster* was dead.

Smiling, she breathed in the resin scent of Killean, tinted with the faint hint of smoke and the taint of a Savage. Simone realized that even after enough time passed for the smell of a Savage to fade, he would always be more Savage than not. There was something inherently wild and dark about Killean, and she loved him for it.

"That other thing is still out there," she whispered.

"But we took out one of its main puppets, and we will destroy it too. I do not doubt that. You shouldn't have thrown yourself on top of me to put out the flames."

Simone snorted. "You're in no position to lecture me, Baldy."

Killean laughed as he wrapped his arms around her and drew her close. Lowering his mouth to hers, he kissed her as he pushed her back on the bed.

"I love you, Simone," he whispered against her mouth.

"And I love you."

~

A FEW HOURS LATER, Killean found Ronan and the others gathered in the barroom. Nathan, Asher, and Logan were with them.

"Would you like a drink?" Declan inquired of him. He was seated at one of the stools lining the bar with a glass of amber liquid before him.

"Yes." Killean settled himself onto one of the leather chairs between Saxon and Lucien.

"How are you feeling?" Lucien asked.

For the first time, Killean didn't sense any anger in his friend's voice. "Much better," Killean answered before turning to Ronan. "If the hunters have a problem with me being here, I'll leave," he said, striking right at the heart of the matter. "I didn't like it in the beginning, but I understand how important this Alliance is, and I won't jeopardize it by being here."

"You're here to stay," Ronan stated.

"They're a little nervous," Nathan said, "but they're accepting it. Joseph's demise helped them adjust faster." Nathan grinned as he lifted his glass in salute to him. "I've never seen a vampire barbeque before, but you pulled it off nicely."

Killean scowled at him, but it didn't last long before he gave a small chuckle. "I hope never to pull it off again."

"I would be fine with that," Ronan said.

Killean met his gaze. Simone had told him Ronan gave him his blood, and that's what helped pull him through the worst of his burns, but he had no idea what to say about it. The sharing of blood between vampires was rare. Until Simone, he'd never shared his before, and he'd wager Ronan hadn't before Kadence. None of the Defenders had ever shared blood between them, until now.

"Ronan—"

"Don't mention it," Ronan said as he sipped his drink.

Killean nodded; that was the most they'd ever say about it, he knew.

Declan walked over and placed a glass of whiskey in front of him. "Thank you," Killean said as he lifted it and took a sip. "I still feel stable," he said when he set the glass down. He didn't want to say the rest, but he had to. "But that could change."

"And if it does, we'll take care of it," Ronan said. "You're back with us, and we *will* stop you from killing any innocents here or on the outside."

Ronan sharing his blood with him had been the act of love between friends, but Ronan would kill him if he believed it necessary.

"Good," Killean said. "So what do we do now?"

"Now we find that thing that was working with Joseph, and we destroy it," Ronan stated. "We also find the mole we have here."

Killean almost choked on the whiskey sliding down his throat. "Mole?"

"Yes," Ronan said and gazed pointedly at everyone in the room. "Someone let Joseph know where you were."

"You don't think we could have been spotted after a hunt and trailed back to the asylum?"

"Do you?"

Killean pondered this before responding. "We were too careful for that to happen. What about Simone's guards? Maybe they messed up."

"It *is* possible," Ronan said. "They were newer, young, and not as highly trained, but I find it unlikely. Joseph would have to know what to look for with them, and the vehicle they were in looked just like any other SUV on the road. No, I think someone working with us might have alerted him. It might also explain how Joseph knew we're working with the hunters now. Yes, one of the hunters he captured could have revealed this, or he could have seen us hunting together one night without us being aware, but it also could have been someone on the inside."

"But who?" Killean asked.

"That is the question. Is it a new vampire trainee? A hunter? We don't know, but we'll find out."

"And they'll regret it when we do," Lucien murmured.

"They can't be a Savage, or we would smell them," Killean said.

"That doesn't mean they're not corrupt," Declan said.

And that, Killean knew, was very true.

"Are we going to move?" Killean asked.

"No. If there is a mole, we'll just be bringing them with us," Ronan said. "And a new place would be more vulnerable. Few know the extent of the security systems we have here, and I trust them all. If this place was attacked, it would not fall easily, if at all, and many of our enemy would be destroyed before they ever reached the more vulnerable residents here."

"Good," Killean said as he thought of Simone. She would be safe here; he was sure of it.

Killean sipped at his drink as they discussed how to discover the answer to who could be the possible mole. After a couple of hours, Kadence and Simone strolled into the room. Ronan rose from his chair, and walking over to her, he clasped Kadence's hand before leaving the room.

Simone came to stand beside him, but Killean pulled her into his lap and held her close. He had no idea what they would uncover in their hunt for the creature he'd seen in the bunker, or how far they would have to go to destroy it, but with Simone at his side, Killean was certain he could keep the darkness in him at bay.

He'd seen himself as so strong before she walked into his life, but he'd actually been weak. She made him stronger by forcing him to face his past and accepting him for who and what he was. He'd never believed himself capable of loving another or envisioning a future beyond the next fight, but he looked forward to every day of their eternity together, and the family they would one day have.

~

***Bound by Passion*, The Alliance Series Book 4, is now available and focuses on Saxon and Elyse. Turn the page for a sneak peek or download now:**
brendakdavies.com/BPwb

~

Stay in touch on updates, sales, and new releases by joining to the mailing list:
brendakdavies.com/ESBKDNews

Visit the Erica Stevens/Brenda K. Davies Book Club on Facebook for exclusive giveaways and all things book related. Come join the fun:
brendakdavies.com/ESBKDBookClub

SNEAK PEEK

BOUND BY PASSION, THE ALLIANCE SERIES BOOK 4

"How ARE we supposed to find anything here?" Lucien asked as he lowered his feet from the dashboard to survey the quiet town they'd entered.

Saxon studied the adjoining storefronts they passed. Most of the stores were brick fronts with red or gray weathered signs announcing a feed and grain store, lawyer, yoga studio, pharmacy, market, veterinarian, and a doctor. The businesses were all shut down for the night, though a few lights remained on in what he assumed were apartments over the stores.

No streetlights illuminated the winding, dark, country road, but as they drove further, a bar with all its lights on lit the sidewalk and part of the street. The bar stood separate from the rest of the buildings, which was a good thing judging by the noise of the music and the shouts of the crowd. The sides of the bar were clear of any trees, but woods surrounded the back of the building, and despite the wintry January night, a group of smokers stood on the deck there.

The snow piled high on the sides of the sidewalks didn't deter a group of young kids scrambling over them in their eagerness to get to the bar. In the driver's seat, Logan slowed the SUV as they crested a hill and left the town behind. Moonlight shone off the icy sheen coating the snow as more countryside came into view.

"Small town," Declan murmured.

"Pull over," Lucien said. He sounded like he'd rather deal with a thousand Savages than one small town.

Logan guided the SUV to the side of the road and put it in park. From the seats behind Saxon, Asher leaned over to study the countryside. "Is this where Kadence sent us?" he asked.

"This is it," Declan said. "We passed the town sign before driving down what I'm assuming is the main section of town."

"Is that *all* there is to the town?" Asher asked.

"How are we supposed to know?" Lucien asked. "We've never been here before either."

"Someone's testy tonight," Asher muttered, and Lucien turned in the passenger seat to scowl at him.

"We have no idea what we're doing here," Lucien said. "Other than looking for some log cabin, and I'd guarantee there are about a hundred of them in these boonies."

"Still not a reason to be a dick," Asher replied, and Saxon stifled a laugh when Lucien looked like his head might explode. For a second, he thought Lucien might jump over them all to strangle the hunter.

"Enough," Declan said from beside him.

Lucien continued to glare at Asher who pretended not to notice as he stared out the windows.

"Kill the lights," Saxon said, and Logan turned off the headlights.

The tick of the cooling engine was the only sound in the night as Saxon stared at the field next to him. Strings of wire ran across the tilted wooden posts stretching over the earth. On the other side of the road, an embankment led into the woods. Wind buffeted the SUV, shaking it as it howled over the land.

The idea of exiting the vehicle and stepping into the chilly night was about as appealing to him as having his toenails ripped out, and he doubted he was alone. They were all dressed similarly in jeans and shirts with jackets that hid the weapons stashed inside their interior pockets. Most of them wore boots, but Asher had opted for sneakers. Even with the jackets and boots, they weren't dressed for these elements.

"Is there any information about the town on the map Kadence gave us?" Saxon asked.

Declan pulled out the map and laid it flat on the seat between them. He tapped the big red circle Kadence had created on upstate New York. The Catskill Mountains ran through the center of the circle, and there was no denying they were in the mountains when another blast of wind rocked the vehicle. He hated the bleakness of winter, but there was something especially desolate about this night and place.

"We're on the edge of the location she circled," Declan said. "The town is about fifty square miles, possibly more."

"So we're supposed to find a cabin out here," Logan said and waved his hands at the windshield. "How many do you think there are?"

"I can find them on my computer," Declan said. "It will take some time, but I'll track them down tonight."

"Maybe she sent us here because she's trying to kill us," Lucien murmured.

"Maybe she's trying to kill *you*, and who could blame her? But she likes the rest of us," Logan replied.

"Especially me," Asher said.

Lucien gave them the finger. "Fuck you both."

Turning, Saxon leaned over the map to study it. In his mind, he saw Kadence spreading it across the table in the library as everyone gathered around her.

Kadence pointed at the circle in New York. "Here."

"And what is here?" Declan inquired as he spun a lollipop between his fingers.

"A log cabin."

"And what is so special about the cabin?"

"I don't know."

Behind her, Ronan folded his arms over his chest; tension emanated from him while he watched his mate. Saxon leaned back on his heels as he surveyed the other marks on the map. Instead of circles, these were pen lines etched onto the map. Each mark had a date written beside it that went back almost three weeks.

He pointed at the first mark and date; it was only fifty miles away, and the date was Christmas. "What are these?"

"That's when I first started seeing markers," she said.

"Markers?" Killean asked.

"Yeah." Kadence turned the map toward her. "Here"—she pointed to the first dot on the map— "there's a church with some of the most beautiful stained-glass windows I've ever seen. And here"—she pointed to the second marker—"there's a bakery with a pink pig on top. I saw the actual town sign for this one." She pointed to the third dot.

"That was when I realized the snippets of visions I was receiving during my dreams were from different towns. I researched what towns had things like what I was seeing and learned the exact locations."

"Why?" Logan asked.

"Because I knew they were leading me somewhere; I just didn't know where or why I was seeing them."

"Why didn't you come to get me to help you with them?" Nathan, Kadence's twin brother, asked.

Nathan had his arm around Vicky, his very pregnant mate. Vicky's twin, Abby, her mate, and their mother and father were arriving tomorrow to stay until Vicky had the baby, which could be any day now.

"Because they were coming to me in dreams, and I didn't know when I was going to have them," Kadence said. "Plus, they were short scenes with one vividly detailed thing that stood out when I woke up. And, like I said, until I saw the town sign, I didn't know what was happening. Once I realized the dreams were trying to lead me somewhere, I searched for the pig and the church, but I didn't know where they were taking me... until, last night."

"And what happened last night?" Simone asked.

"It came to an end."

"And how do you know that?" Killean asked as he ran a hand through his short, dark brown hair. It had taken some time, but his hair and eyebrows had grown back after being burned off almost seven months ago.

Kadence's fingers played across the marks on the map as she spoke. "Because my dream last night had a sense of finality to it, and I *knew* this is where the visions have been leading me."

Saxon studied the circle in New York. "And what did you see in this last vision?"

"The town sign, and then it switched to a cabin in the center of a clearing. Light shone from the windows of the cabin, and it had a farmers porch. The interlocking logs of the cabin were a light wood color, and there was a large, snow-covered field behind it."

Like a million other cabins in the world. Saxon kept the words to himself as he studied the map and then Kadence. She had to know trying to find a cabin in the mountains would be like looking for a needle in a haystack. Granted, it wouldn't be a huge haystack as they had a general location, but she was the only one who knew the exact appearance of this cabin.

"And why is this cabin important?" Nathan prodded.

"I don't know," Kadence said. "I only know something has been guiding me to this town. Why? I have no idea. What's there? Not a clue. There could be another bunker Joseph established to hide out in before he died, it could be a group of Savages, it could be vampires, or it could be nothing."

"You don't believe that," Ronan said.

"No, I don't. There's something there; I just don't know what." She bit her lip as she stared at the circle. "Once we get to the town, I might—"

"I think it's best you stay here," Ronan interrupted.

Kadence turned toward him, and Saxon could see her gearing up for an argument, but Ronan spoke before she could. "We have no idea what is up there; it could be something dangerous, and I don't want you involved."

"I'm already involved in it; I'm the one who saw the cabin."

"And someone else can find it," he said.

"But they won't know what it looks like."

"I think you've described it well enough."

Saxon clamped his mouth shut against the snort of laughter he almost released. One thing he'd learned since Ronan and Kadence became mates was *not* to interfere in their relationship. Ronan was usually pretty in control, but anything having to do with Kadence could push him to a breaking point.

"I have not," Kadence said.

"Someone *else* will find it," Ronan insisted. "Besides, the baby is going to be here soon, and you don't want to miss it, do you?"

Low blow, but Saxon had to admire Ronan's use of the baby to derail her. They would have fought over this for hours, and

Saxon could see it resulting in them being sent out to find this cottage without Kadence's knowledge. Ronan would have paid dearly for it, and Saxon would have preferred to be locked in a room while someone blasted disco for twenty-four hours than be in Ronan's shoes, but Ronan would have sent them.

"The baby," Kadence murmured as she turned to Vicky and her brother. "I could probably find it in a couple of days."

"Don't worry," Declan said. "We'll find it. Won't we, Lucien?"

Lucien rolled his eyes. "Yeah, it should be easy to locate a cabin in the mountains."

"It won't be any problem at all," Saxon lied.

"We'll come with you," Asher said and waved a hand at Logan who nodded.

"Be careful. I didn't see anything bad there, but...." Kadence shrugged as she held up her hands in a helpless gesture. "But I don't know what's there."

"We'll be fine," Saxon assured her

And now, sitting in the middle of nowhere, he wished he was sleeping in his bed or preferably someone else's. He hated the cold, and this place looked as inviting as Antarctica.

Continue reading Bound by Passion:

brendakdavies.com/BPwb

Stay in touch on updates, sales, and new releases by joining to the mailing list:

brendakdavies.com/ESBKDNews

Visit the Erica Stevens/Brenda K. Davies Book Club on Facebook for exclusive giveaways and all things book related. Come join the fun:
brendakdavies.com/ESBKDBookClub

FIND THE AUTHOR

Erica Stevens/Brenda K. Davies Mailing List:
brendakdavies.com/ESBKDNews

Facebook: brendakdavies.com/BKDfb

Erica Stevens/Brenda K. Davies Book Club:
brendakdavies.com/ESBKDBookClub

Instagram: brendakdavies.com/BKDInsta
Twitter: brendakdavies.com/BKDTweet
Website: www.brendakdavies.com

ALSO FROM THE AUTHOR

Books written under the pen name

Brenda K. Davies

The Vampire Awakenings Series

Awakened (Book 1)

Destined (Book 2)

Untamed (Book 3)

Enraptured (Book 4)

Undone (Book 5)

Fractured (Book 6)

Ravaged (Book 7)

Consumed (Book 8)

Unforeseen (Book 9)

Forsaken (Book 10)

Relentless (Book 11)

Legacy (Book 12)

The Alliance Series

Eternally Bound (Book 1)

Bound by Vengeance (Book 2)

Bound by Darkness (Book 3)

Bound by Passion (Book 4)

Bound by Torment (Book 5)

Bound by Danger (Book 6)

Bound by Deception (Book 7)

Bound by Fate (Book 8)

Coming 2022

The Road to Hell Series

Good Intentions (Book 1)

Carved (Book 2)

The Road (Book 3)

Into Hell (Book 4)

Hell on Earth Series

Hell on Earth (Book 1)

Into the Abyss (Book 2)

Kiss of Death (Book 3)

Edge of the Darkness (Book 4)

The Shadow Realms

Shadows of Fire (Book 1)

Shadows of Discovery (Book 2)

Shadows of Betrayal (Book 3)

Shadows of Fury (Book 4)

Coming 2022

Shadows of Destiny (Book 5)

Coming 2022

Historical Romance

A Stolen Heart

Books written under the pen name

Erica Stevens

The Coven Series

Nightmares (Book 1)

The Maze (Book 2)

Dream Walker (Book 3)

The Captive Series

Captured (Book 1)

Renegade (Book 2)

Refugee (Book 3)

Salvation (Book 4)

Redemption (Book 5)

Broken (The Captive Series Prequel)

Vengeance (Book 6)

Unbound (Book 7)

The Kindred Series

Kindred (Book 1)

Ashes (Book 2)

Kindled (Book 3)

Inferno (Book 4)

Phoenix Rising (Book 5)

The Fire & Ice Series

Frost Burn (Book 1)

Arctic Fire (Book 2)

Scorched Ice (Book 3)

The Ravening Series

The Ravening (Book 1)

Taken Over (Book 2)

Reclamation (Book 3)

The Survivor Chronicles

The Upheaval (Book 1)

The Divide (Book 2)

The Forsaken (Book 3)

The Risen (Book 4)

ABOUT THE AUTHOR

Brenda K. Davies is the USA Today Bestselling author of the Vampire Awakening Series, Alliance Series, Road to Hell Series, Hell on Earth Series, Shadow Realms Series, and historical romantic fiction. She also writes under the pen name, Erica Stevens. When not out with friends and family, she can be found at home with her husband, son, dog, cat, and horse.

Made in the USA
Monee, IL
21 August 2022